Dear Reader,

Summer is a time when life slows down, the days stretch out . . . and the imagination runs wild! This summer, let Silhouette Books be your travel guide on a reading adventure. . . .

In 1992, *Silhouette Summer Sizzlers* offers you love in three exotic corners of the world. Visit the sun-drenched coast of Mexico with Linda Lael Miller's dramatic "The Leopard's Woman," in which two radically opposed personalities and cultures meet and clash—making sparks fly! Paula Detmer Riggs will take you on an incredible adventure in the lush tropics of Hawaii in "Night of the Dark Moon," in which a mad dash through the impenetrable jungle is almost the last thing a lovely photographer and her unwilling bodyguard do. In "The Barefooted Enchantress" by Ann Major, a movie star and her young son are whisked away to a castle in Scotland where there are some very strange goings-on—and an irresistible rogue in the center of the mystery.

These three bestselling authors are known for their sizzling sensuality and action-packed prose, so wherever you go this summer, be sure to make *Silhouette Summer Sizzlers 1992* your traveling companion. You'll never be without a sizzling romance and a hot-blooded hero.

Enjoy!

Isabel Swift
Editorial Director

® S I L H O U E T T E ®

SUMMER Sizzlers 1992

ANN MAJOR
PAULA DETMER RIGGS
LINDA LAEL MILLER

Silhouette Books®

Published by Silhouette Books New York

America's Publisher of Contemporary Romance

SILHOUETTE BOOKS
300 E. 42nd St., New York, N.Y. 10017

SILHOUETTE SUMMER SIZZLERS 1992

Copyright © 1992 by Silhouette Books

All rights reserved. Except for use in any review, the reproduction
or utilization of this work in whole or in part in any form by any
electronic, mechanical or other means, now known or hereafter
invented, including xerography, photocopying and recording, or in
any information storage or retrieval system, is forbidden without
the permission of the publisher, Silhouette Books, 300 E. 42nd St.,
New York, N.Y. 10017

ISBN: 0-373-48241-8

First Silhouette Books printing June 1992

The publisher acknowledges the copyright holders of
the individual works as follows:

The Barefooted Enchantress
Copyright © 1992 by Ann Major
Night of the Dark Moon
Copyright © 1992 by Paula Detmer Riggs
The Leopard's Woman
Copyright © 1992 by Linda Lael Miller

® and ™: Trademarks used with authorization. Trademarks
indicated with ® are registered in the United States Patent and
Trademark Office, the Canada Trade Mark Office and in other
countries.

Printed in the U.S.A.

CONTENTS

THE BAREFOOTED ENCHANTRESS

Ann Major

Dream Vacation

Sometimes my idea of a dream vacation is an airline ticket as far from South Texas and my routine of chores as the plane will carry me. The minute I step on board, my mind erases all the lists of things that were so pressingly important to do that day. Once, when I was in this mood, I booked a trip to Scotland for my husband, Ted, and myself.

August in cool, misty Scotland is very different from the humid heat of the Texas coast. Ted and I spent two weeks touring this land where the Campbells slaughtered the MacDonalds, where an eellike monster named Nessie is supposed to dwell at the bottom of a loch, and where Bonnie Prince Charlie's cause is still alive.

Vacation time always seems to move at a slower pace than it does at home when I'm racing about, and I remember the things I do on trips more vividly. Ted and I took long walks in the mountains and glens. We loved the gorse and the heather of the moors, the castles, the narrow, twisting roads with their quaint stone bridges.

I especially loved the ruined monasteries and the Isle of Skye. When my editor asked me to write a Summer Sizzlers story about a dream vacation, I wondered if I could set the story in a cool country like Scotland. And she said, "As long as the romance sizzles..."

And since Ted and I rediscovered each other in Scotland, I thought a cold country might be the perfect setting for a hot summer romance....

Prologue

As Tamara Howard stared wildly around at the movie crew, she knew she was being stalked. Her horse sensed her nervousness, and pawed the earth. Actresses were fair game—especially redheaded, voluptuous ones with zany, sexy, screen images who came from psychic, flamboyant families.

The man Tamara had met the night before had seemed smoother than the slick opportunists she was used to in Hollywood, and it upset her more than usual that such a man had formed an erroneous impression of her. One of the supreme ironies of her life was that even though she was a film sex goddess, she was still embarrassed by her love scenes. And she found it difficult to keep from blushing on the set.

That was the problem. Last night she'd believed herself alone in the glen as she'd lain on her blanket rehearsing the all-important final love scene for *Fair Maid*. She'd been pantomiming the most passionate part like a breathless wanton, when suddenly a deep voice had drawled, "Very nice."

Crimson cheeked, she'd sprung to her feet, her skirts falling demurely, but not before he'd seen too much bare leg and her bare feet.

He had black hair and black eyes, and he was startlingly handsome—clichéd Hollywood handsome. Experience had taught her to be wary of handsome men. His elegant suit flawlessly molded a lean body that was tall and heavily muscled. His face was tough, too, and yet there was an indefinable elegance about him that was both arrogant and aristocratic. He seemed to inhabit not only his own body, but to dominate a much larger, invisible space around him. He acted as if he considered himself king of the castle. In her bare feet she had felt like a peasant.

When his bold gaze had roved the length of her body clad in clingy, soft cotton and lingered upon her slim, naked ankles, her heart had begun to pound.

"So you're the actress who has taken over my castle?" His black brows had lifted and the insolent dark eyes came slowly up her body again as if she were an object he was appraising before deciding to purchase. "You're not what I expected," he murmured in that low, sensual tone. He moved closer. "Why don't we rehearse together?"

The shadows from the shivering trees had given his face a shimmering look. She'd emitted a frightened gasp. When he'd reached for her, she'd run, leaving everything, her script, her blanket, even her shoes, behind. But his raspy, contemptuous voice had followed her. "I will have you, Miss Howard. And why not? I'm sure there have been many others before me."

Many others. His words had chilled her.

Now, this next morning, she had almost had a nervous attack when she had found her script and blanket and shoes tidily stacked outside her room. He knew who she was, where she slept, and she hadn't the slightest idea who he was.

The worst of it was she couldn't get him out of her mind, because she hadn't set him straight. And because she couldn't, everything had gone wrong today.

Killiecraig Castle with its gray walls, turrets and dark slate roofs loomed over the golden rhododendron tree that flowered beside Tamara and her mount, and she had the uncanny feeling that he was up there watching her from some high window.

Scotland was beautiful, but she scarcely noticed the romantic setting of verdant hills, sparkling seas and twin castles on their craggy cliffs. If men like the man she'd met last night thought she was fast, it was because directors kept picking her for light, sexy roles. The more she thought about the man, the more nervous she became. She impatiently fluffed the great white collar scratching her neck.

"Don't fidget, Miss Howard," the girl from wardrobe admonished softly. "The director's nearly ready."

Tamara's worried dark eyes flashed. "Sorry." Her horse shied restlessly as she withdrew her bejeweled hand and clenched the reins of her mount once more. She hated horses, especially lively ones. She hated this elaborate, low-cut Elizabethan costume of satin and itchy gold trim that cut off her breath and pushed up her breasts.

Tamara's apricot-colored hair was braided into elaborate coils, and pins were sticking into her scalp. Onto this ridiculous hairdo was pinned an even more ridiculous white cap trimmed with blooming white heather that seemed to attract every buzzing insect in the countryside.

The director yelled to everyone that this was the tenth take and that they were losing the light. The cameramen widened their lenses. Grips began rushing about. The wardrobe girl adjusted the folds of Tamara's gown.

She tried to draw a deep breath and relax, but the stays beneath her tight bodice cut into her waist like knives.

Jack Brodie, her director, came up. "You've got to concentrate, babe." He told her for the tenth time that this was the final scene and she was to ride across the moor to meet her true love. She refrained from telling him how tired she was of being treated like a moron and typecast into such silly roles—even if the roles had made her very, very rich. What she had always wanted more than anything was respect.

Her eight-year-old son, Will, dashed over to wish her luck. And just as he did, a bee buzzed out of the rhododendron tree straight at the heather blossoms in her hair.

She had always been terrified of bees.

She let go of the reins and swatted wildly. Which was a mistake.

Everything went wrong at once. The bee buzzed in crazed, chaotic circles. When her horse reared, she screamed in shrill terror, not for herself but for her son.

"Will, get back!"

Her frightened screams were cut off as her horse bolted. Jack lunged to save her and was nearly trampled. She clung to her old-fashioned saddle, to the horse's coarse mane, holding on in breathless terror as the animal raced wildly through the extras and then away toward the cliffs and sea. Then the beast veered from the broad green fields and hedges into the woods and thick brambles. Her cap was torn loose and fell to the ground. Her face was scratched and her braids yanked free.

She managed to reclaim the reins and pull on them, but the frightened beast spurted in a mad gallop, heading for the cliffs that plunged down to the sea.

Dear Lord. Her strength was slipping away. If they reached the cliffs, all would be lost. She was fainting. Only vaguely was she aware of the thunder of hooves behind her.

The reins slipped weakly through her numb fingers. The world blackened, but just as she was about to fall, strong arms drew her from her horse onto another. In that last breathless second, when she was safely held next to a great muscular body by arms that crushed the breath out of her, she fainted.

When her eyelids fluttered open, she was lying in lush tall grasses. The world was quiet and still and very cold. She saw gray walls, cathedral-like arches and windows, and open blue skies. She was lying near an ancient grave in the hush of a ruined abbey. When she stirred, the grasses felt cool and wet against her cheek.

"Don't try to move," a man's deep voice murmured.

She shivered at the sound of that oddly familiar baritone.

His hand gently caressed the bloody places on her face, and the warmth of his callused touch was infinitely pleasant.

Brilliant, fiery sunlight streamed through the windows behind him and made it difficult for her to make out more than the fact that he was tall and broad, raven-haired—and that he, too, was dressed in a costume from the Elizabethan age.

Then he knelt nearer and she saw that his eyes were black and shining, his skin dark from the sun. He had high cheekbones and a haughty aquiline nose.

Haughty. With sudden dawning horror she knew who he was. He was the same loathsome aristocrat from the night before. His bold gaze swept hotly over her in the cynical male way that told her his opinion of her was still as low as ever. Then she remembered how skimpily her outlandish costume was cut at the bosom and she tried to cover her breasts with her hands.

He took her frantic hands in his. "Why bother?" he asked cynically. "Women like you invite a man to do more than look."

Pure fury infused her, and she was about to protest. But when she tried to speak, her stays were so tight, she could only gasp helplessly. Mercifully he began to blur—first his cruelly beautiful, cynical mouth, then the rest of him. He pulled a knife from a scabbard. The last thing she saw was the glittering blade in his hand. She was aware of him examining her expertly again, his fingers sifting beneath her hair, and she was too weak to fight. "Lovely," he whispered in those honeyed, melodic tones that stirred her. Then she knew a delicious, wanton warmth as his lips covered hers. Even if he was odious and ill-mannered, he had a marvelous mouth, and she felt a soul-jolting thrill as he used it to nibble her lips with consummate skill.

"You are not hurt," he said. "But this dress is so ridiculously tight you can't breathe." He lifted her from the grass. With one careless movement, his knife sliced deftly through the laces at the back of her gown, and the satin material parted like unwanted peels from lush, ripe fruit.

His hand moved lingeringly, possessively, against the naked flesh of her back and he pulled her close against himself and kissed her again with the insolent confidence of a skilled lover who knew how to arouse the kind of woman he imagined her to be.

There were shouts from behind the walls. Running footsteps. "You owe me more than chaste kisses for saving you," he taunted silkily. "And I intend to claim my reward."

She breathed deeply, and reviving gulps of icy air rushed into her lungs. But when she opened her eyes to push him away, he was already gone.

Will and Jack were there along with all the others. She searched all the faces, looking only for his hateful, chiseled visage.

"Are you okay, Mom?" Will demanded worriedly.

Jack helped her sit up, and she leaned against the tombstone. "A man pulled me from that horse."

"What man?" Jack demanded. "Your costume's in shreds!"

"Didn't you see . . . ?"

No one had seen him.

While Jack quizzed her, Will read the inscription on the grave. "Sir Ramsay MacIntyre. Golly! This is old! This guy died in 1587."

Someone suggested that she be carried into the castle gallery to recover, and soon she found herself in a long, tall, darkly paneled room lit by several high lead-paned windows. A single shaft from the setting sun illuminated the portrait of a man in Elizabethan dress.

There was a trancelike unreality to the moment as she stared wordlessly. In any light, in any costume, the man with those excessively handsome, excessively cynical dark features would have been instantly recognizable. As she studied the high cheekbones, the aquiline nose and the full sensual lips, she grew warm

all over. She told herself her reaction was due to rage
and outrage. His costume, too, was the same.

"That's him!" she breathed only to Will.

"Who?"

Numbly she moved nearer. "The man in that
painting is the man who saved me!"

Will went to the little sign under the painting and
read. When he looked up, he gave his mother an odd
look. Then his face changed to awe and to new respect.

"Mom, he's the same guy whose name is on that
tombstone. See, he died in 1587! Mom!"

A woman in a white apron and cap approached
him. "Och," said the servant proudly, "that be none
other than Sir Ramsay, the famous ghost of Killiecraig Castle."

*She had seen a ghost. She was psychic after all—like
the rest of her crazy family!*

No! This couldn't be happening! All her life Tamara had been afraid of something like this, and she
felt doubly unlucky that her psychic encounter should
be with such an abominable ghost.

"You're a very lucky lady, ma'am." There was a
definite note of awe in the older woman's voice. "He
hasn't been seen in nearly five years. Not since he terrified Lady Katherine by floating out of this very
painting. She ran and nearly fell down the . . ."

"Down the what?"

"Never mind what happened to poor Lady Katherine. You're very lucky, ma'am. He's known for
mischief, not heroics. His favorite game is to scream
in the gallery, or make bloodstains appear on the rug
of his room on the exact date his head rolled on the
executioner's block. Sometimes he throws bottles and

fills the wine decanters with ink. Once he interrupted a game of cricket by tossing his head across the lawn."

"He sounds...ghastly."

"The ghastly ghost of Killiecraig!" Will began to jump up and down, elated. "Mom, did you really see him? I can't wait to tell Grandma! She'll be so proud!"

That thought jolted Tamara back to reality. All her life she'd been the black sheep of her family because she wasn't psychic and, worst of all, didn't want to be. Unfortunately Will didn't share her aversion to psychic phenomena. He looked wildly excited.

Tamara rubbed her head, determined to downplay the incident for Will's sake. "Obviously I bumped my head harder than I thought when I fell off that horse." Truly puzzled, she stared at the painting. "You say...he's buried in the abbey?"

"That's correct, ma'am. He was a rake—until he married. He usually haunts the ladies."

A shudder ran through Tamara. *Why me?*

She went cold. He had lain her next to his grave. He had kissed her, and even though she had thought him haughty and despicable, the handsome cad had made her feel as she had never felt before.

"Who is the woman in white hanging beside him?"

"It's *his* lady, ma'am. She disappeared. She went riding one day, and never returned. Broke his heart, they say. That's why he doesn't rest in his grave. He be looking for 'er. All the MacIntyres are exceptionally fond of their ladies," she said softly. "I'd say you favor her."

"No! But my dress is nearly like..." Tamara's voice broke as she remembered her costume had been a copy of a design in a period painting.

He was dead!

The less she thought about him and his lost lady the better. And she wasn't going to tell anyone that a ghost had kissed her. Not when everyone thought she was a screwball. Not when she came from a crazy psychic family. Not when she wanted to be normal and lead a normal life more than anything! Not when she wanted to be taken seriously by the film community.

Suddenly she wished she hadn't told Will anything, because unfortunately he had inherited her family's dreadful fascination for ghosts, a trait she didn't want to encourage.

Again she shook slightly, but as she looked at the man in the painting, she touched her cheek where Sir Ramsay had caressed it and then her lips where he had kissed her.

"I think I imagined him," she said.

"Mom! You said you saw him!"

"Well, I didn't. How could I? He's dead! And that's the end of it."

But, of course, it wasn't. It was only the beginning.

From the top of the landing she heard a man's deep-throated, husky laughter, which was followed by a low, sibilant whisper.

"What was that, Mom?"

"The wind," Tamara replied, but she was trembling as she clutched her son to her so he wouldn't run up the stairs to investigate.

"It be the ghost, ma'am. I daresay he's taken a special fancy to you." The older woman was looking at her oddly.

Tamara shivered, and she was unsure whether it was from excitement or dread. No matter. She was deter-

mined to leave at once and forget her abominable
ghost.

But the next afternoon, as she was leaving the castle, she discovered a postcard of the painting of Sir
Ramsay for sale in the gift shop. Again she studied the
slashing line of that cynical, haughty mouth and was
mortified at herself when she was unable to resist
buying the card....

Chapter One

The party was loud, and everyone was having a wonderful time. Everyone except Tamara, who had a headache. All three stories of her Vail ski chalet were filled to the brim with guests. The windows were thrown open to let in the cool summer air, and still the house smelled more of cigarettes, exotic perfumes and delicious foods than of pine and spruce.

Large tables were laden with sumptuous hors d'oeuvres. Champagne flowed from fountains. The Hollywood crowd had flown out for a private screening of Tamara's soon-to-be-released *Fair Maid,* and they were sprawled about the den watching it.

Tamara's mother, as well as Zenda, Tamara's sister, had simply popped in wearing their usual flamboyant red scarves and bright Gypsy bangles—a surprise visit. They wanted to say goodbye to Will before he and Tamara took off on a three-week holiday.

"Because you never bring him to see us, daughter dear," her mother had said mischievously.

"Because you encourage him in the wrong interests, Mother dear."

"Psychic talent should be developed at an early age," her mother had replied with such twinkling eyes that Tamara had felt deeply suspicious as she watched her parent whisk Will off for a private grandmotherly chat.

The more Tamara worried about what her mother and Will might be plotting, the more the pulse in her temples seemed to pound. Oh, why couldn't she have had a normal family? She didn't really fit into her own. Not that she had wanted to. But Will would have fit—with the slightest encouragement. Will was highly imaginative, lively, a difficult child to handle. It was Tamara's opinion that her family made him more so.

Oh, how her mother would have burst with familial pride had Tamara confided in her about Sir Ramsay MacIntyre. For that reason, Tamara had never spoken to anyone about him, least of all her mother. Not that Tamara had forgotten. On the contrary. Nothing disturbed her more than the fact that she couldn't forget him, that he'd seemed so real, that the experience had been so powerful and his spirit so compelling that she still thought of him constantly. She even carried that postcard of him in her purse and would find herself compelled upon occasion to study his cynical smile.

Fortunately there had been no more fresh supernatural events in her life since that one, so she was beginning to think that taking a sabbatical from her acting career and leaving L.A. was a move in the right direction.

After her quiet year in Vail, Tamara was so relaxed and Will was so happy that neither of them wanted her to go back to acting. Unlike many artists, she had such a shrewd business head and she was so talented at deal making and handling her investments that she would never have to worry about money again. Thus, she was free to retire and do as she liked. She could be a mother. She could do what she'd always dreamed of doing—write.

For the past few months, she had even been dabbling at writing a serious film, but every time she talked to Jack or anyone in the business about it, they just laughed at her. Long ago they had typecast her as a sexy, lightweight female.

Tomorrow the film crowd would fly back to California, and she and Will would set off for their relaxing holiday. All she had to do was live through this party and try not to worry about what her mother and Will might be planning.

She rejoined the crowd in the den just as a flickering image of herself in white satin raced across green fields. Everyone in the room clapped when she got off her horse and ran into the arms of her leading man. It was the love scene she had been practicing by herself in the glen when Sir Ramsay had come and offered to help her rehearse. She remembered the way he had slashed her dress in the abbey, the way his haughty lips had scorched her skin, and she felt a strange tremor go through her. It was an effort to smile casually when Jack came to her.

His gaze went over her body in that assessing male way she hated. "Babe, I've got the perfect picture for you."

"Have you even read my script?"

He had the grace to blush even as he ignored her question and poured himself a glass of champagne. "Babe, you're an actress, a star. Writers are a dime a dozen. Your script's too tame. Not enough sex or violence for our foreign markets."

"I'm not coming back, Jack."

"Babe, what the hell happened to you in that abbey?"

She bit her lips and tried to appear calm. "Nothing. I just moved to Vail. I wasn't getting anywhere in Hollywood."

"Right," Jack said. "You were just the biggest actress out there."

"I was doing the same thing over and over again."

"Who isn't?"

She touched his arm confidingly. "The pressure got to be too much. When I first went to California, I was a fun-loving kid who was running away from my crazy home. But I laughed all the time. Then I met Adrian. We got married. We had dreams. He wanted to be the special-effects wizard of Hollywood, and I wanted to be the decade's sexy funny girl. When my career eclipsed his, neither of us could handle it. He did brilliant things, and I did idiotic stuff, but I was the star. When he walked out, I was surrounded by sycophants. Success like that can be a curse. I became rich and famous, but I lost myself. The men I met didn't want me—they wanted the hot sex symbol I'm portrayed to be."

"That's Hollywood, babe—and not just Hollywood." Again he looked at her in that way she hated. "You're every man's fantasy."

"Which is the last thing I want to be. Will is getting older. I want him to have a stable life, to go to school, and I don't want to leave him behind to film on location. Most of all, I want him to respect me. I'm not a kid anymore. I have different dreams. And I don't know how to make them come true. I don't know who I am anymore. Or what I want to do. But I think I just want a simple, normal life. Every boyfriend I've had since Adrian has either wanted to use me as a rung on the career ladder or to brag that I'm some new notch

on his sexual gun belt—so there haven't been any
boyfriends. In Scotland I realized that I couldn't remember the last time I'd laughed.''

''Okay, babe, okay, but if you ever want to come
back to lala land, you call me before you call anybody else.''

''You'll be the first, Jack.''

The party was still going strong upstairs, but a puzzled Tamara, now in ragged jeans and a sweatshirt,
stood over her open suitcase. It was hard to pack when
she didn't know where they were going. Tomorrow
morning Will and she were just walking out to the ga-
rage, getting into the car and driving away for what
she hoped would be a dream vacation.

If Will didn't object, she planned to head south, so
she grabbed a couple of pairs of shorts. She was
throwing them into her suitcase when Will dashed into
the room carrying a large, suspicious-looking envelope.

His red hair was mussed and in need of a washing,
but what worried her was the gleam of excitement in
his eyes. Every freckle seemed to be dancing on his
nose, but maybe that was because he wasn't standing
still. He smiled brilliantly, charmingly, guiltily, and
scratched one of his ears. She felt a vague prickle of
alarm. He was up to something. She should never have
left him alone with her mother for so long.

''Mom . . .''

''Yes, hon.''

He kept scratching his ear in that nervous way of
his. ''You did say we could go . . . anywhere.''

Again she felt that warning prickle, stronger now.
''I have a feeling this is leading somewhere.''

He blurted it out in a single breath. "We won the trip!"

"We won... What trip?"

"I entered a contest, Mom. And I won! I mean, *we* won!" He thrust the brown envelope into her hands, and she jumped back as if it were a snake. "Look—two tickets. A trip to the most haunted castle in Great Britain."

"And that's good?"

"Great! You said we could go anywhere we wanted." He was talking very fast, so she couldn't interrupt. "I put down the dates you said we could be gone. Here are the airplane tickets and everything! Invitations to a masquerade ball. Wow! A limo, too! We're going back to Killiecraig Castle."

"Killiecraig Castle!" She fingered the tickets and realized they were genuine.

Unbidden came the memory of a haughty knight and his taunting aristocratic voice. *I will have you, Miss Howard. I intend to claim my reward.*

"No!" she screeched, almost throwing the tickets at him. "This is supposed to be a vacation. We said somewhere warm. Somewhere with a beach—where I can relax. Mexico. Not Scotland! We have everything here they have in Scotland—mountains, cold air."

"But, we don't have ghosts, Mom."

"I hate ghosts!" *Especially a certain ghost!*

"That's just 'cause Grandma likes 'em so much."

"She's in on this, isn't she?"

Will looked guiltily down at the floor.

"You invited her out here—just so you'd have an ally in this battle if I said no, didn't you?"

"I don't know." He stood pigeon-toed and shame-faced, tugging on his ear again, but he was too clever to admit anything.

"All my life I just wanted to be normal," Tamara moaned.

"Ghosts *are* normal, Mom, for psychics like us."

Tamara groaned. The situation was hopeless. "There's no way we can pack and get to the airport on time. Who would drive us in to Denver?"

"I'm already packed, and Grandma said she'd drive us."

"I'll just bet she did."

Will took Tamara's hand and pulled her into his bedroom. His room was immaculate—a first. A ploy to win her over, no doubt. Tamara pretended not to notice.

He pointed proudly to the nine suitcases lined up neatly against the wall. "Grandma helped me pack." On top of one suitcase was a book called *The Amateur Ghost-hunter*.

Tamara went to it and picked it up. Her mother had given her a book just like it when she was a child. "Where did you get this book?"

"Grandma."

"You knew you'd won, and you didn't tell me—you told her?"

"'Cause I knew she'd understand. I was waiting for the, er, right moment to tell you. I want to go!"

"No! Absolutely not! This is not what I planned."

"You didn't make any plans, Mom, because you said plans would ruin everything. That's another reason I didn't tell you. Grandma thinks it's a great idea. She says old castles are the ideal environments for psychic phenomena."

"The ideal…" Tamara flung the book down. "That settles it! Will Howard, we're not going. And I'm sending your meddlesome grandma packing, too. This is an absolute no. I mean it. We're going to Mexico."

Killiecraig Castle loomed above them, darkly magnificent against the background of blue sea and green hills.

"We're here, Mom! We're here!"

Tamara nodded sleepily as their white stretch limousine pulled up beside a tour bus painted to look like a giant red-and-gold tartan. When her chauffeur got out and began unloading their twelve bags, she rummaged for her shoes and Will dug frantically under the seats for his books and games.

Then the chauffeur opened her door, and she stepped out and warily looked up at the carved gargoyles over the arched doorway—vicious, cruel-looking beasts that seemed to warn her away.

Her gaze traveled farther up to the machicolated towers and their crenellations. A light came and went in a tower window, and she thought she saw a stealthy movement behind the curtain there. Quickly she looked away, but the uncanny feeling that she was being watched lingered. *Her ghost?* A disquieting sensation tickled through her. As she drew her heavy sweater more tightly about her shoulders, she told herself it was only the cool breeze rushing up the cliffs carrying the scent of the sea that chilled her.

Even though it was summer and she was dressed warmly in a pair of her favorite jeans and a long-sleeved cotton shirt that downplayed her voluptuous figure, she felt exposed standing there in the open. Perhaps she really had that extra sense that ran in her family. To distract herself from that horrible notion, she struck up a conversation with her son, who was counting his suitcases to make sure none was missing.

"What did you pack in all those bags?"

He looked up quickly and gave his ear a nonchalant tug. "Stuff."

"What kind of answer is that?"

"Special-effects stuff I borrowed from Dad to catch your ghost with, and a few things from Grandma."

"Oh, no!" At the mention of her mother and ex-husband, Tamara felt her panic level begin to rise. "Will, there are no such things as ghosts."

"Then why were you so scared about coming back here?"

The light came on in the tower window and winked at her—almost mischievously. Tamara twirled a strand of her red hair on her fingertip and forced herself to stare defiantly up at the window. "I don't believe in ghosts, and I'm not scared."

But when the light went out, she jumped.

"What's wrong?"

"Nothing. Absolutely nothing...."

"Then let's go look at *his* picture."

"No. And that's an absolute no. I mean it."

Mother and son were standing again in the gallery after dinner beneath *his* portrait. She was tense; Will was excited. All evening these emotions had been playing against one another and building.

The painting was lit; the rest of the room was filled with shadows. Tamara was acutely aware of that painted visage even though she had avoided looking up at him—which was ridiculous. Why should she be afraid of a painting?

In the grand room, Tamara became aware that she was still wearing her jeans and sweater.

"Do you think we were dressed too casually at dinner?" she asked to avoid talking about the painting. "All the other tourists were wearing elegant dresses."

Her son's dark eyes left Sir Ramsay and flashed at her admiringly. "Old ladies have to dress up. They don't look as good as you."

She was touched by his compliment. So touched she momentarily forgot the danger of where she was. As if pulled by a magnet she let her eyes be drawn to the painting. Once caught, she couldn't tear them away. She stared wordlessly, shamelessly, into those devil-black eyes, and again she felt the riveting pull of his dangerous spell, despite the centuries that separated them.

He had saved her life.

No. *He was a ghost.* No! He wasn't even that! She had imagined him.

Unbidden came the memory of his thrillingly sensual kisses and of his claim that she owed him more than such kisses. More imaginings? And had she imagined the knife and the severed laces of her dress, as well?

He was everything she hated most. Not only was he a ghost, and the last sort of creature she wanted any kind of a relationship with, but like so many of her modern admirers, he saw her as nothing more than the embodiment of some torrid male sexual fantasy.

Why then was he able to fascinate her as no man ever had—not even Adrian? Her slim hands clenched. Hatred was a powerful emotion, she told herself. As powerful as love.

Perhaps this was the curse of being born into a psychic family. Maybe she had tried to deny this fatal talent because she had sensed the disastrous power it might have over her.

Nearby, there was a sibilant whisper. Tamara and Will both jumped.

They were not alone.

Then the door beneath the painting opened quietly, and a shadowy figure appeared. In the breathless silence, Will clutched for his mother's hand, bravely releasing it the instant he recognized Selma, the same servant who'd served their dinner tonight, the same talkative servant who had shown them the painting a year ago.

Selma wiped her hands on her white apron. "Your ghost has been up to mischief this past week," she said.

Will and Tamara both spoke at once.

Tamara was trembling. "He's *not* my ghost."

Will was jumping up and down. "Hey, that's great!"

"He stole all the keys. Bloodstains appeared on the carpets again.

Tamara didn't want Will hearing more of Selma's overly imaginative stories, so she quickly said goodnight and dragged him up several flights of stairs to their adjoining rooms. The minute they were alone, she began again, "Will, there are no such things as ghosts."

He crossed his arms over his chest and stood as still and as stubborn as a miniature Napoleon. "But Grandma says—"

"Will! She's wrong. We've come all this way... for nothing. We don't have to stay here, you know. We could take that tour into Edinburgh tomorrow with the old ladies. There is nothing to do here. There are no kids. You are going to be bored out of your skull."

He thrust out his chin and kept his arms laced. "There's lots to do. You can read your investment magazines and forget all about me."

He went to a suitcase and began unpacking, carefully setting items on a bureau in the methodical manner of his father. She saw masking tape, scissors, sacks of flour, string, rope, nuts, marbles, makeup kits... "It's going to take me a while to get ready," Will said brightly.

"To get ready for what?" she asked suspiciously.

"Your ghost."

"Stop calling him that!"

Will plopped down on his bed and started leafing through *The Amateur Ghost-hunter*.

It had always been impossible to talk Adrian out of a project he was enthusiastic about. Why was she trying to talk Will out of his? She would have to find another way of convincing him. So, while he read and calculated and sifted through his bags, she unpacked her lingerie and got ready for bed. While she showered, her son locked and taped all the doors and then spread strings across her bedroom in the area between her bed and the door. One window wouldn't lock, so he nailed it shut. The key to her door was missing and therefore couldn't be locked. So he nailed it shut, too. Before he locked his own, he put marbles out in the passage. Then he sealed his door with tape. He rolled back the rugs and sprinkled flour between their beds and their doors.

When he was in bed, he explained, "If he isn't a real ghost, he'll come through a door and leave footprints."

His eyelids drooped sleepily and she kissed him good-night. "How very reassuring."

"But if he's a human, I'll catch him for you, Mom."

"Believe me, that's the last thing I want."

Will closed his eyes and was instantly asleep.

Tamara returned to her room. In a swirl of diaphanous gown, she went to the tall window. One of the incongruities in her nature was that while she liked to wear jeans by day, she adored sexy lingerie underneath them and filmy negligees at night.

The well-kept lawn sloped down to the cliffs and the sea. In the distance she could see the abbey and the gravestones shining eerily in the moonlight. Against her will she remembered him.

Her heart raced crazily. It seemed to her he was very near.

Quickly she withdrew her elbows from the window ledge and went to her bed. She turned out the light, and the room melted into darkness.

If he's human . . .

Hateful thought, she assured herself more adamantly.

Unbidden came the memory of his warm kiss.

If he's human . . .

That would only make her hate him more than ever.

But when she fell instantly to sleep, the smile that curved her lips was shamelessly rapturous.

Chapter Two

The same silvery moonlight that gilded the abbey and its tombstones streamed into Tamara's bedroom. In her dream she was in the abbey again. It was terribly cold, and she was shivering from what she imagined must be the coldness of his open grave.

Suddenly her ghost was there, enormous and standing near. Then he was kneeling and pulling her into his arms, holding her close. He placed a beautiful gold rhododendron blossom in her hair. Velvety petals tickled her skin. She felt the warmth of his hand tenderly stroke her cheek, and she moaned softly, reveling in his touch, yearning for more.

With a roughened fingertip he slowly traced the line of her throat to her neck, setting fire to her senses. With another soft little sigh of pleasure she wrapped her arms around his broad shoulders and lifted her face for his kiss.

Her gallant ghost, ever ready to give her what she wanted, lowered his head to hers.

"You are everything I imagined and more," he whispered in that low, raspy, faintly insolent tone she remembered so well.

He was on top of her, the muscular, unforgiving length of his powerful body pressing down upon her much-slimmer frame. They fitted together perfectly. His arms were hard about her. When his lips covered hers in a long, demanding kiss, her mouth opened instinctively to let his tongue slide inside. His kisses were delicious and thrillingly hot. She threaded her hands through his hair and drew him closer.

His hair was as soft as silk as it curled untidily about her fingertips.

It was all so real.

"Tamara . . ." His haughty voice had deepened and was huskily warm. No one had ever spoken her name so charmingly, so urgently. His unsteady breaths tickled her throat.

Her eyelids fluttered drowsily open. He caught her chin with the edge of his hand and tipped it back, forcing her to look up at him, and as she stared into the fierce, possessive glitter of his black eyes, she froze.

He was there. Really there! And even more marvelous looking than before. He had straight, even features, a lean jaw and a beautifully shaped mouth.

Her room was very cold, and in her thin nightgown she began to tremble. She turned away wildly. The moonlight illuminated the unbroken expanse of Will's tape that crisscrossed and sealed her door, as well as the untouched expanse of white flour between her bed and the door. He had left no footprints.

Her ghost was real.

"You must go," she whispered. "You have no right to come here like this! I don't want to be psychic! I won't be! Go and haunt somebody else!"

His beautiful mouth curved, but he didn't speak. She was her mother's daughter after all, and she couldn't resist the terrible impulse to reach out and touch him. She sucked in her breath for courage as she moved her hand closer.

Her fingertips hovered a faltering mere inch from his lips when a scream of sheer terror erupted from the passage. There was an awful thump.

From the next room she heard Will spring from his bed. "Yippee! Mom! I've caught your ghost for you!"

Her ghost smiled down at her sardonically.

Was there another one?

"Will! Don't go out there!" She threw back her covers even as her son's running footsteps told her he had disobeyed her—as usual. She heard him panting as he struggled to unfasten his taped door.

Her ghost had arisen and was slowly backing into a darkened corner and dissolving into the shadows.

She got out of bed and rushed to Will's room. Moonlight shone on the tumbled sheets of his empty bed. She saw her son's footprints in the flour, the gaping door, the black passage.

"Will!"

"It's just Selma, Mom," Will said sulkily, profoundly disappointed.

Tamara flew out into the passage. Selma was sprawled in a sea of marbles as helplessly as a beached whale on a rocky shore.

Tamara knelt beside the poor woman. "Oh dear, I'm so sorry. I'm afraid this is all my fault. Take my hand."

Selma struggled to her feet with a groan and limped to the light switch. "Marbles!" She leaned down and picked up a shiny agate one and glowered down at a wide-eyed Will. "Someone's been up to mischief, and I bet I know who."

"Not mischief. I just wanted to catch the ghost," Will explained weakly.

"It's me you caught, young man. With these bruises and my bad back, I'd say you're a lot more dangerous than any ghost."

"Pick up those marbles, Will," Tamara commanded gently.

"But . . . what if he comes?"

"He'll just float right over them," Selma said with some asperity. "It's *people* that fall and break their necks. Don't you know anything about ghosts? He could be standing here right now—invisible—laughing at us."

Will was deeply insulted by her last remarks and dragged his feet about picking up the marbles. But at last he finished, and within minutes Tamara had him tucked into his bed once more and was back in her own room. Her bedroom was still much colder than Will's. Shivering, she turned on the light.

There were no footprints in the flour. The doors and windows were still sealed with tape. Her room was ice-cold.

Had Sir Ramsay come? Or had she only imagined him? Did she imagine as well his warm, male scent that seemed to cling to her skin?

She went to her bed, more determined than ever to convince herself he was nothing but a horrible figment of her highly active imagination. But when she threw back the covers and was about to get into her bed, she saw it.

She gave a startled gasp.

On her pillow lay a single golden rhododendron blossom.

Soft summer sunlight sparkled on the damp leaves of the rhododendron tree. Bees were dipping in and out of the sweet, nectar-laden flowers. Tamara had just said goodbye to the old ladies who were off to Edinburgh for their day-long bus tour. Will was in a drawing room eagerly quizzing Selma about the ghost.

Tamara held her blossom up against a clump of blossoms on the tree and saw that the delicate gold petals were an exact match. Well, the flower was real, and it appeared to have come from this tree.

Just as she made that realization, a bee buzzed toward the blossom in her hand and she screamed.

"Oh, dear me!" said a sharp, annoyed voice from the other side of the hedge. "What's wrong?"

Tamara walked around to the other side. A portly lady with snowy white hair was kneeling on a towel before a flower bed. Her plump figure was as tightly girdled as a seamless navy sausage. She looked the way Tamara had always imagined Mrs. Santa Claus would look.

"Bees!" Tamara explained in a low, embarrassed tone. "I'm scared of them."

"Don't you know anything about gardens, child?"

"I'm afraid not."

"Then you must learn. Bees are a blessing in the garden," said Mrs. Claus, who was dressed rather formally for gardening in navy blue and pearls and goatskin gardening gloves. She set her spade down firmly in the black dirt and rose with some difficulty.

"Please don't get up," Tamara said.

"I'm Lady Emma MacIntyre," she said briskly.

"Delighted to meet you." Tamara held out her hand with the flower in it.

Lady Emma regarded her plucked blossom with a deep frown. "Dear me, child, you mustn't pick the rhodies."

"I didn't. I found it on my pillow last night."

Lady Emma examined it closely as if looking to see if it had wings or legs. "How on earth did it get there?"

"I was wondering the same thing myself."

"Dear me. I always hate strange things happening. The servants, especially Selma, will blame it on our ghost. Selma is so enthusiastic about the ghost." A pause. "I like life to be orderly...predictable...like my garden."

"Yes, that would be lovely."

"You're that actress, aren't you?" Lady Emma did not seem pleased. "My son, Ramsay, is a great fan of yours."

"A fan?" Tamara knew what that probably meant, and she blushed. "Ramsay?" The name sent a cold chill through her. "Isn't that the same name as the ghost's?"

"I'm afraid so." A shadow passed across Lady Emma's face and then was gone. "Unfortunately my Ramsay's as dark as his unlucky namesake ever was. There's more than one ghost in this family, my dear. There are stories I could tell you, stories of misguided ambition, tragedies..." She broke off. "But I'm sure you are not interested in our family history."

"Oh, but I am."

"My first son was our favorite."

What a dreadful thing for a mother to say. "Was?"

Again a shadow passed across the woman's plump face. "Ian died—a hunting accident. Ramsay took over running the estates. He's had his share of trouble. It was a dark angel who cursed Ramsay. Poor Ramsay even looks a bit like our famous ghost. Selma was always especially fond of Ramsay—perhaps for that reason. She played a part in spoiling him and turning him into the arrogant devil he is.''

So, there was a flesh-and-blood Sir Ramsay Mac-Intyre, who was so disreputable that his own mother couldn't recommend him. As she pretended to study her blossom, Tamara's mind filled with new doubts and wild speculations, as well as a certain sympathy for him.

Lady Emma knelt down again and explained that she was tucking cloves into the rose bed to prevent slugs. ''So you liked our castle enough to come back, did you?''

''My son won a dream vacation here.''

''I didn't know about any contest.'' Lady Emma looked baffled. ''That must be Ramsay's doing. Although he's perverse about most things, he's quite clever at managing the estate. He's ambitious, you see, which is not always a bad thing.''

Tamara frowned at the golden blossom.

''Child, you must come to tea. I'm sure Caroline and Ramsay would love to meet you.''

''Caroline?''

''Our delightful neighbor from Mount Woraig. She's a very special friend of Ramsay's.'' Lady Emma's eyes sparkled. ''Lately they are constantly together.''

''You look pleased.''

''I am. Ramsay's usual female companions, shall we say, are of a different caliber. But never mind about that! They grew up together. She is as beautiful as he is handsome. And she's an excellent gardener.''

''It sounds like a fairy-tale match.''

"She has a fortune. Perhaps that's why he finally noticed her. She's respectable. He has a title. She has always loved this magnificent house."

"I see." Tamara looked wistfully up at the castle.

She felt a vague sadness for the flesh-and-blood Ramsay, the ambitious dark angel. His future marriage sounded about as romantic as the most materialistic of Hollywood deals.

Chapter Three

It was cool and so late that the shadows in the abbey were long. Tamara still had an hour before tea, so she had taken a walk and ended up too near the ruined, lichen-covered walls and tumbledown tombstones to avoid them. A cool, crisp breeze whispered in the trees. Even in broad daylight with a modern jet painting a white trail across the sky, there was a sense of gloom and decay about the ruin.

She tucked her golden rhododendron blossom in her hair and, removing her sandals, tiptoed barefoot across the tall, wet grasses toward Sir Ramsay's grave. Like the others, his tombstone was a little crooked, the carved letters blurred by time, but she could read them clearly. "Sir Ramsay MacIntyre."

There was a whispery sound from behind her. A tall shadow fell across the grave.

She whirled.

And there he was, standing in vaporous mists, with his thick black hair and scorching black eyes, his too-handsome face and sensual mouth smiling a dazzling white smile. As he raked her with his bold hot gaze, she was completely unnerved.

A chill wind gusted through the abbey. The mists dissolved. Her face went chalky white.

"Good afternoon," he said in a deep, melodious voice that seemed to burn through her. "You were remembering me . . . fondly?"

"No!" She blurted the word a bit too wildly.

"I can see that you are a woman who would deny the truth."

"You are as haughtily arrogant as ever."

He grinned at that.

Instinctively Tamara began backing away from him. She stumbled into Sir Ramsay's tombstone and fell across the grave. The blurred letters seemed to mock her. She read the inscription again, jumped up and screamed. He laughed at her discomfiture. In her haste to get away from him, the golden blossom and her sandals fell into the high grasses that covered his grave.

She began to scramble away from him in earnest, but he moved quickly, more quickly than she, and blocked the yawning archway that would have been her escape. He didn't touch her, but she was aware of the subtle power of his tense body.

"Don't be afraid," he commanded, but his husky voice, vibrant with desire, made her more so.

Her heart was beating like a rabbit's, but she was determined not to act afraid. "You took me by surprise."

"I saw you come this way and I followed you here."

He wore the tweed jacket of a modern British gentleman who lived in the country. With an effort she recovered herself. "You're real."

"Very real."

"I mean...alive!"

He laughed. "I should hope so." His dark eyes gleamed. He stooped to pick up her things, and she leaned down at the same moment. His hand touched hers, and her stomach fluttered. "Would you prefer me dead?"

"No," she said breathlessly, but she drew back.

He moved nearer.

"But the ghost?" she asked.

"A foolish legend the servants repeat to lure tourists and intrigue inquisitive little boys."

"But you look like him!"

"Surely you didn't think that *I* was the ghost?"

"No! Of... of course not!"

A wry smile crooked his haughty mouth. "You did! Didn't your mother tell you there were no such things as ghosts?"

"No! I... I mean, of course, she did. Don't all normal mothers..."

He laughed at her obvious confusion. "You're lying, and it's not something you do all that easily. Tell me about this mother who taught you to believe in ghosts. Tell me—" he paused as his eyes drifted over her body "—how an actress with your... talents still blushes as easily as a girl?"

Tamara was trembling, too conscious of his searing gaze. It was no use trying to hide the truth. "My mother is psychic. I'm not. I was a great disappointment to her."

"I see you and I have something in common—unusual mothers. Mine is a tyrant in the garden and would arrange my life as she arranges her flower beds. I, too, have been a bit of a disappointment to her. Unfortunately I'm not as docile as her dahlias."

"That's easy to believe."

Again he laughed. "I'm glad you came back."

"It was my son's idea, not mine! He won..."

"Ah, yes. The contest." Sir Ramsay's eyes went over her. "He's a lucky little boy."

"And unfortunately, like the rest of my family, Will's overly interested in psychic phenomena."

"He should be happy here. This is reputed to be the most haunted castle in Great Britain."

"It was you who saved me then, and not the ghost?"

"I was out riding, and then I saw you go flying by." He grinned. "Anyone would have done the same."

"But why did you pretend to be the ghost?"

"I didn't. Can I help it if I resemble a certain painting of him?"

"You were even dressed like him."

"I was on my way to Caroline's masquerade ball."

"Your special friend?"

A muscle twitched in Ramsay's cheek. "My mother's phrase."

"She has a fortune—you have a title."

"You *have* been talking to my mother." His voice was grim. "She arranged my first marriage and plans to do so again. She sees it as my duty to marry well."

"And was your first marriage a success?"

"In some ways." His quiet tone held a faint edge of bitterness. "But I'm a widower now."

She saw that he was not a man who easily revealed himself. "I'm sorry." An awkward pause. "I'm afraid my son, Will, is going to be very disappointed there's no ghost."

"The last thing I want is for either of you to be disappointed." His deep voice seemed to flow over her.

"Last night, you came to my room."

His chuckle was warm. "To welcome you."

"An unconventional welcome."

Again he smiled. "For an unconventional... lady."

The soft irony in his last word was so close to an insult that she blushed. "My door was locked," she said quickly. "How did you get in?"

"You would know all my secrets?"

"You kissed me...."

Again, that white smile. "You did not seem to object."

"Why did you do that?"

He moved closer. A new fire kindled in his eyes. "For the same reason I want to now. Dear God, you are lovely...."

"No...." She tried to move away.

Effortlessly he caught her to him. "I'm sure you usually say yes."

"I'm not that kind of woman!"

Hard hands imprisoned her against his body. "You don't have to play the innocent with me," he murmured. "I like your kind of woman and the simple relationships a man can have with them." Then he bent her back over his arm and kissed her as if he were starving.

For one horrible moment she forgot to struggle, and she clung to him, opening her mouth to his, returning his kiss with hot trembling lips that betrayed a need as fiery as his own. Until she remembered where she was. And who he was. And what he obviously thought of her.

Then she flung herself free, and her golden blossom fell to the grave again. "I have to go, or I'll be late... to meet your mother... and Caroline for tea."

His black brows arched. "You and I are better suited to this kind of dalliance than to tame tea parties, my dear."

He reached for her again, but this time she eluded him. "Think of Caroline."

"She is the last thing on my mind at the moment."

"You should be ashamed."

"It's easy to judge when you don't know the facts."

"I know enough. It is all too obvious you are the type of man who makes love to one kind of woman and marries another."

"I admit only that I was enjoying myself immensely with you. And so were you." His dark eyes flashed. "Are you hinting that if I married you, you would no longer be adverse to my lovemaking?"

"It's no use talking to you."

"Good. There are other things I'd rather do with you than talk." His softly spoken jeer was a sensual invitation.

Mortified, Tamara raced past him.

He seemed in no hurry to follow her. With a leisurely air he stooped and picked up the golden flower and pinned it onto his lapel.

"Our Miss Howard is really quite famous," Lady Emma said as Tamara autographed a napkin for Caroline.

The afternoon had grown even cooler. Despite the brilliant sunshine slanting across the lush garden from beneath dark clouds, there was a mood of impending storm. The three women were sitting in deck chairs that had been brought from the conservatory out onto the brick terrace.

Caroline, blond and icily beautiful, was dressed in flawlessly cut riding clothes. She took the napkin haughtily when Tamara had finished and tucked it into her purse. "My maid will be delighted. She is a great fan of yours."

Tamara, who was beginning to wish she'd never accepted this invitation, bit her tongue to keep from making a catty return. Still in her jeans and sweater, she felt too casual for this tea. When neither Ramsay nor Will had showed up on time, the three women had run quickly through their small talk and moved on to Lady Emma's favorite topic—gardening. She discussed her hydrangeas, pampas grass and bamboos with great enthusiasm. She then explained that the sequoias and other conifers had been planted at the edge of the garden to shelter her rhodies and other tender plants from fierce winter winds.

Her garden *was* lovely, Tamara decided, with the austere castle towering over the flowing paradise of climbing roses and sweet-smelling honeysuckle. Straight paths met precisely at a sundial that was overrun with lavender and thyme, sage and parsley. There was the faint smell of peat burning—its essence golden and smoky, like whiskey.

Lady Emma was droning on about her garden when Tamara saw Selma coming toward them in her starched white apron and cap. The poor woman could barely manage the silver tray laden with blue china cups and a silver tea service. When Tamara jumped up and took the tray from her, Caroline looked vaguely startled and then smugly pleased. Selma thanked Tamara and then returned with an even heavier tray loaded with plates of scones, bread and butter, biscuits, tiny griddle cakes, jam, clotted cream, thinly sliced ham, little golden iced cupcakes and watercress sandwiches.

"There's enough food for an army," Tamara said, jumping up to help Selma again.

"That's because Ramsay's coming," Caroline said softly.

A damp wind gusted, and Tamara shivered apprehensively.

"Did someone call my name?" the conceited devil in question called out jauntily. He whispered something into Selma's ear which made her hug him and laugh before she scurried away.

Both Lady Emma and Caroline jumped up, delighted. Tamara coldly concentrated on setting down the heavy tray. Ramsay kissed Caroline and his mother lightly on their cheeks and drew a chair up beside them, basking in their attention. But all the time, Tamara was aware of his eyes taking in her struggles with the tray. Before he sat down, he leaned over to help her.

"I was managing quite nicely without you," Tamara said coolly.

"Indeed?" His smile gleamed and his dark eyes flashed mockingly. "Nevertheless, it is my duty as a . . . gentleman." He seemed to say the word with difficulty.

"Why do you even bother to pretend to be one," she whispered into his ear, "when we both know you're a scoundrel?"

He laughed softly as she released the tray into his hands and sat down mutinously.

Under his breath he murmured, "You're lucky I am. Gentlemen are too stuffy a breed for a . . . lady of your talents."

At this fresh insult, Tamara saw fire.

Lady Emma introduced them.

Ramsay ignored Caroline and concentrated on Tamara. "Delighted," he said, taking Tamara's hand in his.

The man was maddening. He'd probably pinned her flower onto his lapel just to taunt her. She yanked her hand from his before his lips could touch it. Fortunately the other two women were so interested in Ramsay they did not notice her anger.

"As I was telling you, Miss Howard, my son is a great fan of yours."

"I'm thrilled to hear it," Tamara said icily.

"The thrill is all mine, I assure you," he countered.

"Well, I've quit making movies," she snapped.

"Why?"

"Because..." She almost said, *Because of men like you.* But she looked into his eyes expecting mockery; instead he seemed keenly interested. She spoke more gently. "I-I never fit into the Hollywood scene. It was too wild for me."

"I find that hard to believe."

"I wanted to be taken seriously."

"You are too beautiful—to be serious."

"Your chauvinistic attitude is the prevalent one there among the men who have the power. All they wanted me to be was a cute, funny bimbo. I just can't do it anymore. You see, in that environment even the laughter went out of my soul."

His handsome face had grown intense. Before he could speak, Caroline took his hand possessively and said, "Then we will have to find a way to amuse her, won't we, darling?"

He was holding Caroline's hand, but he had eyes only for Tamara. "Indeed we will." His voice was low, intimate.

Tamara felt drawn to him despite firsthand knowledge that he was abominable. Caroline seemed to think there was an understanding between them, even while he flirted blatantly with another. Tamara was appalled. She was on the verge of excusing herself when Will appeared. There were more introductions. Lady Emma began to fuss excessively as Will helped himself to scones and jam and milk.

When her son had finished eating, Tamara said sweetly, "Will, you see that I was right, after all?"

"What do you mean?"

"I didn't see a ghost."

Will's eyes widened with dismay. He began to finger his ear nervously.

"It was Lady Emma's son, Ramsay, who saved me." Tamara glanced toward Ramsay. "He was dressed up like the other Sir Ramsay for a masquerade ball. I mistook him for his ancestor in the painting."

Will studied Ramsay with new interest. And as his young face grew very glum as reality sank in, Tamara's became exuberant.

A few minutes later, when the weather grew misty, Will asked to be excused. Tamara escaped with him.

Chapter Four

Tamara sat on Will's bed and pretended to read a mutual-fund prospectus. In reality she was watching Will pack with a smug, motherly, didn't-I-tell-you-so-dear air. She was pleased that his book, *The Amateur Ghost-hunter,* lay forgotten in one corner.

"You're sure you want to go?" she asked him solicitously, setting her prospectus aside.

He pitched a couple of stray baseball cards into a suitcase. "There's nothing to do here, Mom."

"Since there are no ghosts, huh?"

"Mom! You said you wouldn't rub it in!"

"Can't I? Not even just a little?"

He picked up a rumpled sweatshirt and threw it at her.

She held up her hands teasingly in a mock gesture of surrender. "Okay. You win."

"No. You won, Mom, and you're gloating."

Tamara almost wished her own mother were here so she could really gloat. This was a victory over psychic nonsense, as well as a victory over a certain appalling man.

Tamara and Will had eaten their dinners in their rooms because Tamara hadn't wanted to risk seeing Ramsay again. Not that she felt quite as hostile toward him as she had during tea. No, now that she was sure of her escape, she could afford to be magnanimous toward everyone in the castle, even him.

Suddenly there was a loud knock on Tamara's door.

Tamara got up and went to her room. "I bet that's Selma here for our trays." She opened the door. "Come in," she said, carelessly turning away, her red hair floating loosely about her shoulders, her night-gown billowing.

"I thought you'd never ask."

She froze at the sound of that deep, familiar voice. Then, in a rush, she grabbed her robe from her bed and pulled it on.

Ramsay's black, haughty eyes watched her fumbling movements. "We missed you at dinner," he said softly. "*I* missed you."

She stiffened. "Will and I were tired. We have a long trip tomorrow."

Ramsay picked up one of her investment magazines, thumbed through it, then tossed it back onto her bed.

"Then you're leaving?"

"See for yourself." Triumphantly she led him to the door to Will's room, where Will was packing.

"But you were supposed to stay three weeks."

"Will is so disappointed that there's no ghost that he's agreed to go somewhere warm—like Spain." She headed jauntily back into her room. "Now, if you'll excuse me, I need to pack—for a real vacation."

Ramsay's footsteps thundered behind her. "If it's warmth you're after, I'll give you warmth." His hand caught hers burningly. As he drew her to him, his gaze raked her with such unnerving thoroughness that she was momentarily mesmerized. Then his mouth fastened on hers.

For a second she yielded to the heat of his firm lips and powerful hands. His kiss was over before it had begun. When he let her go, she fell away from him, shuddering weakly, her heart fluttering wildly, the taste of him lingering.

"Don't go," he commanded. "We haven't had a chance to get to know each other."

"It's for the best."

"How can you be sure?"

"I've met too many other men who think about me as you do." Her shamed voice was a hoarse whisper.

"I'm sure you have." His gaze went over her flushed cheeks, her flaming hair, her heaving breasts.

"You see what I mean."

"What would any man think?"

"You remind me why I've stayed single and celibate so long."

"Celibate? You?"

"See, you're surprised. Just the way you say the word is an insult. The way you look at me..."

"You're an American sex goddess."

She groaned deep in her throat like a frightened animal. "That's my Hollywood image! I'm not that person. I have a brain, a personality. I'm not just a body! Quit looking at me like that."

"I'm looking at you because I want you so much."

"What you want...I cannot give so easily as you seem to think."

He took her wrist and put his finger to her leaping pulse. "Even though you are attracted?"

"I'll admit...to a little crazy chemistry," she said weakly, pulling her hand free. "But I'm looking for more than that in a relationship."

"Why?"

"I want love."

"Love!" He shrugged. "That's a word."

"You are wrong," she said softly. "It's two people sharing the same values, sharing their lives and more."

"Stay and teach me then," he whispered. "Maybe it's not too late for me to learn your definition of the word."

"I don't think I'd find you a willing pupil. I rather think you'd try to instruct me with lessons of your own."

"Like so many others, you judge me before you know me," he said harshly.

Like so many others. Had he, too, suffered the same thing she had? Curious, Tamara studied his closed, darkly handsome features. He had not been the favorite son. Was his haughtiness a defense? He was ambitious, virile. Even though he had come on too strong, she had the impression that he had hidden depths. No other man had ever caused the kind of emotional upheaval inside her that just his voice, his touch, could cause.

"Please . . . don't go," he said.

Some powerful emotion flared in his eyes before he quickly subdued it. She felt almost irresistibly attracted to him. Fortunately, just as his large hands closed gently over her shoulders to draw her nearer, Will bounded into the room.

"It's Will's decision," she said, flushing with guilty embarrassment as she turned primly away. "I'd better pack."

Ramsay growled impatiently. Then he started on Will.

Silently Tamara listened to his arguments.

But it was no use. Since there were no ghosts, Will had decided to please his mother and go someplace where she could have a real vacation.

At last Ramsay gave up—rather too easily, Tamara thought.

And when he said goodbye, some perverse instinct made her wish he would drag her into his arms and kiss her fiercely again until he made her know that she could never leave him.

Instead he said a terse goodbye as if he had something more important than her on his mind, and walked out the door.

As she turned back to her packing, it was strange how lonely and deflated his coldness made her feel. Strange that she almost wished he had turned out to be a sexy ghost, after all.

In a distant passage in the castle a clock struck midnight. Tamara stirred uneasily in her bed. At the twelfth chime a bloodcurdling, otherworldly howl erupted from Will's room.

Terrified, Tamara sprang awake in the dark. "Will!" The castle was so still she thought she'd been dreaming. Then the dreadful scream was repeated. When its echoes died away, the silence that followed was like death.

Dear God! Will!

Tamara rushed toward his room. She collided with her son in their doorway.

"Mom! Mom!" He threw himself into her arms.

As she held his shivering body close, she noticed that his room was ice-cold. He was too excited to endure her cuddling long. He pushed her away and flicked on the light. The room was empty except for them.

"Did you see it, Mom?"

"What?"

"The ghost."

"I thought we agreed that there is no such thing," she said gently, hopefully. "There's nobody here but us."

"But there was!" He couldn't contain his excitement. "It was green, and headless, and it howled. It came out of the air, and it floated away!"

"Will, you had a bad dream."

"No! I saw it! Just feel the air! It's cold—air from the grave!" he spoke in a dramatic spooky voice that was uncannily like the overly dramatic tone his grandmother used during séances.

Psychic genes? No! Will didn't have them! And neither did she!

"Will, please! Calm down."

There was a thunderous knock at the door. Will jumped back into her arms. Round eyed, they both watched the handle turn. "I bolted the door from the inside," Will whispered.

They kept clutching each other and watching the door as if they expected a phantom to float through it. Tamara was the first to recover. She went to the door and unbolted it.

The minute she saw Sir Ramsay standing there, she realized she was in her nightgown. When she raced back into her bedroom for her robe, he followed her inside.

"I thought I heard something," Ramsay said, his voice grave. "Is anything wrong?"

Tamara didn't want him to know. "We're fine now," she said shakily.

"No!" Will shouted. "He came!"

"Who?" Ramsay demanded.

"The ghost! He came to my room!"

"You're sure?" Ramsay's voice was quiet as he knelt to the child's level.

"He was green, and he howled!"

"He sounds dreadful," Ramsay said comfortingly in a gentle tone.

"No, he was wonderful," Will exclaimed. "I can see ghosts! Just like Grandma! And Mom heard him, so she's psychic, too."

"There must be some rational explanation," Tamara said.

"I'm sure there is," Ramsay agreed.

His dark face was unreadable in the shadowy room. Did she only imagine that he sounded faintly amused?

"No!" Will said adamantly.

Tamara lashed out at Ramsay. "This is all your fault!"

He looked startled. "What do you mean?"

"If you'd told me who you were when you saved me that time . . ."

His expression held grim relief. "You fainted, remember?"

"Well, this is the very worst thing that could have happened."

"No, it's the very best!" Will contradicted. "Grandma was so sure this would be a good environment to explore psychic phenomena."

"I hate your ghost and your legends, Ramsay MacIntyre. I'm afraid that it's going to be hard to convince Will to leave tomorrow," Tamara said passionately.

"Impossible, Mom. We're staying, and that's final." Will sounded very determined.

"Will, we are *not* psychic, and that's what's final."

"I never thought I would feel gratitude for our famous phantom blackguard," Ramsay said, and this time she was sure of his amusement. "But if his appearance keeps you here, I am grateful." To Will he said, "You're a very brave little boy. You must guard your mother with great care. Like most women, she is naturally terrified of a headless ghost."

"I am not terrified!" Tamara shouted at them both indignantly. "I don't believe there was a headless ghost!"

"Nevertheless, we men must guard you," Ramsay said conspiratorially.

"You're not helping, Ramsay MacIntyre! All I want you to do is leave me alone!"

Ramsay turned to face her fully. "Which is the very last thing I will ever do," he countered softly, an ardent fire darkening his eyes, which she refused to meet.

Soft sunshine streamed into Will's room as Tamara struggled breathlessly to roll back the heavy rug so she could search the floor for a trapdoor.

Beneath the carpet she found nothing. Bitterly disappointed, she sat up and stared at the stone walls.

Ramsay had come to her room one night without using the door. So had the headless phantom. She wondered if the two appearances had been engineered by the same unscrupulous individual. Not that she was about to voice her suspicions to either Will or Ramsay—not yet. The last thing she could have readily admitted to Will was that Ramsay had appeared in her bedroom and she had let him kiss her. And with Ramsay, she knew it was best to keep him off balance.

She was concentrating so hard she didn't hear Ramsay push the partially opened door wider.

"What are you doing?" he demanded as he strode inside.

She started guiltily. "Oh . . . nothing." She began to roll the rug back into place.

"You were obviously looking for a trapdoor or something."

Her dark eyes flickered guiltily in her white face. "N-no. . . ."

"Well, there isn't one," he said emphatically.

A slow anger was building inside her. He had wanted her to stay. Had he used her son to keep her here?

"And I'm sure you know every inch of this castle," she said. "All its secrets."

"As a matter of fact, I do."

She swallowed nervously. "I want to know how that thing or that person got into Will's room last night."

"Then you believe there was something?"

She hated this pretense. Still, she wasn't ready to confront him. "I heard it myself."

"Maybe Will—"

"What?" This time she couldn't keep the fury out of her voice. "Do you think I don't know my own son's scream?"

"He seems to be a highly imaginative child. It is not so unusual for children to see things, for them to have imaginary friends, is it?"

"I don't call sneaky green monsters that glow in the dark and howl like raving lunatics imaginary friends. I heard something, and it wasn't Will. His room was ice-cold. If there was something—or someone—in this room, there must be a logical explanation. I don't like the idea of anything threatening Will. Something like this would have terrified most children."

"I see your point. No mother would. But Will wasn't terrified. He was thrilled." Ramsay's deep tone gentled. "And he wasn't in any danger. I promise you, he's safe here."

"How can you be sure?"

"I just know. Trust me," he said quietly. "Do you think I would ever let anything frighten or endanger your child?"

Something in the steady way he looked at her sent an odd shiver through her. He was the very last man she should trust. And yet she did.

"Will wanted to see that ghost and he enjoyed seeing him," Ramsay continued.

"I don't want to encourage his interest in the paranormal."

"But if he enjoys it . . ."

"Not all enjoyable things are good for one," she said primly.

His assessing gaze skimmed Tamara from head to toe caressingly. "Then we have opposing philosophies."

"For once I find it easy to agree with you."

"Perhaps you would find that there are more topics we could easily agree on—if we got to know each other better." He picked up one of her magazines on mutual funds. "For instance, I share your interest in making wise investments."

Again that caressing gaze moved over her. Again her skin quivered in reaction to the brief pleasure of it. "Oh, no . . ." she began.

"Oh, yes." His voice was suddenly husky. "I didn't come up here to look for the castle ghost."

She had to smile. "I'm sure you didn't."

"I came here to see if you would like to drive out into the countryside with me. Since you're staying, you might as well enjoy yourself. I could show you the village. We could take a picnic lunch—"

"No." She was instantly on guard. "Absolutely not."

"Why?"

"There's Caroline. She might see us together."

"Then she would know who I am really interested in. If you come with me, I will explain Caroline."

"I can't leave Will alone."

"He's not alone. He has all the old ladies in such an uproar with his tales about the glowing green ghost that they refused to go on their tour today. Right now he is down in the garden with them. Mother is telling them all about the castle, its history, its legends, its ghosts. I believe they plan to spend the day trying to find Will's ghost."

"You have an answer for every argument."

"A year ago I saved your life. If you come out with me now, that could be . . . my reward."

"That's blackmail. Sometimes I think you would stop at nothing to get what you want."

His arrogant features grinned down at her. "You understand me better than you know."

Chapter Five

Ramsay's long, tapered fingers gripped the wheel of his low-slung, black sports car in a surge of excitement as Tamara came out of the castle and walked toward his car. Her full-bosomed, slender-hipped figure was exactly to his taste. Her skin was the color of honey, her hair the color of flame. She was perfect in every way—except for her stubborn rejection of him. But he was going to change that today. More than anything he wanted to make love to her so he could get her out of his system—once and for all. For a full year she had haunted him, day and night.

He got out to open her door. Her long-lashed eyes lifted briefly to his. At his hungry look her creamy complexion glowed with rose before she lowered her gaze.

Damn. So she was still determined to play that game.

"I wasn't sure you'd come," he said.

She got in silently, reluctantly.

"Relax," he whispered.

"How can I with you waiting to pounce?"

"I'd think with your experience you'd be used to that reaction in a man." He smiled lazily.

She ran nervous fingers through her luxuriant hair, which shone like copper in the sun. "That doesn't mean I like it."

Her act was so convincing he almost began to doubt she was playing a game with him when she acted the innocent. No. He was sure she'd be different when he got her away from her son.

He slammed her door. "Look—"

"You saved my life. I'm here. I'm going for a drive and a picnic with you. And that's all." She managed a tight smile. "Then I owe you nothing."

His gaze touched the darkness of her eyes. "Of course." But he was angry. He hated playing games, wasting minutes when he had such a short time to accomplish his mission, such a short time to enjoy her.

"I-I feel we're being unfair to Caroline," Tamara said.

"Caroline can go to the devil!" He turned on Tamara. "Listen to me. Caroline is nothing to me. The sooner she knows that and you know that, the happier we'll all be. I will not be forced into another marriage. God knows I've been forced into enough things and then held to dark account because I was."

Tamara whitened at his harsh words. When he started the car, he took off like lightning. Soon he was driving fast, too fast, because he needed the challenge of the twisting road to keep his mind off the challenge of the beautiful, silent woman whose red hair was streaming against his bare forearm.

He was aware of her fear, of the way she held on to the door of the car, of the way she clung to her seat every time the tires squealed around the curving cliff road. Once she even grabbed his arm, clutching him as she had when he'd kissed her, stirring him more than he wanted her to—before she remembered she was more afraid of him than of his driving and removed her hand.

Gradually his dark mood passed and his speed lessened. He felt guilty. Hadn't he promised himself he would never drive like that again? When he slowed the car, Tamara relaxed and was so charmed by the Scottish countryside and the magnificent view that she forgot to sulk. Their argument receded from his mind.

On one side of the road were verdant hills and cloud-dappled peaks, on the other sheer cliffs that plunged to tumbled rock and a foaming sea. The powerful car slowed fractionally through the tiny whitewashed villages, but didn't stop.

Finally they came to a particularly beautiful place of old crofts and pastures, which were deserted and wild. This was his favorite spot, a favorite of the inhabitants of Mount Woraig, too. Slopes of bracken and white and pink heather ran down to the sea. Tamara must have forgotten her determination to do nothing but stoically accompany him, because she touched his arm again and pointed toward Killiecraig Castle and Caroline's smaller "great house" on the opposite side of the cove.

"It's all so beautiful," Tamara breathed.

He was inordinately pleased that she liked it.

It was hotter than usual, but he deliberately stopped the car in the sun instead of beneath a shady tree.

She pretended to remember her fear of him and withdrew her hand from his arm. Her eyes grew enormous when he took the keys out of the ignition. "What are you doing?"

He had to steel himself against those big, imploring eyes. "Our picnic," he murmured, pocketing the keys.

"Do you mind if I stay in the car?"

He minded the bloody hell out of it. "Suit yourself." With savagely controlled movements, he got out, took out a blanket, an ice chest and a picnic hamper, then stalked a short distance away. He spread the blanket over a patch of white heather in a shady spot that was hidden from the road.

He popped the cork of a vintage bottle of champagne and splashed it into a flute. Then he lay back and sipped it. If she was stubborn, he could be more so. When he had finished his first glass, he drank a second. Then he closed his eyes for a nap in the balmy sun-spotted shade. He'd let her bake awhile. It wasn't long before he heard her uncertain footsteps in the heather.

She exhaled softly. "Just what do you think you're doing?"

His black eyes opened slowly. His pulse began to throb at the sight of her shapely body back-lit by the sun. He'd been dreaming of that honey-colored body quivering beneath his.

Now there she was, looking as she'd looked a year ago—like an exquisite being of warmth and love and radiance, who invited him to leave his world of darkness and join her.

He felt hot and alert to the core in every male cell. "What was I doing? Why, waiting for you to join me," he said casually.

Her soft, delectable mouth tightened. "We've been here too long. I'm hot."

Oh, so was he. "That's your fault, not mine." He crossed both strong hands and pillowed his head beneath them. "I'm quite comfortable here."

"I want to go."

"You promised you'd picnic."

"That's what I thought you were doing."

"I fell asleep waiting for you."

"You are impossible."

"I was dreaming of you. You are a beautiful woman." His gaze slid over her. "Beauty is wasted unless it gives pleasure."

"Don't start that again."

He ignored her harsh tone. "Would you care for champagne?"

"No. I'm afraid you'll try to take advantage of me."

"I won't force myself on you, if that's what you're thinking."

She stared down at him with doubt-filled eyes.

"What if I promise that I won't even touch you—unless you touch me first?" he asked. *Stupid idea, Ramsay.*

"And will you promise?"

You are a fool, Ramsay MacIntyre. You should take her here, today, and be done with it. "Yes," he murmured. He sat up, took the bottle from the ice chest and poured her a glass. He held it up to her.

Still she hesitated. They both studied his outstretched hand and the glass in it, where warm sunlight glimmered in the golden bubbles.

She was the first to smile. "I do believe you're stubborn enough to hold it there forever."

"You may be right."

"I could test you and see."

"It would be a waste—" his black eyes flicked over her "—of good champagne." He kept holding the glass, offering it to her.

When she licked her lips, he saw that she was thirsty.

"It was a very good year," he said, tempting her.

"Oh, all right. Since you promised…" With a great show of reluctance she took the glass, her fingers brushing his, and sank slowly down on the blanket beside him. Not too near.

But near enough so that he could breathe in the dizzying smell of her. Near enough so that he was tantalized by the temptation to touch the luscious, velvet skin, to run his fingers through the flaming, silky hair, to ease the soft cotton over those pale shoulders. It was all he could do to drag his gaze away from her breasts, her slim waist, her flaring hips. Desperately he swallowed. *He had promised her.*

"It was hot in the car," she admitted. "Too hot. Why didn't you park in the shade?"

"Then you wouldn't have joined me."

She brought the glass to her lips. "Are you always so calculating?"

He was watching her lips. "Always—when I want something badly."

She sipped her champagne, feeling safe because of his promise. "You might as well give up on me."

His black eyes flashed. "I never give up."

"You really must."

She was so thirsty she drank a second glass of champagne. Her cheeks were soon aglow, her mood mellow, but since he'd made that foolish promise, he couldn't push his luck.

"This really is a beautiful spot for a picnic. How you must love it here," she said, relaxing.

"Yes, my family has lived here for centuries."

"I can't imagine being part of something that goes on and on."

"It can be dreadful."

"How?"

"In a place like this, you can never be free of the past."

"In America, especially in Hollywood, things are too transient."

He smiled. "But there's a freedom and a beauty in that."

"What do you mean?"

"A freedom to choose. You can be anything you want. Look at you. You're an actress. I've read that you're trying to write, that you've made a fortune and invested it wisely."

"Believe me when I say that I became more than I ever wanted to be." Her voice was sad. "I don't suppose one's life ever turns out the way one wants it to."

"No..." A pause. "But you're an international star. You can marry whom you want."

"What good did that do me?" she asked wistfully. "My husband walked out on me."

Ramsay's voice hardened. "You could easily find another. I was born to traditions that have been followed for centuries. One wrong step, and you're an outcast forever. There are rules that govern one's life here."

Her beautiful dark eyes stared into his. "Such as?"

"I wanted to be an engineer."

"Then why aren't you? This is the twentieth century."

"When my brother died, I had to take over here."

"Surely—"

"How can I make someone like you understand, you who can have the world, what it's like to be confined to one small part of it?" he murmured. "What it is to be obligated by duty... by guilt."

"I don't want the world. I just want a normal, simple life. I want to be married, to have more children."

He had thought her the free-and-easy kind of woman, the kind of woman a man found temporary passion with, not the kind of woman a man married. His hungry gaze studied the way the pale cotton molded her body, the way her hair spilled over her shoulders like wild flames. He still thought she was that kind of woman. Yet her voice had been filled with yearning....

"Why is it so impossible for me to believe that those things would ever satisfy a woman like you?" he asked dryly.

"Believe it—because I know from experience that fame and money and my career are not enough. Because illusion can be stronger than reality. That is a truth everyone in the movies learns sooner or later. You believe in my image." A pause. "You were saying that you had to take over here."

"I did what the family expected of me—for once."

"You sound bitter," she said.

Why was he talking to her? Certainly he had not brought her here for that purpose. Still, he could not seem to stop himself when her great, dark, sympathetic eyes seemed to absorb his every word. And he felt oddly calmer, more relaxed than usual after confiding in her.

"It was as difficult for my parents as it was for me," he continued. "They didn't want me here—any more than I wanted to be here."

"What a dreadful thing to say!"

"I was a necessary evil. When it turned out that I was actually talented at running the estates everyone was amazed."

"But why?"

The old anger filled him. "I had been wild, irresponsible."

"You were young," came her gentle, understanding response.

"Ian had always been their favorite. I suppose I was wild just so I could get their attention."

"Ian was your brother?"

Ramsay nodded. "When he was killed in a hunting accident, they were left with me. There were those who blamed me for his death. But no one blamed me more than I blamed myself."

"What happened?" she asked softly.

Ramsay clenched his hands. "We were hunting together. He set his gun down to climb over a low wall. But he fell on it, and the gun went off." Ramsay unclenched his fists and stared helplessly at his empty palms. "I heard the shot, but he was dead before I reached him."

"Your brother's death was an accident," she said fiercely.

His eyes were shuttered. "I inherited because of it. I am alive and he is dead, and for years I wanted to be dead, too."

"You must not let an accident destroy you," she said again in that soft, comforting tone, her eyes sad.

"The talk died down," he went on grimly, "but when my wife died two years ago, it was revived."

"Why?"

"I was driving the car she was killed in. It was raining—the road was slick. A drunk driver didn't make a turn." Ramsay swallowed hard. "I couldn't stop. She was pregnant . . . with my son."

There was a long hesitation, and it seemed to Ramsay that the fate of his very soul hung in the balance as he waited for her reaction.

But again her eyes filled with sympathy, not loathing. "How awful," she whispered.

"I inherited again—because of a death. She was an heiress, you see, and our marriage had been arranged. It was known that I had not been in love with her, that at first we had been unhappy together. Then we became so reconciled to one another that for a while I put death and guilt aside. After she died, the guilt was worse than before. For a time I thought I couldn't go on. But then..." He looked at Tamara. *Then he had come upon a barefooted enchantress in his forest, a creature of light who made him forget his darkness.* "I blame myself," he said aloud.

"You shouldn't. Terrible things happen to everyone."

There was no contempt in her voice, nor in her manner, only empathy.

She doesn't hate me. He felt relieved, elated, as he realized that, if anything, she seemed to like him even more than before.

"I can't imagine bad things happening to you," he said in a softer tone.

"But, of course, they have. I blame myself for my divorce. When Adrian married me, I thought our marriage would be like a fairy tale—happily ever after. But he walked out on me because of my success. He couldn't handle my image. Men don't see me. They see some fantasy." She reached out and touched Ramsay's face very gently.

His hand closed over hers, and he stared deeply into her eyes. "Sometimes it is hard to know what is real and what isn't."

"You know the hurt is real, though," she said.

Her slim hand in his seemed the only reality that mattered. He pulled her to him and began to stroke her hair. "Yes, the hurt is real."

"And the loneliness," she said.

"What could you possibly know about loneliness?"

"Everything," she whispered. "I'm not what you think." She nuzzled his chest with her cheek, pressing her ear very tightly against his pulsing heartbeat. "Everyone thinks that I'm some sex goddess, but I'm not."

"Then what are you?"

"Just a woman," she said in a low, intense voice.

He enhaled the delectable scent of her. He felt the heat of her skin against his own, and he felt a warm wave of emotion. "You are so much more than that."

He had craved her these past twelve months. He thought she was the most beautiful, the most sensual woman he'd ever seen. He had believed she was the kind of woman a man in his position could have and enjoy without having to make a commitment. He had believed that, after he had her, he could then forget her.

He was beginning to wonder if she wasn't a great deal more to him than all that.

His eyes locked on her exquisite face, on the ripe softness of her curving mouth.

She flushed. "Why do I have the feeling you're about to take advantage of me?" Her throaty giggle brushed every erogenous part of Ramsay's body.

A white smile flashed against his tanned features. "Because you just remembered that you touched me first and we can forget my promise," he whispered teasingly before his mouth closed over hers.

"No!" She struggled to push him away. "I don't want to forget it."

Her warm breath on his skin sent a shaft of desire pulsing through him.

"Of course, you do, darling." He caught her shoulders and held her still. His mouth hardened its ravaging claim on hers. He kissed her until she was breathless, until he felt her arms wind around his neck; until he felt surrender quivering through her limbs; until he felt his all-engulfing heat ignite an answering heat in her. She half opened her mouth, and he bent her head back. He kissed her lips tenderly, stilling her fears with soft caresses and sweetly murmured endearments until she closed her eyes and lay still.

Nearby, a horse whinnied and stomped the heather, but neither Tamara nor Ramsay heard. Several passionate minutes passed in this mutually blissful manner before the horse made that obnoxious sound again, louder this time. Tamara was lying in his strong arms, completely responsive to every nuance of his lovemaking. She glanced drowsily past him and saw the stray beast grazing near the heather.

Ramsay started to kiss her again, but she covered her mouth with her hand.

"No... no... How did things get out of hand so quickly? What must you be thinking of me?"

"I was thinking you are delectable, darling."

"I can't believe that I nearly let you...that you..."

He swore silently as Tamara's torpid eyes slowly focused on the voracious munching lips of the mare.

Tamara sat up grimly and smoothed her tangled hair. She kept her eyes lowered as if she couldn't bear to look at him. "I won't be some girl you seduce with a glass of champagne in a bed of white heather."

He was filled with hot rage. "What would you be, then?"

"More than that." Tamara brushed the wrinkles from her clothes. "All you want with me is an affair."

"Would it be so awful to have an affair with me?"

Her face was very pale. "As a matter of fact, yes."

"I want you, Tamara."

Her dark eyes were bleak. "For how long?"

"Does that matter?"

Tamara got up slowly, and the drawn look on her beautiful face tore at his heart.

"To me it does," she said softly. "I may look the part—directors like casting me that way. But I don't lightly indulge in affairs. You need to find another woman to go picnicking with whom you can seduce, Sir Ramsay, if that's all you want." A pause. "If you're smart, you'll call off your ghost, and let Will and me go."

He shrugged in anger and frustration at this new accusation. "Ghost? What the hell do I have to do with that?"

Quietly she choked back her tears. "I'm warning you, if you don't stop haunting Will and trying to seduce me, you'll be sorry."

Ramsay's black gaze narrowed and slid with hateful emphasis over her luscious body. "You're just angry because if that nosy mare hadn't stumbled over here, damn little *seduction* would have been necessary. You are every bit as sexy as your image. You would have given me everything I wanted and begged for more!''

Tamara's cheeks flamed, and she drew back sharply as if his jeering words stung. "I'm not usually like this. Only with you. You're wrong about me!''

"Am I?" He laughed softly and reached out to touch her.

She jumped up to go, but the strap of her purse caught in the heather and bracken and fell to the ground, spilling its contents. She scrambled to pick up her scattered things.

Her wallet, her lipstick, her keys lay on the ground, but the first thing she reached for was a tattered post-card.

Curious, he grabbed it before she could.

She lunged wildly at his brown hand, but he held the card securely and turned it over to discover why it was so precious to her.

Instantly he recognized the haughty smile of his notorious ancestor. Ramsay burst out laughing.

"So this is your treasure!" With a conceited grin Ramsay released the card.

She tore it to shreds.

"I'm immensely flattered," he drawled lazily. "Did you carry that around for a year because it looked like me?"

She was throwing her other things into her purse. "You bastard!"

"That's a bad choice of insults. Remember, I can trace my lineage back a thousand years."

"I could think of a dozen others."

He laughed a sudden, ringing, free laugh—because he was enjoying himself immensely again. Fighting with her was almost as much fun as making love to her. "I'm sure you could."

When she had gone to the car, he got up slowly. He could still taste her. He still wanted her—now more than ever.

He liked talking to her, kissing her, deviling her, fighting with her. Everything he did with her was enjoyable.

I'm not usually like this, she had said. *Only with you.*

He had been haunted by her for a year.

She had carried his picture, too.

What did it mean?

All he knew was that there was no way he could allow her to walk out of his life.

Not yet.

Not until he had her.

Chapter Six

Still furious, as well as mortified and hurt, Tamara ripped off her soft cotton blouse and skirt and threw them onto the bed. Her reflection in the mirror showed her that her hair was a wild, livid scarlet and her face as paper white as it had been when she'd come back from picnicking with Sir Ramsay. All the old ladies had been worried at dinner that she was ill, and she had used that as an excuse to return to her room before Will.

It was nearly nine now, and she peered out her window and clicked her nails impatiently. The stubborn sun lingered above the horizon and cast a dull lemon glow on the sloping lawns. *Would it never go down?* She yanked on a black sweater and covered her bright hair with a black scarf, and all the time she could think of nothing but him.

For hours she had been obsessing about Sir Ramsay MacIntyre.

He was as bad as they came. He wanted her in the same hateful way that every producer and director had wanted her when they'd promised her a serious role and then invited her for a romp on their casting couches. She'd turned them down cold and escaped Hollywood untainted, untouched. She told herself she was just as determined to make a fast and honorable exit from Killiecraig Castle. But first, she would teach one very arrogant individual a lesson.

She slipped into a pair of skintight black jeans, but when she zipped them, her hands were shaking so much she couldn't button them.

They were shaking with rage, she told herself, struggling furiously with that stubborn button.

Not just with rage, taunted a secret voice, the voice of her soul. *With hurt, too.*

"No!" she whispered. "No!"

Yes! came the voice.

A single confirming tear slid down her cheek.

Angrily she brushed it away and sank onto her bed in despair. Another tear followed the first.

She would not cry over him.

Still another defiant tear trickled down her cheek.

Fool that she was, she did not want to leave Ramsay even though he was proud and stubborn and impossibly arrogant. Even though he only wanted her physically. Even though his own mother had warned that he was a dark angel. Even though he was determined to shut out love. When he'd told her of his brother dying and his wife and child dying, too, and that he and others had held him responsible, she'd felt his pain as if it were her own, and been drawn to him against her will. She did not believe that ambition had driven him to any dark deeds.

For some inexplicable reason, he affected her emotionally, as other men who had wanted her in that same quick way he wanted her had not. But she longed for his tenderness, not just his fire. His heart, not just his body. And most of all, most impossibly of all, she wanted his respect.

But how could she get these things when he was blinded by the voluptuous screen image Hollywood had created for her? He saw only her breasts and her

tiny waist, her long legs and honey-colored skin. To
him she was a body who could bring him shallow,
physical pleasure. He couldn't have cared less about
her soul or her heart or the person she was. He came
from a centuries-old noble lineage. He saw her as a
sensual being of transient glamor and easy morals.

She would have to forget him. That was all. But
first, since he had stooped so low as to use her son's
desire to believe in the paranormal to keep her near,
she would use him to prove to Will and her mother,
once and for all, that there were no such things as
ghosts—not even at the "Most Haunted Castle in
Great Britain." Tonight, if Ramsay dared make an
appearance in their rooms in his headless contrap-
tion, she would be lying in wait to expose him.

The moon was a sliver against an ink-black sky, and
Will's room was cast in almost total darkness. Tamara's bright head had slumped to her chest, where
she had fallen asleep during her vigil in a shadowy
corner. Will's flour and tape gleamed faintly—he had
set his traps as usual before falling into a deep sleep.

From the wall, stone whispered against stone, but
neither sleeping occupant noticed. An icy coldness
stole into the room. There was a silent footfall. As the
castle clock began to strike midnight, a shadow fell
across Will's bed.

Tamara came awake suddenly and saw a glowing
figure standing at the foot of her son's bed. Terrified,
she brought her fingers to her lips and choked back a
scream.

It was even more horrible than Will's description.
Its huge body was a glowing green. From its bony fin-

gers dangled a hideous green head with gaping sockets where the eyes should have been.

For one awful second she watched, paralyzed, as the thing moved stealthily, silently, ever closer to Will. Then with a cry she sprang.

The thing jumped back from the bed and raced toward the wall. She followed just as quickly, but it vanished into the gloom.

Suddenly the walls behind her groaned together, shutting her in total, icy blackness. She turned wildly around, pressing frantic fingers to the stones and failing to budge them.

She was trapped. In some secret passage with stale, frigid air, and unable to get back into Will's room.

The green monster had disappeared. She was alone. Panic seized her.

"Will!" She beat on the stone wall. "Will!" Her voice made terrifying, hollow echoes as if she were in a cave. But no matter how hard she beat or how loudly she called to him, the wall did not open, and her son did not come.

Dear Lord! She sank weakly against the cold, damp wall, her courage and her enthusiasm for this adventure completely gone.

The darkness wrapped her like an icy shroud. She forced herself to slide her feet along the floor and realized she was standing at the top of a dangerously steep, winding staircase. Very carefully she groped down the uneven steps, hoping against hope that they would lead her to some door and she could escape.

So tautly strung were her nerves that her legs soon ached from the effort of climbing blindly down so many stairs. The farther she went, the more terrified she became. There was no door. Nothing. Only chilling gloom that made her feel claustrophobic. What if no one ever found her?

Down, down those endless stairs she crawled until she was so numb with fear she no longer thought about what she was doing.

Suddenly her foot stepped into nothing.

A stair was missing.

She lunged wildly for the railing. It was gone, too.

The last sounds she heard as she spun into that spiraling darkness were her own echoing screams. Then everything was black and silent.

"Tamara..."

Ramsay's beautiful voice called to her hoarsely, as if from a great distance.

Tamara came awake slowly. In her deep, unconscious state she had been sinking helplessly in that dreamy, black nothingness and chased by a glowing green monster.

Her lashes fluttered. The first thing she heard was Ramsay's voice crooning; the first thing she felt were his hands gently stroking her brow.

She opened her eyes and saw that she was in an immense bed with elaborate hangings. *His bed.*

She raised her head, and his eyes melted into hers.

With an agonized cry of joy and relief his strong arms lifted her, cradling her against his chest. He dropped his dark head against the curve of her neck. Weak though she was, she clung to him.

"If anything had happened to you..." he muttered in furious self-loathing, crushing her closer. "My darling. My beautiful, brave, foolhardy darling."

He had called her his darling. She wanted to weep with happiness.

As his mouth kissed her hair, her forehead, her cheeks, her lips, as if she was infinitely precious to him, she grew even more aware of his joy.

She was safe. In his arms. And he was deeply glad.

"I followed the green thing and got locked in an awful passage," she babbled as incoherently as a child.

"You little fool," he said, brushing a strand of her fiery hair back from her eyes.

Her logical mind heard the insult; her heart heard the love and tenderness.

"I was terrified," she whispered shakily.

"You were very brave," he said gently but with fierce pride. "And bold. The bravest and boldest of women."

She felt confused, disoriented. "I thought you were the ghost, but you saved me from the ghost. How did you do that, Ramsay?" Her fingers moved up and touched his cheek.

He turned slightly, and she saw a guilty-looking Selma hunched in a low chair by the window.

"I really wasn't much of a hero. When you accused me of being the ghost, I started thinking. You see, I had suspected that Selma had given our ghost a helping hand by staging some rather dramatic appearances through the years, but I always turned a blind eye to her mischief—perhaps because it helped the tourist trade."

"Ramsay…"

He couldn't meet Tamara's loving gaze. "When I saw how concerned you were about Will, I decided to find out tonight, once and for all, if I was right to suspect Selma, so I followed her. When I saw her sneak into the passage, I should have stopped her, but I wanted to see what she was up to. I chased her through the passage and watched her go into Will's room, but I didn't know that you followed her out of it. I was too busy chasing her myself." His low voice grew bitter with self-contempt. "As usual I played both hero and villain. Thank God I heard your scream when you fell and I went back."

"You were after the ghost, too—" With wide, uncertain eyes Tamara studied his handsome, contrite features.

"Yes. But the minute I knew the truth I should have put your safety and peace of mind first. I was ordering Selma to quit haunting Will when you screamed," he admitted with guilt-stricken reluctance. "If only I had acted sooner, you wouldn't have been hurt. Because I didn't, I nearly caused another dreadful accident. Darling, when I saw you lying there..."

She felt his terrible remorse.

"Don't," she whispered.

He took her face between his hands and tilted it back. His thumbs traced the soft curve of her lips lovingly. "I would never have been able to forgive myself if something had happened to you because of me."

"Hey, I'm okay." What was wrong with her? Tamara wondered. She should remember that Ramsay's basic feelings for her were too shallow ever to satisfy her. Why, then, did she touch his mouth as lovingly as he touched hers?

She had wanted to expose him—to prove to Will that there was no ghost, to prove to Ramsay she knew he was an odious trickster and that she was no fool. Then she had planned to leave him forever.

Well, there was no ghost. She had proved that. But if Ramsay wasn't a hero, he was hardly the villain she'd imagined, and this moment that should have spelled triumph over him was not at all as she had planned.

He got up reluctantly and crossed his bedroom, returning sheepishly with Selma, who guiltily held up glowing green robes and a hideous chartreuse head.

"The paint is phosphorescent," Selma explained contritely. "I'm sorry. So sorry, ma'am. But Will, he did so want there to be a ghost."

"I understand, Selma."

"It weren't Sir Ramsay's doing.... He's had so little happiness, I wanted to help him. It weren't fair the way they favored Ian over him. The way they blamed him for... When I saw the way he felt about you, I couldn't let my Ramsay end up all alone again. I never thought you would be hurt."

Ramsay folded his arms comfortingly around Selma for a long moment. "There, there, no real harm has been done."

After a while, when Selma was feeling better, she left.

Tamara watched her go, and sank back against his pillows in a state of bewilderment.

"So now we've found our ghost," he murmured.

She stared up at him. Why did she feel on the verge of some infinitely more profound discovery?

"You have every right to hate me," came his quiet voice as he knelt beside her once more. "If I had confronted her a long time ago with my suspicions, none of this would have happened."

This was a different Ramsay. A changed Ramsay. A humble Ramsay, and he was looking at her as if she was very precious to him.

"I suppose just a bit of Selma's crime should be on your conscience," Tamara agreed. But when he took her hand in his and kissed it, she did not pull it away. "And since you did know I didn't want to encourage Will's interest in psychic phenomena, if you suspected Selma, you should have at least mentioned to me—"

"Until I actually saw her tonight, I wasn't sure she... I hate to accuse someone unfairly, especially Selma." Ramsay lowered his head.

"Will!" Tamara jumped up and flung back the covers. "I was so upset, I forgot all about him. My poor boy. He must be terrified."

Ramsay seized her hand and pulled her back, and just his touch sent a shiver through her.

"No, Will's immensely excited," Ramsay quickly reassured her. "My mother is with him. He knows you are fine. He's very proud of you for chasing the ghost. He thinks I rescued you. So I am a hero, too."

"I must tell him the truth."

"Yes." Ramsay took her hand. "I'm almost glad about tonight. If you hadn't been hurt, I would never have known..."

With soft, wide eyes, she stared at him. "Known what?"

He seemed unsure, different as she waited for his answer. He looked away. "Never mind."

"Please tell me."

"I'm not sure I know myself," he admitted. "Everything seems to happen so fast when I'm around you. All I can say is that when I saved you last year, I felt something for you that I'd never felt for anyone before."

So had she.

"I figured it was just a powerful physical attraction, and I thought I would forget you," he continued huskily. "But tonight—"

"I was determined to forget you, too," she said.

"Instead I found myself watching your old movies and wanting you more than ever. I read every magazine article about you I could find. I was obsessed with you. Once I was on my way to an important business meeting in London. I passed a theater showing your movie and went in, instead. I couldn't watch the love scenes though..." He broke off, his face wretched with jealousy.

She blushed. "I can't even watch them myself."

"The thought of another man kissing you, having you—even on film—drives me crazy."

She touched his face. Her eyes pleaded for him to believe what she was going to say. "There *is* no other man—not in real life."

He gripped her tightly. "Maybe I wasn't the ghost. But I did play one trick. On impulse I made up that contest brochure and sent it to Will. He was the only entrant. I never really thought you'd come, but when you did, I thought it might be because you'd been attracted to me, too, and probably wouldn't object to a brief vacation affair."

"How did you get our address?"

"From the producer who had contacted me about using the castle in the first place."

"So you planned . . . everything?"

"It seemed the only way. I had to have you or I'd never forget you."

"You are a rogue."

"You are right," he said agreeably. "But many a rogue has ruled Killiecraig wisely and well through the centuries."

"I should flee the minute the sun comes up."

He took her hand and kissed it tenderly. Her flesh tingled at his touch.

"I would strongly advise it," he murmured, continuing his kisses.

"You only want me so you can forget me. That's the most unromantic thing I ever heard. I should go to my room and pack at once." She paused. "Then why...?"

He studied her mouth with an intensity that made her breathless. "Why what, my love?"

"Why am I going to stay?"

"You tell me."

"Maybe," she began gently, "I want to prove to you that I really am a sex goddess. That once you have me, you'll be like all the heroes in my movies and worship me forever."

He kissed her then. His hand curved around the back of her neck and pulled her to him. He slanted his mouth against hers, nuzzling her lips tenderly for a brief moment before deepening his kiss.

"I'm probably going to regret this in the morning," she whispered a few moments later.

"Probably," he agreed. "But the most wonderful nights are those you regret in the morning."

He was wrong for her, so wrong. This wasn't some movie role; this was real life. She wanted a man who related to her as a person and who respected her, but he touched some wellspring deep within her that she had never known existed. He awakened needs that were too all-consuming to deny.

"Philosophy from a true rogue," she heard herself murmur even as she lifted her face so his seeking mouth could claim hers again.

Then there were no more words. There was only a wild, primitive explosion that shook them both. Marriage had not prepared her for these lips that could turn her whole body into responsive flame, for these hands that could arouse such mindless ecstasy.

No, nothing had prepared her for the soul-jolting thrill of Ramsay. If his mouth was hard and ravaging, it brought such exquisite pleasure that she was all soft sweetness melting in his fire like sugar above flame. The delirium of passion that passed between them was wilder than any film fantasy.

Within seconds they were both naked, their clothes ripped off and flung onto the Aubusson rug. And as his body plunged into hers and brought her to ecstasy, she surrendered not only her body, but her soul, her heart, every cell in her being.

And as she did, she wondered how she had lived before this night. How had she endured without him? He made her whole, complete. What would she have done had he not been alive, had he not forced her to come back to Scotland, to him?

Afterward, she lay spent and numb in his arms, knowing that she was irrevocably changed. He had made her live up to her wanton screen image, and the experience had been more shatteringly wonderful than she had ever imagined.

She began to weep senselessly. Why did she weep when at last she felt such peace? He had made her a woman.

He began to kiss her gently, tenderly. "Are you happy? Or sad?"

She spoke through her tears. "Happy." And then she giggled.

He laughed, too, and brushed her damp hair away from her forehead. "So am I."

"Three weeks won't be long enough," he murmured.

She rolled over and faced him. "I've never had an affair before. How long is long enough for you to forget me?"

She felt his warm, dark eyes melting into hers. With a groan he pulled her to him and buried his lips against her throat. "You're not what I expected," he murmured. "Not even remotely what I expected."

Her next words were muttered shudderingly against his chest. "Does that mean you're disappointed?"

"You're sweeter than I ever believed a woman could be," he muttered. "And hotter, too. You set me on fire."

"A real sex goddess," she said, laughing.

Gently he began to kiss her, and again it was as though he set her whole being aflame. The second time was more incredible than the first. It did not seem possible that he could bring her such joy. Afterward he slid his arms around her and pulled her close. When she drifted to sleep wrapped in his arms, she knew that she wanted to stay with him forever.

A new sun was brightening the lead-paned windows when Tamara awoke, tangled in Ramsay's arms and legs. She blushed when she remembered all that he had done to her the night before, and she touched the pulse at his throat just to make sure he had survived it.

Beneath her fingertips, his heartbeats were hard and strong. He opened his eyes.

And she said, "I love you. I know I probably shouldn't say it—since you want to forget me."

"Probably not," he agreed.

The sunlight was in her hair.

"My God, you are beautiful," he whispered. Then he crushed her to him.

A long time later he said, "Last night you said I was the first man you'd had an affair with. Was that the truth?"

"Yes."

He placed a gentle kiss on her tousled curls. "Then I intend to be the last."

"What?"

"Did you really mean it when you said you wanted marriage, a family, that you wanted to give up acting and try to write?"

She nodded. "But what are you saying? I thought you just wanted to get me out of your system."

"Damn it. Forget what I said."

She nodded sweetly, obediently and then caressed his muscular chest with light fingertips. "Ramsay, you're confusing me. You say one thing, then another."

"You little fool, haven't you realized that everything's different now?" he thundered.

For him, too? She smiled, content.

"You could write here, couldn't you?" he asked evasively.

"I'm not sure." She breathed the soft words into his ear. "With so much virile temptation around to distract me..."

"Damn it," he roared, tightening his arms about her possessively.

"Ramsay, are you asking me to be your wife?"

"If you will have me," he admitted on a note of raw desperation.

"If..." Her joy was too great for coyness, and she showered him with fervent, enthusiastic kisses.

"That was yes, I presume?" he whispered with conceited male triumph.

He was her humble Ramsay no longer.

She nodded, anyway. "But you said you didn't believe in love."

"I believe in what I felt last night, in what I feel now." His black eyes gazed cravenly at her.

Sex. Was that all she still was to him? All she could ever be... to the man she loved? Quiet tears filled her eyes and lashes. He didn't love her. It was just her earthy appeal as a wanton that aroused him. For her, his lovemaking had transcended the physical.

She turned away so he wouldn't see her hurt. Quickly she used her acting skills to compose herself. *He wanted her enough to marry her.* She would have to settle for that, because she knew now that she loved him too desperately to risk losing him. She had only to feel his eyes upon her, to know his touch, to be filled with electric, contagious excitement. Marrying him would give her one last chance to win him.

That secret, inner voice whispered, *Fool. This is not a movie. When his passion is satisfied, how will you hold him?*

She brushed his lips with her fingertips. "I will marry you because I don't want to live without you." A pause. "You must explain to your mother and to Caroline."

"How can you possibly think of them now?"

"Because I am so happy—I want everyone to be happy."

"You are sweet, so sweet," he whispered.

Then he rolled over, and she was beneath him again for a delightfully lengthy and very wanton time.

The rest of that glorious day was the happiest Tamara could ever remember. The antique emerald engagement ring that Ramsay gave her fit perfectly. As he slid it reverently onto her slim finger, he said, "This has been in the family for centuries."

Will was thrilled when they showed him the ring and told him of their marriage plans. He was especially pleased at the thought of staying in the haunted castle forever. Even Lady Emma seemed perfectly reconciled to the idea after a private talk with Ramsay. When Ramsay rode over to tell Caroline, Lady Emma came to Tamara to discuss preparations for the wedding.

"I think a garden wedding would be lovely," Lady Emma began.

The two women were still talking amidst the flowers and beautifully sculpted flower beds when Ramsay returned and said that Caroline had understood and had offered her congratulations. Caroline even thought it would be wonderful to announce the engagement at her masquerade ball.

Later, when Tamara was alone with Ramsay, she confided that she had brought nothing to wear to a masquerade ball.

He smiled mischievously. "You would make a beautiful Lady Godiva."

"Be serious."

"I was never more so." He touched her arm, and she felt a shock go through her body.

"You're high voltage," he murmured, pulling her into his arms and kissing her in that hot way that ignited every cell of her being.

"So are you."

"We're going to have the most incredible marriage."

"We were discussing costumes."

His arms tightened around her. "But this is so much more fun."

She pushed him firmly away. "No more kisses until we finish . . . our discussion."

"In that case. . ." His black eyes teased her. "There are all sorts of things in the closets and attics. We will go as Sir Ramsay and his lady. You will wear white heather in your hair."

"No bees, though."

"No bees," he agreed. "And we will travel by car—not on horseback."

"Poor Will," she said. "I'm afraid he's going to grow very bored now that we've retired the headless green ghost."

Ramsay grinned. "Perhaps we shouldn't retire him."

"What do you mean?"

"Does it seem fair that we should be so happy while Will grows bored? Now, if we were to take over Selma's duties and haunt the castle together at night, that would keep him thoroughly entertained. He could spend his days snooping about, laying traps—while we enjoyed each other." Ramsay's black eyes were kindling with insistent passion.

"Ramsay MacIntyre, you're an incorrigible rogue."

"But what do you think of my idea?"

"I would feel guilty—encouraging his belief in psychic phenomena."

"It would be so much fun—for all of us," Ramsay said.

"I would still feel guilty."

"We would retire the ghost after the wedding." He paused. "Your mother would approve."

"That's the worst argument you could have made."

"Would you rather spend your days chasing after Will—or entertaining me?" A slow smile, laden with sensuality, spread across his face.

She felt a familiar heat creeping up her neck. "Define entertainment," she said, weakening just a bit.

"With pleasure." Ramsay enfolded her in a crushing embrace, both defining and persuading her without words.

"Ramsay..." she whispered pleadingly. "I really don't think..."

His eyes turned warm and dark. His mouth sought hers.

"I guess it really won't hurt him...."

Then he kissed her.

Chapter Seven

Weary from dancing, Tamara raced breathlessly in her white gown out into the dark garden and sank against a shadowy pillar. A cold sea mist was drifting in, cloaking Caroline's vast, gray stone house so that some of the plantings were already completely hidden.

An electric excitement seemed to infect the masked guests as they swirled in the ballroom in their costumes. Women in elaborate headdresses and sparkling gowns mingled with feathered Indians and cowboys and gentlemen dressed in tunics and capes.

Tamara's engagement to Ramsay had been announced to thunderous applause. Ramsay was inside dancing with a lovely masked woman dressed as Cleopatra, who had come up to him to congratulate him.

From where she stood, Tamara could see into the ballroom. Mount Woraig, although not as magnificent as Killiecraig Castle, was festooned with flowers and decorations. There were tubs of bluebells, richly scented exotics, camelias and roses. The brocade curtains at the long windows were a pale blue. Fabulous crystal and silver glittered from low tables.

Tartan-clothed tables overflowed with meat pies, sliced beef, chicken and fish. Several bars had been set up, and liquor and champagne flowed.

Tamara had been too excited to drink or eat anything.

Suddenly two more breathless ladies strolled out into the garden. The mists were thickening. Not wanting company, Tamara shrank more deeply into the shadows so that she was completely concealed.

Tamara heard their voices as they came closer.

"It's easy to understand what he sees in her," a haughty voice said. "And it's not her mind. But he's always been so clever about indulging that appetite—without a marriage. He's so calculating that I'm surprised he isn't putting his family and estate first—the way he usually does."

The next voice was Caroline's. "Oh, but he is. Lady Emma explained that this actress, for all her shortcomings, is extremely rich—far, far richer than I."

"These misalliances with shallow beauties rarely turn out well. He will soon tire of her, my dear."

"He will have her money to console him."

Tamara blanched. Then a quick heat washed and ebbed in her cheeks, leaving her cold and pale and clammy. Her heart hammered with quick, tortured beats as she watched the women return to the ballroom.

It had never occurred to Tamara that Ramsay might be marrying her for her money. He had seemed forthright about desiring her, about wanting to make love to her so he could forget her. Then their lovemaking had been beyond either of their expectations, and she had almost forgiven him for marrying her for physical passion alone. Almost—because she had come to revel in their passion as much as he, and it had not seemed such a shallow thing.

He had felt passion for others without loving them.
Or marrying them.

Was she a fool to have hoped their passion would
endure and he would come to love her?

Tamara wanted desperately to be alone to think this
new torment through, but the waltz ended. From her
desolate spot she could hear the guests' laughter.

Ramsay came out into the garden to look for her.
When he called to her, his voice raspy and unsteady as
if with desire, she felt a constricted feeling in her
throat and hid.

He found her immediately. "There you are!"

Her heart began beating wildly.

Did she only imagine the fierce joy, as well as the
passion, in his deep voice? Was she being unfair to him
not to give him the benefit of the doubt? She stepped
bravely into the light, and the silver threads in her
white silk dress sparkled.

He caught her to him. "I apologize," he whispered
fiercely, holding her tightly. "I didn't want to leave
you alone." He placed a swift kiss on her unsuspect-
ing mouth.

At even this brief touch of his warm lips, her pulses
leapt. "I-I was tired from dancing," she murmured
with downcast eyes, pulling away.

He was all concern. "If you're tired, we could
leave."

The last thing she wanted was to be alone with him.

"No," she managed lightly. "It is not yet midnight."

He laughed. "Our green ghost's favorite hour to
haunt Will."

She turned away. "You know I feel guilty about
that."

He pulled her back, kissing her eyes, nose and mouth very tenderly. "We will tell Will the truth soon—after we are married."

After we are married... The phrase brought back all her doubts.

Blood pounded in her ears, whether from his kisses, or from her despair, she did not know. "I want to dance," she said suddenly, urgently, racing past him into the softly lit ballroom.

While they waited for the next number to begin, he placed his fingers beneath her chin, lifting her gaze to his own dark one. "I thought you were tired."

"Not any longer." She found it hard to look into his eyes. "I want to dance. And dance. And dance."

"You're in an odd mood," he murmured as the music began and he spun her effortlessly among the other dancers.

They swirled past pillars. Potted palms. Other dancers.

She threw back her head and flicked a glance up at him through her long, curling lashes as if she were playing a scene in a movie. "Am I?" she asked in that light, flirtatious voice that was not her real voice at all.

Frowning darkly, he crushed her to him.

On the way home from the party, Tamara sat silently in Ramsay's car twisting her engagement ring round and round on her finger while the cold wind whipped through her hair.

"Did you have a good time?" Ramsay asked, his low voice guarded.

"Wonderful," she lied politely, as if to a stranger.

"So did I." But his fingers had tightened imperceptibly on the wheel.

They lapsed into an awkward silence. The powerful car sliced through misting chill, tires squealing as he took a dangerous curve. She kept twisting her emerald ring.

"You're driving too fast," she whispered.

He frowned at the road ahead, his eyes narrowing on the flying mists and forests. "Am I? And is that really what's bothering you?"

"Of course," she lied again. "It must take a great deal of money to run a castle," she said casually after a moment.

He shot her a hard, curious glance as the car whipped over a narrow bridge.

"A great deal," he agreed.

"Your mother said you were talented at managing the estate."

"One of her rare compliments," he replied curtly. "Like you, I have my talents."

"So . . . how important is money to you?"

"Very important. Isn't the need for money an ever-present reality in modern life?" His voice had grown harder.

She thought of all the ambitious producers who had tried to use her for financial gain. Was Ramsay like them? Was she no more than a property, a lucrative investment, to him?

She felt the tears pricking behind her lashes. "I suppose so."

His assessing gaze flicked briefly to her again before he turned his attention back to the road. "Like you, I try to make wise investments," he countered smoothly.

"Like me?" Her voice sounded choked, tiny.

"I've read about you, remember. I know how successful you are. Why do you ask?"

The car snarled ever faster, and she drew a sharp breath. "Oh...no reason."

"Right! No reason!" He braked violently in front of the castle. Gravel spun as the car ground to a standstill. Then he swung around on her.

She shrank back against the seat.

"Something's wrong," he muttered in a harsh, goaded undertone, pulling her roughly into his arms.

She twisted away. "I'm just tired."

His gaze locked on hers. "Did something happen at the ball?"

"No...."

"Something upset you."

"I said—"

"If you think I believe your bloody lies..."

He edged dangerously close to her, and she could smell the clean, male scent of him. But even as her body warmed to his nearness, she set her mind against him with more determination.

"I have to go...inside," she said, her voice barely a whisper.

"Right." Instead of opening her door, he slid even closer. "You just want to get away from me."

His glittering gaze held her captive as his lips moved nearer. As always she was drawn to him as if by an irresistible magnetic force. Her heart began to pound violently. When his mouth came down on hers, her every instinct cried out for her to surrender. He had only to kiss her to stir her body to that warm restless need.

She let him lift her face to meet the seeking, probing force of his mouth. For one long moment she opened her lips to his.

He tasted warm, delicious. Then he touched her with fingertips of fire, and she felt a hot tidal rush of excitement. Dear God, how she wanted the unbearable, exquisite pleasure he alone could give her! She understood how she had believed he could be marrying for this alone.

Just one kiss, and she was as limp as a rag doll. *No!* She closed her eyes and sank her teeth into her bottom lip.

It was all she could do to bring her tiny palms to his huge chest and push him weakly away. "I-I said I was tired," she managed icily.

He pulled back, enraged, his body hard and tense. He clenched his hands into fists to keep from touching her again. He closed his eyes as if the mere sight of her brought him pain, and he cursed viciously, silently, to himself.

His warm breath fanned her cheeks. Her unhappy heart thudded painfully in her breast. Oh, how she longed to run her hands up and down his magnificent corded muscles. How she longed for his kisses, for his wildness that brought such soul-destroying ecstasy, and for the peace she found sleeping in his arms afterward.

She thought of the terrible loneliness this night would be without him, and the rest of her life loomed before her in an endless black vacuum of empty days and empty nights.

At last he shuddered and looked up at the cold stars. "Too tired to haunt the castle? Too tired to come to my room afterward?" He ground out the words.

Her glance flitted to the hard, sensual line of his grim mouth, and again she ached for that mouth and his kisses that inflamed all the secret desires of her heart and soul.

"I just want to be alone," she said.

He made a dark, scornful grimace. "There's more to it than that!"

She lowered her lashes and said nothing.

"Damn!" A furious, barely controlled pause. "Look at me!" he commanded.

She shrank away.

He drew a deep, angry breath. Without a word, he leaned across her and opened her door.

Chapter Eight

Tamara's heart was filled with stupid, soul-crushing self-torment, but she steeled herself against tears.

"Shut the suitcase and stick it under your bed," she, the taller ghoul, whispered shakily to the smaller one.

The shorter ghoul was dancing with excitement in front of his mirror, studying the horrendous effects he'd achieved with spirit gum, face powder, nose putty and crepe hair. He tugged an ear and giggled wildly, thrilled with his horrid self. "Dad would be so proud! I sort of borrowed this idea from his movie *Witch Doctor*."

"Will!"

The short ghoul let go of his ear and snapped dutifully to attention. Then he grabbed his still-open suitcase and shoved it under the bed. When three wigs, a pair of eyeballs and a plastic skull fell out, he pitched them under the bed, too.

Will seized a bunch of rubber bats and a bottle of fake blood from the dresser and turned to the taller ghoul. "Have you got Dad's explosives?"

Tamara tried to forget the stark longing in Ramsay's black eyes as she deftly pressed the spring in the stone wall.

"You bet!" she replied grimly, patting her pocket.

The stone walls parted and icy blackness spiraled downward into the bowels of the castle.

Just for a moment she wondered if getting revenge on Ramsay was really worth this.

"Wow! That's...that's dark!" Will drew a deep breath and jumped back. "Are you sure about this, Mom?"

She waved her flashlight with renewed determination. "I showed you I could open this door from both sides. We won't be trapped."

"I meant, should we really scare him? I mean he's old. He might have a heart attack or something."

She remembered Ramsay's formidable prowess in the bedroom and was glad her purple makeup concealed her fiery blush.

"He's not that old! And he's in excellent shape. Besides, a heart attack would serve him right. He was haunting you, wasn't he, hon?"

"But so were you, Mom."

She winced. "Please, don't remind me. I'll feel guilty about that till the day I die."

"I thought you were neat in that spooky nun costume. Grandma would have been proud. Was a nun really walled up alive—"

"Don't you dare ever tell your grandma! She'll think I'm frustrated because I'm not psychic and feel sorry for me."

"Which one of you made the bloodstains in the gallery under his picture? Those were neat! What did you use for fake blood? It wasn't honey and red food coloring, 'cause I tasted it."

"I borrowed some of your A-B blood."

The stone walls were closing behind them.

"And who turned the old ladies' hot toddies into ink? That was terrific!"

That had been Ramsay's inspiration. As she thought of him and the fun she'd had with him, all that she was losing, her heart began to slam in slow painful strokes.

Her flashlight wavered.

"Will! We have to concentrate!"

In his green, headless-ghost costume, Ramsay raced carelessly up the black stairs of the passage toward Will's room. It was almost midnight, and he had to hurry.

What the hell had been wrong with Tamara?

She'd been fine at the ball—glorious and lovely in her shimmering white dress. Her eyes had lit up every time he'd looked at her. Then in the car she'd been a white-faced stranger, freezing him out every time he glanced at her, shrinking away when he touched her. He tried to remember the exact moment he'd first known she was upset.

She'd been fine until he'd left her alone to dance with Lady Julia. He'd noticed the change in her when he'd found her afterward in the garden. Was Tamara jealous? Of Julia?

That was insane.

Damn. *Women.* Why couldn't they be more like men and just come out with what was bothering them?

Well, she was going to come out with it, Ramsay decided furiously—and tonight—if he had to throttle her to get it out of her. Because if she didn't, she'd cost him a night of lovemaking and cuddling afterward. Ramsay was determined to go to her as soon as he finished haunting Will.

His frustrated thoughts were thus occupied when it happened.

Suddenly out of the blackness two purple-faced ghouls floated toward him, their mouths dripping foul black blood. Behind them were explosions of horrifying hellfire. A dozen bats dove at him.

On a scream of stunned amazement, Ramsay stumbled on a step. He lost his grip on the railing, and his green head went bouncing down the stairs behind him like a basketball, vanishing into nothingness.

As he fell, he had a last, chilling thought.

The bloody castle really is haunted!

When Ramsay came to, he was lying on cold damp stone, the sharply edged stairs biting into his neck and back painfully.

When he became aware of hushed voices, his lashes parted slightly, warily. The two ghouls were leaning over him, talking anxiously. Mute with horror, he closed his eyes and lay very still, sure he had died and gone to hell.

"I told you he was old and he might have a heart attack, Mom."

Ramsay's lashes flicked irritably. *Old? Who the hell was that purple-faced brat calling old?*

Then Ramsay realized who they were and that he was alive. For some reason Tamara and Will had turned the tables on him and haunted him.

He was alive!

Ramsay almost laughed out loud.

"He didn't have a heart attack!" Tamara said. "He slipped and probably hit his head. Hard though it is, he must have knocked himself out." She paused, then said in her "mother" tone, "I told you I wanted *flash* powder, not black powder bombs."

"I thought the bombs would be okay."

"Kids are supposed to do what big people tell them to. He could have broken his neck."

"Well, you ought to be happy, 'cause you sure got your revenge."

"Will," Tamara began mournfully. Ramsay felt her fingers comb back his hair with great tenderness. "You know I didn't really want to hurt him—no matter how much he had it coming."

"Mom, you said—"

"I just wanted to pay him back for all the tricks he's played on me before we left tomorrow."

Left tomorrow? What was she talking about? Why the hell did she want to go, anyway? No way was she leaving tomorrow. No way was Ramsay ever spending another day of his life without her.

Not when he had one last trick up his sleeve.

He groaned pitifully and opened his eyes.

"Ramsay, it's me," Tamara whispered tenderly, taking his hand.

He squinted and groaned again in seeming agony at the flashlight shining in his eyes.

"Will! Put that light down. We've got to help him to your room. Then we can call for help." She turned desperately back to Ramsay, her voice softer. "Ramsay, dear, you've got to try to stand. Ramsay, can you hear me?"

He lay very still, closed his eyes and pretended he couldn't.

"Ramsay!"

He didn't move.

"Oh, my God." Her voice went low with terror. She lay her head miserably upon his heart. "He's still alive," she breathed in relief. "Ramsay... darling..."

She sounded so pleasingly distraught that Ramsay decided to ease up on the poor girl—just a bit.

He opened his eyes again and gave her a weak smile.

"Ramsay, dear, we've got to get you to Will's room."

He nodded.

When she bent over him, her breasts jutted into his chest, causing an unwanted thrill to course through him. He muttered a strangled curse, and she thought it was because of the effort it cost him to stand.

"I know it hurts," she whispered, all sympathy as she helped him to rise.

He liked her attentiveness, her total concern, and he moaned unabashedly and leaned heavily on her to obtain more of it. In this pleasant fashion it took them a long time to reach Will's room. And an even longer time to get him to his own.

Once there, he wasn't about to allow her to leave.

Tamara stood beside Lady Emma as she knelt over Ramsay, who appeared to be dozing tranquilly. Tamara was thankful to the bottom of her heart that he was going to be all right. Not that his mother seemed worried. The doctor who had examined Ramsay, alone, had gone after informing Tamara and Lady Emma that one of them had to stay with him for the rest of the night.

"This sudden collapse isn't like Ramsay at all," Lady Emma said suspiciously as she tucked the covers beneath his chin. She patted the white pillow beneath that black head. "I still can't believe he has a concussion." She was studying her darkly handsome, wayward offspring with narrowed, vaguely skeptical eyes. "I keep thinking he's up to something. He's usually as robust as a horse." She turned to Tamara. "You say you were in the secret passage dressed as two ghouls and you scared him?"

Tamara nodded guiltily.

Lady Emma's eyes sparkled at such mischievous goings-on. "Really, my dear, you mustn't blame yourself. I can't imagine that Ramsay would be frightened of the devil himself. Like all male Mac-Intyres, he has more courage than an army of fools. It's an unfortunate trait that on several occasions has almost ended their ignoble lineage."

"I'm afraid we really were quite convincing," Tamara said, deeply ashamed.

"I'm sure you were, my dear. It's just that Ramsay's such a dark angel I can't imagine he'd be concerned over a ghoul or two."

The dark angel's lips twitched in an effort not to smile, but fortunately neither woman noticed.

"He's not as bad as you think, Lady Emma. He can be quite . . . charming when he wants to be."

The old lady's sharp eyes studied her with keen interest. "Then why did you give me the emerald ring back?"

"Because . . . because I'm not the right sort of wife for him. He lives in a castle. He comes from a long line of—"

"Rogues and fools," his mother finished. "You're much too good for him."

"I come from a crazy family, and I've made all those silly movies."

"Ramsay adores your movies, and if the rest of your family is as charming as you are, I can't wait to meet them."

"I'm afraid they are all—" Tamara's heart filled with dread to admit the truth "—psychics."

"How absolutely splendid! I've been wanting to talk to Ramsay's father for simply ages."

Tamara would not be sidetracked. "People around here will never accept me as the right sort of wife for him. They won't respect me. Caroline—"

"Nonsense," Lady Emma interrupted in her headstrong fashion. "Who cares what people think? We respect you."

"You do?"

"Of course. You're perfect. Not that I saw it at first. You see, I'm afraid that I have a natural prejudice against anyone who isn't too keen about gardening."

"You don't think Ramsay would tire of me?" Tamara asked wistfully.

"Believe me, my dear, Ramsay has thought this thing out, or he would never have asked you to marry him. He is ruled by his head, not his emotions."

Which was a thought that made Tamara's stomach tighten. So all was as she'd thought. He was marrying her coldly—for her fortune.

"I'll just have to teach you and Will to garden, my dear," Lady Emma said with one of her breezy, confident smiles.

Tamara took Lady Emma's hands in hers and led her to the door. "You must be very tired, Lady Emma," she said gently. "Since I caused the accident, I'll stay with him."

"That's very sweet of you. It has been rather an exciting day for someone my age—the ball, two ghouls, Ramsay's accident."

"But after he's well," Tamara continued, "I won't be staying or learning to garden. It's over between Ramsay and me."

Lady Emma pressed Tamara's hands and looked very sad.

A loud groan erupted from the bed, and Tamara rushed anxiously back to their newly restless patient.

"Do you think he's in pain, Lady Emma?"

"Over, you say?" mused Lady Emma to herself, her face brightening when her son moaned loudly again and she guessed his tactics. "Not if my dark angel has a say," she said too softly for Tamara to hear. Then she shut the door so Tamara and Ramsay could be alone.

"The pain's better when you're near," he murmured in a low, sickly tone to the hovering Tamara.

She leaned closer to catch his pitifully weak words. "Can I get you anything?" she asked.

His dark hand emerged from beneath his sheet and wrapped around her slim fingers.

"No, I have everything I need," he murmured on a deeply contented smile.

"I'm so sorry I scared you, Ramsay."

"I forgive you," he said very gallantly.

Two days had passed, and Ramsay didn't seem to be getting any better. He lay in his bed, wiling away the long hours, utterly listless unless Tamara was near.

Tamara was worried sick. Her guilt compelled her to stay near him constantly, to tend him. She read to him, talked to him, brought Will in, and the child found a hundred little ways to amuse Ramsay during their brief visits. She lived for Ramsay's weak smiles, his feeble attempts to pretend he was better because it pleased her so. She begged him to see another doctor, but he stubbornly refused.

"Are you still mad at him?" Will asked that third morning as she put on her makeup, readying herself to go down and fetch Ramsay's breakfast tray.

She set her lipstick down and snapped a brush through her hair. "Of course."

"Then why do you act like you adore him? You never treat me this good when I'm sick."

"Will, I don't adore him! And we're leaving as soon as he's better, if that's what you mean," she said stubbornly, tying her hair with a blue bow that made her look particularly young and pretty.

"Aw, Mom. I love this place. And I like Ramsay, too. Even when he's sick."

Tamara turned toward him, struggling with the bow. "I do, too."

"And I think Ramsay was cool to haunt me. Grandma says it was the most romantic thing she ever heard of—his pretending to be a ghost and printing that brochure just to win you."

"You told her! When?"

"She called. And she says you should marry him."

The blue ribbon knotted, and Tamara turned back to the mirror in disgust.

"She would!"

On the fourth morning Tamara went to Ramsay's room earlier than usual, so great was her impatience to find him better.

Only to discover his bed was empty.

She stared at the tumbled white sheets, her eyes widening with fright that something terrible might have happened to him. *She should never have left him alone.*

Then she heard merry male whistling from the shower. His bathroom door was open a crack. He turned off the water. The shower door opened, steam seeping from the crack, as he began to sing a bawdy Scottish love ballad.

On an impulse she shrank back behind his curtains.

Wrapped only in a towel, he strode jauntily out into his bedroom. The dark muscles of his big body rippled with every movement, and his great physical power struck her like a blow. She watched the swell of his powerful shoulders still wet from his shower with a longing so intense it frightened her.

She remembered the thrill of those arms crushing her against that body. For four lonely nights she had lived without that.

He stood in the sunlight and stretched lazily, like a great dark panther flexing his muscles. She could almost feel the shower heat coming off of him.

Where was his limp?

He was as fit as a fiddle. *As healthy as a horse.* His mother's words.

The handsome blackguard had been tricking her— *again.*

She leapt from her hiding place. "You fraud!"

He had the decency to look startled when he saw her. Then his bold black eyes wandered to her lips, and he grinned. "Good morning."

"You're well!"

His smile widened. "You're a very good nurse."

"You were never sick," she said coolly.

"Why do you constantly doubt me?"

"I'm tired of playing games."

"And so am I." He moved nearer.

Her breath rasped painfully in her throat. "Why did you pretend you were hurt?"

"To keep you here."

"Well, you have tricked me for the last time."

"I agree. We need to talk—like a normal couple. Rationally, for a change."

"No. I'm leaving you and that's final."

"Why?"

"Because you would break my heart and Will's, too, if we stayed."

"I've asked you to be my wife because I want you more than I've ever wanted any woman."

Did he want her because of her fortune? Deal making in Hollywood had taught her a lot about what men would do out of greed.

"I'm sure you do." She turned away from him. "But you don't love me."

"Maybe I'll even own to that," he said quietly.

She looked away from him, stricken. "I know you'd say anything to keep me here."

He came to her and put his hand under her chin, turning her sad face to the light and looking for an intense moment into her eyes. She gazed up at him, all the longing of her heart in her eyes.

"Yes, I would," he said. "I love you. And I know I'll grow to love Will, too. I lost my own son...."

The pang of fierce yearning was sharp and sweet and dreadful. Her mouth quivered. She hated him more than ever for that tender moment, for reading her emotions, for playing on them, for making her want to believe him.

"Damn you," she said. "Damn you for being so good—you're as skilled as any actor in Hollywood."

"Don't go," he murmured.

"Nothing will change my mind. How can I believe anything you say? You rigged the contest. You even faked your injuries."

"Because . . . I love you," he said heavily.

"You're just using those words because you know how much I want to hear them."

"No. I do love you."

Near tears, she listened to his words, hardly breathing, wanting to believe him, unable to do so. "I . . . I don't think so. I think you are cold and calculating," she began in a rush. "You told your mother I was rich. . . ."

"How do you know that?" he demanded grimly.

"Caroline said so."

"So that's what's been bothering you!"

"Of course, it's been bothering me. Many other men have wanted me for the material things I could give them—a start in show business . . ."

"You little fool—that's not why I want you," he said, reaching for her, dragging her into his arms. "Tamara, listen to me." He framed her slender face in his hard hands. "I was managing these estates successfully long before I met you. True—I have to keep up with the times and pay close attention to financial matters. I admit it's a constant battle."

She remained silent.

"I don't want to lose you," he went on. "I can't bear to lose you. If I lose you, I lose everything—again. Only this will be worse than before."

She held herself rigid. "You'll just have to find another heiress," she whispered. "Because you've already lost me."

The dreadful finality in her voice matched the dreadful finality in her heart, and the last feeble glimmer of hope that had lit his eyes was snuffed out. His arms fell to his sides slowly, reluctantly.

When she was sure she was free to go, she drew a ragged breath and ran stumbling out of his room, out of his castle.

Out of his life.

Forever.

Chapter Nine

Killiecraig Castle loomed in the mists above the limo, as darkly magnificent as ever against the backdrop of cold, gray sea and velvety green hills. When Tamara, half sobbing, came out of the castle, she saw that Will's nine bags were open, and some of his things were strewn messily in the lush grasses. He was refusing to shut his bags so the chauffeur could pack them.

Tamara was too dispirited and too brokenhearted to wage another battle. She got into the limo, sank back against the leather seat, closed her eyes and began to shiver.

No sooner had she settled back than they both rapped on her window. She looked up into two angry faces peering in at her.

The chauffeur's blotchy face looked furious. His hat and uniform were askew. "Ma'am—"

"Mom!" Will's freckled nose was mashed flat against the glass. His nostrils looked huge.

More than anything she wanted to close her eyes again and ignore their breathless spill of words.

She rolled down the window.

"He won't close his suitcases," the chauffeur said in a tone of utter exasperation.

"Because I can't find it!" Will shouted in his loudest outdoor voice.

"What are you looking for, Will?" she asked gently.

"The book Grandma gave me—*The Amateur Ghost-hunter.*"

"Will, get in the car. I'll buy you another one."

"But Grandma wrote me a note in that one."

"She can write you another note."

"It won't be the same."

"Will, we're going. Now!"

He folded his arms across his chest in his miniature-Napoleon stance. "Not without Grandma's book!"

She thought, *Why is motherhood such a constant job? I can't take this. Not now.*

"Will, please . . ."

Will thrust out his chin like a general facing a long siege.

"Will, I absolutely mean it. Get in the car."

Tamara was flying desperately up the dark castle stairs. She had capitulated and decided to go after the book herself, because like all males, Will could never find anything—even when it was right under his nose.

She opened the door to his room and then shrank back into the shadows when she saw Ramsay slumped dejectedly in a chair by the window that looked out over the lawns. His handsome face was as gray and haunted as her own. In one hand he held *The Amateur Ghost-hunter*. In the other he held a photograph—a publicity picture of her in that ridiculous white Elizabethan gown and cap of white heather.

She should go back and make Will come up for his book, but for some ridiculous reason she was almost afraid to leave Ramsay. If ever a man looked heartbroken, it was Ramsay MacIntyre.

Why? Was he grieving for her fortune or for her? Hesitantly she stood there, her heart filled with doubts. Could it be possible that she was wrong about him?

His face blurred. But her tears were those of hope. She sighed softly, and at this soft sound from her, he started.

"Tamara . . ."

"Ramsay . . ."

At first she saw his terrible bleak pain, his utter desolation. All the dark, lonely misery in his heart. Slowly his face brightened.

She smiled uncertainly through her unshed tears.

The joy that came into his shining black eyes dazzled her. "You came back," he whispered huskily. "To me."

"No!" said her voice, although her heart thrummed a different song.

She started toward him, wanting to run into his arms.

But some shred of feminine pride stopped her. There was still her wounded pride that must humble her haughty Ramsay before she could let him claim her.

"Just for Will's book," she managed tightly.

Something in her eyes must have told him otherwise, because he put the book and the picture down and rose slowly to his feet.

"No, you came back to me," he said with the glimmer of his beautiful smile, his haughty smile.

"A girl would be a fool to love you, Ramsay MacIntyre."

"Indeed she would be," he said coming nearer and enfolding her tenderly in his arms. "Dare I hope . . . ?"

She stared up at him lovingly. "Indeed I am that fool," she whispered.

"No. You are no fool. You are the most beautiful, the sweetest woman I have ever known. I worship you. I adore you. And most of all . . . I respect you."

"You're just saying that because you know I want that more than anything."

"I am saying it because for the first time in my life I am in love."

"If only—"

"You are way past 'if only,' my love. All your dreams have come true and so have mine."

"You don't want my fortune?"

He grinned down at her. "Must I be adverse to it?"

She kicked him lightly in the shin.

"I am a practical man, my love."

She struggled. "I don't want to be loved for my money."

His teasing stopped abruptly. He grazed her forehead lightly with his hand as if she was very precious to him. Then his lips met hers in a hot kiss.

Several hushed moments later he tore his mouth from hers long enough to utter, "You're not loved for anything except your lovely self. Oh, you're definitely not. And I'm going to prove it to you once and for all."

She offered her lips to him, and again he kissed her. Then he picked her up in his arms and carried her out into the passage that led up to his room.

They were in his vast bedroom, standing before his bed with the silk hangings.

"I love you, Tamara," Ramsay said reverently, gently, unbuttoning her blouse. "Don't you know that

until I knew you, not your screen image, I thought you
were all wrong to be my wife? I could have married
Caroline if I had wanted a fortune. But I wanted you.
Only you. You were so sweetly sympathetic on our
picnic. After you chased Selma through those dark
passages to protect your son and expose me, I saw you
in a very different light. You were so fiercely brave.
When I saw you lying unconscious, I knew I would
have died if anything had happened to you."

"And when I scared you the other night..."

"I *wasn't* scared."

"Yes, you were. You're just too macho to admit it."

"My family has lived with its ghost for centuries
without fear...."

She laughed, not quite believing him.

"But we have the rest of our lives to argue about
that," he murmured. "For now I want to prove to you
just how much I need you, just how much I love you."

He pulled off her blouse and his gaze set her whole
being aflame.

She lay down on the bed and looked up at him, her
own eyes blazing. "And how are you going to do
that?"

He lay down beside her, his lips instantly on hers,
his hands moving down her body, and the building
ecstasy she found in his arms was like nothing she'd
ever felt before.

"You just get better and better," he whispered as his
great body covered hers.

She closed her eyes. "Don't talk..."

Then her own words were crushed back by his
kisses, and she was swept away by the sheer power of
her sweet, bewildering hunger for him.

She couldn't get enough of him. To have him in her arms again, to be close, to be free to kiss his eyelids, his brows, his lips. To be able to caress his magnificent body everywhere with her hands. To know that she could be a wanton in his bed and he would still respect her in the morning. To know that it was their love for one another that made their passion so exquisite. To know that he was hers—forever.

Then he buried himself in her, and all consciousness was snuffed out like a flame.

He loved her.

As she loved him—completely, irrevocably, with body and soul.

Epilogue

Despite the cold gray day, the small summer wedding was lovely. Will dashed about. Tamara wore her white gown and white heather. Ramsay's smoldering eyes followed her everywhere.

Although one mother-in-law wore navy blue and pearls and the other red scarves and bangles, the two adored one another. Tamara's mother had flown over to help Lady Emma baby-sit Will while Tamara and Ramsay took off for a month-long honeymoon to Italy.

"We will go somewhere warm," Ramsay had said of Italy. "Our honeymoon will be the kind of vacation you wanted in the first place."

"This has been a true dream vacation," Tamara had said, pressing a kiss to his lips.

Just when Tamara thought everything was going well and she and Ramsay were about to depart, her mother began with her mischief.

"I'm sure it will take the two of us to handle Will," she said to Lady Emma. "But I know how to keep him amused."

"Mother!"

As always, her mother was impossible to repress. "I've seen *him*, you know."

"Who?" Tamara asked, even though she had a sinking feeling that she already knew.

"*He* floated out of his painting."

Tamara pressed her lips together. "Who did what?"

"The most marvelous ghost! He looks like you, Ramsay dear. I'm afraid he confessed to having lived the most dreadful life, but for your sake, Tamara, I've made him a promise."

"For my sake you should have ignored him," Tamara said, as Will began jumping up and down beside her.

"How could I, when I know how you hate ghosts? So you see, while I'm here baby-sitting Will, we're going to find his lady so that the ghost can rest in peace. Then you will be rid of him forever."

Tamara was horrified. "Mother!"

Will was very excited. "Oh, great! I *knew* he was real! Can I help you, Grandma?"

"Most certainly, young man. It's time you had a real expert show you how. Your mother has been too busy catching a husband to do anything a boy your age would consider useful, such as snagging your very own ghost and putting him to rest."

"Selma'll help me too, Grandma! She knows all the secret passages."

"That'll be fine—if she'll promise not to be too creative. Ghosts don't always like to be imitated by mere mortals."

Tamara turned desperately to Ramsay. "Perhaps we shouldn't go on our honeymoon. Perhaps we should stay here and look after Will."

Ramsay took his bride's hand firmly and pulled her quickly into the limo. "The boy will be fine," he whispered, bending his head and kissing her. "It'll be a comfort knowing Will is having fun, too."

"Not to me. You know I don't like to encourage his interest in the supernatural."

Ramsay traced her lips with a fingertip. "Trust me. Will must learn what is real and what is fantasy for himself—the way I had to."

A light like candle flame lit Ramsay's black eyes as he looked at his wife.

"I'll trust you forever," she murmured, warmed by the bright glow of his love.

And those were the last words she spoke for a very long time, because he had pulled her close against him again.

Ann Major

I used to talk to myself and wonder—was I crazy or was I a writer?

Or was I both?

I have always spent a great deal of time in an imaginary world that's all my own. Since childhood, I have gone around talking to myself. As a child I would dress in strange costumes and sit before the mirror in my bedroom and tell myself stories.

I have always liked to lie in bed right after I awaken and let my mind travel down fascinating paths just to see where they go. Not that it ever occurred to me that any of this daydreaming might ever prove useful.

I was a teacher of writing before I was a writer. My writing career began the day after my first son was born. I was lying in the hospital bed weeping with postpartum blues and consoling myself with a romance novel.

The story was such a great comfort to me I thought, "If only I could write a story as wonderful as the one I am reading." So, as soon as I adjusted to my new role of retired teacher and stay-at-home mom, I began to write—rather desperately—between bottles and diapers and more babies.

I wrote a million words before I sold one, but every unsold story was a thrilling challenge. I believed in those stories, even the ones I never sold. I lived them, and working on them helped me to learn my craft.

Fantasy nurtures our psyches and helps us face reality. I am deeply grateful that I have been published, that I have been able to touch other people's hearts and souls and imaginations. People read and write romances for all sorts of reasons, but most of all, we do it because we love these stories.

Ann Major

NIGHT OF THE
DARK MOON

Paula Detmer Riggs

The Vacation From Hell

"Go spelunking? In a cave? Me? You've got to be kidding. I get claustrophobic in a phone booth."

"C'mon, Paula. It'll be fun."

My college roommate was scientifically oriented. That is, she only dated guys in the Science Club. I, on the other hand, loathed classes that ended in -ology, even though Miami University, in its infinite wisdom, was forcing me to take my share in order to graduate.

"I'd like to, Elaine," I said in my most placating tone. "But I have this English lit mid-term and—"

Elaine waved aside my objection with a freshly manicured hand. "It's only for a day. Besides, you need the exercise and fresh air. You look positively haggard."

Haggard? The very thought sent me racing to the mirror.

It was true! At eighteen, I was already looking matronly. Perhaps an adventure *was* exactly what I needed.

That's how it started, the vacation from hell.

There were twenty of us, packed like overdressed sardines into three cars. Eighteen men, Elaine and me.

We left at dawn, before the air was properly oxygenated. It was November and cold. By mid-morning, when we reached our destination in the hills of Kentucky, I was cold, hungry and furious. Elaine, on the other hand, was cozied up to the only decent-looking guy in the club. If she was hungry, it wasn't for food.

It had recently snowed in the hills. The cold winter sun glinted off the ice crystals encasing the bare tree branches. A nearby stream seemed frozen solid. There was absolutely no sign of civilization anywhere, just a yawning black entrance to the cave that was our destination.

"Isn't this terrific?" one of the scientific types exulted as he was hauling this strange wire-mesh box out of the trunk.

"Uh, what's that thing?" I asked naively.

The budding genius gave me a disdainful look. "The cage for the bats, of course."

"Bats? What bats?"

"The ones we came to collect." Dummy.

I turned white. Elaine giggled. Murder flashed through my mind. Unfortunately for me, my roommate was much larger than I was. She also played center on the women's field-hockey team.

Glumly, I examined my options. I could sit in the car, longing for room service at the nearest four-star hotel while slowly freezing to death. Or I could tag along and hope for the best.

I tagged along. There was no best.

By their very nature, caves are dark. Not middle-of-the-night city dark, where there's always a faint glow to the blackness. No, cave dark is ink black and smothering thick.

Caves smell, especially caves housing homesteading bats. I used my wool muffler to cover my nose. It helped some, until my breathing froze the fabric solid.

Caves are treacherous, with narrow passages and water hazards that usually come right after one has squeezed through a passage the size of a spare tire on one's hands and knees.

By the time we found the bats' cavernous bedroom, my best slacks were irreparably torn and caked with mud, and my gloves were frozen to my hands.

I fumed. Elaine giggled. The intrepid scientific types trapped their precious bats, ugly, noisy, smelly little creatures that they are.

By the time we finally trekked footsore and bone chilled to the mouth of the cave, fresh snow had all but buried the cars. We were snowbound. No way were we going to get home that day.

Someone remembered a farmhouse a few miles down the road. Reluctantly, the farmer and his wife took us in. The guys slept in the living room. Elaine slept with her friend. I slept with the bats.

Chapter One

The sky was as black as a mourning cloak. Swollen clouds hung low over the Big Island of Hawaii. A *kona* wind whipped the Pacific to foam and tore at the coconut palms like an angry hand. The quarter horses in the main corral of Sinclair Ranch were restless, unable to settle. A storm was coming.

Alone in his office in the sprawling ranch house, Quinn Sinclair listened to the wind howl and thought about the fences that would need mending in the morning.

"Quinn, are you listening?"

Quinn tucked the phone receiver between his shoulder and ear. Bracing one booted foot against his great-grandfather's priceless koa wood desk, he balanced his chair on two legs.

"Sorry, buddy," he drawled in a voice that was still graveled from too many cigarettes at too young an age. "Storm's comin'. Might be a problem."

The man on the other end of the line snorted. "What about *my* problem? I didn't call you in the middle of the night here in D.C. to get a weather report."

"Hell, Eddie, I'd like to help you, but Meg handles the guest-ranch side of this operation. I just run the cattle on the working side."

"Don't give me that. You own the whole damn place. All...what? Two hundred thousand acres?"

Quinn stifled a yawn. His day had started before the sun was even a glimmer in the east and wasn't finished yet.

"Something like that."

"So pull some strings with that sweet sister of yours and get Anne a room."

Anne. Was that the woman's name? Quinn hadn't been listening all that attentively. He was dead tired. His thigh muscles were beginning to seize up on him, and his back hurt. He'd been in the saddle from dawn for five days straight, riding fence and tallying beef.

In its heyday, Sinclair Ranch had needed a crew of forty *paniolos* to run it. Now he had nine, including himself. The payroll only stretched so far each month. From now until May, the height of the tourist season, he would be forced to make do with even fewer hands. Quinn rubbed the stubble on his jaw and thought of the ranch books he hadn't opened in three days.

"Problem is, Eddie, we only have twenty-five beds for paying guests, all of which, according to Meg, are taken for the next three months."

"What about the room next to yours? The one Candy and I slept in?"

Quinn's mouth thinned at the memory. Eddie's wife had come on to every man on the place. To him, too, before he'd let her know he wasn't interested.

"Give me a break, Eddie. The family wing's the only place I can go to get *away* from the tourists."

Five thousand miles away, in the icy slush of a Washington winter, Assistant Attorney General Edward C. Franklyn sat in a cluttered corner office of the Justice Department. In front of him was a thick file folder, marked with the yellow flag of the Witness Protection Program.

On the top was a candid photograph of a woman dressed in rumpled khaki shorts and an army-surplus shirt. Her hair was tousled, blond and naturally wavy. A camera of professional quality was slung around her neck, as much a part of her as the infectious grin on her face and the sexy little cleft in her chin.

Her name was Anne Oliver, age thirty-three, a freelance photographer of some renown. At the moment, she was Franklyn's greatest concern. Trouble was, his friend Quinn was a hard man to con, especially when it came to women. And Franklyn needed that room.

He decided to try another tack. "That's what I've been trying to tell you. The lady is almost family. One of Candy's best friends, in fact. They...work together in New York."

Deception was the one aspect of his job that he'd learned to tolerate but never liked—especially when he was forced to lie to a man he respected as much as Quinn Sinclair. Forgive me, buddy, he thought. Someday you'll understand.

"Tell you what, Eddie. I'll call around, get Candy's friend a reservation at one of the other resorts."

Static crackled over the line. Then Franklyn said, "Consider it a personal favor. Okay?"

Quinn heard the slight change in his old friend's tone. A favor, he thought. As in payback time?

His gut twisted before he controlled the surge of sudden emotion, just as he controlled everything in his life these days. Ed Franklyn had a right to ask a lot more of him than a room.

"What the hell?" he said, his voice resigned. "Let me know when the lady arrives, and I'll send the chopper to the airport in Hilo to pick her up."

"She'll be there at four o'clock tomorrow afternoon. And *the lady's* name is Anne Oliver. You can't miss her. Tall, blond. A real knockout."

"I said 'send,' Eddie. I don't intend to pilot the damn thing myself."

There was a pause. "I was hoping you'd take a personal interest in her. Show her around. Make sure things go smoothly."

Quinn dropped his feet and sat up. "Jeez, Ed, I'm a stockman, not an escort service."

"It's nothing like that, Quinn." Franklyn's voice took on a richer note. "Anne is special. She needs some . . . delicate handling."

"You mean she's a gold-plated bitch like . . . well, never mind who she's like. I get the picture."

Franklyn cursed the burst of patriotic zeal that had led him into government work. "Let's say I need you to put that temper of yours in cold storage while she's there and treat her like a VIP."

Quinn's gaze shifted to the wall that separated the two large bedrooms that made up the master suite.

A model, he thought. Tall and blond. No doubt she would have every hand on the place falling all over himself to light her cigarettes and saddle her horse.

"I'll make sure the lady has no complaints, Eddie. You have my word." He hung up before he changed his mind.

The DC-9 out of Honolulu landed in Hilo ten minutes early. Every seat was occupied. Anne's hope of a nap had been dashed when her seatmate had turned out to be a wispy octogenarian from Pasadena who was terrified of flying.

Even before the wheels had left the ground, Anne had found herself holding tight to the frail woman's hand. Every time the conversation had lagged, the woman had veered toward panic. Anne was nearly hoarse from the nonstop chatter.

The mood in the plane was lively as the soon-to-be vacationers slowly moved up the aisle. Even though the cabin was refrigerator cold, Anne felt as though she were sweltering.

As she made her way down the steps and across the tarmac to the terminal, she told herself to ignore the weakness making her muscles feel like twanging rubber bands.

Oliver women never fainted. It was so undignified. Heck no, Oliver women were of good Scottish stock— strong, stoic and certainly not given to embarrassing displays of weakness.

Trouble was, she didn't feel all that strong right now. Ten days in the hospital had left her pale and unsteady on her feet.

Inside the terminal, the waiting room was small and crowded. Tour guides with professional smiles dropped wilted leis over the heads of their wide-eyed charges before herding them into groups. Family members greeted each other joyously in a mixture of languages. Everyone seemed to have someone but her.

"Don't worry about a thing," Franklyn had said just before he'd put her on the plane at Dulles. "Quinn will take care of you."

At the time Anne had hated the very idea that anyone had to take care of her, let alone some reclusive stranger halfway round the world who thought she was someone she wasn't.

Her pale mouth curved into a self-conscious grin. A model, for Pete's sake. Someone who pranced on the wrong side of the camera lens. What the heck, Annie? she thought. You can do anything for two months. Right?

And then she would return to Washington, to a courtroom in the federal courthouse, to sit across from four vicious, sadistic killers who wanted her dead.

Anne's mouth went dry. Fear twisted in her stomach until she forced herself to relax.

So, she thought. Where are you, Mr. Sinclair? Tough-looking guy, Franklyn had said. Half Polynesian, from one of the oldest families in the islands. Big, he'd added, with diver's shoulders and a don't-bother-me look she was told to ignore.

"Hell of a place, that ranch of his," Franklyn had promised. "Very romantic. Popular with honeymooners. You'll love it. But you can't tell him why you're there. You can't tell anyone."

Feeling dizzier and dizzier, she scanned the features of a dozen men. More. None of them remotely resembled Franklyn's description.

Settling her bag more comfortably on her shoulder, she spotted an empty seat and headed in that direction. She was almost there when she sensed someone behind her.

The now familiar rush of fear tightened her throat, and she whirled. "What do you want?" she demanded.

Accustomed to men her own size, she found her gaze settling on a V of very dark, very soft-looking chest hair framed by the rumpled lapels of a chambray shirt that snugged powerful male shoulders and emphasized the breadth of a hard male chest. A blood-red lei was slung over one enormous shoulder.

She jerked her gaze upward. The eyes that raked her face were too dark to be called brown, and yet they weren't quite as black as the silky lashes framing them. His hair, windblown and thick, was the same indefinable color that gave his eyes a suggestion of mystery.

His face was more angular than square, although his jaw had a stubborn jut. His skin was tanned a deep bronze. His mouth was resolute, strength trapped in the corners, misleading softness in the curve of his lower lip.

"Whoa, easy now. I didn't mean to scare you." His voice was slightly hoarse.

Anne's heart thrummed in her throat, and her hands were shaking. "Well, you did," she said, trying to regain her composure.

His mouth slowly formed a smile, as though the muscles of that part of his face were little used. "Sorry about that. I'm a little big to be sneaking up on anyone. I thought you saw me."

Anne felt a shadowy feeling of some elusive emotion pass through her. It seemed like desire. She was certain it wasn't.

"Let's forget it, okay?"

"Sure. I'm Quinn Sinclair."

The quick look he shot around and the subtle flex of his wide shoulders told Anne that impatience was as much a part of this man as the unknowable darkness in his eyes.

Feeling as though she was suddenly moving in slow motion, Anne forced her facial muscles into what she hoped was a friendly smile and extended her hand. "Call me Anne."

Instead of taking her hand, he took the lei from his shoulder and looped it around her neck. "Welcome to Hawaii," he said before bending to brush a kiss across the swell of her cheek. His lips were hard and cool.

Anne felt her breathing change. It wasn't voluntary, nor, she discovered, could it be controlled.

"Uh, *mahalo*. Thank you. And thank you for finding room for me."

"No problem."

Quinn had expected a beautiful woman. He hadn't expected one with dark shadows under her eyes and skin so pale it seemed almost transparent.

Her eyes, framed by curly wheat-colored lashes, were a clear hazel without a hint of green. Tipped at the outer corners, they had a sleepy cast, like a cat too long in the sun. Her mouth had a soft look of fragility that drew his gaze.

Her hair was sun-streaked, no doubt artfully done every few weeks in one of those pretentious places in Manhattan. At the moment it was pulled back into a severe twist of some kind that made her look very cool and sophisticated.

Champagne style and subtle vulnerability, he thought. Class and a shimmering sensuality. It was a hell of a combination. No wonder Ed had called in a favor.

Tension began riding his spine. A heavy pressure invaded his groin. The involuntary response made him irritable. What a man couldn't control usually ended up causing him trouble.

Two months, he thought. And she'll be sleeping right next door. Terrific, Eddie. Thanks a lot.

"Ready? I want to get back to the ranch before dark."

"Mind if I collect my bags first?" she asked with the faintest suggestion of humor in her low voice.

His mouth twitched. "Not unless you make me carry them all."

"I've only got two and this." She touched the strap of her tote.

One of his eyebrows lifted. Anne had a feeling she had surprised him.

"This way," he said, nodding toward the corridor. He lifted her tote bag from her shoulder and hefted it over his. The purple-and-pink bag looked much smaller when he held it.

"Is your car outside?" she asked as she forced herself to keep up with his long, impatient strides.

"No, I brought the chopper."

Chopper. Anne's stomach lurched, and the little warmth remaining in her face turned to ice. She hated helicopters. "Is it far? Your ranch, I mean?"

"Twenty minutes."

Twenty minutes, she echoed silently. A lifetime.

An updraft caught the chopper, shaking it from side to side. Quinn adjusted the craft's trim and watched their shadow splash across the broad, open pit of Halemaumau. The ancient volcano, dormant now, but once a seething pot of lava, was like a beacon, guiding him home.

Polynesians had been on Hawaii for uncounted generations when Josiah Sinclair, a seaman from Maine on a whaling clipper, had jumped ship on his first trip to the islands, lusting for excitement and fortune. He'd found both, dying a wealthy man sixty years later.

Quinn and his sister, Meg, were the last of old Josiah's direct descendants. She had inherited the house. The ranch was his, the only thing other than his sister that he cared about.

Once, however, when he'd been eighteen, he had rejected his heritage and the responsibilities that went with it for a life at sea, just as Josiah had done.

He'd spent fifteen years as a Navy SEAL. Having barely scraped through high school, he began as a lowly seaman apprentice. But his own ambition coupled with a steely resolve to carry out every assignment to the best of his considerable ability had won him a commission when he'd been twenty-four.

Six years ago, after a stupid mistake had blown his career out of the water, he'd come home to heal, his soul and spirit battered.

He'd succeeded, but the cost had been a loneliness he'd learned to accept. At age forty-one, he was content with the life he'd struggled so hard to put back together again.

The only jarring note was the lack of funds that made it necessary for him to open the ranch to paying guests. Someday though, four, maybe five years by his calculation, he would have his mammoth debt reduced to a reasonable amount. And then he could return to the private life he craved.

He shifted in the hard seat and concentrated on the instruments. The sooner he got the lady to the ranch, the sooner he could get back to work.

Beside him, Anne managed another look at her watch. Ten minutes to go. Overhead, the rotors clattered and shook, jarring the breath from her lungs and battering her eardrums. Below her, Hawaii was a blur of green. Behind her were six empty seats.

Next to her, Quinn Sinclair slouched awkwardly in the bucket seat that seemed too small and too low for his big frame. His long legs moved restlessly, as though the tension she felt in her tight muscles was somehow showing.

With the impersonal eye of an artist, she noted the flat belly and lean athletic hips, the soft, comfortable fit of worn denim over heavy thighs, the scuffed, dusty boots. Nothing fancy, nothing to impress. A working man's clothes. A working man's body. Strong, powerful, built for endurance and stamina.

Eyes slitted behind the traditional aviator sunglasses, he flew the ungainly craft with the reckless confidence of a combat veteran—or a man with a death wish.

A loner, she thought. Content with his own company. Not an easy man to like. But then, Franklyn didn't say she had to like him.

The chopper hit a spot of turbulence, tossing them upward and then down. "Oh," she gasped. Quinn glanced her way, catching her gaze on him. His mouth compressed, as though he were annoyed about something.

"Great view," she said, forcing a smile that felt transparently phony.

"See that crater?" he said into the microphone attached to his headset. "That's where Pele lives."

Anne looked down, her stomach lurching. She saw a deep conical hole in the midst of a barren moonscape. Surrounding the crater was a rippled ocean of gray lava.

"Pele was the goddess of fire, right?" she murmured, returning her gaze to Quinn's profile.

"Right. According to legend, she used a sharp stick to dig a hole on each island, which she filled with fire. But her older sister, Na Maka O Kaha'i, was jealous and filled each pit with water to put out Pele's fire."

"Sibling rivalry, even among goddesses."

One eyebrow arched above his dark glasses. "Sounds like you have a sister."

"Four, actually. I'm the oldest. I grew up on a farm in Missouri."

Quinn could feel the friendliness radiating from her and told himself not to trust it. "Just another all-American girl, I suppose?"

"'Fraid so. When I was growing up, they called us the Oliver girls. The mercantile used our picture to advertise back-to-school clothes. My poor daddy spent most of his money keeping us in dresses and shoes."

"Is that where you got interested in modeling?"

"Something like that."

Anne hated lying. Heat rose in her face, and she fervently hoped he wouldn't notice.

Something shifted in his eyes. What little warmth she had felt from him disappeared. She looked down, trying to see a house. A landing strip. Something.

Don't move, she told herself with false confidence as he guided the chopper lower. If you don't move, everything will be all right.

Without seeming to, Quinn watched the tip of her tongue run over her bottom lip. She was obviously terrified and trying hard not to show it. A sudden need to protect her caught him by surprise. He told himself to ignore it. He'd been trapped that way once before, and it had nearly destroyed him.

"There's the ranch," he said. "On your right."

She looked right, pretending an interest in the land whizzing by beneath them. An irregular clearing had been cut into the trees like giant brush strokes of pale green crisscrossed by thin rust-red lines she took to be dirt tracks. Mountains rose on either side of the valley like ragged lines of crumpled black paper. At the far end a cluster of white buildings nestled in the shadow of the tallest peak.

According to Franklyn, the area was remote, unspoiled, even primitive in places. The inhabitants of the mountain villages still clung to the old ways and the ancient language. Time was relative, judged more by the sun and seasons than the clock. Secure as any safe house, Franklyn had promised.

Secure or not, she considered it better than the dreary bungalow in Maryland where they had tried to stash her. The tiny rooms and tall fences had made her stir-crazy. When she'd threatened to find her own hiding place, Franklyn, bless his heart, had come up with this one—if she didn't end up dead before she got there.

Anne took a deep breath, but the landing was perfect. Sinclair cut the engine and, while waiting for the rotors to stop spinning, efficiently carried out some kind of post-flight checklist.

One by one Anne relaxed the fingers mangling the soft suede handbag in her lap. Beyond the window she saw a huge white house that would have been ugly if it hadn't been so classically Victorian. Three stories high. Gabled, adorned with gingerbread on nearly every surface. It even had a turret, the rounded kind with a steep conical roof.

As she watched, an orange golf cart with a fringed canopy sped toward the chopper. The dark-haired, deeply tanned young man driving it wore a wild yellow-and-pink aloha shirt and white-duck pants.

Quinn removed his headset. He hung it on the hook under the window and indicated that Anne should do the same.

"Ron will take you to the house and get you registered."

Ron? The thought of facing yet another stranger was too much after a trip that had seemed endless.

"But I thought you . . . Ed said you would handle everything."

Quinn felt the contentment of being home evaporate. So Eddie had passed along his promise to give her the VIP treatment.

"Well, hell, Ms. Oliver, we sure wouldn't want you going back disappointed." His words had razored edges, but Anne was too exhausted to care.

He slipped from the seat and brushed past her to slide open the door. Anne followed, her balance precarious, her ears ringing.

He jumped down and extended his hand. Anne took it. Just as she stepped down, the scene in front of her began to whirl. The cement pad seemed to lurch. She had a sensation of tilting. Of hitting something solid. Of Quinn Sinclair's hard mouth forming words she didn't understand. And then . . . nothing.

She was on a bed. Not her own. The mattress was too soft. The air smelled different from her own town house in St. Louis, too. Something was wrong.

"Call the damn doctor, Meg. She's been out too long."

Anne turned her head toward the low, rumbling voice edged with impatience. Sinclair. The sexy cowboy with the moody eyes.

"You heard what Eddie said when you called him," whispered a woman's voice. "She's suffering from exhaustion. That's why she's here—to rest."

In the dim light Anne saw Sinclair and a woman nearly as tall as he was standing by a long, narrow window. His sister? Wasn't her name Meg? Her usually excellent memory was strangely fogged.

Anne drew a deep breath. Life was returning to her body in stages. Fingers, toes. Arms, legs. Finally the rest of her.

"Why the hell didn't he tell me that to begin with?" Sinclair whispered, his voice rougher than Anne remembered. "Damn near scared me to death when she fainted."

"There's something you should know," Anne muttered, drawing their attention like the crack of a whip. "Oliver women never faint."

"Couldn't prove that by me," Sinclair muttered.

"Don't pay any attention to my brother," the woman told Anne as she came toward the bed. "He's not used to feeling helpless. And when you took that header into his arms, he didn't know what to do."

Quinn scowled. "Who do you think brought her here, then, if I'm so damn helpless?"

His sister ignored him. "I'm Margaret Sinclair, Meg to my friends," she said with a smile that twinkled eyes remarkably like her brother's in shape and color, but not in hardness. "I've been looking forward to meeting you. Eddie Franklyn is a particularly good friend of ours."

Anne tried to clear the cotton from her mouth. "I'm sorry I'm so much trouble."

Using her elbows, she pushed herself upward, only to discover, as the coverlet fell away, that her blouse was unbuttoned, allowing the lace and satin of her bra to show. That Quinn had noticed, too, was obvious after one hasty look at his face.

His eyes glittered with the kind of heat that was unmistakable. She averted her gaze, but not before she had seen the slow, sardonic lifting of one of his black eyebrows.

"Meg did it, not me," he drawled. "In case you're wondering."

"I wasn't," she snapped too quickly. She hated the heat climbing into her face. Oliver women never blushed. She forced herself to button her blouse one slow button at a time.

Meg Sinclair glanced from one to the other with a speculative look on her face that disappeared as soon as she returned her gaze to Anne's pale face.

"How do you feel?" she asked. "Are you hungry? Can Quinn get you a drink of something? Brandy, perhaps?"

Anne shook her head. "I'm fine," she said. "Just a bit jet-lagged." She pulled up the coverlet and made herself smile. "All I need is a good night's sleep."

A frown lined Meg's broad forehead. She was a stately woman in her late thirties with a look of compassion warming her smile. Anne liked her face. She liked Meg.

"Are you sure?" Meg persisted. "I could make you a sandwich."

"Leave the woman alone," Quinn interjected, a scowl pulling at the corners of his mouth. "She's a big girl. If she said she's fine, she's fine. Right, Ms. Oliver?'' His gaze shifted to her face and stayed there. But his body still remembered the soft warmth of her breasts against his chest when he'd carried her into the house. For such a tall woman, she'd felt amazingly fragile in his arms.

Blood was pounding in her temples, and her face felt hot. She was beginning to feel off balance, the way she always felt when confronted with new and treacherous terrain. She didn't like the feeling. She wasn't sure she liked the man generating it, either. Just being near him made her jittery and tense.

"Right, Mr. Sinclair," she said. "But thank you for your concern. And your help. If I *had* fainted, that is. Which, of course, I didn't."

The look that flashed in his eyes was brief, but Anne had trained herself to look for the tiniest details that made her photographs unique. Amusement, she thought. The man can laugh. Why doesn't he?

"If you need anything in the night, just give a holler. I'm right next door." His gaze directed hers to a door to her left. It was closed. The ornate brass lock had no key.

"Next door?" she repeated. Fatigue buzzed in her head and slowed her thinking.

The sudden grin he gave her changed his face from interesting to dangerously attractive. "Yeah, didn't Eddie tell you? You and I are sharing the master suite. We're the only ones at the end of this wing."

He turned and walked toward the door leading to the hall. "Sleep well," he said as he went out and closed the door behind him.

Chapter Two

*G*unfire.

They had found her! She was going to die.

Anne jackknifed into a sitting position, her heart slamming against her rib cage. Brilliant light angled into her eyes, blinding her. Acting on instinct, she threw off the sheet and dove to the floor. Her elbow banged the hard wood, sending pain jolting through the newly healed flesh in her upper arm.

She cried out, then froze, flattened against the rough straw mat, face down, afraid to move. Afraid even to breathe.

What...? Where...? She looked around in a panic.

The big airy room with the old-fashioned furniture was quiet. Sunshine splashed the polished wood beneath her bare thighs and warmed her skin. Beyond the gabled windows, the sky was a clear, innocent blue.

There were no men in camouflage with automatic weapons. No protective FBI agents. No one in the room at all—but her.

And then she heard it, the clatter of metal on dirt. Horses' hooves.

"Terrific, Anne," she muttered into the woven floor covering beneath her cheek. "If you're a basket case now, what will you be like two months from now?"

Before she'd left the hospital, the doctors had offered tranquillizers for the rough times they told her to expect. Shakes, nightmares, extreme anxiety. Post-trauma stress, they'd called it. Common in gunshot victims. She'd refused the pills. Her emotions were sometimes too strong for her own good, but at least they were hers.

Needing to fill her lungs with fresh air, she hauled herself to her feet and hurried to the window. The panes opened outward, like old-fashioned casements, and she flung both windows wide.

Birdsong greeted her, along with the rustling of wind in the coconut palms. Beyond the neat fences, cattle grazed. Horses frolicked in the corral by a big white barn that looked more Yankee than Hawaiian.

The day smelled of something spicy. Ginger blossoms, maybe. Or plumeria. The dawn air was washed clean and felt cool against her bare arms. Below the windowsill, leftover raindrops glistened on the palmetto leaves, bright as crystal prisms.

She took another deep breath, then another, savoring the feeling of freedom. *You're alive, and it's a glorious, wonderful day,* she told herself. *Don't think about anything but enjoying it.*

It was early. The distant mountains were still shrouded in shadow. Best shot in black and white, she registered automatically, to show the dramatic silhouette of the peaks.

Closer to the house, however, she saw a montage of color. Exciting, vivid color—flowers, birds, even the clothes worn by the ranch hands in the corral.

In an instant her eye framed the picture. The men should be the focal point, with the horses they were saddling behind them. She would use fast film, a long lens.

Cowboys in Hawaii, she thought. Lean, wiry men who looked tough enough to have stepped from the pages of the Zane Grey novels she'd devoured as a child. Their faces, burned to leather by the tropical sun, were a polyglot of racial mixtures, Hawaiian, Chinese, Japanese, Anglo—too many to identify.

Paniolos, they called them here. According to the guidebook she'd read in the hospital, the name came from the first Spanish cowboys on the islands. The cattle had come from Texas, gifts from Captain George Vancouver to King Kamehameha.

Very Hawaiian, she thought. English sea captain, Polynesian king, Spanish ranch hands. A blending of cultures, still dynamic and functioning, a hybrid blossom stronger than the root stock.

Perfect, she thought, excited at the possibilities. A story told in pictures. Her specialty.

She hurried to the bags lined up neatly next to a huge armoire. Last night, after Quinn and his sister had left, she'd unpacked the basics from the smaller bag, changed into her nightshirt, brushed her teeth and fallen into bed again. Everything else was still packed.

Eagerness welling inside her, she opened the larger bag and took out the only camera Franklyn had allowed her to bring, a vintage Nikon that looked anything but professional.

Purchased when she was thirteen with money she'd made baby-sitting, the Nikon was older than she was. It was a familiar weight in her hands. Her best friend. Sometimes she thought it was her only friend. The only one she could trust without reservation, anyway.

The camera was a part of her, sometimes the best part. Her way of forcing order into a disorderly world.

Its eye, unaffected by emotion, was more sensitive than hers. Life was manageable when it was viewed through the length of a lens.

From the smaller bag she took a telephoto lens and fitted the two together. She slipped the old Nikon around her neck and returned to the window.

The onshore breeze caught her flaxen hair, whipping sleep-tangled strands into her eyes. She raised a hand to push it aside, and as she did, she caught sight of a rider cantering toward her across one of the fields.

He rode with one arm relaxed, the other holding the reins with an ease that made the powerful copper-colored stallion an extension of his will.

His straw Stetson was pulled low, hiding his features, but his skin was Polynesian dark and the hair that curled over his collar was as black as the stallion's mane.

It was Quinn.

She took a hasty step backward, reluctant to have him see her. Not that she was afraid, she told herself, even as her heartbeat took on a more agitated rhythm. Nor was she excessively modest, but she *was* standing there in a thin cotton nightshirt. And he was very male.

No doubt he'd received his share of "offers" from unattached female guests. A vacation fling was almost expected these days. For others, perhaps, she thought, absently rubbing the newly healed scar on her upper arm. Not for her. And certainly not with a man who looked as unbroken and dangerous as the stallion he rode. Right now, all she wanted to do was survive until April.

"Yo, boss," one of the men called out as Quinn approached the corral. "You got a minute?"

Anne didn't hear his reply, but the waiting men laughed, and one of them pushed open the corral gate, allowing the horse and rider to enter.

Inside, Quinn dismounted with the supple motions of a man used to the saddle. After removing his gloves, he tucked them into the low-slung waistband of jeans that had seen better days.

One of the hands took charge of the stallion, leading him into the barn. The others gathered around, talking and gesturing, respectful, but oddly boyish at the same time.

As Quinn listened, he swept off his Stetson and wiped his brow with his forearm. Even though he was surrounded by his men, he seemed apart from them. Not so much alone, Anne decided, as solitary.

Her natural curiosity took over. Was he a loner by choice or experience? Or did he feel superior to the men he commanded?

Perhaps, she mused. There was something intriguing about the set of his powerful shoulders that suggested an inner confidence and an innate toughness, the kind experience and struggle put into a person.

Still in shadow, Anne lifted the camera to her eye. With skill so practiced it was now instinctive, she framed the picture with meticulous precision until she got exactly the right combination of light and shadow.

An instant before she clicked the shutter, Quinn's head came up and he turned toward her. A hundred feet or more separated them, but the skillfully ground lens brought his face so close that she could see his mouth compress.

A scowl pulled his thick black brows into a V over the bridge of his nose, shadowing his eyes and reminding her of the storm clouds that gathered over the mountain peaks. His eyes narrowed, as though he were seeing her with equal clarity, although she knew that was impossible.

A sensation like warm water slid down her spine, and she snapped the picture. An instant later she stepped out of sight, the only part of Quinn Sinclair she wanted trapped forever on film.

The clock was striking seven when Anne descended the stairs to the main floor. She was dressed in white slacks and a long-sleeved yellow shirt, both old favorites.

The house was so quiet it seemed to be holding its breath as she reached the foyer and turned left, her sandals silent on the floor mats.

The lobby was deserted, the desk unattended. The plantation blinds were tilted upward, allowing light to enter but screening out the heat. The twittering of the morning birds and the nickering of the horses in the corral drifted in with the breeze.

The seductive aroma of strong coffee led her to a large airy room looking out on an exotic garden in full bloom. Tables set with flowers and damask clothes were cleverly scattered amidst flourishing plants as tall as small trees. The tables and chairs were empty. The room wasn't.

Quinn was standing in front of the massive nineteenth-century sideboard, pouring himself a cup of coffee.

He had discarded the hat and smoothed his hair into rough order. His shirtsleeves had been rolled another turn, revealing forearms corded with lean muscle. Sunlight streaming through the window turned the curly hairs on his arms to soft brown.

From the corner of his eye Quinn saw her come in. She stopped when she saw him, a look of uncertainty crossing her face. An instant later he caught a whiff of her perfume. It was subtle, making him think of spring rain and wildflowers.

Her long thick hair was braided and caught up by a frilly bow at the back of her neck. Sunlight found the lightened strands, turning them to gold. He was tempted to release that braid and watch the silk of her long hair fall loose against her neck. It would be slippery and warm against his rough fingers, like the rare lace ferns that grew only in the high country.

"Am I in the wrong place?" she asked. For the first time he noticed that she spoke with a faint accent. Not exactly Southern, but certainly not native New York. The cadence was easy on the ear. Perhaps too easy.

"No, just early," he answered. "Service starts at eight. Tourists sleep late."

"I don't mind waiting to eat, but I would kill for a cup of that coffee," she said with a hopeful look at the pot in his hand.

Quinn turned over another cup, found a saucer and poured. "Black, no sugar," he said before turning to look at her. It wasn't a question.

"Yes, how did you know?" Anne's voice was husky, and her breathing was too rapid, the only outward signs of nervousness she couldn't control.

"You look like a woman who takes her pleasures straight."

Pleasures. The word excited a dozen different images when he said it, all of them erotic. She told herself to ignore them.

"Hmm, a cowboy psychologist. I'm impressed," she murmured, fervently hoping that the heat blooming in her face wasn't visible.

"Naw, just a country boy, ma'am." He tilted his head and did his best to look humble. Anne thought he looked like a too-sexy, too-masculine little boy.

She burst out laughing. "I'll bet."

"True story. I learned to ride before I could walk."

"That I can believe. Your legs have that slightly bowed look."

His gaze dropped to the long expanse of soft, faded denim sheathing legs thick with saddle muscles. "The hell they are!" he grumbled.

Even as she grinned, she was admiring the symmetry of sinew and bone that formed his long, powerful body. Somewhere deep inside, something softened, like a sigh.

"Seems to me you'd be a good two inches taller if you could straighten those knees of yours," she mused. "Maybe three."

"Mainlanders. What do they know?" he groused. But he looked different somehow as he replaced the pot on the warmer, then spooned sugar into one of the cups. Younger, she thought. More relaxed. She had a feeling the boss worked harder than his men. Certainly he had been up earlier.

"Join me?" he asked, indicating one of the tables by the window.

"Thanks. Uh, *mahalo,* I mean." It had been a long time since she'd felt so...normal. It was a good feeling.

He carried both cups to the table, then stood by one of the chairs, watching her walk toward him.

The lady had style, he thought. No wonder she made her living showing others what to wear. Even though she was overdressed for the islands, the tailored outfit seemed absolutely right somehow. On her, anyway.

Her shirt, loose flowing and extremely feminine, brought out the gold in her almond eyes. Her slacks, cut in classic lines, bagged round the hips as though she preferred her clothes a size too big. Not that they detracted from the decidedly feminine curves they covered, he decided. Just the opposite.

His imagination was working overtime, trying to define the exact shape of her hips and thighs beneath the soft white material.

To Anne's surprise, he held her chair for her, seating her with impeccable courtesy before hauling out his own chair and settling into it.

Hidden sophistication, she decided. Rough on the outside, polished to a smooth hardness inside.

"You look better this morning," he said. "Your face has some color." And freckles spattered over her nose. Had the elegant model with the cool composure once been a tomboy, climbing trees and skipping rocks in a stream? he wondered.

She lifted one eyebrow and looked at him directly. "Why does that sound more like an insult than a compliment?"

His mouth, so hard a moment ago, took on a strangely vulnerable slant. "Maybe because I'm out of practice."

Anne wrapped her hands around the bone-china cup and waited for the hot liquid to warm her palms. "If you're out of practice, it's because you choose to be."

Quinn was surprised at the accuracy of her guess, but he didn't let it show. "Probably," he said, his gaze falling to the snowy tablecloth.

"Why?"

Quinn wasn't used to directness in a woman. He wasn't sure he liked it. Or trusted it. "No time."

Anne tilted her head and studied him. His eyes were more brown than black in the morning light and edged with a circle of gold. She'd seen eyes like that before, on a rare Tibetan leopard she had stalked for weeks before getting close enough to capture the perfect shot.

Powerful, solitary, the big cat had tolerated her for reasons of his own. But he hadn't trusted her, even after weeks of familiarity. And when she'd gotten too close, he'd turned on her, wrecking her best camera and nearly mauling her before he'd suddenly changed his mind.

She shook her head slowly. "No, I don't think time is your problem."

"Hmm. Then what is?"

Sipping her coffee slowly, she thought about the dark, masculine features she had seen in the viewfinder. His face was lean, his nose aquiline, his bronzed skin stretched taut over strong bones. His mouth hinted at an elemental sensuality so powerful it bordered on frightening. His eyes compelled attention and, in some, obedience.

Aesthetically, his face was too harsh, too asymmetrical, too strong. Artistically, his face was a treasure, a portrait painter's dream. Or a photographer's.

But the man himself was an enigma. A rugged man of the land with rare moments of sensitivity and a hint of shyness. She sensed integrity there, and immense strength, the quiet unassuming kind that didn't parade itself for praise.

She was drawn to the man more than she should be. Excitement thrummed through her, and she tamped it down.

"You like women, but you don't trust them," she said over the rim of her coffee cup. "You don't trust me."

It had been a long time since anyone had read him so well. It made him edgy. "What makes you say that?" he asked before he could stop himself.

"Woman's intuition." And twenty years of studying faces.

He shifted in his chair, crooking an arm over the top rung and stretching out his legs. Dust still clung to the frayed jeans. His boots were worn down at the heels and scuffed at the toes, but the leather was first quality and the workmanship superb.

He looked up to find Anne watching him, a faint smile playing over her lips. The lady had a mouth made for kissing. Or was that an illusion, too?

He cleared a sudden thickness from his throat. "Eddie tells me you're a model."

He told me the same thing, she wanted to say. She didn't. This wasn't a game to be taken lightly. Her life was at stake.

"Yes, I'm a model."

"You live in New York?"

Anne took a sip of coffee. "When I'm not traveling. I spend most of my time out of the country." That, at least, was true.

Quinn toyed with his coffee cup. Usually he took his morning coffee in the kitchen with his sister and

Auntie Genoa, the ranch's chief cook. Bone china and linen tablecloths weren't his style.

"Ever been to Hawaii before?" he asked, because the silence unnerved him.

"Yes, about four years ago. But I never made it off Oahu."

"On a shoot?"

So he knew about modeling, she thought. Or at least the right word to use. Interesting. "Yes, on a shoot. In July, I think."

"Swimsuits, no doubt," he said, his mouth jerking slightly. Just thinking about her body dressed in little more than two scraps of material made his mouth dry and his groin hot.

"I wore a suit, yes," Anne admitted. But only because she had spent most of her time underwater, photographing the strikingly beautiful flora adorning the reefs. One of her photographs had won a prestigious award.

"Stayed at the Royal Hawaiian, I imagine."

Naturally, that was what he would expect of a highly paid model, she realized with a private moment of amusement. In fact, for most of her stay she had shared a room with her scuba instructor's twin daughters. They still exchanged cards at Christmas.

"Of course," she murmured.

"Nice life, if you like that sort of thing."

"I suppose I must."

One of his ebony eyebrows lifted slowly, and his expression clouded, as though he were considering her words. His very deliberation made her uneasy.

She turned her head and pretended to study the silent dining room. "This is a fantastic room," she murmured. "It has a friendly feel to it."

He looked around, his interest casual at best. "This used to be the solarium," he said. "My mother's favorite room."

"Is that Josiah?" she asked, indicating a large portrait hanging in a place of honor between two windows.

Quinn's gaze lifted to the thickly varnished portrait. Josiah Sinclair stared back at him, lines of wisdom etched into his austere Yankee features.

"Yeah, that's the great man himself."

Anne studied the face in the portrait. There was character there, she thought. And wisdom. But little kindness.

"You resemble him. Around the eyes, especially."

Quinn looked at the painting he'd seen every day of his life for years but never really studied. The portrait had been painted when Josiah had been well into middle age.

Crusty old bastard, he thought. Looked as hard as the Maine hills where he'd been born. Not a man a woman would take to if she had a choice.

His gaze returned to Anne's face and lingered. She had a quietness about her, a restfulness that he didn't expect from a woman who made her living in the fast lane. She had a way of relaxing a man just by sitting across from him. And exciting him just by lifting a cup of coffee to her full, soft lips.

"Family legend says that he jumped ship because he was about to be hanged for stealing the captain's rum. Took a keg with him, they say. Traded it to the first King Kamehameha for land and one of the king's stepdaughters."

Anne laughed. "That's terrible." She aimed another quick look at the stern face in the portrait.

"Shame on you, Josiah. I hope she ran you a merry chase."

Slowly she turned back toward Quinn. "Something tells me the man had a houseful of children."

"Eleven."

She grinned. "Good Yankee stock," she murmured. "How long were he and the chief's daughter married?"

Quinn lifted one eyebrow very slowly. "Who said they were married?"

Anne pretended to be shocked. "Is that why you're still a bachelor? Family tradition?"

"I'm divorced." Like a smothered flame, the glow that had appeared in his eyes went dark.

"Oops," she said. "I think I hit a nerve."

"It's been over for a long time." His voice was flat. Clipped.

Perhaps legally, Anne thought. But not emotionally. The residue was still there in the tension riding his shoulders and in the hard compression of his mouth.

"Sorry I brought it up. I'm way too nosy sometimes, mostly because I always want to know what makes people tick."

Quinn saw a look of concern cross her face. Did she sense the bitterness that his divorce had left him? Probably, he thought. She had a knack of slipping beneath a man's guard, enticing him to reveal far too much of himself.

In too many ways, the expensive model from New York wasn't what he had expected. Cool elegance one minute, fragile vulnerability the next. And now, consideration and charm, a potent combination. One that had trapped him once before—until he had discovered that those things, too, were illusions, created to entice.

What would she say, he wondered, if she knew that his distrust of women was caused by a beguiling, sensuous woman very much like her?

His hand reached out and captured hers. Ignoring her soft protest, he turned her hand palm up and studied the long slender fingers. They looked graceful and yet capable. Surprisingly, the nails were cut short and left unpolished. He liked the way her hand fit into his.

"You took my picture this morning," he said, lifting his gaze to her face.

The darkness in his eyes held her. Gray, she thought. Or black flecked with brown? Too many colors to label accurately, she decided. And far too expressionless for the violent emotion she sensed in him.

"Yes. If you like, I'll send you a copy when I... when the drugstore develops them."

Her gaze was direct. Too direct. He was used to evasion in a woman. And deceit.

He ran his thumb over her life line, and her fingers tried to close. Her wrist was delicately formed, with small bones and thin skin. Surprisingly dainty.

"Why take a picture of me?"

She felt strength in his touch. His hand was callused, the skin warm and dry, the easy control in his fingers absolute.

"You have an interesting face. Like Josiah's. I was curious."

He let his fingers play over the back of her hand. An urgency like the jittery feeling she felt in an electrical storm ran up her arm.

"Do you always get right to the point with a man?"

"With everyone. I find life more interesting when I don't have to deal with phony images."

Something stirred inside Quinn, a longing he'd thought dead a long time ago. He refused to trust it.

"Strange. Isn't that what you do for a living?" Sarcasm, quiet and suggestive, edged his voice. "Create phony images? Use sex to sell overpriced things to suckers who aren't smart enough to know they're being conned?"

Use sex. Anne's back teeth ground together. She had never used sex for any reason. Not in her work. Not in her personal life.

Oliver women never lose their tempers, she told herself. It's so exhausting. And sometimes very destructive, especially when it led to hurling things like expensive bone china at men who made insulting remarks.

Her gaze shifted to the cup and saucer in front of her, and her mouth took on a thoughtful slant. No, Annie, no, a voice warned. You like Meg Sinclair, remember.

Slowly, her eyes narrowing and her face freezing, she withdrew her hand and got to her feet.

"Thanks for the coffee, Mr. Sinclair. I'll see you around." Slanting him a cool smile, she turned and walked out of the dining room.

Chapter Three

Quinn couldn't remember the last time he'd slept past sunup. A few years back, probably, after one of the binges he used to go on when the rage inside him became too dangerous to handle sober.

Striding impatiently toward the kitchen and his first cup of coffee, he rolled one shirtsleeve another turn and started on the other. It was almost seven. No doubt his men would be wondering if the boss had tied one on again. Naw, fellas, he thought, the boss is just havin' trouble sleeping.

The kitchen door was closed. As he approached, he heard a burst of female laughter. It was a happy sound, but it only served to deepen his black mood. He hit the door with the flat of his hand, sending it flying inward.

Meg was there, and Auntie Genoa Kamae. He'd expected them. He hadn't expected Anne to be there, too, laughing with the others as though the three of them were fast friends.

Meg saw him first. "'Bout time you showed your face, big brother. I was beginning to worry about you."

Quinn's bad mood sharpened. "Don't bother."

"*Aloha,*" Auntie Genoa called out when she caught sight of him. Large of body and even larger of heart, Auntie Genoa always had a smile for the boy she'd helped raise.

She was coring pineapples for breakfast. Anne was helping, eating almost as much as she sliced. She was dressed in a silky purple jumpsuit, with the pant legs rolled halfway to her knees, showing shapely ankles tanned a golden brown. Next to her suntanned skin, the rich color looked exotic and sexy.

Quinn felt the muscles of his jaw bunch. The kitchen was off-limits to guests.

"Morning," he muttered. His gaze met Anne's, and he nodded.

The violent emotion she had sensed in him was close to the surface now. Well hidden, to be sure, but she saw the signs. A slight narrowing of his dark eyes. Tension running along the hard curve of his mouth. A stillness in his face.

For two weeks she had stayed out of his way. Actually, it hadn't been difficult. She had learned very quickly that Quinn rarely mingled with the guests.

"Only under threat to life and limb," his sister had confided. "These days my brother likes his privacy."

Anne understood that very well. She, too, had a craving to be alone at times—to order her thoughts and listen to the quiet meanderings of her mind. But she also liked the company of others. Men, women, old, young—she had trained herself to discover something unique in each one.

"You were up late last night," she said, eyeing the deep lines in his face.

"Was I?"

"The floorboards creak," she said. "I heard you pacing."

Quinn allowed himself a brief look at her mouth. The corners were tight, but her lower lip promised a softness that most men would find irresistible. He felt a quick hit of desire surge through him and steeled himself to ignore it.

"Sorry it bothers you." He walked past her to the huge stainless-steel coffee urn that was always on, even in the middle of the night.

"We have a problem, Quinn," his sister said as he filled a mug with coffee. "The helicopter is out of commission."

"Since when?" The first swallow scalded his tongue, and he muttered an explicit obscenity.

"Sometime yesterday. Zach told me last night."

"Last night when?"

"Right after he made love to me. Not that it's any of your business."

Quinn felt heat climb up his neck. His sister and the ranch's pilot, Zach Hogan, had been lovers for years. He told himself he neither approved nor disapproved. It wasn't his place to judge. But he didn't much like hearing about his sister's sex life.

"What's wrong with it?"

"Something to do with the fuel line. Zach has to fly commercial over to Honolulu this morning for a part before he can fix it."

Quinn ran over the balance in the ranch account. This time of year, things ran close to the bone. "He'd better check with me before he spends any money."

Meg frowned. "We have to have the chopper, Quinn. Our entire activities program is planned around it. Today I was supposed to take a group to Volcanoes National Park."

"So plan something else."

"That, dear brother, was exactly what I was doing when you came barging in here. Anne has agreed to lead a photo safari."

"*Anne* has?" His gaze swung in her direction. "For a lady who makes her living on the other side of a camera, you take a lot of pictures. Half my hands spend more time getting haircuts than they spend working."

He leaned against the counter and crossed his legs at the ankles. Anne noticed that he was wearing another pair of beat-up jeans. The hem was frayed and the knees nearly worn through. His shirt was missing a button.

The man needed tending, she thought, then smiled to herself. He hadn't exactly asked for volunteers. Nor would she be first in line if he did. Still, the thought was intriguing.

Anne felt her cheeks warm and hoped he was too far away to notice the color that must be rising. "All models know a lot about lighting and composition," she hedged. "And photography has been my hobby for a long time." She nudged her chin higher. "Besides, since you won't let me pay for my room and board, I have to do something useful around here or I'll feel like a freeloader."

Quinn thought about the credit-card bills he was still paying down. And the divorce settlement that had all but put him into bankruptcy. He had learned the hard way that no woman ever gave a man something for nothing.

"Suit yourself," he told her. "Just stay away from my wranglers. They have better things to do than pose for pictures for a bunch of tourists."

"Thanks for the advice. I'll keep that in mind." Anne finished the last of the pineapple and began licking the juice from her fingers, drawing Quinn's attention to her lips.

She had the kind of mouth that made promises, even when she wasn't speaking. Promises that made a man hard and hurting. Promises that lied. Or did they? Suddenly he wasn't as sure as he needed to be. Uncertainty was new to him, and it made him irritable.

"I've got work to do." He drained his cup and rinsed it carefully, the way Auntie had drummed into him years ago.

He left without saying goodbye. A second later they heard the back door slam. Meg and Auntie Genoa exchanged looks.

"First of the month is a bad time for something to go wrong," Meg said.

"What's wrong with the first of the month?" Anne asked.

"That's when Quinn has to write out his alimony check."

Anne drew herself another cup of coffee. "I didn't think the courts awarded alimony anymore."

Auntie snorted. "They do when the wife hires a shark for an attorney."

"I could strangle that woman with my bare hands," Meg muttered, her voice seething. She caught Anne's eyes on her and attempted a smile. "In the old days a woman like that would have been stoned."

Anne lifted her cup to her mouth and drank deeply before asking in a casual tone, "Are you talking about Quinn's ex-wife?"

"Yes. Her name is Liz. Elizabeth Chesterton. Maybe you know her? She's a model, too. A friend of Candy's, in fact. Like you."

Auntie took another pineapple from the basket and whacked it in two with a cleaver. "Nonsense," she snorted. "Anne and her are nothing alike. That woman never helped out a soul, 'lessen it was for money."

Anne dropped her gaze. "The name sounds familiar, but I don't know her."

"Just as well. She's a gold-plated bitch." Meg crossed to the stainless-steel refrigerator and took out a large bowl of eggs. From a shelf she took down another bowl. Anne lowered her cup and picked up an egg. Cooking wasn't high on her list of pleasures, but she did know how to scramble eggs.

"Why didn't he fight it? Offer a settlement instead?" she asked, tossing the shells into the sink.

Meg's smile had bitter edges. "He did. Or rather, his attorney did. She got that, too." She whacked another egg on the edge of the bowl, spattering herself and the counter with yolk.

"No wonder he doesn't have much use for models."

Meg stopped mopping the counter to eye her warily. "How'd you know?"

"From something Quinn said the first day I was here. I got the impression he didn't think much of...my profession."

"Don't take it personally, Anne. He's carrying around a lot of hurt. Has been for years. I'm not sure he'll ever get rid of it."

"I know," Anne said softly. "It's in his eyes."

"He makes me so mad sometimes!" Meg exclaimed. "As a kid he was unbelievably sweet in spite of that big, scary body. He didn't even date much in high school. Girls scared him, I think. I should have known he'd fall hard when he fell."

Yes, Anne thought. His feelings ran deep and strong. "How did they meet?"

"When he was in Newport for officers' training school."

"Worst thing that ever happened to him," Auntie proclaimed. "That she-bitch never would have married him if he'd still been an enlisted man."

Meg nodded. "That's for sure."

Anne wiped her hands and reached for her coffee, only to discover that her cup was empty. She moved past Meg to draw another cup. "Why did he leave the navy?"

Meg's mouth tightened. "He didn't. Not voluntarily, that is. They kicked him out."

Anne's hand jerked, spilling hot coffee on her fingers. "Ouch," she muttered, grabbing a towel. "Whatever for?" she asked, nursing her scalded fingers.

Auntie Genoa stopped chopping and looked at her thoughtfully. "You like him, don't you? I mean, this isn't just idle curiosity."

Anne frowned. Did she like Quinn? Or was she merely attracted to him? "No, I don't think I like him. But I . . . care about him. Does that make sense?"

Auntie looked sad. "Exactly how I feel about him these days," she muttered as she resumed her chopping.

Meg took a whisk from a hook overhead and began beating the eggs. "Quinn would kill us if he knew we were telling you these things. He doesn't talk about the past. Not ever."

"If you'd rather not—"

"No, I think you should know." Meg sighed. "I wish Zach hadn't made me stop smoking. I need a cigarette." She cast a hopeful look in Anne's direction.

"Sorry," Anne murmured. "I don't smoke."

"Smart lady." Meg paused, then said in a quiet tone, "Quinn and Liz had been married about eight years when he left for one of his special super-secret assignments. He was gone six months. When he got back his adoring wife was eight weeks pregnant."

Anne's eyes filled with pain. "Not by him, obviously."

"Obviously," Meg echoed in a dry tone. "Liz swore that she'd been raped by another officer, a friend of Quinn's."

"Oh, no," Anne murmured, her cup frozen halfway to her mouth.

Meg banged the whisk against the edge of the bowl, shaking off the last of the beaten eggs. From the rack over the stove, she took a huge frying pan and slid it onto one of the front burners.

"Quinn's always had a temper. Over the years he'd learned to control it, but this time he couldn't. He went after the guy. Put him in intensive care. Nearly killed him. Navy investigators arrested him for attempted murder. He was court-martialed."

Anne was too stunned to say anything. Meg's brief smile told her that she understood. "It was a circus. Your friend, Ed Franklyn, was Quinn's attorney. He put enough doubt in the board's mind to get Quinn acquitted of attempted murder. But the navy gave him a dishonorable discharge for striking a superior officer. He was lucky he didn't end up serving time in the brig at hard labor."

"And his wife?"

"She divorced him. Turns out she'd been cheating on him for years and finally got caught. Her lover refused to accept responsibility for the baby, which apparently made Liz panic."

"She lied?"

Meg nodded, her eyes growing stormy. "She knew that Quinn had a temper. She used it to get back at her boyfriend."

Anne groped behind her for the counter and tried to steady her shaking knees. "Oh, my God."

"He came home a changed man. Rarely talked, never laughed, kept to himself mostly. If it hadn't been for the ranch, I'm not sure he would have made it. Trying to make this place pay again saved him."

Auntie nodded. "Poor boy was in a bad way for a long time. First year he never left the ranch. Looked like he never slept more'n a few hours. A lot of nights he drank too much. But gradually he started putting himself together again."

"You're right," Anne said emphatically. "Someone should have strangled the woman."

Meg burst out laughing. "I like you, Anne. We think alike." She hesitated, then added, "You would be good for Quinn. He needs a woman like you."

"Hold on! He doesn't even *like* me." Anne felt her face warm and rushed to add, "Even if I were interested in him, which I'm not."

"He likes you," Meg said.

Anne looked down at her toes. "Could have fooled me."

"That first morning you were here he had Manola saddle a horse for you. He'd planned to take you riding after breakfast, and that's something he'd never done with a guest—not even once in the four years we've had the place open to tourists.''

Anne lifted her gaze and searched Meg's face. "He never said . . . I didn't know.''

"Like I said, Quinn's always been shy with women. He was probably working up to asking when you walked out on him.''

Anne's jaw dropped. "How did you know?''

Meg hopped down from the table and picked up her clipboard. "I was just coming down the stairs when I saw you charge out of the dining room. A few seconds later Quinn followed, looking as though he was about to explode. He slammed out of the house so fast the windows rattled.''

Meg filched a piece of pineapple from the now brimming bowl and gave Anne a knowing grin. "I'm glad Eddie pulled strings to get you here, kiddo. If anyone can shake my big brother out of that deep freeze he's been in for so long, it's you. I'd bet my half of the ranch on that!''

Anne returned her grin, but her eyes were thoughtful. "Don't,'' she warned. "I wouldn't want you to lose.''

The silence was magical. Anne rested her back against a smooth, cool boulder and watched the afternoon sun play over the velvet grass. The perfume from the flowers surrounding her was intoxicating. The breeze was gentle, scarcely disturbing the peace of the secluded grotto she'd come to consider her own private sanctuary.

A few yards away, Sadie, the spirited pinto mare Manolo had reserved for her exclusive use, grazed contentedly. Hummingbirds drank from orange flowers shaped like tiny trumpets, and butterflies of all sizes painted the air with color.

Anne pulled up one leg and rested her chin on her knee. All day, even as she had talked to a group of her fellow guests about light and shadow, composition and structure, she had been thinking of the things Meg had told her earlier. Dishonorable discharge. Even the words hurt.

"You're going to get wrinkles if you keep frowning like that."

Anne turned so quickly she felt a twinge of pain in her neck. Less than twenty feet away Quinn sat astride his big bay, watching her. Sadie nickered, acknowledging the presence of the two dominant males.

"Wrinkles don't bother me," she said, hugging her knees. "They give a person character."

"Character, huh? Is that in fashion these days?"

"It's always in fashion."

Quinn shifted in the saddle. One hand rested on the saddle horn; the other gentled the nervous stallion.

Anne found herself fascinated by those hands. His fingers were long and lean, the veins fanning the back prominent and strong, his wrists thick with muscle. And yet, when he tended the stallion, his hands were as gentle as a woman's. She raised her camera and snapped off a series of shots.

Quinn frowned and tugged his hat lower. "Meg tells me your picture safari is a hot ticket. You're booked solid for tomorrow."

"I had a great bunch of students. It was a kick."

His black eyebrows rose slowly. "Yeah, well, I thought you were supposed to be resting instead of working."

"Teaching isn't working. It's fun. I haven't felt this relaxed in years. No wonder you love it here."

Stillness froze his face. "Who says I do?"

"Don't you?"

Instead of replying he dismounted. The stallion shied, suddenly nervous, but Quinn held him easily. "Whoa, son. Let's you and me take a break." He led the stallion to the far side of the glen and tied him to a sturdy bush.

"What's your horse's name?" Anne asked as Quinn walked toward her.

"Kanaloa."

This time her smile was spontaneous and genuine. "That's perfect. Did you name him?"

He nodded. "He's named after—"

"—the Polynesian god of the underworld," Anne finished for him. "Some of the books call him the 'devil-god.'"

Quinn hesitated, then sat down on a large flat rock and extended his long legs in front of him. He swept off his hat and wiped his damp forehead with his forearm.

Anne caught a whiff of sweat and dirt—rough, masculine scents that should have been distasteful. Instead, she found the combination oddly exciting.

"Been reading up on local history, have you?" he asked as he tossed his hat aside.

"Of course. Usually I do that before I...travel to a place, but this time I...the trip was arranged in such a hurry." Anne watched speculation settle in his eyes and rushed on. "I know there are four main gods. Ku, Kane, Lono and Kanaloa."

She smiled at the dubious look crossing his face. "Kane is the most powerful, since he's the one who

created the world by using the seeds from a calabash.
Seeds for the clouds and rain and wind. Other seeds
for the stars and the moon and the sun.''

She lifted her face toward the warming rays and inhaled slowly, savoring the mingled scents that were so
strong they were almost intoxicating. She heard the
wind in the lacy branches above and the rhythmic
swish of the horses' tails. It felt good to be alive. To be
safe.

''Right?'' she asked, turning toward Quinn.

He inclined his dark head in a brief nod. ''What
about the mountains and valleys?''

Frowning, she searched her memory. ''Those he
made from the flesh of the gourd.''

''So they say.''

He seemed relaxed, but his eyes were guarded. Now
that she knew why, she wanted to tell him that she understood, but instinct told her that would be a mistake. A man as proud as Quinn would mistake
empathy for pity.

He rested his elbows on the rock and leaned back.
His frayed shirt pulled taut over his lean belly. Anne
wondered how those hardened muscles would feel
against her palm.

Before she realized what she was doing, she snapped
off several more shots. Of the lazy glint in his eyes. Of
the play of light and shadow over his powerful torso.
Of the taut disapproval flattening his mouth.

She lowered the camera and rested her elbows on her
knees. ''Then along came Lono. He was a farmer at
heart and also, I think, a poet. Anyway, he's the one
who made the flowers grow and the grass green. He's
the one who created the delicious smells and colors
and tastes that make the islands so special.''

Something changed in Quinn's eyes. The blackness seemed to shift, revealing an emotion that she had never seen before. Before she could define it, however, his silky lashes wiped it away.

"You have a good memory."

"I also enjoy immersing myself in the essence of a place. It helps me... in my work."

At the mention of her work, his head came up again, and she saw that the hard measuring look was back in his eyes. "What about Ku? Did you read about him?"

Anne leaned back and rested both palms on the cool grass beneath her. "Now that guy was the problem. For some reason, he decided that this beautiful paradise needed people to enjoy it. So he created man, and all the troubles that man brings to a world."

Quinn found that he was looking at her mouth again. The softness drew him, tantalized him, teased him. "Funny. I thought the trouble didn't start until he created woman."

"Spoken like a true Polynesian chauvinist," she said.

"Half-Polynesian."

"*Hapa-haole*," she echoed. "Half-white."

"Yes." The terseness of his answer didn't surprise her. From the three or four times they'd been together, she had learned that he rationed his words even more rigidly than his smiles.

Anne plucked a handful of grass and let it sift through her fingers. Across the glen Kanaloa suddenly snorted and pricked his ears. Two squirrels, chattering madly, chased each other through the drooping leaves of a giant bird of paradise.

Without thinking about it, Anne caught a picture of their romp. When she lowered the Nikon again, she found that Quinn was watching her with a strange look on his face.

"Do you ever go anywhere without that thing?" he asked, indicating the camera.

"No. It helps me understand things around me."

"The camera never lies, huh?"

"Not to someone who is willing to look honestly."

She shouldn't be so easy on the eyes, he thought. But she was, with her hair tossed into wildness by her ride and her eyes half-closed with the pleasure of the day.

His pleasure was more basic. He wanted to be inside her, those sleek thighs locked around him, her sweat drying on his skin.

He shifted his position, but the heaviness in his groin remained. A man could lose his soul to a woman like that if he wasn't careful.

"What does your camera tell you about this place?" He trailed his gaze around the grotto.

"That it's safe here." She glanced his way, catching a look of surprise in his eyes. Speculation.

"Safe?"

Alarm shivered through her. He was coming too close. And close meant danger. In more ways than one, she realized.

"I mean, it's very special, very spiritual. This particular place is very old, but time has no relevance here."

He sat up and let his folded hands dangle between his knees. "You must have been talking to my sister."

Anne felt a chill. "About what?"

"This is an ancient *heiau,* a temple, where the people came to pray."

To pray. Was that what she'd been doing? Praying for strength? For courage? For Quinn's deep wounds to be healed?

"So that's why it's so peaceful here," she murmured, lifting her shoulders and letting them fall.

"Legend has it that the *kahunas,* the priests, are still here."

"Is that why you come? To pray?"

"Not anymore," he said, rising. He leaned down to retrieve his hat and put it on.

Anne sensed that their time together was ended. She scrambled to her feet and brushed bits of grass from her seat.

"Time I was leaving, too," she murmured with a trace of regret. "I promised Mrs. Bronsky I'd be a fourth for bridge this afternoon."

"Sounds like fun." His tone suggested that he thought it was anything but.

"Bridge isn't your game, I take it."

A shadow crossed his face. "Too tame."

Quinn walked with her to the spot where Sadie had been waiting patiently. The mare snorted when they reached her side and nuzzled Anne's shoulder, eager for another run.

Anne laughed and produced a carrot from the pack strapped around her waist. "Half now, half when you get me safely back to the barn," she said as she broke the carrot in two.

"This old girl's gonna be sorry to see you go," Quinn said with a chuckle. "Manolo tells me you've got her as spoiled as a pet and about as tame these days."

His hand smoothed the pinto's mane. Anne's stomach fluttered.

"I'm not sure about that. She tossed me on my bottom this morning."

He looked down at her, a trace of worry moving across his face. "Something scare her?"

"Yes, a barking dog. How did you know?"

His hand came up to finger a stray lock of Anne's hair that curled against her neck. "Since she was a foal, she's shied at sharp noises. That's why Manolo has orders never to let novices or children ride her."

His fingers brushed the thin skin beneath her jaw. Fire spread from the spot. "She didn't go far," she murmured.

"She never does."

"She's been trained well."

"Yes."

It seemed so natural to lift her gaze to his. He took a step closer. Or perhaps she moved first.

"I'd better go," she murmured, even as his thumb began a gentle exploration of her cheek.

"Not yet." His fingers flattened against her jaw. It seemed so right to tilt her head toward his touch.

He lowered his head a few more inches until his mouth was slanted directly over hers. "God help me, I have to do this," he whispered. Before she had a chance to refuse, his mouth took hers.

Sudden, unexpected sensations jolted through her. Surprise, desire, a promise of something even more powerful.

At first he merely tasted, exploring her mouth slowly, thoroughly, with his. His lips were warm and coaxing. Perhaps she could have withstood a demand, but the sweet persuasion of his surprisingly gentle kiss was more difficult to resist.

She swayed, suddenly unsteady on her feet. He kept the kiss soft and lingering, but his hands stole around her, holding her gently, as though she were very precious to him.

Needing to touch him, she smoothed her palms up his arms to his big shoulders. His powerful body shuddered, as though it had been a long time since he'd been touched by a woman.

He pulled her closer, but the camera hung between them, keeping them apart. With a growl of irritation, he lifted it over her head and hung the strap on Sadie's pommel. The mare snorted and tried to nose between them.

Quinn grinned, even as he concentrated on her mouth again, this time with the urgency of a desperately lonely man. The shock of the impact shimmered through her, and her fingers tightened on his arms. His mouth brushed hers, lifted, returned with more pressure.

His lips were warm, his body warmer, but she thought only of his mouth. Of how it was making her feel. Of the desire building in her.

His tongue moistened her lips, sending slow waves of pleasure rolling through her. Her heart thudded in her chest as his arms tightened until his lower body was aligned with hers. Denim pressed against denim. The hard evidence of his growing need pressed against the softest part of her belly.

Her legs went watery, and she clung to him, her fingers pushing against hard, lean muscle. Gradually, skillfully, he deepened the kiss until her pulse was roaring in her ears.

Fire flickered inside her. Did he feel the heat in her? she wondered.

She went on tiptoe, trying to get closer. To get inside that place no one was allowed to know.

Quinn felt his body swell to full arousal and his control waver. He had known desire for a woman, but he had never felt driven to take and take and take until he was filled with the taste of her and the feel of her and the warmth of her.

He traced the line of her soft mouth with his tongue, his heart hammering violently against his rib cage. Trapped behind the fly of his jeans, the hard bulge she had caused throbbed to the point of pain.

Every day, since seeing her in the terminal at Hilo, he'd wanted to taste her soft, impudent mouth. Every day he thought about stroking the satiny skin that grew tanner and tanner. Every day he tried not to notice the long sleek thighs and rounded bottom. And every day he failed.

He ran his hand down her back to cup the tight buttocks that teased him into a foul temper every time she paraded across the yard in those damn tight jeans.

He had known that her body would fit perfectly against his. Soft curves, long graceful angles. Neatly, perfectly, and yet not submissively.

God help him, he wanted to take her here in this sacred place, where such things were forbidden. He wondered how he had lived so long without her.

Locked against him, Anne felt his body rock against hers. Hard, insistent, distinctly male. Small darts of need shot through her, and she moaned.

Quinn heard the small helpless sound and knew that he was close to crossing the line between choice and demand. He was sliding into quicksand with this woman. In another few seconds it would be too late.

He jerked his mouth from hers. He was breathing hard. So was she.

Anne slowly opened her eyes and looked up at him, the hazel depths soft with the same need that was throbbing through him. He saw no hardness in her, no calculation, no coy pretense. Because he wanted to believe that so desperately, he knew he couldn't let himself take the chance.

"Aren't you going to stop me?" he demanded, his eyes feverish with a hunger he was powerless to hide.

His harsh tone hit her like a sudden torrent of icy water. The temper she told herself she didn't have fought with an acute wave of disappointment.

"Yes, I'm going to stop you," she said, twisting out of his arms. "And don't ever do that again."

She turned, but before she could mount, Quinn lifted her in his arms and deposited her in the saddle as though she weighed no more than air. He gathered the reins and put them in her hands. He wasn't smiling.

"Don't ever give a man like me orders," he warned, his voice graveled. "I'm the one with the key to that damn door between us, remember?"

Before she could answer, he swatted Sadie on the rump and the mare surged forward. All Anne could do was hold on.

Quinn was alone, a bottle of rum at his elbow, a glass in his hand. Moonlight filtered through the blinds, leaving stripes like prison bars on the age-darkened floor of his bedroom.

"Here's to celibacy," he muttered, pouring the last of his drink down his throat. The liquor was rough, burning all the way to his gut.

He reached for the bottle and refilled his glass. The clink of glass on glass reminded him of nights better forgotten, nights spent in this room alone, a loaded pistol in front of him offering relief from the humiliation burning in him.

Tonight, however, it wasn't the past tormenting him. It was Anne Oliver. The taste of her. The feel of her. The soft look of desire in her golden eyes.

In his office, when he should be working on the books, he found himself remembering the light in her eyes when she talked of her feelings about the *heiau*.

In the pasture, when he should be on the lookout for strays or busted wire, he found himself wishing she was there to watch the sunset with him.

In this room, with only a door between them, he found himself hard and aching with a need that he couldn't seem to banish, no matter how many cold showers he took.

He kept remembering her in the grotto this afternoon. She had made him see his land in a different way—the way she saw it. Enchanted. Special. Enduring. And she had made the ancient legends come alive again.

He had known her only a few weeks, spoken with her only a few times, yet he was always aware when she was near. He scarcely knew her, yet he sensed that he changed when she was around.

She raised longings in him that he'd thought he'd put aside years ago. Longings that made him want to trust again. To trust in the things he saw in her eyes.

With one quick movement he downed the last of the drink before slamming the glass down on the desk. At the same moment the ornate Victorian clock that had been a housewarming gift to Josiah and his bride from Kamehameha tolled the hour.

Midnight.

Biting off a curse, he left his bedroom and headed for the wide, curving staircase where five generations of Sinclair wives had waited for their husbands. But no one waited for him.

His long, saddle-toughened legs took the stairs two at a time, the thudding of his heels muffled by the runner. The foyer was illuminated by the moonlight shining through the etched glass.

He jerked open the door, leaving it ajar behind him. Lava stones crunched under his boots as he headed for the barn. Moments later he emerged astride Kanaloa.

He gave the stallion his head, and Kanaloa bolted, heading for the treacherous trail leading to the foot-hills. The wind, spiked with the first drops of the storm, lashed Quinn's face as he galloped into the waiting blackness.

Chapter Four

They were big, brutal men in camouflage, silhouetted against the edge of the precipice. Two in front, unarmed, hands raised. Four behind, with rifles.

Cold winter daylight dulled the ice crystals carpeting the hard ground. Drab gray clouds pressed down.

"No!" Anne screamed. "Don't!"

Her cries were obliterated by the explosion of gunpowder. The men in front jerked, their bodies absorbing slug after slug. Blood spurted, congealing in the frigid air.

The echoes of the shots faded. Silence settled. The rifles aimed toward her. Fear spiraled, clutching at her throat. Her legs were leaden, her breath icing into vapor in front of her.

She turned and ran. Her Jeep was in sight when a bullet caught her in the arm. She spun crazily, pain spiking hot in her flesh. She managed to jerk open the door, start the engine, drive. She wouldn't die. Not here. Not like this.

"No," she choked. "I won't. I won't."

"Easy, Anne. Relax. It was just a dream."

Rough but gentle fingers stroked her cheek, bringing warming blood back into the icy flesh. Still swimming toward consciousness, she turned toward the comforting touch. Beyond her closed lids she sensed light. Warmth. Safety.

After an eternity, she managed to open her eyes. Quinn was sitting on her bed, wearing only his jeans. His face was lined with tiredness, and those unreadable black eyes were rimmed with red.

The connecting door was open. Beyond, she saw a massive bed and rumpled sheets. The pillow was indented where his head had lain. No doubt the crisp cotton was still warm from his body.

His nearly nude body, she realized, taking note of the broad, bare shoulders and the massive chest furred with soft, dark hair arrowing to the waistband of unbuttoned jeans.

"I have this dream ... It's so aw-awful."

Like vivid photographs, the images haunted her. The faces of the two men. Their eyes. Their mouths open, screaming. They hadn't wanted to die. No one wants to die. Not like that.

She began to shake. Her teeth began to chatter. "I'm not u-usually like this," she murmured. "I'm always so g-good at...at coping, but this..." She broke off, her gaze clinging to his. "S-sorry. This isn't your problem."

Quinn hesitated, then lay down beside her and took her in his arms. Before she could draw a breath, she found herself cradled against his wide chest.

Anne stiffened. "Quinn—"

"Shh. Go back to sleep."

Anne murmured a protest and tried to sit up. Quinn's arms tightened. She tried to hold herself separate, to hang on to her need to be brave. But the heat of his body was like a sedative, enticing her to relax. The scent of soap clung to him, clean and reassuring. His furred chest rose and fell in a hypnotic rhythm, lulling her.

Her lashes drifted closed, her cheek resting on his wide, smooth shoulder. His big hands began combing through her hair, spreading it across her back like a silky fan.

She snuggled closer, cushioned by the lean, hard muscles beneath her. Her arms curled around his waist, and her lips curved into a drowsy smile against the downy chest hair tickling her nose.

"I just figured something out," she murmured.

"What's that?" Even half-asleep, she knew that his voice held a smile.

"Deep down, under all those frowns and bad temper, you're really a very sweet man. I'm glad Ed sent me to you."

His hand stopped moving, and he seemed to stiffen for a moment before his fingers burrowed into her hair to rest on the sensitive spot at the nape of her neck. His touch was intimate and yet nonsexual, the touch of a friend more comfortable with actions than words.

"Go to sleep, Anne," he ordered in a gruff voice. "I'll keep the nightmares away."

She smiled. "I wish you could. But you can't."

A few minutes later, she was asleep.

In the half-light of dawn, Quinn lay motionless, cradling Anne against him. She was using his chest as a pillow, and her hair was a soft blanket warming his skin. She was asleep, her breathing even and quiet.

Moving slowly so as not to wake her, he raised one arm and tucked his hand under his head. He hadn't intended to fall asleep. A man was vulnerable then, especially in someone else's bed.

Quinn inhaled slowly, intensely conscious of the soft feminine body curled against his. Until his marriage, he'd never spent a night with a woman without making love to her.

With Anne, everything was different, especially the need he felt to be with her. Awake, asleep. Talking, not talking.

She had a way of reaching down inside him and pulling out things he had vowed to keep hidden. And that scared the hell out of him.

The mistrust his ex-wife had put in him was still strong. He wasn't sure if anything or anyone, even Anne and her soft smiles and willing kisses, could exorcise it.

Slowly he eased from beneath her and rolled out of bed. He went into his own room, clsoing the door quietly behind him.

He was halfway to the bathroom and a cold shower when the phone by his bed buzzed. The blinking button indicated his private line.

"This better be important," he snarled into the receiver.

"It is."

Quinn recognized Ed Franklyn's voice. He also recognized the deadly urgency in his tone. He sat down on the bed and rubbed his morning beard. "What's wrong?"

"Are you alone?"

Quinn glanced at the closed door. "Yes."

Silence hummed over the line, broken by intermittent static. Quinn waited, his gaze narrowed and his mouth hard.

"There's a problem," Franklyn said, breaking the silence.

"I'm listening."

Huddled in a phone booth three long, cold blocks from his office, Ed Franklyn stared at the swirling flakes of snow hitting the glass. His eyes were bloodshot, and his tongue was fuzzy from the endless cups of coffee he'd drunk.

"You remember when I told you I had taken a job in the Justice Department after I retired from the navy?"

"Something about immigration statutes, wasn't it?"

"Not exactly." There was a pause before he added, "I'm in charge of the federal Witness Protection Plan."

It took Quinn less than a second to realize his old buddy had used him. "Anne," he said in a cold, clipped voice.

"I've always said you were quick."

"Not quick enough, apparently. You set me up."

A weary sigh hissed along the line. "It was necessary."

"That's crap and you know it."

"I know how you feel about that ranch of yours, and I was afraid you would have refused if you thought the place might get shot to Swiss cheese."

"You've got that right." Quinn drew a calming breath, reining his temper tight. "Tell me about Anne."

"Have you ever heard of the Aryan American Brigade?"

"Vaguely. Neo-Nazi bunch of idiots, aren't they? Hate-mongers?" Quinn stared at the red ball that was the rising sun.

"Exactly. Currently based in Colorado. Our best estimates put their numbers at close to twenty thousand, divided into cells located mainly in the western states. Their leader is an ex-marine named Marvin Draygon.''

''I've seen pictures of him. Charismatic son of a bitch.''

''Yeah, along with being ruthless and vicious and hell-bent on destroying anyone whose pedigree doesn't come out white Anglo-Saxon Protestant.''

The muscles of Quinn's spine tightened. ''What's Anne got to do with bastards like that?''

''Well, first off, she's not a model. She's a free-lance photographer. She was doing a piece on a species of endangered deer in some godforsaken place in Colorado when Draygon and three of his lieutenants took a couple of FBI undercover agents into a field and turned their AK-47s on them. Anne saw it all.''

Quinn muttered a vicious curse. ''No wonder she has nightmares.''

''What's that?''

''Nothing. Go on.''

''Because of her, we have a good chance of convicting Draygon and his buddies of first-degree murder. Trial starts April second—if she lives to testify.''

''*If?*''

This time the silence was tense. ''We had a female agent acting as a decoy in a Silver Springs safe house. Looked enough like Anne Oliver to fool her grandmother.''

''What happened?''

''Six bastards in full combat dress got past two of the Bureau's best. Killed the decoy and split, but not before they got a good look at her face. They know she wasn't Anne Oliver.''

Quinn bit out another vicious curse. ''Get somebody here. *Now.*''

Franklyn's voice turned defensive. "We're working on it."

"Not good enough," Quinn shot back, his voice instinctively taking on the steel of command.

There was another silence before Franklyn admitted, "We have reason to think there's a leak in our secure network. If we send someone to get her, they might follow."

Quinn's hand gripped the receiver so tightly the plastic nearly cracked. "What do you want me to do?"

"Fly her to Pearl Harbor in your chopper. Turn her over to Navy Intelligence. They can take care of her until I can make secure arrangements."

Quinn stared at the sunshine spattering the floor, his stomach slowly twisting into a hard knot. "The chopper's out of commission. Busted fuel line."

"Coincidence?"

"Probably," Quinn conceded. "You want to bank on that?"

Franklyn's reply was obscene and to the point. "Any ideas? I'm fresh out."

Quinn closed his eyes and visualized the island he knew as well as he knew his own body. "There's a small patch of deserted beach on the Hamakua Coast between Keokea Beach and Waipo Bay. We take the guests there sometimes to snorkel. It's rough country, no roads. You have to get in by sea or air."

"Spell those two names for me."

Quinn obliged, then continued, "I'll have her there at dawn on Thursday."

"But the chopper—"

"We'll go by horseback."

"Horseback? That seems damn risky, Quinn."

"Don't worry. The country between here and there is about as wild as it gets. I have relatives living in places in the hills that the *haoles* and the other tourists don't even know exist. Once I get her there, we should be safe enough."

There was a pause before Franklyn said curtly, "Sounds workable. I'll make the arrangements. I'll be coming to get her myself, so she won't be scared spitless."

Quinn stared out the window at a sky that seemed an innocent blue. "What about Meg and the others?"

"Odds are the Brigade doesn't know where she is. Even if they did, I doubt they would chance another all-out attack."

"I can't risk my sister and the others on a guess, Ed. Get some protection out here."

"As soon as I can. In the meantime—"

"In the meantime I'm posting men in the house. They'll be visible, and they'll be armed."

Franklyn sighed. "One more thing you should know, Quinn. Ms. Oliver took a bullet before she managed to get away from Draygon and the others. God knows how she managed to survive, but she did. We can't lose her now."

Lose her...

Quinn went deadly still. His eyes took on the texture of slate. "You won't lose her," he said. "Count on it."

"I will." There was a pause before Franklyn added tersely, "Let's keep all this just between you and me. She's a gutsy lady, but she's already been through one trauma. We need her wits about her when she testifies."

"That's damn cold-blooded, Franklyn."

"It's my job."

"It's still lousy." Quinn hung up and headed for his closet. From the top shelf he took a large brown metal box. Inside were his service medals, his lieutenant-commander's shoulder boards—and the piece of paper condemning him to live the rest of his life with shame in his gut.

His mouth tightened, but his hand was steady as he pulled out the worn holster containing his father's .45 and a box of ammunition.

Chapter Five

Anne lifted her face to the shower spray and let the hot water cascade over her. She sudsed herself slowly, her thoughts turbulent.

Quinn had slept with her. He hadn't made love to her.

She was grateful. She was also, she discovered, disappointed.

After the kiss in the glen, she'd stopped pretending that she wasn't sexually attracted to him. She was. Intensely. So much so that she couldn't stop thinking about that hard, nearly naked body next to hers. So much so that she was soft and aching inside.

The few serious relationships she'd had had been on her terms, controlled as carefully as the composition of her photographs. But that would be impossible with Quinn. No woman controlled him. She doubted if anyone, woman or man, ever had.

Impatient with her own thoughts, she threw back the shower curtain and reached for the towel. Through the open window she heard the now familiar sounds of the ranch coming to life. Horses neighing. Pickup trucks clattering down the lane. Deep male voices calling out morning greetings.

Finished drying, she drew the towel around her like a sarong. Her skin was still damp, but the air was warm. Humming to herself, she tucked one end of the soft terry between her breasts before she left the bath-room.

Two steps into her bedroom she stopped short, a soft gasp of surprise escaping her lips. Quinn was standing by the dresser, rummaging through the top drawer.

His jaw was freshly shaved, his hair shiny and clean, his clothes slightly less disreputable than usual. Little shivers of awareness took over her stomach and tight-ened her throat. Did it show? she wondered. The hot, fluid need he aroused in her?

"Looking for something?" she managed.

The raw, pink scar on her arm hit Quinn hard and low, like a sucker punch. He wanted to wrap her in his arms and promise to keep her safe. He wanted to kiss the violated flesh until pleasure obliterated the mem-ory of the pain she had suffered. He did neither. It was safer that way—for both of them.

Returning his gaze to the open drawer, he shoved a handful of silky underthings into the worn saddlebag looped over one arm. The flimsy garments seemed very fragile in his big hands.

"We leave in ten minutes. Better hustle." He closed the top drawer and opened the next. He pulled out two shirts and began stuffing them in the bag.

"Just where is it we're going in ten minutes?" she asked.

"To a wedding luau."

"I must have missed the part where we discussed this."

Her shower cap was still wet. Drops of water were beginning to dribble onto her forehead. With an im-patient frown, she pulled off the cap, allowing her hair to cascade to her shoulders. Quinn watched without moving, but inside, low and deep, he felt a ripple of desire.

"Wear jeans and boots," he ordered. "And a hat. It's a day's ride there, a day back. Plan to spend the night."

He tried not to notice that the skin above the skimpy towel was still dewy from her shower.

"No, Quinn. Thank you, but . . . no," she said, allowing a trace of impatience to show. "I promised Meg I'd lead another photo safari this morning."

Quinn watched her chin take on that slight tilt he was coming to recognize as determination. The lady certainly had her share. But so did he.

"That's not a problem. The chopper is fixed. Meg won't need you after all." The lie came hard, but Quinn told himself it was necessary.

He closed the drawer, slung the bags over his shoulder and came toward her. He stopped an arm's length away, his expression revealing little.

"Take your camera along to the luau if you like. There will be traditional food and dancing, the way it should be done, not the watered-down show Meg gives the tourists. Most *haoles* never get a chance to see something like this. Most wouldn't even notice the differences. You will."

Anne hesitated, poised to voice another, stronger refusal. But the lure of witnessing a genuine island celebration conducted in the age-old way was nearly irresistible. Even so, a night with Quinn was sure to test what little resistance she had left.

She forced herself to meet his eyes. "About last night . . ."

"Last night you needed a friend," he said, his voice bare of emotion. "I was the only guy around at the time."

The bed they had shared was only a foot away. She knew it was there. So did he.

"And tonight?"

"Tonight is up to you." One quick step closed the distance between them. "But I won't pretend I don't want to make love to you, because I do."

His hand came out and hooked around her neck. At the same time his mouth descended, opening over hers in an unmistakable demand.

Anne stiffened, but the resistance she tried to summon melted into the pleasure jolting through her. Her lips softened under his.

His fingers flattened along her neck—not quite caressing, and yet no longer controlling. His free hand pressed against her back, arching her toward him until their thighs met.

His thumb stroked the soft skin above her breasts, sending urgent darts of sensation deep into her. She pushed against him, rising to her toes so that she could feel more of that hard mouth. Her hand caught him behind the neck, her fingers digging into the thick ropes of muscle. His hair felt surprisingly silky, almost too soft for such a hardened man.

A groan rumbled from him, and his body surged against her. Only a towel and a thin layer of masculine clothes separated her skin from his.

Heat rushed through her. Yes, yes, she thought. Nothing seemed to matter but the flood of wonderfully warm, tingling feelings surging through her.

Her body was fluid, pliant, ready to mold to his. His was hard and thrusting and blatantly aggressive. She moaned at the thought of being filled by him.

His tongue dove deep, and she met it eagerly with hers. He probed; she suckled. His hand pressed her spine, forcing her closer, closer, until she felt his heart beating a violent rhythm against her breasts.

His mouth lifted, and his hand released the pressure on her spine. Anne swayed, her lips still parted and moist from his mouth. Her skin felt hot, and her breathing was erratic. Her hands clutched the slipping towel.

"Here, let me," Quinn said, replacing her hands with his. He snugged the knot tighter, his fingers brushing her breasts. The nipples hardened, showing clearly through the soft towel.

Quinn's eyes changed until they seemed to smolder. "I want you, Anne," he said in a rough voice that was more demand than plea. "But the choice is yours. I won't force you."

He brushed her mouth, then stepped away. "I'm leaving in ten minutes. Are you coming?"

Anne ran her tongue over her tingling lips. He waited, a stillness in his eyes, the tension in his face drawing her. The distance was there, the wall that he put between himself and the world, but something was different. Something important. Something inside him. But what?

"Yes," she said with a smile that trembled only slightly. "I'm coming."

"Welcome to Kaliwea," Quinn said as they entered a large clearing that seemed to have been scraped by a giant hand out of the side of the mountain. By Anne's watch, it was a few minutes past four.

They had been riding most of the day. At first the trail had been clearly marked. But now there was no trail at all, only the one in Quinn's head.

With each mile they'd traveled, they had gone higher, and the air had become thinner, the foliage thicker. Anne felt hopelessly lost.

Overhead, the sun was hot, but they were sheltered from its rays by a cooling canopy of trees. The shade, a dark emerald, smelled musty, like freshly plowed earth after a rainstorm.

"Is this part of the ranch?" Anne asked as she guided Sadie onto the rutted lane.

"Used to be. I sold it to Mama Chloe a few years back."

"Is she our hostess?"

"Yes, my father's second cousin. She's a self-taught expert on traditional Polynesian culture. Has this thing about preserving the old ways before they're gone forever. She intends to build a replica of an ancient village up here. Bus in the tourists. Put on authentic dances. Serve traditional food. Tonight you'll be sleeping in a hut with a grass roof."

"Sounds like fun."

His gaze flicked her way. His eyes seemed to smile, and Anne wondered if she was imagining it.

"Don't get too excited. Primitive life means no indoor plumbing and no electricity."

"Oh."

"Don't worry. Mama wants her guests to come back. She's made a few compromises with authenticity."

Anne looked down at her dusty jeans. "Thank goodness," she muttered.

Quinn laughed. It was the first sign of relaxation, of trust, she'd wrung from him. She wanted to shout for joy at the special gift he'd given her. She wanted to be in his arms.

Silly, she told herself. It was just a laugh.

They rode slowly, the clatter of the horses' hooves mingling with the call of birds and the whisper of the wind. On three sides they were surrounded by lush screens of overgrown brush. Directly ahead lay a large brown bungalow on stilts nestled in a grove of giant tree ferns.

Six steps led up to a wooden veranda, where handmade chairs with brightly flowered cushions were lined along the front facade. Under the veranda's weathered floorboards, plump chickens sporting exotic plumage in iridescent shades of bronze and green scratched for grain. Anne raised her camera and snapped off several frames.

"We'll pasture the horses here," Quinn said as he swung from the saddle.

Anne started to do the same, then winced at the stiffness in her thighs. Quinn tied the stallion to a sapling and then, to her surprise, lifted her to the ground.

"Sore?" he asked, his hands lingering at her waist.

"A little. It's nothing serious," she said. Her heart was pounding in her throat, making it difficult to speak.

He hesitated, then removed her hat and hung it on the mare's saddle horn. "I like your hair better the way it was this morning."

One twist of his hand and her hair fell free of its neat coil, brushing her neck and cascading over his wrist. His fingers lightly massaged the nape of her neck, evoking sensations of pleasure and warning.

"When you first arrived, I knew you were going to be trouble." His gaze was searching. The dark centers of his eyes were flecked with the gold of some powerful emotion.

"I don't mean to be."

He moved closer until his chest was only a deep breath away from her breasts. His hand exerted pressure, forcing her face to tilt toward his.

"When you cut me off at the knees that first morning, I thought you were playing hard to get."

She saw the tension in his face and the restraint he imposed on the firm mouth that looked as though it wanted to smile.

"I don't play games," she murmured, her voice too husky.

One side of his mouth angled upward, drawing her gaze to the lips that refused to yield to a smile. "I know that now. I don't, either."

Her mouth went dry. "I know."

Anne lifted a suddenly trembling hand to his chest. Her fingers clutched his shirt. To push him away? To pull him toward her?

He waited, his breath warming her lips. All she had to do was turn her mouth aside, she realized with sudden certainty, and he would stop. She knew, too, that he would withdraw from her then. Utterly. Irrevocably.

He wasn't a man who gave second chances. Not to himself. Not to anyone else.

"Quinn," she whispered, her mouth meeting his. To her surprise, he kept the kiss brief, almost chaste. His hands framed her face, keeping her from getting closer. She frowned, her breath coming too fast, too hard.

Just then the door opened and people spilled out. The screen door slammed, and Anne jumped, her heart racing and her eyes going wide.

He lifted his mouth from hers and turned them so that his body was sheltering her. "I've always had lousy timing," he muttered.

Anne was suddenly conscious of the intimacy of his thighs and hers. She stepped back and tried to brush some of the wrinkles from her shirt. "Are . . . are they all your relatives?"

"'Fraid so." Without seeming to, his gaze swept over the group, looking for unfamiliar faces. He saw aunts, uncles, cousins and cousins of cousins. No strangers. Some of the tension left his braced muscles.

Large and small, adults and children, they whooped and hollered as they ran toward them. Anne heard his name. Other words.

"*Aloha,*" they called in ragged unison.

"*Aloha nui,*" Quinn answered, besieged by hugs and kisses.

He did his best to introduce Anne to everyone. He used her first name, nothing more. Island friendliness? she wondered. Or a gesture, signaling that she was to be treated like more than a friend?

She shook hand after hand, trying to match names with faces, engulfed in a sea of welcome. Their surprise at seeing Quinn was obvious. Their surprise at seeing her was even more so. But their clamorous delight in having their reclusive cousin visit more than made up for the initial awkwardness.

Loni, the bride, was short and plump. Her eyes were soft and shy, but her excitement was almost palpable. To Anne's amazement, she discovered that the bridal reception, the luau, preceded the actual ceremony that was to be held at noon the next day.

"You sure you want to do this thing?" Quinn asked his cousin as he enfolded her in a bear hug.

"Are you kidding?" Loni returned with a mischievous grin. "It took me three years to land that stubborn man of mine. I'm not going to give him up."

Quinn shook his head. "Poor Cully's in for a hell of a life, I can see that."

Loni slapped at his shoulder, but she was still grinning as she turned to shyly acknowledge Anne's good wishes. "I'm pretty nervous, I have to admit."

Anne smiled. "Would you mind if I took your picture? And pictures tomorrow, of the wedding? As my gift to you and Cully?"

Loni's eyes shone. "Are you a photographer?"

Anne felt the blood rush to her face. "Uh, I work with cameras a lot in my career."

"I'm told that Anne is a model," Quinn put in, watching Anne's face. "Right, Anne?"

"Right," she said, feeling sick inside. She stepped back and framed the shot. Loni wet her lips and fluffed her hair, looking pleased and uneasy at the same time.

"Say mai-tai," Anne called out, snapping the picture just as Loni obeyed.

"Lovely," Anne said as she slipped the cover over the lens.

"Let's not stand out here wasting time," the woman who'd been introduced to Anne as Mama Chloe urged in a musical voice. "Come on up to the house. We have coffee and cake." She took Anne's elbow and steered her toward the steps.

"I hope I'm not putting you out," Anne murmured politely, returning the woman's infectious smile.

"Lordy, no. 'Sides, Quinn's never brought a lady here before, so you must be special to him, and that makes you special to us, too."

"I...thank you." Anne wondered if Quinn had heard Mama Chloe's words and couldn't help turning around to catch his reaction.

If he'd heard, he gave no sign. He was now surrounded by the children of the family, all talking at once. Two of the tallest boys were trying to wrestle him to the ground, while a shy little girl hung on to his hand.

For a split second, when he looked up and their eyes met, she saw that he was laughing, his face relaxed, his eyes unguarded. She saw sweetness there and an innate gentleness, the kind only a strong man can possess.

She smiled, but her lips trembled as she raised her camera and snapped a shot. The laughter in his eyes faded, and a look like frustration hardened his mouth.

Anne felt as though the sun had dipped behind a cloud, even though it was still blazing brightly over the clearing.

"I don't know why Quinn changed his mind about coming for the party, but I'm glad he did." Anne turned to see Mama Chloe watching her, a smile curving her lips. "And brought you along."

Anne's grin faltered. "Changed his mind?" she echoed. "I don't understand."

"Never mind. I'm sure he had his reasons. Quinn never does anything without a reason."

Chapter Six

The luau began at sundown in a quiet, secluded grotto a half mile from the house. The setting recalled the celebrations of earlier times, before American missionaries changed island life forever.

Burning torches turned the twilight into golden daylight. Mats of pandanus leaves served as a table and chairs. The traditional poi and other staples were served in wooden calabashes and on platters.

Coconut milk for the children and a home brew made of fermented taro root known affectionately as *okolehoa* were served in coconut halves. Banana leaves served as plates. Men, women and children ate with their fingers.

Anne had never seen so many exotic dishes—pineapple brought first to the island by Captain Cook in the eighteenth century, wild bananas native to the islands and the large, juicy mangoes she had come to crave.

In the place of honor sat an enormous wooden platter containing the pig that had been roasting all day in a pit lined with banana leaves. The tail was a black corkscrew curl. The crusty brown face seemed to be smiling at her.

With the exception of the modern clothing, the only intrusions into the nineteenth-century atmosphere were Anne's camera and the wristwatches worn by most of the guests.

As the guests of honor, Loni was sitting at one end of the long mat, her husband-to-be, Cully, at the other. Anne was sitting cross-legged near the middle. Mama Chloe sat to her right, occasionally translating the names of some of the dishes she passed to Anne. Quinn was on her left, stretched out full-length, his head propped on his hand.

Torchlight streaked his hair with the same golden hue as the sun-bleached hair on his arms. He seemed to be enjoying himself, although Anne noticed that he was drinking milk instead of the potent home brew, and that he ate very little.

After the first few courses and her first tentative sips of *okolehoa*, Anne began to relax and enjoy herself. At first the island liquor had tasted like sour apple juice and been difficult to swallow without grimacing. Now, she realized, she was beginning to like the tartness. Certainly it was going down much more easily.

Definitely delicious, she thought, as she raised the Nikon and framed Loni's face in the viewfinder. The girl was dressed in a white muumuu, and flowers were entwined in her dark hair. The happiness on her face gave her a radiance Anne envied.

"Take one of Cully before the *okolehoa* makes his mouth too numb to smile," Loni requested, beaming at her groom.

Anne had liked Cully Hayward on sight. He was only an inch or so taller than his bride, with thinning sandy hair and a face only his mother or a woman in love could call handsome. But his smile was engaging, and his compact body radiated masculine sex appeal.

Dark eyes gleaming, the groom raised his coconut shell, grinned, then downed half the contents in one swallow. The guests hooted and applauded as Anne captured his triumphant expression.

Nice people, she thought, smiling to herself. Happy. Friendly. Had Quinn been like that as a boy? she wondered. Had his dark eyes flashed with humor instead of pain? Had he laughed easily?

Her thoughts directed her gaze to his face. He was watching her impassively.

"Something wrong?" he asked in a voice too low to intrude into the general conversation.

"You're not drinking," she whispered. "Isn't that against the rules?"

One side of his mouth slanted. "I have my own rules."

"Me too," she said, taking another long swallow. "Mine say that all rules are off during wedding luaus."

Across from her, Loni's older brother, Tino, produced a ukulele and began to tune the strings. Someone else began strumming a guitar. Soon everyone was singing, the words melodious and oddly sad. Anne closed her eyes and let the music flow over her.

More alert than he wanted Anne to know, Quinn scanned the area, looking for signs of trouble. No one had followed them. He'd made certain of that. But that didn't mean they were safe.

He'd known men with uncanny tracking skills. Men with almost supernatural abilities to find the enemy. He'd been one of those men himself once, a long time ago. Too long ago.

His combat skills were rusty; his emotional edge had been blunted by his years on the ranch. He could handle dying alone. He couldn't handle watching Anne die.

Completing his visual check, he allowed his gaze to linger on Anne's face. The flickering torchlight brought out flaws—the faint shadows under her eyes, a chin that was too square, a mouth that was too generous for the fragile bone structure.

And yet she was so lovely, so utterly feminine, that it took his breath away to look at her. He wanted to bury himself and the regrets that tormented him inside her softness. He wanted to forget all the reasons why that would be a mistake.

"Quinn?"

His gaze searched her face before settling on the soft mouth so close to his. "What?"

"Can I ask you something?"

Her breath carried the same tangy scent as the numbing liquor he had denied himself. The hunger in him grew, clawing deep. "Why do I think I'm not going to like this?" he muttered, but his tone was indulgent.

She shook her coconut shell and gave him a hopeful look. "I'd like a teensy bit more, please," she murmured, sliding her tongue between her lips.

One dark eyebrow rose, and his mouth twitched. "If you have any more *okolehoa*, you won't be able to focus your eyes, let alone that camera you love so much."

Swaying to the music, Anne squinted at the nearest torch. The flame flickered sensuously. When one flame became two she would quit, she promised herself as she waved her coconut under his nose. "I've had stronger," she murmured over the slow, sultry throb of the music.

"Have you?"

"Hmm. In Brazil I drank goat's blood. Tasted awful, but the Indians who were my hosts were so sweet to me I didn't want to offend them, so I drank it all. 'Course, I was pretty sick for a while."

"Don't say I didn't warn you," he said as he sat up and reached for the nearest gourd. He filled the coconut half-full and corked the gourd.

"Don't be so stingy," she murmured.

Quinn shook his head and poured more. "You are one stubborn lady, Anne Oliver," he muttered. "Too stubborn for your own good."

Watching intently, Anne noticed that his eyes were crinkling at the corners. When he wanted, he could be a very charming man. Too charming, she realized, taking a quick sip.

"And you're not, Quinn Sinclair?"

He turned his head slightly, and the torchlight played over his mouth. His hard, unyielding mouth. The mouth that had plundered hers.

"I learned a long time ago that the pleasure isn't always worth the pain. Seems you haven't learned that yet."

Anne drank deeply from the coconut, then licked the last drops from her lips. "But isn't that my choice?"

"Yes. As long as you know the risks you're taking." He got to his feet and extended his hand. "Time to turn in."

Mama Chloe turned her gaze from the musicians and uttered a cry of protest. "You two can't leave yet. It's time to begin the dancing."

For some reason Anne had a feeling Quinn knew that already. Didn't he want her to watch?

"We'll pass. Anne's had a long day, and—"

"No, I haven't," Anne put in. She swung her gaze from Mama Chloe to Quinn. "I'm having so much fun, and I don't want to miss the dancing. You said there would be dancing."

"You make it hard for a man to take care of you." There was an edge to his voice, but he resumed his place next to her.

Mama's words had released a murmur of anticipation. Three of the men stood and disappeared into the thick tangle of ferns to the right.

Two others left the circle, only to return almost immediately carrying a variety of drums. Some were made of scooped-out logs with what looked like sharkskin stretched over the top. Others had been fashioned from large gourds.

Two of the women settled drums in front of them. A third took two of the gourds from one of the men. Anne heard a rattling sound as the woman returned to her place.

"What are those?" she asked Quinn.

"*Uliuli.* The Polynesian version of castanets."

At a gesture from Mama, the drumming began. Rhythmic, throbbing, intoxicating. Anne felt her heart beating faster, echoing the pounding urgency of the beat.

The same urgency built inside her until she was breathing faster and faster. And then, from the darkness, three figures leapt into the circle of the flares.

Nearly naked, their bodies gleamed in the firelight. A cloth of tapa bound their loins in the traditional way. Bracelets of boar tusks encircled their upper arms. Rattles of dog fangs jangled on their ankles.

The quick, menacing moves and the frantic thudding of the drums indicated a war dance. Anne had read enough to know that the dance was symbolic—simulated spear thrusts that ended a hair's breadth from an unprotected chest, deadly kicks and chops of the hand that would have killed if they'd connected. Even so, the power of the mock battle was enormous.

Anne found that she was holding her breath, and she let it out slowly. She longed to capture this moment on film, but that might break the spell for the others.

Instead she contented herself with leaning forward to get closer. To absorb every nuance of the ancient movements. To draw the pounding rhythm inside her until she felt a part of the dancers.

Gradually she became aware of a change. The tempo slowed. The movements became more graceful. The drums were muted. Sharp, staccato steps became flowing. Arm and hand movements spoke of wooing instead of war. Graceful gestures promising rapture instead of death.

Lean male hips swayed suggestively. Provocatively. Tension stretched inside her, the same hard, painful tension that tightened Quinn's face.

His gaze met hers. Hot, dark need blazed in his. In hers, too? she wondered, looking away quickly.

One of the men held out a hand to a young woman who immediately rose and joined him, matching her movements to his. The second chose, and the twosomes began to dance. And then the third man came toward Anne, his hand extended, palm up.

Enthralled, Anne placed her hand in his and let herself be pulled to her feet. The lights became a blur. The music was inside her, compelling her to move.

Freedom, she thought. That was what the ancients had. Uninhibited, joyous freedom to express their emotions. Eyes half-closed, she whirled faster and faster, her heart racing, her blood surging.

In her mind it was Quinn who was dancing with her. Quinn's wooing that was exciting her. Quinn's spirit that was reaching out to her.

Anne stumbled. A strong hand held her until she caught her balance. Dazed, she glanced up, intending to murmur her thanks.

Her breath caught. For an instant she wondered if she was drunk. Were those truly Quinn's eyes she saw blazing with longing, Quinn's hand holding her, Quinn's mouth descending toward hers?

She swayed, and her hands clutched at his shirt. Through the material, she felt the heat of his body and the pounding of his heart.

With a harsh groan, he lifted her into his arms and walked out of the intimate circle of light and into the darkness. Anne pressed her face to his neck and inhaled the musky man-scent of his skin. Anger radiated from him, along with something more. Something as elemental and powerful as the dancing. Sexual hunger as urgent as the long strides taking them farther and farther from the others.

Lulled by the motion of his body, she was nearly asleep when, suddenly, she felt herself falling. She cried out, opening her eyes at the same time. She had a split-second image of a dimly lit room before she sprawled on her back against something soft. A bed.

Looking up, she saw a thatched roof, steeply sloped. Just as Quinn had promised, she was in one of the huts designed as future quarters for the tourists Mama hoped to attract.

Quinn was standing by the bed. His arms were folded. This time she had no trouble determining the color of his eyes. They were as black as the sky overhead, lit from within by a powerful emotion, held at bay by the control she had come to expect from him.

"You're angry with me," she murmured, defiantly meeting those dark eyes.

"Am I?"

"Is it because I was dancing?"

"What do you think?"

Anne sat up. "I think I'm having a wonderful time tonight."

Her hair tumbled over her shoulders, silky and thick. Her cheeks were pink, and her eyes were glowing. Her mouth, free of lipstick now, looked almost too tempting to resist.

Quinn felt the air grow thick. Suffocatingly thick, the way it was underwater when his air supply was nearly gone.

"Go to sleep, Anne. It's late."

She looked to one side, then to the other. There was only one bed in the room. "Where will you sleep?"

"On the floor," he said in an even tone.

"Why?"

"You're not in any shape to make decisions we both might regret," he said in that low, even tone. His gaze slid up the tense line of her neck to her face. Lingered. In the half-light, the angular lines of his lean face seemed too powerful, too compelling.

Anne sensed that the lack of emotion in his voice was deceptive. Instinct told her that Quinn was very much like the volcanoes that had created the islands, with crusts as hard and cold as dead ash on the outside, seething with explosive power within.

"I was thinking of you," she murmured. "When I was dancing. I want you to make love to me."

Quinn sat down on the bed and tried to steady his pulse. His throat was dry, and his blood seethed.

"I can only give you tonight. No promises of tomorrow. No strings."

"I'm not asking for promises," she said softly. "Only tonight."

His breath came out in a shudder. "I'll make sure you don't get pregnant." His voice had a rusty quality. Painful memories? she wondered.

Her mouth went dry. "It's all right. I'm on the pill. Because of my... schedule. Traveling and all." To places where feminine hygiene wasn't even a concept.

Before she'd met Quinn, having to take that little pill every morning had been a nuisance. Now she was grateful her gynecologist had insisted.

One by one she undid the buttons of his shirt, then slipped her hands inside and flattened her fingers against his skin. It was smooth and warm, inviting a slow exploration.

Quinn watched her pupils grow wide and heard her breath catch. The warmth of her breath on his face sent pulses of hard need shooting deep. He felt his blood hammer in his head and pool in his groin.

"You can trust me, Quinn," she murmured, touching the tense line of his jaw with fingertips that trembled slightly. "I won't hurt you."

Quinn heard the gentleness in her husky voice. A hot urgency licked at his belly, and his breath suddenly felt too explosive for his lungs to hold. Slowly he lifted her fingers to his mouth. He kissed the tips. Her palm. The pulse throbbing at her wrist. Then he pushed her hand above her head and held it there.

"Hold me," she whispered as her fingers slowly caressed his massive shoulders. "Keep the nightmare away again."

His skin rippled in reaction, and the hard muscles beneath contracted. Above the intensity of his dark eyes, his eyebrows drew together as though he was feeling a sudden pain.

"It's been a long time. I don't want to hurt you." He flattened all emotion from his voice, but she heard the yearning buried there.

"You won't. I trust you."

"Tonight we both trust," he murmured on a rasping breath. Slowly he grasped the hand still clinging to his shoulder and pushed it over her head to join her other hand. She was completely helpless now. Vulnerable. Trapped.

He brought his head down slowly, and she found that she was holding her breath. His mouth brushed her throat, exploding the breath from her in a helpless rush.

"Sweet," he murmured before sliding his mouth to the tender skin below her ear. Then he let his tongue explore her ear, flicking in and out of the sensitive whorls.

He flattened her palms with his, then entwined their fingers. Anne turned toward his exploring mouth, impatient to feel those hard lips tasting hers. She lifted one leg and tried to twist toward him, but his heavy thigh captured hers, holding her.

He drew back, struggling to hang on to his concentration. To his control. Desire spiked hot and heavy between his thighs, urging him to drive deep into her soft, pliant body.

Her face was flushed, her eyes glittering with the same desperate need to touch and be touched that was surging in him like adrenaline.

His mouth firmed over hers, firing a hungry response from her lips, which surprised him into a harsh groan. His hands grew possessive, sliding over the fragile bones of her throat to her shoulders, then her breasts.

Anne gasped as his fingers kneaded her already hardened nipples, exciting sensations of both pain and pleasure. Pain, because it had been so long since she had been touched so intimately; pleasure, because his touch was achingly gentle, almost adoring.

"Yes, oh, yes!" she cried against his hard, hungry mouth.

In answer his tongue plunged deep, rasping hot against hers. Quinn sensed the wildness that lay waiting just beyond the boundaries of her control. His own control threatened to shatter with each kiss, each soft moan his mouth was drawing from her.

"Patience," he managed to say between gentle, wooing kisses. "Or this will be over before we've started."

Anne heard the strain in his voice and smiled, even as she moaned in protest.

Because every nerve ending in his body was driving him to haste, he forced himself to undress her slowly, savoring the feel of her soft skin beneath his palms as he drew off her shirt. Her bra was silk and lace, utterly feminine and seductive. She moaned as his hands slipped it from her. Her breasts were luminous in the dim light and tipped with dark nipples.

Quinn's mouth replaced his hands, his tongue as deliciously caressing as his fingertips had been. Anne writhed, her hands eager, stroking down the corded length of his belly, tangling in the arrow of silky hair.

Her nails rasped against denim. Her fingers pushed beneath the constriction, and he gasped, his breath warming the moist cleft between her breasts.

Suddenly he rolled away, his breathing harsh and ragged. He stood and yanked down the tight jeans. Her own breathing rapid and shallow, Anne sat up and eased out of her slacks.

Her hands were on the elastic of her panties when he stopped her. "Let me," he whispered harshly. "I want to see all of you."

He kissed the curve of her belly, then slid the silky panties from her. Anne shivered and reached for him.

The bed dipped under his weight, and then she was enfolded in heat again. Heat from his body. Heat from hers. His leg slid between hers, rough where the hair curled dark against his bronzed skin, hardened by lean muscle and sinew.

His hands roamed over her, his fingers finding sensitive places that were as new to her as they were to him. Flashes of desire burned over her skin where his mouth and hands had prepared her.

Quinn felt the tremors running along her thighs where his hands stroked. His fingers suddenly trembled as they slipped inside her. She was warm silk, moist, ready.

Need clawed at him, more powerful than the hottest rage, more engulfing than the most potent bitterness. Feelings he had ruthlessly deadened for years threatened to erupt. Protective feelings. Tender feelings. Feelings too dangerous to be acknowledged.

With a groan that felt torn from him, he moved over her, his patience gone. He entered her slowly. The cords on his neck were distended with the effort he was expending to keep his cries of pleasure locked inside.

Anne clung to him, her legs wide, her body opening willingly to admit his. Pleasure spiraled inside her like a vortex, whirling faster and faster until she was consumed, her cries mindless, ecstatic.

Her nails raked his back, urging him to move. His first gentle movements released the last of her will. She gave herself over to him, her heat mingling with his, her body melting into his.

She opened her eyes, needing to see his face. His eyes were closed, the thick black lashes quivering slightly against the hard planes of his cheeks.

His skin glistened with dampness. His breathing was labored, the sounds of pain and pleasure mingling as though torn from his deep chest.

She moaned, trying to match him thrust for thrust. And then the vortex within her was out of control, spinning, spinning, until she was a part of it. Mindless, breathless, her pleasure was a long-drawn-out cry that Quinn caught in his mouth.

His body convulsed, the muscles bunching and straining against her skin. She thought he cried her name, but the waves of pleasure taking her made it difficult to know for sure.

And then she was falling, drifting in warmth, Quinn's head cradled against her breasts, their bodies joined.

Her fingers stroked his thick, soft hair. In the muted light, it seemed as black as the moonless sky, but, like the Hawaiian night, the strands felt warm against her fingers.

She sighed with the pleasure of the afterglow, filling her with a serenity she hadn't felt in a long time.

Violence and hate and fear seemed far away. No one could find her when she was cradled in Quinn's strong arms. Nothing could hurt her while he was with her.

"Mmm, lovely," she murmured.

She felt the muscles of his cheek tighten against her breast and thought he must be smiling. He wasn't. In fact, when he raised his head to look at her, his mouth was hard with tension. "Did I hurt you?"

"No, of course not," she murmured, running her fingers over the forceful line of his mouth. Her body tingled in private places, wonderful places.

"No regrets?"

He let his fingers gently push through the thick, pale curls framing her face, until the softness brushed his wrists. Beneath the rough pads of his thumbs, he felt the blood throbbing in the veins beneath her satiny skin.

"No, no regrets. You're a very generous man, when you let yourself be."

His hands clenched in the rumpled silk of her hair, the only part of him that moved. "No," he said, his voice dull. "I'm not."

She smiled; the feel of his mouth was still imprinted on her lips. "You're really a lot gentler than you want people to know," she said, turning to kiss the strong wrist so close to her cheek.

His pulse leapt. "Anne, there's nothing in me that you would want. I wish there was."

"I'm not so sure. I think there's more in you than you know. Good things. Things to be proud of."

His mouth compressed. "You're crazy, that's what you are." An emotion he couldn't define thickened his voice and tightened his gut.

She laughed, feeling wonderful. "No, I'm just happy. Life is very good when the nightmares stay away."

Quinn thought about the men of the Aryan American Brigade who even now might be trying to find her. To kill her. His Anne.

Rage spiked with frustration twisted in his gut. The bastards would never get her. Not while he was alive.

He turned onto his side and settled her against him. "Go to sleep, *ipo,*" he murmured.

Anne snuggled against him, her mind running through the Hawaiian phrases in her guidebook. Sweetheart, she thought. He'd called her sweetheart.

Anne woke to an unfamiliar quiet. She was marvelously relaxed, even though her body ached in private, intimate ways that brought a warm rush of pleasure to her face.

Dawn was hovering, casting just enough light into the hut to show her that Quinn was still asleep. He was sprawled on his back. One hand was tucked under his pillow. The other was curled over her thigh, as though, in his sleep, he needed to be connected to her.

His big chest rose and fell easily, and his breathing was steady. The sheet was bunched between them, covering her but not him.

In sleep, his body was totally vulnerable. And yet, the long, muscled length of him suggested power and strength. He was partly aroused, as though he were replaying their lovemaking in his dreams.

She lay perfectly still, studying the deeply etched tension that never left his face, even in sleep. His jaw was dark with whisker stubble. His brow was scored with faint lines that never disappeared. Unlike her, he had no scars on his body. No obvious marks of suffering. But they were there, inside, where healing was the most difficult.

It made her sad to imagine what life must be like for him. The loneliness he had condemned himself to endure. The bitterness that ate at him.

From somewhere close she heard the mournful call of a dove. It was a lonely sound. An answering sigh eased from her lips.

Today they would attend Loni's wedding. Together they would toast the young couple's happiness. Perhaps they would spend one more night alone—here, where the world seemed far away.

And then what?

As though hearing her question, Quinn frowned and muttered something in his sleep. His brows drew together, and a long, heavy breath like a groan escaped his parted lips.

Anne wanted to kiss away the demons that were disturbing his sleep, but she felt suddenly shy. In many ways he was a stranger, this man who had discovered depths of passion in her that she hadn't even dreamed existed.

He knew her body, but he didn't know her. To him, she was a rich, snooty fashion model like his ex-wife. Anne shook with a sudden chill. She had asked him to trust her. Would he feel used when he discovered she had been lying to him?

A woman's lie had nearly destroyed him once. She didn't want him to be hurt again.

Franklyn was wrong. Quinn did need to know the truth about her, and he needed to know now. As soon as he awoke, she would tell him.

Flattening her hand against the cool sheet, she slid her fingers under the pillow, searching for his strong, warm hand. She needed to touch him. To feel the life in his skin and the security of his strength next to her.

But instead of his hand, she touched something cold and hard. Frowning, she pulled it out from under the pillow.

It was a pistol. A big, ugly, deadly revolver. And it was loaded.

Chapter Seven

Fear ignited in her stomach, making her queasy. Scarcely daring to breathe, she eased to a sitting position and clutched the sheet to her breast. Awkwardly, using her free hand, she wrapped the sheet around her. Her other hand tightened around the grip made for a bigger hand than hers.

She took a deep breath. Calm down, Annie. Lots of men carry guns. For... for snakes and things. Except there were no snakes in Hawaii. No predatory animals running wild. No real dangers at all. Except for the human kind.

She cleared her throat. "Quinn? Quinn, wake up."

His lashes fluttered, then lifted. She saw a smile in his eyes—until he noticed the gun barrel pointed at his chest.

His face went still. His gaze remained riveted on the pistol. "Anne, that trigger has a very light pull."

"Something tells me this isn't a wedding gift."

"No."

The pistol was surprisingly heavy. But then, the bullets were lead, weren't they? And there were six of them in the cylinder. She wet her suddenly dry lips.

"Do you always travel with a gun?"

"Not exactly." Quinn watched her, trying to decide how to handle her. He wasn't kidding about the pull on the trigger. A mere twitch would be enough to blow a hole in his chest the size of his fist.

"Exactly what *is* it doing under your pillow, then?"

"Give it to me first and I'll tell you."

Anne shook her head. "Not until you explain why you brought it."

Quinn tightened the muscles of his spine and legs, but he made himself lie motionless. "Anne, I know about the Brigade. And I know why you're in the Witness Protection Program."

Anne gaped at him, growing colder and colder. The gun barrel wavered. "How do you know?"

"Ed Franklyn told me."

She paled. Suspicion clouded her eyes. "I don't believe you. He wouldn't. Not when he made me promise not to say a word."

"Call him."

Doubt flickered across her face. "There's no phone here."

"We'll go up to the house. Mama Chloe has a phone." Mama Chloe's house was on the other side of the clearing, beyond the grotto where the luau had been held.

Anne searched his face. She saw tension there. And a steady, patient look in his eyes. But his mouth was set. His body had a stillness that was chilling.

"Okay, but I'll get dressed first. Don't move till I tell you to." Her clothes were scattered over the floor where Quinn had thrown them. His were there, too. Mixed with hers.

Still holding the gun steady with one hand, she managed to get to her knees and clutch the sheet to her breasts. Quinn's expression didn't change. Still, she had never felt so vulnerable, so exposed.

Awkwardly, she crawled backward. Her foot tangled in a fold of the sheet, tipping her sideways. Quinn moved so quickly that she had no time to cry out before his powerful fingers clamped around her wrist.

He pushed her arm upward just as her finger instinctively tightened. The gun went off with an explosive force that drove her backward and made her ears ring.

His curse was equally explosive. Pain shot through her wrist as Quinn wrested the gun from her and thumbed on the safety.

"You could have killed both of us!" she shouted, rising to her knees again and facing him. She forgot, for the moment, that she had lost the protective covering of the sheet.

"*Me?*" he shouted. "Are you crazy, woman? I wasn't the one waving the damn gun around."

"You should have known how I'd react if I saw it! You could have told me."

"I had a reason—"

Suddenly he heard a sound that froze the rest of his explanation. Chopper blades. High-pitched, like a gunship, coming in fast and low.

"Get dressed," he ordered, giving her a shove before he vaulted from the big old-fashioned bed and snatched up his jeans.

Anne watched with a stunned expression. "What?"

"Hear that?" he asked, nodding in the direction of the sound that was rapidly growing louder. "Might be friendly, might not be. I'm not taking any chances until I know one way or the other."

Still holding his revolver in one hand, Quinn shoved his legs into his jeans and jerked them over his thighs. He had fastened enough of the metal buttons to anchor the soft denim to his hips and was already heading for the door when Anne scrambled off the bed.

The mattress was higher than normal, causing her to lose her balance and stumble against the night-stand. By the time she had regained her balance, Quinn had the door open and was searching the sky through the thick tangle of tree branches overhead.

"Be careful," she shouted, but he was already pulling the door shut behind him.

"Oh, God," she muttered. "If he gets himself killed . . ."

Biting her lip, she snatched clean underwear from the saddlebags and dressed as quickly as her shaking hands would permit. She was shoving her feet into her boots when the door slammed open and Quinn burst through at a dead run.

"Get down!" he shouted, even as he dove forward. His body crashed into hers, and they sprawled to the floor, his chest crushing her breasts and driving the air from her lungs.

Through a gasp of pain and outrage, she heard a roar overhead. Noise pounded her eardrums and made her teeth rattle. The floorboards vibrated, and the windows shook.

In one violent motion Quinn wrapped his arms around her and rolled them both under the bed. At the same moment bullets strafed the hut.

Lead slugs thudded into the double layer of mattress and box springs above them and ripped into the floor as though it were canvas, leaving a trail of holes like stitches. Bits of thatch and splintered wood rained down. Glass shattered, shards exploding inward.

Anne tried to scream, but she found she couldn't draw breath. Her lungs burned. Her body shook. Her fingers clutched Quinn's shirt. Just when she knew she was going to die, the roar began to fade. Anne inhaled deeply, greedy for air. Still gripped by terror, she was afraid to move.

"Are you all right?" Quinn asked, his breath warm and reassuring against her neck.

She nodded, and his arms tightened. "Is...is it gone?" she whispered when her throat relaxed enough to allow speech.

Quinn raised his head and listened. "Sounds like it. Better give it a few more seconds to make sure."

"Thank God," she murmured, closing her eyes.

God had nothing to do with it, Quinn thought with a private, cynical smile. God was never there when you needed Him.

"It's the Brigade, isn't it?" she asked against the comfort of his warm neck.

"Looks that way. Probably tracked us from the ranch, then radioed for the chopper." He bit off a curse. "I blew it, Anne. I had intended to scout around last night after the luau, but I... fell asleep."

"You expected them?" she cried.

"I... knew it was a possibility, yes."

"How did you know?"

"Eddie called."

"When?"

Quinn hesitated. She was withdrawing from him. He could feel it. "Yesterday morning. Early."

Anne let go of him, her hands shaking. "That's why you brought me here, isn't it? To protect me. Not because you wanted my company. The sex was just a bonus."

Quinn's eyes flashed dangerously. "You know better than that."

"Do I?" Her voice was thick and wavering. Quinn sensed the hurt shimmering beneath the anger. It was better that way, he told himself, even as he fought a need to kiss the pain from her eyes.

"I told you where I stand, Anne. The choice was yours." He rolled free and stood up. The room was ruined. Furniture splintered. Walls blasted. The mattress that had saved their lives pockmarked.

Outside, a pair of roof-high palm trees had been chopped in two by the hail of high-powered machine-gun shells. The surrounding ferns had been shredded like paper. The air smelled dusty.

Anne eased out from under the bed and sat up. Her stomach was jumping uncontrollably, and her mouth was so dry it was hard to swallow.

"That was close," she said with a shudder she couldn't quite master. She rested her back against the bed and tried to ignore the spinning in her head.

"Close enough." He snatched up his shirt and shrugged into it. "We got lucky."

"They'll be back, won't they?"

Quinn passed a critical eye over her face. Her lips were white, her skin so pale it seemed translucent. Her hair was a tumble of curls. She looked shaken, but controlled. He hoped that she was tough enough to take the truth. If she wasn't, they were both in trouble.

"Right now, the bastards are probably landing about six miles from here in a meadow near Cook's Ridge. If they're as good as I think they are, they'll double-time back here to make sure we're dead. We've got an hour, maybe less, to get as far away from here as we can."

"What...what about Mama Chloe? Oh, God, Quinn, what about Loni? We have to warn them.

To . . . to do something.'' Anne scrambled to her feet and started toward the door. Quinn hauled her back.

"Easy, honey," he ordered, his fingers restraining her.

Anne struggled to free herself. She had to warn them. "Let me go! I can't let it happen again. I can't . . ."

Quinn pulled her hard against him and wrapped his arms around her. Her body shook against his. "These men are pros, Anne. They have a job to do—kill a potential threat to their leader. Anything else isn't part of their mission."

"But—"

"As long as we stay away from the house and the others, they'll be safe."

Anne stared up at him, her heart racing. "This . . . this is just like my nightmare. I . . . can't wait until I wake up."

One side of his mouth saluted her try at levity. Under the stubble, his jaw was set. "Me, too."

His mouth came down on hers. His kiss was demanding, bordering on desperate. His arms wrapped tighter, pulling her hard against him. She dug her fingers into his shoulders, trying to get closer. Her mouth moved under his, answering his demand with one of her own. She felt herself begin to tremble. From need this time.

Quinn felt the small tremors take her body. His own was none too steady. He knew that they needed to leave. He knew that the hunger that surged in him couldn't be satisfied.

He deepened the kiss. His breath rasped against hers. His thighs rubbed hers. His hands roamed greedily.

The promises he wanted to make and couldn't, the words she deserved that weren't in him to say, the longings he was too proud to express—those things he put into his kiss.

Quinn was breathing hard when he finally managed to relax his grip on her. He waited for her to open her eyes. When she did, he saw that she was as aroused as he was. Her lips parted, still rosy from the pressure of his, and she smiled.

"Think you can ride now? There's a village a long day's ride south of here, with a sheriff's substation. We'll head there."

Anne managed a shaky nod. "Much as I'm enjoying myself, I guess we'd better go."

Silently, his hand in hers, he led her to the dresser. Still without speaking, he looped her camera over her neck, grabbed the saddlebags she had hastily packed and led the way to the door.

Neither looked back.

"I used to love the rain," Anne said with a deep sigh. "But that was when I was curled up with a good book in front of a roaring fire, eating warm brownies and drinking cold milk."

Resting her elbows on her crossed knees, she watched a steady drizzle pelt a bush that had large leaves shaped like elephant ears.

"Me, I'd rather have brandy and a cigar," Quinn said without opening his eyes.

"Right now that sounds wonderful, even the cigar," she muttered, wiggling her toes. Her boots were soaked; miraculously, her socks were dry.

The shelter where she and Quinn had taken refuge was enclosed on three sides by walls of lava rock a yard thick. The roof sloped downward from a height of ten feet or so to the entrance, where it was only a few inches above Quinn's head, giving the small area a cavelike feeling. Unlike a cave, however, the floor where they had spread their saddle blankets was man-made of flat lava stones, laid close together like tiles.

Crude though it might be, it kept them dry and relatively warm. Oblivious to the steady downpour, the horses grazed nearby, hobbled to prevent them from straying too far.

It was late afternoon. How late, Anne could only guess. She hadn't seen the sun since midmorning, and her watch had been smashed when Quinn had thrown her to the floor.

The rain had started several hours after they'd ridden away from the ruined hut, heading south along a narrow, twisting trail. Unlike most of the afternoon showers Anne had become accustomed to, this one showed no sign of stopping.

By the time Quinn had indicated that they were to stop, she had been shivering and miserable. A change of clothes had warmed her skin, and she'd used her discarded shirt to dry her hair. But she couldn't do anything about the empty feeling in the pit of her stomach.

"Is this what you call a monsoon?" she asked, propping her chin on the heel of her palm.

Quinn opened one eye and inspected the sheet of water cascading over the eaves like a waterfall. He was sitting a few feet away with his back against his worn saddle, one leg drawn up at the knee. The stubble on his jaw had darkened, giving him a slightly disreputable appearance that Anne liked.

"If this was summer, yeah," he said finally. "Now I call it a damned nuisance."

Anne heard the irritation in his voice and thought about the apple they had shared at noon. It was all either of them had eaten. She was hungry, but a man of his size had to be ravenous.

"Are you sure it's safe? To stop, I mean?" she asked.

"Safe or not, we don't have much choice. The trail thins out about a mile south, and then it's straight down. It's too risky for the horses in the mud."

"If it's risky for the horses, it has to be risky for... anyone following us, right?"

"Depends."

"On what?"

"On how they're following. If it was me, I'd get a fix on the subject's direction, then search the area by chopper."

"Subject," she echoed. "Is that what I am?"

Quinn sat up and flexed the tired muscles of his back. "To them, yes."

Anne glanced at the sky. The clouds were so low they obliterated the tops of the tallest trees. Thank God it was rotten weather for flying. Or was it? She decided she didn't want to know.

"I've been a real problem for you, haven't I?" she said with a smile.

"Yes." The drawn, strained edges of his mouth told her more about his mood than the curt answer.

"I'm sorry."

"Don't be." He hesitated, then added in a rough tone, "For what it's worth, I think you're one brave lady. I wouldn't want to take on a bunch of goons with just a camera."

Surprised, Anne stared at him. Something in his eyes brought a strange flutter to her throat. She wanted to believe that it was love. She knew she didn't dare.

"Have you ever been afraid, Quinn?" she asked in a low tone. "Deep down in your soul scared?"

"Yes." His answer was gentle, encouraging her to continue.

"When?"

"On a dive in Australian waters when a twelve-foot great white was trying to decide whether or not to have me for dinner."

"What did you do?"

"Tried not to pee my pants and did my best to look unappetizing."

Anne laughed. "It must have worked."

"Guess it did." The lazy slur of amusement in his voice warmed her.

Anne got to her feet, too tense to sit any longer. She walked to the entrance and held out her hand.

The rain was cold. She waited until her cupped palm was full, then brought it to her mouth for a drink.

"It's good," she said. "Not as good as *okolehoa*, though." She looked over her shoulder and gave him a slightly abashed grin. "Now that was good! You should have had some."

"I've had my share."

Anne let her grin widen. "I'll just bet you have."

Watching her, Quinn wondered why he had thought he could resist her. Why he had wanted to try.

He got to his feet and stretched, then joined her at the entrance. "Hell of a day for a wedding," he said.

Anne sobered. "I hope nothing's happened to your family."

His fingers rubbed the tender place in the middle of her back. "Strange as it sounds, guys like Draygon have a strange sense of honor."

While he'd been branded as dishonorable, Anne thought. She inhaled deeply, filling her lungs with the damp air. It smelled musty.

"What is this place, anyway?" she asked, needing to fill the silence.

"It's called a *puuhonua*. Roughly translated, it means sanctuary." His arm circled her shoulder, and she leaned into his hard, solid body.

"Like a church?"

"More like a refuge, although there was a priest here. In the old times, if you broke *kapu* by stepping on the chief's shadow or eating forbidden food, you were sentenced to death. By stoning, usually."

"Good Lord," Anne muttered. "I take it they didn't have much of a crime problem in those days?"

His laugh warmed her. "More than you'd think. But there was an appeal process, a sort of court of last resort."

"Even then?"

"Even then. If you made it here without being killed on the way, the priests would purify your soul, and you were forgiven. They also did the same for escaped prisoners of war or disgraced warriors."

"Just like that?"

"Just like that. Things were . . . simpler then." The strange note in his voice drew her gaze. He was staring fixedly at the sodden walls enclosing the grassy area, and she knew he was thinking of his past.

"Is that why you came home?" she asked softly. "For refuge? After the court-martial?"

His gaze met hers. Held. Narrowed. His arm dropped from her shoulder, leaving her feeling cold and abandoned.

"Who told you?"

"Meg." He frowned and she hastened to add, "Don't be angry with her. She knew I wanted to understand you better. She thought knowing about your past might help."

"That sounds like Meg."

Once, she would have considered the hard slant of his smile cruel and unfeeling. Now that she knew him better, she sensed that his coldness was a defense against feelings so strong they had once nearly destroyed his life.

"You made a mistake, Quinn. It's a very human thing to do."

"Oh, I'm human, all right," he drawled, his mouth twisting. "When I'm around you, I'm very aware of just how human I am."

He moved closer. His hand tested a stray curl, rubbing the silky strands between his fingers. "You have a way of making a man want to take chances he shouldn't," he said, curling his hand around her neck.

He kissed her gently at first, but his restraint soon broke. His big hands roamed her back as though he was trying to memorize the soft curves and angles of the body pressed against his.

Anne stretched closer, her hands framing his face, her lips moving enticingly under his. This might be the last time they were together. The last time she could love him.

Taking his time, as though this was the most important task he had ever performed, he kissed her with slow, deep movements of his tongue.

His leg slid between hers until she rode his muscle-thick thigh. He moved slowly, sinuously, sending velvet spikes of pleasure thrusting into her with sweet insistence.

Quinn heard her small feminine moans of pleasure, and his body clenched at the feeling of savage possessiveness that ripped through him. Two centuries had passed since his people had been warriors, but the instinct to defend his *ohana,* his family, to the death still burned in him.

Anne was more than family. She was a part of him. His soul.

Quinn was breathing hard when he finally managed to relax his grip on her. He waited for her to open her eyes. When she did, he saw that she was as aroused as he was. Her lips parted, still rosy from the pressure of his.

The rain beat down steadily, forming a curtain enclosing them in the shelter. The air smelled fresh. Beyond the opening, the grass was a vivid green.

"Wow," she murmured, her voice thick.

"I'll say," he muttered, lowering his head again. It was like the first time, a gentle exploration that excited her as much as the fiercest demand. More.

She clung to his shoulders, the pounding of her heart almost as loud as the rain. Quinn knew that she was his—for the time left to them.

He forced patience into his hands as he worked at the buttons of her shirt. His knuckles moved against her skin. She inhaled in a rush, her eyes going very dark and turbulent.

"Hurry," she whispered, trying to help him with the last button.

"Not a chance. This has to last me a long time." He brushed kisses over her face before he pushed her shirt over her shoulders. It fluttered to the floor in a slither of soft cotton. Her bra was next.

The air was cool, making his hands seem wonderfully warm as they molded her breasts. It hurt to breathe. It hurt to wait. Her nipples swelled until they were hard and exquisitely sensitive.

Eagerly, impatiently, she leaned into his callused palms, rubbing against him. His chest lifted in a deep, shuddering breath.

And then he was stepping back to shuck off his own shirt, baring his wide, hairy chest. Anne leaned forward to kiss the hard, rounded cap of his shoulder. His muscles leapt under her lips, sending ripples over his skin.

Quinn pressed his lips together to stop the groan rising in him. He closed his eyes, enduring the wash of pleasure he was helpless to resist. All she had to do was touch him and he lost the iron discipline over his mind that had kept him strong. He hungered. He needed. The emotions were elemental, savage, not to be denied.

He lifted her into his arms and she curled against him, her arms around his neck. His mouth brushed hers over and over, his tongue darting between her lips to taste and tease.

When he could wait no longer, he took her to the floor and settled her gently on the saddle blanket. He pushed her backward, then unzipped her jeans and tugged them free to reveal a thin wedge of white satin curving high over her hips.

His hand cupped her intimately, causing her breath to catch. His hard fingers rubbed expertly, sending pleasure surging through her.

She moaned and arched against him. Her hand caught at his arm and she tried to pull him closer, moaning out her desperate need. His muscles contracted against her fingers, but he didn't give in to her demands. Instead he slipped a finger beneath the elastic to stroke and rub until she trembled.

Quinn was drunk on his need, his head swimming, his body swollen and hot behind the fly of his jeans. The pressure was excruciating. Yet he couldn't get enough of her. He took her nipple in his mouth and sucked.

She moaned, arching off the blanket in a spasm of need. His own need was clawing at him. Hands shaking, he drew back to struggle out of his boots and clothing.

Anne reached for him, her eyes dark and wild, her lips trembling. He came toward her quickly, his need now a savage, twisting demand.

Her body arched; her thighs opened. She reached for him, and he surrendered, thrusting deep and hard into her. Her body stretched to accept him, sending a shudder deep into him.

Sensations he had never felt before surged in his blood, like a fire out of control, eating at him, warming him. He kept his gaze on her face, hungry for the sight of her response.

Her cheeks were flushed, her lips parted and swollen, her lashes quivering on her cheeks. As he watched, her tongue licked across her lips, making his own mouth hungry again.

Anne's body was heavy, quivering. With each slow, shuddering thrust of his body, Quinn was releasing needs in her that she had ruthlessly denied, needs that now consumed her.

She cried out, her breathing rushed. Still he held back, needing to give her all that he had, all that he longed to be.

Sweat from his body and hers mingled. Skin slid against skin. He shuddered, struggling to hold back until she climaxed. And then they were both out of control.

Anne cried out, pleasure suffusing her. Quinn's cry was torn from him, exploding against her damp neck. And then they were spent, clinging together.

"Until you leave the island, you're my woman," he whispered, his smoldering gaze boring into hers. "I'll kill anyone who tries to hurt you."

"Yes," she murmured. "I'm your woman."

Careful to keep their bodies fused, Quinn rolled onto his back, cradling her against his warmth. She snuggled against him, her breath warming his neck, her softness like a drug.

As long as he held her, the dishonor and shame he'd lived with for so long seemed like a distant nightmare, no longer able to torment him. As long as he held her, he was at peace.

Chapter Eight

The deep pulse of high-speed rotors woke Quinn at first light. The chopper was heading northeast to southwest, flying a grid pattern, most likely. Methodically searching the area for two riders. Smart, he thought. Professional.

If the brush hadn't been so dense, Anne probably would have been dead by now. Him, too.

He'd heard the rain stop a few hours before dawn. If he'd been alone, he would have saddled Kanaloa and taken his chances. But he wasn't alone.

Slowly he turned to look at the woman using his shoulder for a pillow. She was wearing two of her shirts and one of his over her jeans. Her hair was disheveled, and her face was sunburned. In the rush to leave, her hat had been left behind, and she'd refused to wear his. They'd wasted ten minutes arguing—until he'd thrown up his hands in defeat.

Obstinate woman, he thought. More than obstinate. Bullheaded. A man would be hard pressed to hold his own against a woman like that. She would give as good as she got. Better, probably.

Emotions he hadn't known he still possessed ripped through him. Savage, primitive feelings he didn't dare name, feelings that were all too alive and twisting in his gut.

"Anne, wake up," he whispered against the tumble of her hair. "We have to go."

Anne sighed and stirred, still more asleep than awake. The air touching her face carried a chill, but she was nestled against Quinn's warmth, covered by his shirt and protected by his arms. Her body was heady and relaxed. It was too much trouble to move.

"Anne?"

"Mmm?" Anne smiled, but refused to open her eyes.

His mouth brushed her smile, surprising her into looking at him. "Sun's coming up," he said, his voice oddly gruff.

"So I see." Ducking her head, she burrowed her fingers under the open collar of his shirt to find the soft hair on his chest and snuggled closer. Beneath her palm, his heart thudded erratically.

"It isn't good for a person to just leap out of bed first thing in the morning. Or, in this case, off this feather-soft saddle blanket you so cleverly provided for us." Her smile curved again, and her fingers worked at the buttons of his shirt.

Hunger splintered through him. "We at Sinclair Ranch aim to please, ma'am." He spoke lightly, but his body was surging to life under her touch.

His shirt was open now. And so was the top button of his jeans. Her fingers ran over the corrugated hardness of his ribs to find the soft whorl of hair surrounding his navel. He sucked in his breath, and the pounding of his heart reverberated through his chest.

Excitement welled in her. Quinn was as vulnerable to her as she was to him. More so, because he couldn't hide his response.

Her fingers dipped beneath the material of his jeans to tangle in hair that was coarser and tightly curled. This time his indrawn breath sounded like a groan.

"I have no complaints," she murmured. "Especially with the special attention from the owner."

"Is that right?"

"Mmm."

Her hand moved lower until she found his hot arousal. This time Quinn couldn't control the groan that shuddered through him. His hand trapped hers.

"Don't, baby," he grated, his voice harsh. "I'm in enough trouble as it is."

Anne laughed and rubbed her cheek against his shoulder. "No matter how you meant that remark, I intend to take it as a compliment," she murmured before trailing nibbling kisses along the slope of his shoulder to the warm hollow of his neck.

"Anne," he warned, but her mouth cut off his protest. She gave herself to him, trying to compress all the years they might have had into this moment. This instant.

Quinn was breathing hard when he finally managed to drag his mouth from hers.

"Time to get going." His voice was rough, made that way by his longing to make promises he couldn't keep.

Silently he rolled away and stood. He extended his hand and she took it. He pulled her to her feet, then bent to retrieve her camera and the saddlebags.

"Five minutes to use the facilities, primitive as they are," he said, looping her camera over her head and settling the worn leather strap against her neck. "I'll saddle the horses."

"I'll take care of Sadie. After all, this is the last day she'll be mine."

"Ed and his people should be at Hamakua by now. Once we get there you'll be safe."

"Yes, safe."

He turned to look at her. His hand came up to gently brush the tangled hair away from her face. Her arms went around his neck, and she swayed toward him. Her mouth was only inches away from his.

An unexpected wave of tenderness nearly drove him to his knees. Through sheer force of will, he kept himself from pulling her into his arms again. "Promise me you'll do exactly as I tell you," he said in a voice he couldn't quite sharpen into a command.

Anne let her fingers play in the unruly hair at the back of his neck. "If you promise *me* that you won't take foolish chances. I love you, Quinn. I don't want you to die."

He started to speak, but found that he couldn't. Instead he pressed his mouth to hers so gently she trembled.

"Don't look at me like that," she whispered. "I didn't plan to fall in love. It just...happened."

"God, I wish—"

Whatever he'd been going to say was cut off by the sudden rumble overhead. The helicopter was back.

Anne's head bobbed to her chest and she awoke with a start. Sadie tossed her mane, her gait slow and steady.

Anne straightened her spine, trying to work out the stiffness in her sore muscles. Her thighs ached, and her bottom felt numb.

Ahead, Quinn and his big bay seemed tireless. He sat in a comfortable slouch, his shoulders relaxed, his thighs fluid, as though the saddle was as comfortable as a favorite chair. The pistol rode high on his belt in a worn holster.

The helicopter was no longer overhead, allowing her to breathe easier. The trail was still treacherous, sloping downward at a frightening angle. A thick snarl of vines and bushes grew close on the left. On the right, much too near for her peace of mind, was a steep drop-off.

In the worst places Anne gave the mare her head, trusting the smart little pinto to keep her footing. But the trail was less than three feet wide in spots, bordered by loose rocks that added to the danger.

"Easy, girl," she murmured to the mare. "We're almost—"

"Son of a bitch!" Quinn reined in so violently that his mount reared. At the same time, he kicked his feet out of the stirrups and slid over the stallion's tail to the ground.

Sadie shied, and one of her hind legs slipped, but she managed to stay on the trail. "Quinn, what—?"

"Ambush!" he yelled as he slapped Kanaloa's rump. The stallion bolted, his ears laid back and his eyes rimmed with white.

Anne had already freed her feet from the stirrups when Quinn's arm encircled her waist and dragged her from the saddle. He shouted something. His hat went flying.

At the same moment Anne saw two men in camouflage, crouching at the edge of the trail, firing directly at her. Bullets kicked at the dirt close to the mare's hooves. Sadie whirled, sending loose rocks rolling down the hill, and took off the way they'd come.

Quinn gave Anne a shove into the thick brush. Whiplike plants tore at her hair and lashed her face.

She fell forward, but the thick mat of vegetation beneath her kept her from breaking an arm or leg.

Momentum sent them tumbling down the steep incline. Foliage closed in behind them. The world was a blur, going by at a sickening pace. She was helpless, as ungainly as a large rock caught in an avalanche, until finally she reached the bottom. Quinn's heavy body slammed against her, smashing her breasts into the ground.

They had landed in the deepest part of the gorge, where the vegetation was thickest. Everything was green, even the moss-covered stones.

Somewhere behind them bullets raked the underbrush. The noise was horrendous. And then—suddenly—silence.

Trapped under Quinn's weight, Anne couldn't move. Her breath was coming in gasps. Her elbow ached where she'd banged it on something. One palm was badly skinned. Her ankle felt bruised. The stench of rotting vegetation was overpowering.

"Have…they…gone?" she managed to grate out.

Quinn shifted his weight, and she was able to breath more deeply.

"No," he answered in a tone that was barely audible. "They're waiting for us to move."

Anne froze. "Are you all right?" she whispered.

"So far. How about you?"

Anne was so scared her mouth was sandpaper dry. "Still in one piece."

His gaze, narrowed now and so dark she saw nothing of the man who had made love to her, traveled swiftly over her.

"Bastards suckered me," he said, his voice very quiet and made raspy by cold anger. "Probably spotted us early, figured out where we were heading, and then stayed away so we wouldn't change direction.''

"How did they get here? I didn't see the helicopter anywhere.''

"Either rappeled down from the chopper or came up the trail from below. There's a spot there where a gutsy pilot could land.''

Anne bit her lip, trying not to show fear. Her elbow was beginning to ache badly, and her back was stiffening.

"Ms. Oliver? You still alive down there?'' a rough male voice shouted from someplace above them.

Quinn stiffened. "Don't move,'' he mouthed.

"Come on out, Ms. Oliver.'' The shouted words seemed to reverberate through her head. "We won't hurt you. We just want to offer you a deal.''

Quinn shook his head. Anne bit her lip and nodded that she understood.

"It's a good deal, Ms. Oliver,'' the voice wheedled. "You ought to think real hard before you turn it down.''

Anne tried to control the frantic gallop of her pulse. Overhead, she heard a flutter of wings. Brush crackled under foot.

"The bastards are moving,'' Quinn told her. "Following the trail we made falling down this damn hill.''

Suddenly the silence was shattered again by the earsplitting retorts of automatic rifle fire. Twenty feet above and to the left of their hiding place, lead slugs ricocheted off rocks and shredded the vegetation.

Quinn pulled her into his arms. She began to shake, and her teeth started to chatter. A scream started someplace inside, but she forced it down.

"Easy, honey," Quinn whispered against her ear. She clung to him, pressing her face against the warm muskiness of his neck. They were going to die. Both of them.

The shooting stopped again without warning. The silence was worse, she decided as Quinn drew away from her.

Moving slowly, cautiously, he positioned himself so that he was on his knees with his head still covered by the green thatch of weeds.

Anne twisted into a more comfortable position, trying not to make a sound. Silence lay between them for several beats before Quinn brushed his thumb across a stinging place on her cheekbone.

"You're going to have a bad bruise," he whispered.

"Good thing I'm not really a model," she said with a smile that wobbled only slightly at the corners.

The flash of emotion in his eyes caught her by surprise. His fingers moved to her neck, and he pulled her toward him, his mouth hot and hungry on hers.

Quinn knew that every second he wasted increased the already lopsided odds against them. But he allowed himself a deep, lingering kiss. Her hair still smelled faintly of flowers, and her lips were soft. So very soft.

Emotion twisted his gut and fired his blood. He pulled back, his breathing labored. Time had run out.

"We have one thing in our favor. The bastards think we're unarmed." He moved, and suddenly the big black pistol was in his hand. Anne managed to keep from shuddering.

"Are they close enough to shoot?"

"Not yet. I'm going to give them a nice big target. I'm gambling they'll get careless and show themselves." His voice was very quiet, but his tone shivered her skin and brought her gaze homing in on his.

"What kind of target?"

"Me." He took her hand and placed the pistol in her palm. "That's when you empty this sucker at 'em."

Anne looked down at the killing weapon in horror. She had never once fired a gun of any kind. Not even for sport.

"No!" she whispered, her voice catching. "That's suicide. They'll kill you."

"Not if I run fast enough. Aim for the chest. You've got six chances to hit at least one of them. I'm betting you'll get both."

She stared at the gun's trigger. "Don't you have more...more bullets?"

"Yeah, in the saddlebags."

Anne shuddered. Six bullets against two military automatics? There was no way. Quinn would be dead before she managed a single shot. She couldn't let that happen. Not to Quinn.

"We could wait until dark, then sneak away," she said, her words tumbling in her haste to convince him. "It's the dark of the moon now. They won't see us."

She clutched his arm, desperate to keep him safe. He didn't shrug off her touch, but his expression didn't soften, either.

"Anne, these guys know that, too. They won't wait."

As though underscoring his words, the men above let loose with another short volley. Shattered foliage crashed around them, less than a dozen yards above them. Anne held her hands over her ears until the noise stopped.

Next to her, she felt Quinn's body tense. He was ready to make his move. No, she thought. She had to do something. Anything. Oliver women never gave up.

"That's *enough!*" she yelled, her eyes smoldering with anger.

Quinn whipped his gaze toward her, shock mirrored in his dark pupils. "Shut up!" Quinn hissed. "This isn't a game."

Anne ignored him. She was too busy trying to save his life. "*Don't shoot!*" she shouted to the faceless, nameless killers above. "I'm ready to deal."

Silence answered her. Just when she thought she would explode, another Southern voice yelled from above, "Come on up here, sugar, so's we can deal eyeball to eyeball."

"I can't," she shouted back. "I . . . sprained my ankle. And my friend is unconscious. I think he's dead."

She leaned closer until her mouth was only inches from Quinn's ear. "When they come close, you can shoot them." She shoved the pistol into his hand. "Aim for the chest."

Quinn didn't waste time berating her. Instead, he cocked the pistol and pointed it to the sky.

The silence stretched again, longer this time. Anne could picture the two men straining to see movement below in order to pinpoint her location. And then she heard the furtive sound of large bodies moving through brush.

She bit her lip, praying that she hadn't made a stupid mistake. Finally the rustle of movement stopped, and a voice called, "We'd be pleased to come on down there to help y'all. Show yourself, sugar, so's we can find you.'' The voice was much closer this time.

Anne's gaze met Quinn's. "Now what?" she whispered.

"Tell them you're scared. Tell them you want them to hold their guns over their heads so you'll feel safe."

"Will they?"

"We'll soon find out." He kissed her hard. "In case I forget to tell you later, I think you're one hell of a woman."

He maneuvered into a crouch, then signaled to Anne that he was ready. Not a muscle in his big body moved as he waited, his attention focused in the direction of the men's voices. He didn't seem to be breathing. Anne had an impression of great force under rigid control, waiting to be released at precisely the right moment.

"Uh, fellas, how do I know you won't shoot me?" she called. It wasn't difficult to force the sound of fear into her voice.

"Why, sugar, we was just trying to flush you out, is all."

The moisture in the ground was seeping through her jeans. Her knees felt clammy. And her hands throbbed where the skin had been ripped away.

Her heart was hammering wildly now, and she couldn't seem to control her breathing. Sweat collected between her shoulder blades, plastering her shirt to her skin.

"Put your guns over your heads so I can see them," she called. "And ... and then I'll stand up."

Anne heard the rumble of masculine voices, and then the man called, "Okay, sugar. You got yourself a deal."

Instinctively, she turned to Quinn. He nodded, his eyes cold, his face set.

"As soon as the shooting starts," he whispered, "get down as low as you can. Head that way." He jerked his thumb toward the south. "Town is only three or four miles from here as the crow flies."

Terrified, she stood. Leaves and branches obscured her view, but it didn't take long for her to spot the killers. They were slightly to the right, about seventy feet away, holding their weapons aloft. Was that close enough for Quinn to shoot accurately? she wondered as she pulled the branches aside so that they could see her.

"Here," she called.

The men folded into a crouch, their rifles coming down at the same time. Quinn lunged forward, shoving her behind him as he fired two quick shots. One of the men jerked and fell backward, his rifle silenced.

One down, Quinn thought, running to his left to draw the other man's fire away from Anne. He wasted two shots making sure the man took the bait.

Bullets tore through the flimsy shield of leaves. The man was good, moving as swiftly as Quinn, firing from the hip.

Anne screamed. She called out Quinn's name, tried to get up, but she was trembling so hard she had difficulty coordinating her arms and legs.

Quinn kept running, his heels sinking into the muck. Lead slugs whistled past his head. He headed for a large palm directly ahead, high-powered bullets thudding into the ground behind him.

Ten feet from the tree, he veered, doubling back so quickly the other man was caught off guard. Bullets continued to slam into the ground in front of the tree for a split second, long enough for Quinn to plant his feet and take aim.

His first shot missed. The second one hit the man in the belly just as Quinn felt something slam into his right side. His right leg buckled. At the same time his gun hand went numb.

He sank to the ground. Anne screamed something he didn't understand, and then silence settled. The air smelled of gunpowder and shredded plants.

"Quinn, oh God, Quinn!" Anne cried, running toward the spot where he'd fallen.

He was lying on his back, his eyes open, his big hand still wrapped around the pistol. One knee was bent. The denim covering the thickest part of his right thigh was already saturated with blood. The splotch of red covering his right shoulder was almost as bad.

Anne sank to her knees and began tearing at his shirt. His left hand came up to grip hers. His fingers were hard, but his strength was nearly gone.

"Don't," he ordered, his voice harsh.

"You're hurt," she cried on a sob of fury. "The bastards hurt you."

"Are they . . . dead?"

Anne cast a swift, shuddering look toward the trampled area where the two men lay twenty feet or so apart. Neither moved. "I think so."

Quinn nodded and closed his eyes for a long instant. Lines of suffering deepened on his face. His skin was slowly draining of color.

"Go," he muttered, his jaw tight. "Hurry. Pilot . . . will come looking. . . ."

Fear settled in her stomach like jagged glass. Her face was going numb. "No, I won't leave you."

His eyebrows drew together. Frustration glittered in his eyes. "You can and . . . you will," he commanded, his voice as cold and empty as a crypt.

"There's something else you should know about Oliver women," she said, her facing growing paler and paler. "We don't take orders worth a damn."

She pulled her hand from his and tugged her shirt-tail from her jeans. She needed a bandage, pressure, something to stop the bleeding.

Assaulted by pain that threatened the boundaries of his control, Quinn fought to keep the swamping weakness at bay.

"Anne, listen to me." Forcing steel into his voice drained his energy. His breath was coming in shudders now. Pain lanced through his chest like a white-hot blade.

Gritting his teeth, he summoned strength from someplace deep. He forced his mind back, summoning an image of his ex-wife's brittle beauty. He kept Liz's face in his mind, blotting out the sheen of worry in Anne's soft, amber eyes. "Drop the Florence Nightingale act, sweetheart. It's . . . wasted on me. Just get your cute little fanny down this hill and out of my life, so I can stop pretending to care about you."

"You're hurt . . ."

"Sweetheart, I've taken worse punishment at the Fourth of July Rodeo and still had enough juice left to screw half the women hanging on me."

The deliberate vulgarity brought a wounded vulnerability to her mouth that seared him worse than the pain of his wounds. But he wouldn't let himself stop. Not while her life was still in desperate jeopardy.

Somehow he managed to block out enough of the agony so that he could sit up. Anne watched him with horror darkening her eyes.

"Quinn, what...?"

He grabbed her by the hair and pulled her toward him. His mouth clamped down on hers, and he savaged her lips until he tasted blood. Hers, his, he wasn't sure.

She whimpered, a wounded, desperate little sound that made him cringe inside.

His right hand didn't want to function. He used his left again, dropping it from a clump of her hair to her breast.

Anne felt his palm grind her nipple without even a hint of his former gentleness. His movements were crude, more like an animal's rutting than lovemaking.

Her mind shouted a denial, but his hand was pulling at her shirt. Buttons tore from their holes. His fingers fumbled with her bra.

Anne struggled, adrenaline giving her enough strength to roll out of his arms.

"Stop it," she whispered, her voice quavering. "You don't mean this. You just...you just want me to leave you. But I won't. I love you."

His mouth twisted. Somehow he found enough strength to run the most important bluff of his life. "Love? C'mon, Anne. You're a big girl. Love is for kids. You and me, we've been around. We're hot for each other, that's all."

Anne stared into his eyes. Sweat beaded his face and tension furrowed his brow, but his eyes were as hard as agate and just as cold. In spite of his wounds, he seemed strong and ready.

"No," she whispered. "I don't believe that's all you felt."

Quinn cupped his groin with his good hand. "C'mon over here, honey," he drawled with a suggestive twist to his hard mouth, "and let me show you what I feel."

Anne felt as though she were drowning. With a muffled cry, she stood up and began to run.

Quinn sat motionless until she was out of sight. Seconds later, the adrenaline that had sustained him began to drain away. He sank back against the ground and closed his eyes, welcoming the sharp, twisting agony taking hold of his body. His one thought before he lost consciousness was of Anne.

Quinn knew he was alive because he hurt. Everything around him was hazy and vague, except the burning agony in his chest. His leg ached like a son of a bitch, too. He seemed to be swaddled in bandages. He couldn't move his right side.

He tried to raise his head to take stock, but the effort was too much. He sank back against the pillow, his head whirling and his stomach lurching. The ceiling was white, and the air smelled of disinfectant. In the distance a muted voice called something over a PA system.

He turned his head slowly to the left. A plastic envelope of some clear liquid was hanging from a shiny metal stand next to his bed, connected to a needle in the back of his hand by clear plastic tubing.

A hospital? he thought. Had something happened? It took a few moments of fierce concentration before he remembered why he was hurting. He'd been shot.

"Anne." His voice came out as a harsh croak. With his one good hand he struggled to grab the bars keeping him in bed.

"So we're awake," a voice chirped. "About time, I'd say."

The nurse hovering over him was spare and capable-looking, with her salt-and-pepper hair cut in a no-nonsense Dutch bob and kind gray eyes. The hand that counted the pulse in his wrist was warm.

"Did she make it?" he demanded, his voice graveled and weak. His mouth was dry, and his throat hurt, as though someone had jammed something hard down his gullet.

"Easy, Mr. Sinclair. Your pulse is about to set a new world's record. In case you're interested, you've had surgery on your thigh and shoulder," the nurse said with more briskness. "Both will mend, but not unless you relax."

Quinn glowered at her. Even that small movement sent needles of pain through him. "Tell me, damn it," he managed. "Anne. Is she safe?"

"Your friend is fine," the nurse said in a soothing tone. "She was suffering from exhaustion by the time she finally got you down the hill to Madison, but a good night's sleep soon fixed her up."

Quinn closed his eyes and let relief wash over him. Anne was safe. For a beat of time he clung to that thought—until the rest of the nurse's words sank in.

"*She* got me down...the hill?" he asked. "How?"

"On a horse, I understand, slung over the saddle like a sack of oats. How she got you on the horse has to be a story in itself."

The nurse bustled around, checking the various tubes attached to him. Finally satisfied, she poured water into a glass, bent a plastic straw and lifted Quinn's head so that he could take a few sips. The tissues of his mouth were so dry that they seemed to absorb the water before he could swallow.

"Where...?" He started to cough, and pain lanced through his chest.

"In the waiting room. I'll fetch her, shall I?" Without waiting for an answer, the nurse hurried out.

Before Quinn could summon the strength to push himself higher on his pillow, Anne was there, bending over him, her hand clasping his. Her face was pale, her mouth even paler. Her hair was a shiny halo in the light, emphasizing the fragility of her features.

"Hi," she said softly. "We were beginning to think you were going to sleep for a week."

"We?"

Anne sensed the strain in his voice. It was an effort for him to speak. "Ed Franklyn is here, along with an army of guards."

"The Brigade?"

"Ed said to tell you they plugged the leak and not to worry about Meg and the ranch. He has people there, too. Just as you ordered, he said." She tried to force a teasing lilt into her voice, but the past seventy-two hours had stripped her of the last of her resilience.

The desperate search for the horses had taken her nearly a mile up the trail. She had found only one, Sadie. The struggle to get Quinn onto the mare's back had taken all her strength and patience, not to mention Sadie's.

The trip out of the gorge had seemed endless. The worst, though, had been waiting to find out if he would live or die.

"Damn it, Anne. You could have been killed," he managed, trying to touch her face. He discovered that his right arm was immobile, encased in plaster.

"I told you, I'm not much good at taking orders. You'd better remeber that."

"Oh yeah?"

"Yeah." Anne traced the line of his mouth with her fingertip. His normally dark skin was the color of ashes, his jaw covered with stubble. His hair was still matted and tangled.

Quinn was having trouble breathing, but it wasn't pain that was tormenting him. "We need to talk. To...get things straight between us."

Anne felt a flurry of fear in her stomach. "Not now, Quinn," she said quickly. "The nurse said—"

"Now." His voice was weak, but it still carried enough force to bring a frown to Anne's face.

His hand gripped hers tighter. "I thought you would be gone by now."

Anne felt a shiver of hurt move through her. "I couldn't leave until I knew you were out of danger."

"Am I?"

"Yes."

She leaned over to kiss him. Her hair fell free of the combs she had used to pull it back, tumbling over his neck. He groaned. Alarmed, she jerked backward.

"Is something wrong?" she asked.

His scowl deepened. "Hell yes, something's wrong."

Anne looked around anxiously, her eyes filled with worry. "I'll get the nurse—"

"No nurse. You're my problem."

"Me?"

Quinn managed a slight nod of his head. "I love you, damn it."

He glowered up at her as though he had just accused her of a heinous crime. Some of the tension pinching inside her eased.

"I know."

"You know?" he muttered, his voice gaining strength. Just being near Anne was the best medicine. "How could you know? I just figured it out myself."

Outwardly Anne beamed, but inside she was shaking. As gently as she could, she sat on his bed and entwined her fingers with his. "While you were unconscious, they wouldn't let me see you. I had to do something or go crazy, so I developed the pictures I took of you."

"Pictures?" he repeated slowly, as though he couldn't quite believe what he'd heard. His lips were dry, and he ran his tongue over them. It didn't help much.

"Yep. My camera was still on Sadie's pommel. Most of my film was in my saddlebags."

"So you...developed them?"

Anne nodded. "They're darn good, of course. But the best ones are of you. The first ones aren't as good, of course, but that was before you fell in love with me."

She felt his fingers tremble, and his eyes grew stormy. "I'm broke, Anne. Everything I have is mortgaged."

"I see." She pursed her lips. "You think I would only want you if you're rich."

He inhaled deeply, then winced at the hot stab of pain. "No, that's not what I think, damn it. I'm trying to tell you why it would never work between us."

Her eyes were soft and steady on his. He wanted to look away. He couldn't.

"Quinn, stop fighting it. We belong together. I love you. You love me. The camera doesn't lie."

"The hell it doesn't," he muttered, tightening his fingers on her. "It's ridiculous, you and me. I would make your life hell."

Anne lifted her free hand to his face and brushed back the tangled hair. "Probably."

"You're too stubborn for your own good."

"Yes."

"We'll fight."

"Definitely." She let her fingers trail down the hard, stubbled plane of his cheek. "And then we'll make up."

Quinn looked into eyes that were cloudy with desire. Something tore loose inside him, like the knot of a noose.

"I tried to make you leave me."

"I know. I figured that out before I even ran far enough to get out of breath. But I figured you wouldn't fuss as much if you thought I was on my way down the mountain."

His mouth tightened. "I don't fuss," he groused.

"No, you grumble and grouse and order me around like one of your *paniolos.*"

She leaned forward and touched her mouth to his. He groaned and his hand came up to trap her. "Damn it, I need you, you crazy woman." The words shuddered from him, bringing a rush of tears to her eyes.

"And I need you."

His mouth found hers. Excitement jolted through her. Soon they were both breathing hard.

Anne felt a tremor take him and pulled back. "You need to rest."

"Later," he muttered. "When are you going back to the mainland?"

Her eyes clouded. "Ed wants to go tonight. He's found me another place until the trial."

"Good idea."

"I want to stay here." Anne tried to nuzzle closer, but he stopped her.

"No. You'll go."

"Quinn—"

He pulled her down for a long satisfying kiss before whispering, "I need time to get used to the idea of getting married again."

Anne's mouth opened, then closed. "I...are you proposing to me?"

Quinn gave a snort. "Son of a gun, I think I am. Must be the pain pills."

Anne let the happiness trapped in her bubble out in laughter. She kissed him this time, then said in a saucy tone, "I accept, on one condition."

"What's that?"

"That I can take as many pictures as I want during my honeymoon."

Quinn groaned and closed his eyes. "I think I'm in big trouble here."

Anne giggled, caressing his face. "You want to have something to show our children, don't you?"

He opened his eyes, his throat clogged with a lump that felt suspiciously like tears. "Children?" he managed.

"Mmm. Maybe not eleven, like old Josiah. But two or three. If you're willing, that is."

For a long moment, Quinn was afraid to speak. A man didn't like to show his vulnerability to the woman he adored. "I'm willing," he said finally.

"There's one more thing you ought to know. Oliver women make terrific mothers."

After that, neither spoke.

Epilogue

Wearily, Quinn climbed the steps of the porch, slapping his hat against his hip to shake off the red dust. It was past twilight, and he was bone-tired from a day in the saddle. Hunger growled in his belly, and his throat was dry.

Another *kona* wind snatched at the palm fronds and bent the slender trunks. At the top of the steps, he paused to take another look at the rolling green pastures. Horses grazed in the paddock beyond newly painted fences. The cattle were settling for the night.

He waited, but the contentment he should be feeling refused to come. For a week now, since the end of Draygon's trial, he'd been restless and on edge.

Now that the Brigade's leader and his cohorts, including the mercenary informer on Franklyn's staff, were safely behind bars, now that the Brigade itself was in disarray and no longer a threat, there was no valid reason for Anne to remain on the mainland.

Still, she hadn't set a date to return to Hawaii.

"Soon," she'd said when he had called. There were so many things to do. Sell her town house, make arrangements for her goods to be shipped, her schedule of obligations to be rearranged.

Automatically, he turned his gaze toward the east. The sky was crowded with dark clouds. What if she didn't come? What if their four months apart had changed her mind? What if she'd decided that a poor

rancher and a quiet life in the islands weren't enough
for her?

Not that he would put chains on her. He wouldn't.
No one had the right to rein in a talent like hers. She
would come and go on her trips, and he would be
waiting.

If she hadn't decided that the feeling she had for
him wasn't really love after all.

Fear knotting his belly, Quinn turned and walked
into the old house. It was quiet. Meg and the tourists
were down by the pool, winding up another luau. He
could hear the ukeleles in the distance.

Shoulders slumped with more than fatigue, he took
the stairs one at a time. He was halfway up the first
flight when he realized he wasn't alone.

Anne was standing on the landing, in the spot where
countless Sinclair wives had waited for their husbands.

"It's about time you got home," she said, the smile
he loved trembling faintly. "I was about to saddle
Sadie and go out looking for you."

"Were you?" Quinn flung his hat toward the peg by
the door. It missed, but he didn't notice. His gaze was
fixed on the welcoming glow in her eyes.

"You work too hard," she murmured.

"I'm the boss. It's my job."

"Part of your job, my darling. The other part is
loving me."

Anne saw the flash of surprise in his eyes. He hadn't
believed in her, she thought. In their love. Perhaps he
still didn't. But he would, she thought with a small
sweet shiver of anticipation. Oh yes, my darling. It
may take me fifty years, but I'll take the pain from
your eyes.

Quinn reached the landing and swept her into his arms. She was soft and warm and smelled like the woman he worshipped. His kiss was hungry and yet sweetly tender. Anne pressed closer, enchanted all over again by the feel and taste and scent of him.

Her island cowboy. Her man.

"Welcome home, Ms. Oliver," he said when the kiss ended.

Anne smiled as she caressed his careworn face. "Mrs. Sinclair to you," she murmured. "Or have you forgotten that an Oliver woman always gets what she wants?"

"Thank God," he muttered before lifting her high off the floor into his arms. Anne wondered if old Josiah was watching. She hoped so.

Paula Detmer Riggs

I'm an only child.

Aha, you are now saying to yourself. That explains it. All only children are weird. Little hermits in training. Born recluses.

Alas, in my case that was indeed true. Not that I didn't have friends. I did. First it was *The Poky Little Puppy* and then later Nancy Drew and the Hardy Boys. I was content—until I was about ten and read *Gone With the Wind*.

It was stirring. It was thrilling. It was enthralling—until the end. When Rhett walked into the mist of Atlanta, I was devastated. Of course, that couldn't possibly be the way it happened, I told myself over and over.

Right? Right. Okay, so what did happen?

It took me weeks and weeks to devise an ending that suited me. I daydreamed through class after class, refining the he saids and then she saids until, finally, I was satisfied. Of course, Scarlett got her man. With that firmly implanted in my subconscious, I could get on with my life.

Years passed. Reading was always my first love—until I met a certain adorable naval midshipman.

My freshman composition prof told me that I had a gift for writing. Did I plan to become a writer? he asked.

My English lit prof gave me a C because I argued with him about Melville's use of symbolism in *Moby Dick*. What symbolism? I kept saying. It's a great example of storytelling, no more, no less. Good thing you aren't planning to become a writer, he sneered. Storytelling has nothing to do with literature.

I graduated, married my naval officer and kept on reading through nineteen moves in five years. When first one hyperactive son and then another came along, I turned to storytelling to keep them quiet long enough to get clothes on them every morning. I told stories in the car to keep them safe. I told stories at night to lull them to sleep. When my boys were teenagers and no longer interested in my stories, I went off to work. One day, I got fired.

Naturally, I went into a deep depression. I ate (mostly chocolate) and I read. After I'd gone through every book in our local library, I turned to the rack of romances.

From the first I was enthralled. I read while I cooked. I read late into the night. I read during the Padres games at the stadium. Hundreds and hundreds of romances. Soon I was haunting other branch libraries, searching for romances I hadn't read. At the time there were sixteen branches in San Diego. I soon had an intimate familiarity with all of them.

Ultimately, there came the day when I was reading faster than the authors could write. What did I do? Of course. I decided to write my own.

It wasn't easy. It wasn't particularly good, either. But it was the greatest high in the world when I finally finished. That book has never again seen the light of day.

My second, however, became part of the Intimate Moments line's "March Madness." The day I got the call remains one of my most cherished memories. I will be eternally grateful to Leslie Wainger for opening the door to the most wonderful part of my life.

At last. The weird, chubby little girl with glasses who always had her nose in a book gets to make up endings happily ever after.

Paula Detmer Riggs

THE LEOPARD'S WOMAN

Linda Lael Miller

The Lure of Mexico

A couple of years ago, I visited Arizona to speak at a writer's conference put on by the Tucson chapter of Romance Writers of America. The day after the conference, our hosts very kindly took me and several authors, Kathleen Eagle and Debbie Macomber among them, to Mexico for a day.

I was intrigued by the bustling marketplace, and I was carefully warned not to buy anything without bargaining first. My initial purchase was a plaid blanket, and I guess I didn't exactly hammer out a great deal, because the merchant ran after me to give me a hug of gratitude!

Being who we are, writers all, my friends and I could not resist speculating on all the romantic dramas that could take place in the raw Mexican countryside. Kathleen Eagle commented wryly, "Remember, girls, this is no place to get yourself kidnapped. The head *bandito* isn't going to carry you off on the glistening back of an ebony stallion and keep you for his own."

We laughed, but as I gazed toward the distant horizon, I gave a small and somewhat wistful sigh. I could dream, couldn't I?

Chapter One

Olivia Stillwell's wrists were bound behind her, and the filthy, rusted floor of the Jeep bruised her anew with every jostle and bump. In that one small corner of her mind that had not yet gone numb with terror, she reflected that this adventure would surely qualify her for a generous bonus—should she survive to collect.

The fierce Mexican sun pounded down, cooking her, unhindered by her sleeveless white cotton blouse and khaki slacks. Her shoulder-length auburn hair clung to the mixture of sweat and dust covering her face and neck, and she was pretty sure she was going to throw up if she had to travel another mile taped up like a lobster on its way to the boiling pot.

Not that Olivia wanted her abductors to stop. *Or* go on to whatever horrifying destination they had in mind, for that matter.

She closed her eyes, trying to retreat into the darkness inside her head, but there was no hiding place there, either. Scenes from B-movies she'd seen years before played in her mind in vivid color.

Olivia couldn't go forward mentally from there, and she certainly found the present intolerable, so she let her thoughts slide backward to the past.

Until that morning, Olivia's life had gone very well, all things considered.

Her Uncle Errol, who wrote fantastically successful romantic adventure novels for a predominantly
female audience, had hired her to work on his research staff five years before, after her graduation
from college. She'd loved the job immediately and
been good at it. Through attrition and a gradual ac-
cumulation of experience, Olivia had eventually
earned the right to direct the other staffers and take
her choice of the research assignments her uncle doled
out.

She'd earned her position through a lot of hard
work and innovative thinking, though of course a lot
of people didn't give her credit for personal effort.
Because she was Errol McCauley's only living relative, because he'd raised and educated her, almost
everyone assumed her exciting career had been handed
to her on the proverbial silver platter.

Even now, under these desperate circumstances,
Olivia yearned for an accomplishment of her own,
however modest.

For about the thousandth time, Olivia's right cheek
thumped against the Jeep floor. Just then, she thought
with desolate wryness, she'd have given her job to
anyone who asked for it.

Tears flooded her lashes, and she was relieved to
know she wasn't dehydrated to the point where she
couldn't cry. She sniffled. Only that morning, she'd
dined happily on the terrace of her hotel room,
shielded from the cruel sun by a bright red-and-white
awning. She'd finished her two-week research assignment—Uncle Errol was writing about a rich American heiress who, after many trials and tribulations,
married a matador—and decided to reward herself

with a few pieces of pottery from a special artists' colony she'd read about.

Olivia had a potter's wheel and a small kiln at home. In fact, she was quite good with clay, and she had aspirations to sell her own work at art shows and in galleries. As much as she loved her job and the adventures it provided, another side of her nature was developing. She wanted a new career, and a baby, not that one had much to do with the other.

After getting directions from a good-natured bellman, Olivia had set out for the compound in her rented car.

Somewhere in the desert, she'd taken a wrong turn, and the horrors that had followed would have sent Stephen King rushing for his typewriter, inspired.

First, the small sedan, which had seemed perfectly reliable when she'd left the secluded resort town of San Carlos, had overheated. The radiator had exploded, making hot water hiss against the underside of the hood, and of course there had been no starting the car again after that.

Still, Olivia had not been overly alarmed. After all, she'd been in similar predicaments in much wilder parts of the world—"soaking up atmosphere," as her uncle called it—places like Colombia and Morocco and Nepal. She'd had a canteen and there was sunscreen in her purse, along with a billed cap, and she'd never doubted for a moment that she'd find the artists' colony if she walked just a short way farther.

Someone there would take her back to the hotel.

Olivia had put on her sunglasses, slathered her face and arms with protective lotion, donned her neon-pink baseball cap and set off confidently down the rutted road. Several alarming creatures had scurried across her path, and she'd made mental notes about their coloring and size. The more details she brought home, the happier Uncle Errol would be; he liked to use a lot of vibrant description in his books.

Even after an hour, though, there was no sign of the art colony. All Olivia could see in any direction was desert and cacti and a very distant mountain range. She was doing some serious sweating by then, and her bravado turned rapidly to plain fear.

Then the Jeep had appeared, far off on the dusty ribbon of a road, flinging up brown plumes of dirt behind it.

Presently, the vehicle had come to a lurching stop beside Olivia, and she had seen instantly that these men, with their rifles and leering eyes, weren't planning to help her. She'd turned and fled into the desert, the sand so hot that it burned her feet even through the soles of her sandals, and they'd caught her easily.

Olivia had screamed and fought wildly, certain they meant to rape her and leave her to die, and the younger of the two *bandidos* had moved to backhand her. The other man had caught hold of his partner's wrist, staying the blow, and shouted furiously in Spanish.

After that, however, they'd pulled her hands behind her back and taped her wrists together. Her ankles were hobbled in much the same way, and a gag put on her mouth. Her cap had fallen off in the scuffle.

Olivia had lost track of how long they'd been traveling; it seemed like days, but she knew no more than a few hours had passed, if that.

She turned restlessly, giving a low moan. Her throat and sinuses burned with bile, and every muscle and bone in her body ached, but it was the fear that caused her the most suffering. She couldn't forget those terrible low-budget movies about young women taken captive in Mexico.

When they came to a jolting, unexpected stop, Olivia's head crashed into the back of a seat. Her heart seemed to collide with her windpipe.

The older man came around to the back, his shirt soaked in sweat, clasped Olivia's arm and pulled her upright. For a moment he wavered, like a shimmery figure in a mirage, and Olivia felt herself slipping into the darkness.

Her captor muttered urgently, again in Spanish too rapid and colloquial for Olivia to understand, untied the bandanna gag and raised a canteen to her mouth. She drank greedily; he scolded her and pulled the blessed water away until she realized he wanted her to sip slowly. She nodded, and the cool liquid flowed over her tongue again, metallic and sulfur-scented and more delicious than ambrosia.

When the *señor* finally withdrew the canteen, he gestured for Olivia to lie down again. She obeyed, since her options were so limited, and he covered her with a striped blanket, the kind sold to *turistas* in the marketplace, along with plaster statues, tablecloths and cheap jewelry. The Jeep set off again.

The heat underneath that thickly woven cover was excruciating in its intensity, but Olivia recognized a kindness when she saw one. Without that shelter, the brutal sun would literally have broiled her alive.

The trip went on and on, and Olivia began to drift in and out of consciousness. There was so much she hadn't done yet—making a place for herself in the art world, getting married, having babies, winning the Publisher's Clearing House Sweepstakes—she wanted to live! On the other hand, if she was about to be sold into white slavery, as she suspected, death seemed preferable.

As if anybody planned to give her a choice.

There was another water stop, but Olivia was in a dreamworld by then. She was back in Connecticut, in the attic of her uncle's wonderful old pre-Revolutionary house, happily spinning pots and vases and fruit bowls to be offered for sale at local craft shows.

The unbearable Mexican heat gradually went away and was replaced by a growing chill that finally revived Olivia, wrenching her back to bitter reality. She wasn't exactly grateful, but she *was* glad for the blanket.

Beneath her throbbing bones, the Jeep trundled mercilessly along, finding every pothole and rut, occasionally making a sudden swerve so that she was flung against the bolts that held the seats in place. She managed to wriggle enough to peer out from under the blanket with one eye, and she saw a galaxy of spectacular silver stars spread across the dark sky like a banner at some cosmic going-away party.

So long, Olivia. Too bad about all you'll be missing.

The idea of dying made her throat thicken with grief. She was only twenty-six, and the world was entirely too beautiful to leave.

The Jeep climbed, descended, climbed again. When it finally stopped and she heard new voices, all male and all speaking the native language, Olivia passed out.

When she awakened, she thought she was dead. Practically everything in the room where she found herself was covered in white linen, with the palest pastels for accent, and the place was comfortably cool. Beyond the open windows, turquoise waves capped in iridescent alabaster flirted with a sugar-white beach.

Olivia tried to speak, but her throat was too sore.

She sat up in bed, ran her hands over the coverlet, then the expensive cutwork sheets beneath. She was wearing a loose percale gown, and the skin on her arms was red and peeling, though swathed in some rich, soothing cream.

Despite the luxury surrounding her—there was a carafe of cool water on the bedside table, along with a crystal bowl brimming with fresh fruit—Olivia was terrified. This could not be a friendly place, not when she'd been brought here by *bandidos*. Maybe she was in a sort of halfway house, about to be sent to South America, or maybe somewhere like Libya....

The thing to do, of course, was to find her clothes, climb over the terrace and make a break for it. She'd travel on foot if she had to; if she was lucky, she would be able to steal a car. Fortunately, she wouldn't need a key—she'd learned to hotwire engines as part of the research for her uncle's last book.

Carefully, flinching at the pain of her bruises and sunburn, Olivia pushed back the covers and climbed out of the fancy four-poster bed. Her knees immediately folded, and she barely kept herself from toppling to the white woven rug.

Groping, she retreated back to the mattress. Her head was pounding from even that small effort, and her stomach was queasy. She had to get away—as horrible as her kidnapping had been, Olivia was certain the worst was yet to come—but she didn't have the strength.

She gasped when the door opened suddenly, but the visitor was only a mild-looking Mexican woman in her late fifties or early sixties. Neither fat nor thin, she was wearing a pale pink cotton dress and no shoes, and her smile was reassuring.

If this woman was involved in white slavery, she certainly didn't look the part. She said hello in Spanish—the first bit of conversation Olivia had understood since leaving the hotel in San Carlos—and approached the bed.

Olivia asked haltingly if the woman spoke English, and the answer was a regretful shake of the head.

"Maria," the woman said, indicating herself by placing curled fingers against her bosom. Then she gestured toward her guest in question.

"Olivia," said the captive.

Maria smiled and poured a glassful of water from the carafe, then held it gently to Olivia's lips.

Olivia drank gratefully, her nausea subsiding. She settled gingerly back against the pristine pillows, staring up at the ceiling. There were so many things she wanted to ask about, but chattering away at the well-meaning Maria would merely tax her sore throat and strain her already taut nerves.

She must have slept, for when she opened her eyes again, the sunlight pouring through the terrace doors was thinner, and it met the stone floor at a different angle. There was a rap at the door, and Olivia, expecting the gentle Maria, was not as alarmed as she might have been.

Until the visitor entered the room, that is.

He was the most beautifully built man Olivia had ever seen, standing just over medium height. His hair was rich and dark and slightly too long, and the sides were brushed back sleekly, like the wings of a bird. His skin was like fine sandalwood, and his teeth were improbably white, but it was the color of his eyes that really caught Olivia's attention. They were not brown or black, like those of most Mexican people; they were a deep, arresting shade of violet.

Olivia had every reason to believe the white slaver had arrived at last, and despite her raw throat, she opened her mouth and gave a croaky cry.

He paused and looked back, as though expecting to see a monster following him, smiled, then closed the door.

Olivia let out another hoarse yelp, scrambled to her knees, groped for the fruit bowl beside the bed and sent a pomegranate hurling across the room. It missed his head and split against the door. "Stay back, you pimp!" she screamed.

He laughed, resting his gloved hands on his lean hips. He was wearing cotton pants with shiny silver buttons lining the outside seams, high black boots and a cream-colored shirt open halfway down his chest. In fact, he looked for all the world like one of Uncle Errol's legendary heroes come to life.

"I'm glad to see that I have bought myself a woman with spirit," he said.

Chapter Two

Esteban Ramirez braced himself for a barrage of fruit, since the bowl beside the bed was still full of apples, bananas, pomegranates and oranges, but nothing happened. His lovely, if parboiled, guest just knelt there in the middle of the bed, staring at him in proud, defiant horror.

He felt a peculiar tightening sensation in a hidden region of his heart and knew he'd turned a corner of some kind, that his life would never be quite the same again.

Esteban brought himself up short. Now he was getting sentimental.

He took pity on the woman, though he suspected pity was the last thing she'd want even under the circumstances, and raised both hands, palms out, in a conciliatory gesture. He sincerely believed he was communicating friendliness and safety.

"What is your name?" he asked in polite, precise English. It was possible, of course, that the combination of her terrifying experience and the relentless Mexican sun had done some damage to her mind, permanent or otherwise.

"What do you care about my name?" she retorted after a moment of blustery hesitation. Her arms were folded across her well-shaped breasts, her chin set at an obstinate angle. Even with blisters and bruises covering her sunburned flesh, she was beautiful in an elemental sort of way, like the varying landscapes of Mexico.

Esteban swallowed hard. He had never encountered such a saucy woman before, even on his frequent trips to the United States, and he was both charmed and infuriated by her audacity.

"I demand that you let me go," she rushed on. "If you don't, I promise you I will find a way to summon the police!"

Esteban laughed, delighted by her fighting spirit and more than a little relieved. The mind behind those pewter eyes was as sharply cognizant as his own. "This is a very remote part of Mexico," he said, giving the last word its native pronunciation. "Believe me, you're better off dealing with me than with the *federales*." He folded his arms. "I ask you again, *señorita*. What is your name?"

"What is yours?" she countered, testy as a cornered scorpion.

He should have been reassuring the woman, he knew that—Maria would have him horsewhipped if she found out he hadn't laid the visitor's fears to rest right at the outset—but he was enjoying the game too much. Just being near this woman was like drinking cold well water after a savage thirst. "Esteban Ramirez," he conceded, lifting one side of his mouth in a smile.

She raised an eyebrow and pushed a lock of beautiful tarnished-copper hair back from her face. "Esteban. That's a version of Steven, isn't it?" She looked him over after his nod, as though deciding whether or not the name suited him. If she decided it didn't, he thought, she just might change it to something she thought fitting. "You're certainly not the kind of guy people would call 'Steve,'" she observed.

Esteban held back a chuckle, but he supposed his amusement showed in his eyes, the dark blue eyes bequeathed to him by his American grandmother. "No," he agreed. "I don't think 'Steve' would suit me very well." He stopped, waiting. Although he was certain he was doing a good job of hiding the fact, she'd shaken him, this fierce invader with hair the color of a tiger's coat.

"Olivia," she finally threw out, but grudgingly. "Olivia Stillwell, though I don't see that it matters. A slave doesn't really need a name."

"You are not a slave, Miss Stillwell—it is 'Miss,' isn't it?" Esteban asked the question in an offhand tone, with a slight and very Latin shrug, but it suddenly seemed as if the *rancho*, his grandfather's silver mines, everything he owned and had ever dreamed of, everything he *was*, depended on her answer.

Remarkable, he thought. I need to get out more.

"Would you let me go if I were married? Because if you expect a virgin, you've got the wrong woman."

Esteban's heartbeat was irregular. He shouldn't have cared whether Olivia Stillwell had ever been with a man or not, but he did. He hoped she had, and at the same time hoped she hadn't. "As I said before, you are not a prisoner. When you are well, you are free to go wherever you wish."

She narrowed her marvelous gray eyes in obvious distrust. "I was kidnapped, Señor Ramirez, brought here against my will. And you said yourself that you bought me!"

"Yes, I bought you. I thought that would be kinder than letting you be passed on to the next prospect, who might not have been so—" he shrugged again "—enlightened."

"I want to go home."

"And you shall. When you have had time to recover from your ordeal."

"No. I have to leave right now. If you'll just let me call my uncle in Connecticut, I'm sure he'll arrange for special transportation."

She didn't have a husband or a lover, Esteban concluded. If she had, she wouldn't have suggested calling an uncle. The realization filled him with a strange joy, but in the wake of that emotion came a quavering despair at the thought of her leaving.

This conflict, well hidden, he hoped, made Esteban furious with himself. He had his choice of women all over the world, far more sophisticated and beautiful ones than she. He did not need this inconsequential redheaded snippet covered in freckles and sunburn and bravado.

Much.

"It is one hundred and fifty miles to the nearest telephone," he said, attempting to speak reasonably. He had already assured Miss Stillwell at least twice that she wasn't a prisoner, but apparently she still wasn't convinced.

It seemed impossible, but Olivia's face actually got redder. "But my uncle will be worried!"

"Things move slowly in Mexico," Esteban said.

She was persistent, which wasn't surprising, really. She had survived an experience that would have devastated most anyone else. "You must have a short-wave radio in case of emergencies. You could relay a message that way."

Esteban sighed. "No," he said. "Here we live much as our grandparents did." He saw her glance at the kerosene lamp on the bedside table, then at the ceiling where a light fixture would have been in another, more modern house. Clearly, she registered the significance of that. "There is a generator to power the hot-water heater and the appliances in the kitchen," he finished.

She shook her head in obvious annoyance. "No radio?" she asked like a skeptical tourist. "No telephone, no TV, no fax machine?"

He chuckled, wanting to go to the side of the bed and take Olivia gently into his arms, but unwilling to frighten her. "Sorry. Things are pretty low-tech around here. Maria has a small television set that runs on batteries. Somehow, though, I do not think you would enjoy Spanish-dubbed reruns of 'Gilligan's Island.'"

She scooted backward, her lower lip jutting out slightly, and hid everything but her head under the lightweight covers. "You haven't been a whole lot of help, Señor Ramirez," she pointed out.

He smiled, reaching back for the doorknob. He was through trying to make his case with the woman, for the time being at least. She didn't believe a word he said, and that irritated him sorely, since the trait Esteban most cherished was his integrity. "Haven't I? If it weren't for me, Miss Stillwell, you would probably be wishing you were dead right about now."

Her eyes went wide at the reminder of what could have happened, but then they flashed with silver fire again. "You'll pardon me if I don't thank you for holding me prisoner in this house," she said stiffly.

Esteban sighed and opened the door to leave, even though her slender figure seemed to be giving off some kind of electromagnetic charge from beneath the loosely woven covers. His whole being, flesh and spirit, strained toward her, and it took all his strength to resist. "I would never expect gratitude from a spoiled American schoolgirl with no better sense than to go wandering in the desert by herself," he replied. The words were sharp, uttered out of self-defense.

A second piece of fruit struck the door just as he closed it behind him. He grinned as he walked down the hall.

The *rancho,* as much as he loved it, could be a lonely place. For the next few days, at least, the energetic Miss Stillwell would lend some pizzazz to his normally quiet life.

Maria brought lunch soon after Esteban's departure, a wonderful gazpacho, and her friendly concern made Olivia ashamed of the fruit pieces scattered over the floor. While she sheepishly consumed her soup, the housekeeper cleaned up the mess, her expressive mouth drawn up in a soft, speculative smile.

"I wish you spoke English," Olivia said when she'd finished eating and Maria was lifting the tray from her lap. "Then we could talk. I could tell you about my Uncle Errol and the prizes I've won for my pottery, and you could tell me about your boss. He's plainly a bastard—Señor Ramirez, not my uncle—but I suppose you probably like him."

Maria was listening politely, even though she clearly didn't understand more than a few scattered words. When Olivia wound down, the other woman smiled again and said something gentle.

After Maria left the room, Olivia got out of bed, her legs still incredibly shaky beneath her, and made her way into the adjoining bathroom. At least the place had indoor plumbing; that was some consolation.

Back in bed, she tried to come up with a plan of escape, dramatic or otherwise, but her thoughts were still too muddled—not surprising, after the way the sun had sautéed her brain the day before. She closed her eyes and slept, awaking hours later to find Maria lighting the lamp on her bedside stand. There was a simple meal laid out on the white wicker table in the corner of the room.

"Buenas noches," Maria greeted her.

The lamplight gave the room a cozy ambience, and Olivia could almost forget that she was virtually a captive in this house. Dinner consisted of rice and a not-too-spicy but very colorful mixture of sliced chicken breast, red and green peppers, carrots and onions.

She made a point of saying *gracias* when Maria returned to carry away the empty dishes and the silverware, and the housekeeper beamed.

For a few minutes, Olivia had been able to forget that she was in a strange and dangerous situation, for all the attendant luxuries. After Maria had left again, however, Olivia felt bereft. She enjoyed the housekeeper's company, even with the language barrier between them, and was grateful for the other woman's help.

It had been Maria, Olivia knew, who had bathed her when she'd first come to the *rancho*—she remembered it vaguely, like a scene from a fevered dream— Maria who had treated her abrasions with antiseptic and her sunburn with cooling lotion. She owed her silent friend a tremendous debt.

Restless, Olivia decided to venture out onto the terrace. Maybe there was a trellis or something, and in a few days, when she was stronger, she could climb down and run away. Maybe she would even discover that the room was on the ground floor of the house, though she doubted that.

She unlatched the French doors and stepped out onto the terrace. A shock of tropical beauty made her suck in her breath almost as though someone had struck her.

This was not the sand-spider-and-cacti Mexico she remembered from before the kidnapping. No, here there were palm trees swaying against a star-spangled sky, and silvery moonlight wavered on water so blue that its color was discernible even in the relative darkness.

Directly below the terrace was a courtyard of brick and marble, complete with an enormous fountain, tropical flowers in Garden-of-Eden pinks and blues and yellows, and white wrought-iron benches. It was all lit by the moon and stars and by chunky candles glimmering inside glass bowls.

Enchanted, Olivia moved along the railing, looking for a way down. There were no trellises or trees; indeed, the only way would be to take a twelve-foot drop into the hot tub, and she didn't feel quite that adventurous.

As she watched, the emerald-colored water in the tub began to bubble and churn. She was completely unprepared for Esteban's sudden appearance; he crossed the tiled deck, magnificently naked, except for the odd shadow, and lowered himself in.

Olivia was mesmerized for a long moment, though she knew she should retreat. Her face ached with color when he looked up, his teeth as white as the snowy orchids that grew in glorious tangles along the edge of the courtyard.

"Would you like to join me?" he inquired.

Mortified at being caught watching a naked man, Olivia took the offensive in an effort to hide her vulnerability. "You bought me. I suppose you could command it."

Esteban laughed, and the sound reached up through the warm darkness like a caress, making Olivia's breasts feel full and heavy and producing a sharp ache in her most feminine parts. "If I commanded you to come down here, would you obey?"

"Of course not."

He spread his hands, still looking up. "There you have it," he said with a sigh of resignation. "It is almost impossible to find a good love slave these days."

Olivia bit her lower lip, glad she hadn't tried taking a dive from the terrace railing. Judging the depth of the water by the fact that it reached just to Esteban's waist, she realized she would have compressed her skull into her tailbone. "I thought you said there was no electricity here," she challenged, desperate to change the subject, because all of the sudden she didn't find the idea of being Esteban's captive all that unappealing.

"This?" He indicated the hot tub. "I told you—we have a portable generator. Several, in fact."

Olivia folded her arms. "I think you're holding out on me, Señor Ramirez. I demand that you release me immediately."

"Be my guest," Esteban said, gesturing toward the great world beyond the edge of the courtyard. "I would advise you to head north, carry as much water as you can and avoid being kidnapped again. You were very lucky the first time."

He was right, and damn, Olivia hated that. The least he could do was be wrong once in a while.

"Yes," she said stiffly. "Well, thank you."

Esteban settled comfortably in the hot tub, resting his muscular arms along the sides. Olivia couldn't tell for certain, but she was pretty sure he'd closed those beautiful, sensual eyes of his, giving himself up to the heat and motion of the water.

"You're welcome, Olivia," he said presently, sounding relaxed and resigned. "Anytime you're staggering through the desert, please feel free to have your abductors bring you here. I will be happy to buy you, though I don't think you would command such a high price the second time."

Olivia knew Esteban was teasing her, and she wasn't amused. "Naturally, I will repay you as soon as I can reach my bank—"

She knew he had opened his eyes, felt his gaze even through the stone railing of the terrace and the thin nightgown she was wearing. "You will indeed," he replied formally, "but I have all the money I need. You'll have to think of some other way to settle the debt, Miss Stillwell."

Chapter Three

Olivia told herself Esteban was only teasing—surely, even in this backward place, he didn't expect her to repay her ransom with her body—but there was enough uncertainty to unnerve her completely. She fled into her room and pushed the terrace doors shut behind her.

Her cheeks were throbbing with a heat far greater than a Mexican sun could have produced, and she stood there in the dim, romantic light of the kerosene lamps, her hands pressed to her face. Although she wanted desperately to disavow her feelings and the images unfolding in her mind, they would not be denied.

Except for a single, highly forgettable love affair in college, Olivia had no real sexual experience. In fact, the one man she'd been with had left her convinced that the whole experience was wildly overrated.

Now, having met Esteban Ramirez, Olivia was beginning to doubt her convictions, not just mentally, but physically. Even being in the same room with him seemed to send a super-charge through her whole body, and it apparently didn't matter whether the conversation was worthwhile or totally banal. In fact, she wasn't sure it mattered if there *was* a conversation.

She climbed back into bed, but she couldn't stop the torrent of imaginings sparked by the sight of Esteban striding naked across the courtyard below, as dangerously graceful as some fierce jungle cat.

She considered the things men and women did together in Uncle Errol's books—they were certainly nothing like the timid encounters Olivia had had with her idealistic poet back at Northwestern—and was shaken by a hot shiver. It was only too easy to imagine doing those things with Esteban, to picture—and God help her, *feel*—his hard, commanding body settling over hers, claiming hers.

Olivia closed her eyes, trying to steady herself against the tide of desire thundering through her. She sank her teeth into her lower lip and attempted to make her mind a blank, but the scenes kept unfurling. Maybe, she thought, it *wasn't* just fiction, the stuff of books and movies, as she'd always believed. She reached out an arm and clung to the bedpost as though fearing she'd be swept away by some invisible flood. Maybe there really were uncharted parts of her nature, places in her being where only a man like Esteban could take her—

"Stop it!" she hissed, now truly desperate to derail her train of thought. Señor Ramirez claimed he'd bought her only to protect her, but he might be lying. He could be a white slaver himself, a link in a chain of criminals, planning to feed and care for her only until she was in a more marketable condition. Why else would he have refused to help her get in touch with her uncle?

Olivia forced herself to relax, but because she'd done so much sleeping during the day, she wasn't the least bit tired. She lay staring up at the ceiling, once again considering her ridiculous plight.

One scenario, being sold to some filthy man as a plaything, or even forced into prostitution, left her chilled with fear. The alternative vision, lying with Esteban in that very bed, doing some of the things she'd read about, made her break into a sweat.

She figured she'd have pneumonia by morning, what with all these abrupt changes in body temperature, if she didn't figure out a way to get a grip.

Somewhere toward dawn, Olivia drifted off, and her dreams were full of whirling colors and churning emotions. When she awakened in the morning, she felt as though she'd spent the night driving railroad spikes into rocky ground.

Seeing her own blouse and slacks lying across the back of a chair raised her spirits considerably. The garments were mended in places, but they'd been washed and pressed, and her underwear was there, too. The prospect of dressing made Olivia feel less like a prisoner.

She took a quick shower, smoothed on the special aloe-vera lotion Maria had been treating her with and put on her clothes. After brushing her hair and teeth and making up the bed, Olivia ventured over the threshold of her room for the first time since her arrival.

The house had a sort of mezzanine with railings on all sides, and below was an indoor courtyard. There were lush green plants in beautiful pots, along with a fountain encircled by a stone bench. Somewhere out of sight, birds sang a muted concert.

Olivia made her way down stone steps, her mind rolling like a wheel spinning downhill. Descriptions of the house would make for authentic detail in her uncle's current book; she wanted to remember everything until she could find paper and pen to write it all down.

Growing bolder with every passing moment, Olivia began to explore, making all kinds of mental notes as she went. There was a big formal dining room, so Esteban probably entertained, despite the isolation of his house. The study walls were lined with books not only in English and Spanish, but French, as well, which meant, to her, that her host was well educated; the substantial, ornately carved desk said he appreciated fine things.

Olivia progressed to a smaller room, outfitted with all sorts of workout equipment, and smiled to herself. That explained, at least partly, why Esteban was so sleekly muscular. He was into pumping iron.

At the front of the house, facing the shining sea, was a magnificent room with floor-to-ceiling windows. The basic color scheme was a clean, soothing beige, accented by splashes of turquoise and pale peach, and the overall effect was one of the room and the ocean being somehow linked in mystical harmony.

Just being there, mentally getting into step with the silent music of the place, gave Olivia a sensation of being touched, healed. She yearned to capture the sumptuous colors and textures, indeed the soul of Mexico itself, in pottery.

"Good morning."

She jumped, startled by the unexpected voice, and turned to see Esteban standing just inside the doorway, at the top of the three stone steps leading down into the living room. "Good morning," she made herself say, speaking in what she hoped was a calm tone. She didn't want him to know how he frightened her, how he haunted her thoughts and the secret places in her soul that she herself had never visited before.

He was wearing dusty riding pants, black, with the same flashy silver buttons along the outside seams, an equally dusty white shirt opened far enough to reveal a sweaty, well-muscled chest, and a short leather vest.

On anybody else, Olivia reflected, the outfit would have looked silly. On him, well, it inspired dangerous fantasies.

Esteban looked down at his splendidly disheveled frame. "Is something wrong?"

Olivia's face heated; it wasn't the dusty grime that had made her stare and he knew it as well as she did. "I guess it's messy work, running a place like this." She paused. "What kind of place *is* this, anyway?"

He smiled, and the effect was blinding. "I thought you knew," he said, leaning against the doorjamb. "This is a *rancho*. We raise horses and cattle here." He stopped to lift one shoulder. "And there are a couple of silver mines."

It could all be a lie, Olivia reminded herself. A cover for white slavery, or maybe drug-running. She retreated a step at the thought, unable to keep her eyes from going wide.

Esteban looked puzzled for a moment, then assaulted her with another of his lethal smiles. "Relax, Miss Stillwell," he said. "If I were going to drag you off to my bed and use you without mercy, do you really think I would have restrained myself this long?"

Olivia was at once injured and relieved. Naturally she didn't want to be dragged off and used without

mercy, as he put it, but she had some very primitive
fantasies where this man was concerned, and it hurt to
realize he would probably find them amusing.

Since she didn't know how to answer his question
gracefully, she simply turned away, pretending to be
absorbed in the view. As breathtaking as it was,
though, Olivia could think of nothing but the man
behind her.

When he laid his hands to her shoulders, she
flinched, for she hadn't sensed his approach.

Esteban's touch was incredibly gentle and tender; he
might have been a poet, instead of a *bandido* with the
heart of a dangerous jungle creature. He turned Olivia, studied her face with mingled bewilderment and
defiance in his wonderful violet eyes, and then he
kissed her.

Olivia stiffened; nothing in her experience, or even
in the night of erotic dreams just past, had prepared
her for this. It was like embracing lightning; the power
jolted her, making her sway so that Esteban's grip on
her shoulders tightened.

He tasted her lips as though they were coated with
honey, then persuaded her mouth to open for him.
The invasion of his tongue was gentle, but it was
compelling, too; for Olivia it was like being conquered, right there in the middle of that sunny living
room. Excitement twisted into a tight spiral within her.

When he finally withdrew, her breasts were still
pressing against his hard chest, the nipples taut. She
was stunned by the incomprehensible force of her desire.

He lifted his hand and caressed her cheek, then
moved the pad of his thumb over her lower lip.

"I'm sorry," he said. "You are a guest here, and I should not have taken advantage of you."

Olivia didn't respond; she was too afraid she would burst into tears if she tried to speak. She was still overwhelmed by the force of his kiss, and by the new and frightening awareness that she had crossed a significant personal threshold. In some unaccountable way, Esteban Ramirez had changed her forever. She felt stronger, vibrantly alive, more truly herself than ever before.

He looked at her for a moment, as though studying a stranger he knew he should recognize but didn't, then turned and walked out of the room, pulling on his leather riding gloves as he went.

Olivia stood for a long time, as immobile as the statue in the middle of the fountain in the outer courtyard, simultaneously willing him to return and thanking God that he didn't. The fires he'd started inside her were still smoldering, and the yearning he'd created was so strong that she feared a violent eruption even then. Just walking across the room would have been a risk.

Finally, however, Olivia recovered most of her composure, if not all, and continued her explorations. She encountered Maria in the kitchen, a large and airy place full of light and color, and was forced to eat a breakfast of fresh cornbread, fruit and something that might have been either pudding or yogurt.

After that, Olivia tried to wash her dishes, but Maria shooed her out, waving her white apron and uttering a flurry of Spanish words. Finding a large straw hat lying on a bench on the portico out back, Olivia donned that as protection from the sun and set out for a look at the surrounding terrain.

Esteban and his men were busy over by the corrals, raising dust and shouting. Still sensitive to the glaring sun, Olivia returned to the house. More explorations brought her to the study, where she began thumbing idly through a series of leather-bound albums. The pages were covered with clippings from newspapers and magazines, both in Spanish and English, touting the exploits of *el leopardo*. The Leopard.

Olivia felt a shiver. The scrapbooks were obviously Maria's work, and she soon divined that *el leopardo* was none other than Esteban Ramirez himself. Shaken, she only skimmed a few of the articles that were printed in English, and she made little sense of their contents. All she'd really grasped was that Esteban had another identity.

Discomfited, Olivia left the house again and started toward the white beach. The Leopard. If she didn't know better, Olivia could have sworn she'd stumbled into one of her uncle's stories. It would have been pretty amusing if it hadn't been so scary, and if she hadn't been so attracted to Esteban.

The nickname certainly fit Esteban, she had to admit that. He had the sleek prowess and deadly strength of a leopard. And he might well share other traits. He might be vicious; he might, like the animal, stalk his prey, run it to the ground, tear out its throat.

Olivia made her way along a path lined with thick tropical foliage and onto the beach, her thoughts in even more turmoil than before.

The Leopard. Perhaps Esteban really was a white slaver or a drug lord, as she'd first thought. Or maybe he was simply a *bandido*. He had been quick to assure Olivia that she could go back home as soon as she had "recovered" and, although he'd teased her unmercifully, he had not brought her to his bed. None of which meant that the men who'd kidnapped her hadn't been working for him in the first place.

Olivia had been in some bewildering situations in her life, but this one set a real precedent.

Coming to an inlet sheltered by palm trees and foliage, Olivia sat down on the ground, removed her hat, kicked off her sandals. The sand was so white and fine, she thought, sifting some through her fingers, that she could have stirred it into her tea like sugar.

There was something calming about the little hidden pool, and Olivia's troubled mind began to quiet down. Despite her misgivings, she had a sense of returning to Paradise.

Presently, when she could no longer resist, she took off her trusty blouse and khaki slacks and waded in. The waist-deep water reflected the heart-wrenching royal blue of the sky, and it was so clean and clear that Olivia could see the fine white pebbles on the bottom. The coolness was like balm to her skin, so she slipped under the surface to wet her hair, too.

When she came up, lashes beaded with water, just beginning to absorb the delicious peace of the place, Esteban was standing on the bank, staring at her.

El leopardo, she thought, in that dazed moment before alarm overtook her. He certainly moved with the same stealth as a leopard.

Chapter Four

Belatedly, Olivia folded her arms across her breasts. It was no comfort that Esteban was obviously just as shocked to find her in the pool as she was to see him standing at its edge; the situation was no less perilous for his surprise.

"What are you doing here?" he finally demanded, resting his hands on his hips. He was covered in dust from his magnificent head to the soles of his expensive leather boots.

Olivia's mouth dropped open. She'd been about to ask *him* that question. "I beg your pardon?" she croaked after another few moments of hesitation.

"This is my private place," Esteban said, and once again, Olivia had a sensation of returning to the Lost Garden. She might have been Eve, and the man standing on the shore, Adam.

She bristled. "I'm sorry."

Incredibly, he grinned. "You don't look sorry."

Olivia was still flustered. "I didn't think I had to ask for permission to swim in the ocean, that's all."

He began stripping off his clothes, his motions practiced and uncalculated. "This is not the ocean," he said implacably. "It's a spring-fed pool." He paused, inclining his head as he studied her. "I hope you will not be so foolish as to swim in the sea, Miss Stillwell. The currents are dangerous, and there are sharks."

Sharks and currents were the least of her problems. "Perhaps you could just come back later," Olivia suggested cheerfully, growing more nervous as he shrugged off his shirt and reached for his belt buckle.

Esteban shook his head, sat down in the sand and wrenched off one of his boots. "*You* can come back later," he countered, removing the other boot and tossing it aside to lie akimbo with its mate. He looked mildly irritated. "*Madre de Dios,* you American women are petty tyrants, for all your talk about independence and personal liberty."

Olivia narrowed her eyes, crouching in the water and trying to cover herself with her arms, painfully conscious that the pool was as transparent as crystal. "That was uncalled for. I didn't attack your masculinity, for heaven's sake. I just suggested that you might want to leave your bath for another time. Besides, I can't very well get out with you sitting there gawking at me, now can I?" She took a breath. "Furthermore, I'll thank you not to insult every woman in my country just because you don't like me!"

Esteban stood again and began removing his pants. He flashed her a dazzling grin before she looked away. "I'm hot and dirty and tired, Miss Stillwell," he said. "I've been looking forward to taking a cool bath in this pool all day. Therefore, if you don't wish to share it with me, you'd better get out." Having made his decree, *el patrón* speaking to the *peón,* Esteban splashed into the water.

Try though she did to keep her eyes averted, Olivia's gaze went right to him like a magnet.

Good heavens, even Michelangelo had never sculpted such a man. Only God could have achieved that kind of grace and perfection.

Soon, Esteban stood only a few feet from Olivia, in the liquid crystal of the pool. It was almost as though time had stopped, and the universe had gone still around them.

"You are very lovely." He said the words like an offhand statement of fact, as though he were admiring a piece of art in a museum.

"Stop looking at me," Olivia snapped, but her response didn't carry the strength of conviction it should have. She was busy struggling to assimilate all the new feelings this man engendered in her.

His laughter was a joyous shout. "Not a chance," he said when his amusement had abated, giving another of his south-of-the-border shrugs.

Olivia edged toward the spot where she'd left her clothes. Then she scrambled out of the pool, grabbed them and delved into the dense foliage, where she began pulling them on over tender, wet skin. It was a frustrating task.

"This is a fine way to treat company," she muttered. "I mean, you'd think, after all I've been through, that I could take a bath in peace, but *no—*"

Esteban laughed again. Olivia couldn't help looking at him, seeing the sun catch in the beads of water in his hair and eyelashes, on his brown chest. "Don't go," he pleaded good-naturedly. "Your virtue is safe with me, I promise."

"Oh, right," Olivia snapped. Her disappointment at being driven from the pond was all out of proportion to good sense. "You're a regular Zorro!"

"Please," he said with a gentle authority. "Stay."

Olivia had fully intended to leave, and in high dudgeon, too, but instead she sank to a sitting position in the warm sand. She wasn't anxious to get back to the real world or, in point of fact, to leave the company of this disturbingly charming and irritating man. Besides, she felt shaky from all that activity.

"I'm not staying because you told me to," she said, lifting her chin. Her clothes clung to her damp skin. "I just want to be here, that's all." The lower half of Esteban's body seemed to waver under the water, like a distorted image in a mirror.

"Of course," he replied, as cordial as Ricardo Montalban greeting a new arrival on Fantasy Island. "Would you mind tossing me the soap?"

It was a simple request, and the bar he'd brought with him was within reach. Olivia complied, but when Esteban began washing his hair, there was something so intimate in the act that she felt they would always be linked by it.

Her blood heated, and her thoughts alone were enough to ensure damnation.

She let her forehead rest on her updrawn knees, willing her heartbeat to slow down and her breathing to be even again. The trouble was, she kept having these images of herself lying with Esteban, not there on the sand, but in a cool, shadowy room between smooth linen sheets. She should just go back to the house right now, she told herself sternly, but she remained as she was, somehow detached from her normally strong will.

Olivia was not prepared for feeling Esteban settle in the sand next to her, his skin cool and wet from the pool. Out of the corner of her eye, she saw that he was wearing a towel around his midsection, but nothing else.

"Oh, God," she said.

He cupped her chin in his hand, gently turned her face, and kissed her. When his tongue entered her mouth, and one of his hands curved lightly around her breast, the thumb chafing her nipple to attention, Olivia figured the inner tumult he caused her would register at least 9.9 on the Richter scale.

She trembled as he eased her backward into the sand and stretched out beside her. Although she spread her fingers across the roughness of his damp chest, she could not, would not, push him away. The attraction was simply too ferocious, but even so, Olivia knew she was *choosing* to make this tentative surrender.

He moved over her, let her feel the hardness and the power of his body without crushing her under its weight, but the towel and her clothes remained between them.

Finally, mercifully, he released her mouth, and Olivia gasped with relief, only to give a whispered gasp as he began nibbling at her neck. When he opened her bodice and bared a waiting breast to his lips and tongue, she wove her fingers into his hair and held him close, unable to protest. The feeling of his mouth on her nipple was fiery and sweet, and she wanted it to go on and on.

When Olivia was writhing in the sand beneath him, Esteban turned gracefully onto his back and drew her along, so that she lay with her breast above his mouth like ripe fruit on a vine. He wedged his thigh between her legs and gently gripped her hips, moving her tantalizingly against the steely muscle. All the while, he suckled hungrily at her nipple.

Olivia was utterly and completely lost.

Something was happening inside her, something Olivia had only read about before. Something on a level with the formation of a new universe.

After an eternity of moments, she reached the pinnacle she'd been straining toward with both body and soul. Her body arched in a shattering explosion of pleasure, and she thrust her head back and shouted hoarsely to the sky. Esteban drank from her until the sweet spasms had finally passed and she'd fallen, exhausted, to the sand beside him.

"El leopardo," she whispered, still too dazed to think coherently.

But Esteban gripped her shoulders hard, and wrenched her into an upright position. "What did you say?"

Olivia stared at him for a moment, still drunk on the release, her breasts still bared to his gaze. "I called you *el leopardo,"* she finally said, confused.

"Tell me why," he rasped, giving her a slight shake.

Olivia was bewildered, and she hesitated to mention the scrapbooks she'd seen in the study. She sensed that they were private, and maybe he didn't want her to know about his exploits.

Whatever those exploits had been.

"I came across a reference to the Leopard, that's all," she replied, her body still thrumming from his skillful attentions. "It wasn't hard to guess it was you."

He released his hold on her shoulders, and she was almost sorry that the contact was broken. It had not been painful, after all, but there had been a certain command in his hold that strong women sometimes go a lifetime without finding.

"You didn't hear anyone refer to me by this name?" he asked after a long time, looking not at Olivia but at the dancing blue-topaz surface of the pool. "You did not see men who looked out of place among the others?"

Olivia touched his shoulder with one hand and distractedly closed her bodice with the other. A tentative smile twitched on her lips. "I don't think so—I don't even know any of your men by name," she pointed out quietly. "What's the matter, Esteban? Why does this upset you so much?"

He thrust himself to his feet, snatched up his pants and let the towel drop to the sand, leaving the choice of watching or looking away to Olivia.

She looked away.

"I cannot explain it now," he answered as he dressed. "You must go back to the house, Olivia, and stay there until I tell you it is safe to move about the *rancho.*"

Olivia couldn't help noticing how much more formal Esteban's English became when he was troubled. She felt a very primitive urge to comfort him, and yet something inside her balked instantly at this new threat to her already limited freedom.

"I won't do any such thing," she said evenly. "I'm not a mole—I need light and sunshine and fresh air. And you keep saying I'm not a prisoner."

Esteban's glare was as fierce as the Mexican sun. "I have said it, and it is so," he told her. "I do not tell lies."

Olivia rose to her feet and faced him, her hands on her hips. "You're not exactly Mr. Communication, either," she retorted. "You want to keep me here—for the time being, at least—but you refuse to tell me why. Now you're intimating that I might be in real danger, but again, you won't explain. Is that fair?"

"It is expedient," he replied, as though that settled everything. And then he started up the path leading to his magnificent house, his shoulders taut with tension. Olivia followed, not because of any desire to obey his dictates, but because the pool and its lush surroundings no longer seemed like Eden.

Esteban could not shake his uneasiness over Olivia's reminder of his days as the Leopard. The hair on his nape was still standing, and he knew now that there had been a feeling of imminent peril in the air since Olivia's arrival on the *rancho*. All his old instincts, still finely honed even though it had been years since he'd led the raids that had earned him a small but lethal army of enemies, had warned that something wasn't right. In his fascination with the American woman, he had simply chosen to ignore the alarm bells in the pit of his stomach and the deeper chambers of his mind.

This was unlike him.

He looked back at Olivia, who was trudging sullenly along the path behind him, and faced the most difficult possibility he could think of. She might be one of them, sent to the *rancho* specifically to take revenge.

Now you're being paranoid, he told himself, turning his attention back to the path ahead. Still, Esteban had not lived to look back on his days as the

Leopard by being naive or by underestimating his foes.
He would find out exactly what was going on, face it
and deal with it.

In the meantime, he would make sure Olivia Stillwell brought no harm to herself or others.

Chapter Five

When Olivia stormed into her room a few minutes later, she found that Maria had been there before her. A simple midday meal of fruit, salad and small delicate sandwiches waited on the glass top of the wicker table, and on the bed was a long, gauzy, emerald-green dress with flowing sleeves and a ruffled, off-the-shoulder neckline.

Olivia's temper cooled slightly as she thought of the housekeeper's quiet kindness, and she took a closer look at the gown. It probably belonged to Maria, but she had taken in the seams, using tiny, perfect stitches, so that Señor Ramirez's American guest would have something to wear besides her own slacks and blouse.

She went into the adjoining bathroom, leaving the pretty gown where she'd found it, and splashed her face with cool water. She was careful not to look at her reflection, however, fearing her eyes would be suspiciously bright and her skin flushed with an achy backwash of passion.

Olivia returned to her table, with as much dignity as if she were about to dine at the White House with her famous uncle as an escort instead of dining alone in what amounted to a luxurious jail cell. She ate the miniature sandwiches daintily, finished with the fruit salad, and then moved the dress to the empty closet, kicked off her sandals and stretched out on the bed.

She was still bruised and sunburned from her ordeal with the kidnappers, and Esteban's kisses and caresses next to the pond had left her so languid that another burst of anger would have been more than she could manage.

Olivia yawned, closed her eyes and drifted off to sleep.

Sometime later, sounds—shuffles and bumps and whispers—began to intrude on her rest. Slowly, they drew her upward, out of the sheltering depths of the dream state, and she sat up, frightened. For a few moments she remembered only the kidnapping, and nothing about Maria's kindness or Esteban's pleasuring beside the turquoise pool, thinking she was still in the hands of her abductors.

Then, when her eyes had finally focused and she'd taken several deep breaths, she recalled where she was. Thus far, despite her doubts and suspicions, she'd been safe in this place, and well treated.

Still, for all the reassurances Olivia offered herself, something new was going on. There were people in the hall.

She went curiously to the door and, after tugging at her blouse and smoothing her hopelessly tousled hair, she clasped the doorknob and turned it.

There were two men in the hallway, dressed like members of Pancho Villa's band, and they both had rifles. Olivia gasped, raising one hand to her chest.

"Where is Señor Ramirez?" she demanded tersely, after gathering her courage.

The guards both spoke at once, babbling in Spanish so quick that the words flew past her like a flock of excited birds. All Olivia knew was that the men had been assigned either to keep her inside the room or someone else out. Neither possibility was very comforting.

"Never mind," she said, drawing on all her bravado. "I'll find him myself." With that, Olivia started through the doorway, only to have the men cross their all-too-real rifles in front of her to make a barricade.

That answered one question. She was being kept in.

Olivia would not let herself panic. She made a stabbing gesture at the floor with her right index finger, hoping it conveyed a certain amount of authority. "Bring Señor Ramirez here!" she ordered loudly, enunciating each word as though that would somehow translate them for her listeners.

The taller of the two men put a grubby hand on Olivia's shoulder and gently pressed her back from the door. Then, in an apparent afterthought, he took a folded piece of paper from the pocket of his vest and held it out.

"These men are here to protect you. Kindly do not drive them insane," Esteban had written in a strong hand that somehow conveyed a smile. "If you are too frightened, you may come and sleep with me. E.R."

"This situation gets more like one of my uncle's books with every passing moment!" Olivia complained, blushing because Esteban had invited her to his bed and because she wanted so much to go. Then she crumpled up the note and tossed it into the hallway, past the mustachioed faces of the guards.

One of them politely pulled the door closed, and a moment after that, a key turned in the lock.

Olivia was overwhelmed by a barrage of emotions—frustration, anger, confusion, fear. She couldn't think about Esteban, because that stirred unwanted sensations in the innermost depths of her person, so she turned her thoughts to her uncle.

Here she was, a captive in Mexico, with God only knew what kind of fate awaiting her, all because Errol McCauley had decided to write a book about a socialite, a matador and a black-market operation. *He* was safely ensconced in his circa-1750 house in Connecticut, or his condo in Vail, or his beach place on the Georgia coast, no doubt sipping white wine and chatting with his longtime companion. In fact, Olivia would have bet her best pair of Italian shoes that neither of them even knew she'd been abducted along a dusty back road and sold to a man people called the Leopard.

Olivia paced furiously, her arms folded. Even worse, when and if she finally managed to get back to the United States and recount the experience, dear Uncle Errol would almost certainly rub his palms together and ask for an accounting of every detail of every moment. Such things were grist for his mill, and instead of sympathy, he would probably just give his niece a fat bonus and an airplane ticket to someplace where she could get herself shanghaied all over again.

She stopped in the middle of the room. Maybe her uncle was eccentric, maybe he'd always been different, but she loved him and missed him enormously. Fifteen years before, when she'd been a very unhappy eleven-year-old tucked neatly out of sight at a rigid boarding school in New England, both Olivia's parents had been killed in a car crash in France. Uncle Errol had immediately come to collect the numb, confused child, and he'd put her straight into a public school in Connecticut, where she wore regular clothes and went home to a regular house every day when classes ended.

Olivia sighed, reflecting. Sure, her life with Uncle Errol had been unconventional—it couldn't have been otherwise, with him and his friend James sitting side by side in the audience at her piano recitals and school programs—but he'd been more of a parent to her than either her father or mother. She'd felt safe with him, and loved, and the town had been remarkably tolerant because there were so many local artists and everyone knew *they* were different.

She sat down on the edge of her bed, brow puckering into a frown. Olivia had always felt a little guilty for loving Uncle Errol so much, for being so glad to go and live with him. It seemed like a betrayal not to miss her parents more, not to grieve for them, but the truth was that Olivia hadn't really known Jack and Susan Stillwell. They'd put her in boarding school the day she turned six, and afterward neglected to call, write or visit. During those vacations when Uncle Errol didn't come to fetch her, she either stayed at school or was shipped off to some mansion belonging to family "friends," where she was ignored by the adults and usually tormented unmercifully by the children.

So it seemed to Olivia that her childhood, which she thought of as a happy one, remarkably enough, had begun at the age of eleven, when her mother's brother had claimed her and made a place for her in his extraordinary life.

Tears brimmed in Olivia's eyes. Uncle Errol had been there for her when she was eleven, and many times since, but she was a big girl now, and she would have to get out of this one on her own.

The question was, how?

Esteban stood before the wall of windows in the living room, watching the tropical sunset breed fire on the restless sea. He had showered after returning from the pool—the cold spray hadn't reached the blazes raging in his groin—but he had worse problems now than the need to bury himself deep in Olivia's softness.

The past he'd thought he'd buried was back.

A decade before, when Esteban had long since completed his studies in England and progressed to the continent, where he gave a new meaning to the term "prodigal son," his grandfather had summoned him home.

There had been no question of disobeying; Abuelito—Grandfather—wielded a much more profound authority than simply being *el patrón* on a remote, if lucrative, Mexican *rancho*. Esteban's father had been the spoiled second son of a neighboring family and had run away without marrying his rebellious young mother. After she was killed in a riding accident, it had been Esteban's grandfather who had looked after him, with a lot of help from Maria.

Esteban's destiny had always been to become *el patrón,* no matter how he might have tried to persuade himself to the contrary. After he'd seen that his grandfather's health was failing and had a few shouting matches with the regal old man in the bargain, Esteban had, as the Americans said, gotten his act together.

He'd learned everything he needed to know, and much more, about raising purebred cattle and fine horses and the management of his silver mines. The latter produced little now, were all but shut down in fact, but the proceeds had been invested wisely almost from the day Abuelito had discovered the ore, and the profits had grown into vast sums, gathering interest in American and Swiss banks.

The isolation of the *rancho* had been a problem for Esteban, however, especially after his grandfather's death. Even though he loved his work, he would occasionally become so restless that he couldn't eat or sleep.

It was during one of those times, when he'd gone to Mexico City for a little R and R, that Esteban had met the American. He always thought of him by his nationality instead of his name, because even though the man had sworn he was called Tom Castleberry, Esteban had never believed him.

Over the coming months, Esteban had encountered the American virtually everywhere he went. Finally, the older man told him a long and intriguing story about a dangerous foreign government setting up a strategic base of operation in the wilds of Mexico. He produced impressive identification and documented proof, and the long and short of it was that Esteban and a few trusted men were recruited for counterespionage purposes.

Esteban smiled bitterly, standing at his window all these years later, remembering. It had been just the kind of offer that would appeal to a hotheaded young man who longed for excitement and adventure.

God knew, he'd gotten those things and more. After the bad guys had started moving in their equipment, and even small missiles, Esteban had led raids on their camp. They'd fought back, all right—he had the scars to prove it—but after a while they'd given up and retreated into Central America.

All this without formally involving either the American or Mexican governments.

Esteban's code name had been *el leopardo,* and he had not heard the phrase since the last time he'd seen the American in the small *cantina* in Mexico City where they'd agreed to meet. The agent's final words to Esteban had been, "Watch your back. Maybe we won this one, but there are plenty of people around here who would have profited from that little missile project, and some of them know who you are. You've made some dangerous enemies."

The words echoed in Esteban's mind as he turned away from the dying sun. It didn't bother him so much that he had endangered himself—he thrived on trouble, because it gave him an edge and kept his wits sharp—but he had inadvertently involved Olivia, and the thought of anything happening to her filled him with a raging terror.

After a moment, he focused on Maria, who had probably been standing there for some time. She smiled, handed him the snifter of brandy he was just realizing he wanted, and spoke to him in Spanish.

"The pretty Olivia was not happy to discover that she is a prisoner in her room. She's been demanding to see you."

Esteban took a grateful and pensive sip of his liquor. When he'd returned to the house, a messenger had been waiting with a message from the United States. Tom Castleberry, the American agent who had dubbed Esteban "the Leopard" in the first place, had been found dead in a cheap motel room. The circumstances had been mysterious enough that the State Department had felt compelled to notify others who might be a target.

He was not afraid for himself, but when Esteban thought of what those vengeful bastards might do to Olivia, especially if they guessed that he cared for her, he had immediately posted two of his most trusted men outside her door.

He handed the empty glass to Maria, with a nod meant to convey his thanks. "Miss Stillwell," he replied, in the soft, musical language of his birth, "may demand all she wishes. I am still *el patrón* and I do not take orders from a woman."

Maria arched one eyebrow. "I think *this* woman is different," she ventured. "She belongs to this place, and to you, the way the lyrics of a love song belong with the music."

Esteban kissed Maria's forehead; she had been his nurse as a child, and now she was his friend. "You've been watching those American soap operas again," he teased, but secretly he was beginning to imagine Olivia in his bed, at his table, beside him as he rode over the land he cherished. He saw her blossoming with his child, and the longing to feel her beneath him was so intense it was painful.

His spurs made a clinking sound as he crossed the central courtyard toward the front door, purposely resisting the urge to lift his eyes to the balcony as he passed beneath. Even when he'd handled this current

difficulty with his old enemies, he thought sadly, there
would be no hope of a future with Olivia. She saw him
as a captor, and besides, they came from two very
different cultures. Two different centuries.

The whole thing was impossible, he decided, and the
sooner he put Olivia Stillwell out of his life for good,
the better off he'd be.

Chapter Six

Olivia was left to stew in her frustration and helpless anger for several tumultuous hours. Then Maria arrived, bearing a stack of richly bound volumes and a small velvet box.

With graceful charadelike movements, the housekeeper managed to convey that Olivia was to rest quietly for a few hours, then dress for dinner. The box contained a beautiful set of antique silver combs, and the books, expensive classics printed in English, were apparently meant to offer much-needed distraction.

Having little choice and feeling enormously grateful for the books, Olivia agreed to Maria's kindly decree with a nod, and settled down to reread *Jane Eyre*. Mercifully, the beloved story kept her mind off her precarious situation for a long, therapeutic interval.

Later, Olivia donned the loose and ultrafeminine green gown Maria had altered for her, pinned up her rich auburn hair and arranged the lovely old combs for accent. Although the cut of the dress was definitely south-of-the-border, the silver ornaments and Olivia's old-fashioned hairstyle gave her a startling Gibson-girl look.

This woman staring back at her from the bathroom mirror was a stranger, a person she had never encountered until that moment. She was sophisticated and sensual, aware of her power as a woman. Able to accomplish anything she set out to do.

It was alarmingly plain that this fresh facet of Olivia's personality wasn't just visiting; she'd come to stay, bringing along a whole steamer trunk full of bright, shiny new dreams, hopes, goals and wishes.

Olivia smiled and, of course, the image smiled back. "I've been waiting for you for a long time," she said softly.

But there was still the matter of her captivity.

Esteban came to collect her himself, and his glorious violet eyes seemed to melt when he saw her. He muttered something in Spanish, and Olivia felt the words like a caress, even though she didn't understand them. She straightened her back.

"I will not be held captive, Esteban," she said in a firm but slightly tremulous voice. "If you don't trust me, then please don't pretend to be my friend."

He looked spectacular, wearing dark trousers, a flowing shirt and a black leather vest decorated with gleaming silver studs. On any other man, no matter how handsome, the outfit would have looked theatrical; on Esteban it was as natural as skin. "I trust you," he said thoughtfully, "though I'll admit I'm not sure why." With that, he held out his arm. "You look very lovely tonight," he said, escorting her past the guards, who stood on either side of the door, their expressions solemn and vaguely disapproving.

Olivia felt a sweet shiver go through her, but she couldn't let her doubts be dismissed so easily. She needed assurances that things were going to be different. "You will send them away?"

Esteban glanced back over one shoulder and spoke quietly to the men, who immediately abandoned their posts.

"There," he said. "They are gone." He did not lead her down the side stairs, but through a pair of arched double doors farther along the hallway.

The suite, obviously Esteban's private domain, was dimly lit with candles, and even though Olivia couldn't see much, she knew the place was huge and filled with substantial masculine furniture. On the far side, another pair of doors opened onto a large terrace; the piece of sky visible through the opening was studded with stars.

Out of the corner of her eye, Olivia made out the shape of Esteban's bed, which was large, with thick posts and a canopy of some sort. She swallowed, filled with a sense of delicious foreboding.

She wanted to stay here, this dangerous new Olivia, and give herself to Esteban in the rich Mexican darkness. She wanted to nurture his seed in her body and bear a child as arrogantly beautiful as his father. She wanted to set up a potter's wheel and a kiln, and capture the raw, stunning beauty of the land around her in clay.

On the terrace, where candles flickered and flowers filled the warm air with their lush scents, Maria had prepared a table. There was a bottle of wine in a silver cooler, and various dishes under engraved covers. Two places were set with Limoges china—Olivia had developed an eye for such things because Uncle Errol was a collector—and heirloom sterling.

Olivia let Esteban draw back her chair in the old-world way, feeling like a completely different person. She'd read her fair share of sensational psychology and wondered if all the trauma of recent days had caused her to develop a new personality.

Desperate to break the spell of Esteban and the moonlight and the dark chamber behind them, she said, "You agree, then, that you won't keep me locked up in my room anymore. It's a barbaric thing to do, you know."

Esteban sampled the wine in that ritualistic way of a true expert, then poured a glassful for Olivia. "The word 'barbaric' doesn't begin to cover the fates that can befall a woman wandering around certain parts of Mexico by herself. And this is one of those parts."

Olivia sighed. She no longer wanted to leave this man and his spectacular land, and yet she had very grave doubts that anything real and lasting could develop between them. After all, they came from different cultures, different backgrounds, different *centuries* for all practical intents and purposes. "I'm not sure any of us are safe anywhere," she mused.

Esteban, to his credit, did not pretend to misunderstand. He, too, cherished his freedom; he loved the *rancho,* among other reasons, because he could range from one far-flung border to another, with no more constraints than a nineteenth-century bandit. *"Sí,"* he agreed. "And perhaps it is not a good thing to be safe all the time."

Olivia took a sip of her wine. It was a delicious vintage; Uncle Errol would have raved, then ordered cases sent to all his friends. "Do you live here all year round?" she asked, feeling more relaxed.

"No," Esteban replied, handling his knife and fork with an élan Olivia had rarely seen in men his age. "I have a place in Santa Fe, and I enjoy traveling."

Olivia thought of all the countries she'd visited, all the cities, and sighed again. "I do, too," she said, "but now I feel like stopping somewhere, putting everything I've seen and heard and felt into my art."

"Art?" Esteban looked genuinely intrigued. They were developing a bristly friendship, they'd nearly made love, and yet he didn't know about her passion for pottery.

She told him, in glowing terms, forgetting for a few minutes the unsettling nature of their relationship, all about her prizes and small successes. "Of course I probably won't earn a lot of money, at least not for a while, but that isn't really a problem. I make a good salary and I've saved quite a sum because I haven't had many living expenses."

He smiled. "Tell me about your childhood," he said. "I'll bet you had freckles, and pigtails, and were constantly skinning your knees."

Olivia laughed. "You're right on two counts, at least. I did have freckles and pigtails, but I wasn't allowed to skin my knees until after Uncle Errol came and rescued me from boarding school." She went on to give a condensed but truthful version of her life, and felt a little foolish when she'd finished. Usually, she didn't divulge a lot of personal details to others, because it was difficult for her to open up.

Esteban reciprocated by telling her about his grandfather, and growing up on the *rancho*. He, too, had been sent away to school, mostly in Europe, but the effect had been very different for him. He had, in essence, learned to balance the old world and the new with an easy grace that Olivia frankly envied.

His words were as smooth and elegant as the wine, blending with her blood in much the same way, and it was too late to steel herself against them. Even though she was ravenously hungry, a sure sign that she was recovering from the rigors of her recent experiences, she might have left Esteban's table for his bed, had he suggested it. That scared her more than anything.

He sat back in his chair when the meal was over, looking troubled all of the sudden, distracted. "You must be very careful, Olivia. There are men . . ."

Olivia's heart beat a little faster as she remembered the clippings in Maria's scrapbooks. How she wished she'd read every word of them. "What men?"

Esteban hesitated for a long time. "Men who are my enemies," he said. "If they've noticed you—and it would be wishful thinking to believe they haven't— they will see you as a perfect means of revenge. They've been waiting a long time for such an opportunity."

Although she felt a chill move down her spine, Olivia felt compelled to argue. "Surely no one could get into the house," she insisted. "The guards would never let them pass."

Esteban thought for a long moment, then conceded, "It is true that I trust my men."

Olivia chewed industriously, eager to reply. "You could always send me back to the States," she said, and it was crazy, how much she hoped he would refuse.

He studied her for a long moment before answering. "Something is unfolding between us. I want to see what it is."

She looked up at the magnificent array of stars, bright as the fancy buttons on the vests Esteban wore in the daytime, and sighed with pleasant resignation. The moon spilled a wash of silver light over the sea, the tropical foliage, the rugged mountains in the distance. "So do I," she whispered at last.

His hand moved to enclose hers, and the dry strength of his touch made Olivia's blood shout in her veins. His thumb, callused and deft, moved over the delicate flesh on the inside of her wrist. "You will be allowed to move freely about the house," he said, his tone hoarse, as if he was making the offer unwillingly. "But you must not so much as step out onto the terrace without an escort."

Olivia cherished this small victory, but something inside wouldn't allow her to be content with it. She raised one eyebrow, took a sip of her wine and asked, "Aren't we on a terrace now?"

Esteban's magnificent shoulders stiffened. "Obviously, I am with you. Manolito and Luis are in the courtyard below. You would not be safe here if this were not so."

Olivia had no idea how to respond, and her emotions were churning. She honestly didn't know which eventuality terrified her more: being abducted by these mysterious enemies of Esteban's, or falling so deeply in love with the Leopard that she was willing to throw off her life in the twentieth century like a thrift-shop dress. Living here, with Esteban, would be like stepping into the pages of a novel...

...where one or more of the major characters could end up dead. The thought dampened Olivia's romantic thoughts, but her body was still seething with volcanic heat. Every gesture Esteban made, however innocent, stirred things up even more.

In the end, to Olivia's great disappointment and relief, he did not carry her to his bed. He simply escorted her, wine-dazed and warm, back to her own room.

She slept only intermittently that night; her hungry body, taught to want satisfaction and then denied it, was restless. In the morning, Olivia made a drastic decision.

All her pretty dreams were just that—pretty dreams. She had to get out of this backward country and home to the world she knew but didn't love before she was as addicted to Esteban's lovemaking as others were to cocaine or opium. Her longing for him was already a deep, primordial need that clawed at her insides, and her only hope was to get away.

Forget.

She washed and dressed in her battered slacks and blouse. Since there was no breakfast waiting on the wicker table like before, she concluded that Esteban had not changed his mind about dismissing the guards. She crossed the room to try the heavy door.

It was unlocked, and there was still no sign of the seedy ranch hands who had been posted in the hallway the day before.

Olivia flew down the stairs. She slipped into the study to see if the scrapbooks containing the clippings about Esteban were still there, but they'd disappeared. She chided herself for not reading the English accounts of the Leopard's exploits when she'd had the chance.

Maybe, a cooler part of her mind retorted, she hadn't *wanted* to know the whole truth in the first place.

Olivia went on to the kitchen.

Maria was there, stirring batter in a bowl, and she smiled and gestured toward a table near a sunny window. Seated on the threshold of the open door was one of the men who worked for Esteban. He had a rifle lying across his knees, and he yawned copiously while Olivia sat down to eat her breakfast.

Even after finishing and washing and putting away her plate and silverware, Olivia lingered. Pretending an interest in the Spanish radio show Maria was listening to while she ironed a pile of cotton shirts that were surely Esteban's, Olivia kept an eye on the guard sitting in the doorway.

Perhaps he had pulled night duty, or maybe he was just plain lazy. In either case, the man kept yawning loudly, and presently he sagged against the jamb. Olivia forced herself to stay calm, knowing Maria was perceptive, not wanting the housekeeper to sense what she was planning.

After a seeming eternity, Maria left the kitchen with the crisply pressed shirts, humming pleasantly. Olivia waited until she'd been gone for at least a minute, lest the woman return for something she'd forgotten, then bolted for the door.

It was easy to slip past the guard, who was now snoring.

Maybe it was feminine intuition that drew her toward the outbuildings—she'd been wanting to explore them. Then again, maybe it was just luck. God knew, she was overdue for some of that.

In any case, when Olivia wrested open the door of the largest shed, she saw an intriguing and very familiar shape under a dusty tarp. Lifting the edge of the canvas, she felt, at one and the same time, a leap of hope and a twinge of very real despair.

Contrary to the impression he gave, Esteban had not totally divorced himself from the modern world. The hidden object was a red Blazer with four-wheel drive and all the options.

Holding her breath, Olivia tried the door on the driver's side, and it opened. To her amazement, the keys were hidden under the floor mat near the gas pedal. She crept back to the door, which she'd left slightly ajar in order to let in dusty rays of sunlight, and peered carefully in every direction.

Then she went back, climbed behind the wheel and, squeezing her eyes shut, turned the key in the ignition.

The Blazer started.

Stunned at her continuing good fortune, Olivia opened her eyes and studied the gas gauge. So much for the benevolence of the gods; the needle rode just a hair above the empty mark.

She shut off the engine and let her forehead rest against the steering wheel while she dealt with her frustration and a vague, nagging sense of joy. She'd found transportation, a vehicle equipped for the rugged Mexican terrain, and the tank was empty.

"Hell and hallelujah," she muttered, for it took both words to cover the broad range of her feelings.

Chapter Seven

If there was a Blazer, not to mention several generators to serve parts of the *casa,* Olivia reasoned, carefully replacing the tarp that hid the vehicle, there must also be a gas pump hidden away somewhere. Unfortunately, she couldn't take the time to search for it, since she was bound to be discovered at any moment.

She looked around carefully before stepping out of the shed. The door was wide enough for a car to pass through, and it opened from side to side. Olivia closed it, drew a deep breath and started back toward the house.

The guard—she'd heard Maria call him Pepito—was still asleep, his big, dusty sombrero scrunched against the doorjamb, but his exuberant snores were turning to snuffles. He was probably waking up.

Olivia slipped past him and took a can of soda from the big generator-powered refrigerator, passing Pepito an innocent smile when he snorted awake, laboriously turned in her direction and gave her a suspicious glance.

She saluted him with the cold drink. "Here's to Los Estados Unidos," she said.

Pepito made a sound that sounded like the Latin equivalent of a harrumph. Obviously, he was no great fan of Mexico's neighbor to the north, and he probably thought baby-sitting a woman was beneath his dignity.

Olivia smiled winningly, turned on her heel and left the room. Unable to face returning to her room, even though it was a pleasant place, she went to the living room and stared out the windows, drinking in the gold-washed turquoise of the sea, the impossibly deep green of the trees, the violent colors of the tropical flowers. She yearned to lie in the white sand beside the pool again, with Esteban's hand on her body, his mouth greedy at her nipple...

She turned, drunk on the view and on her own thoughts, actually uncertain whether she could remain standing or not, and he was there.

"No wonder they call you the Leopard," Olivia said. She'd tried to make the observation sound like a joke, but she knew she'd failed. She had been too weakened by the realization of his presence; her voice was too small and too meek.

Esteban was covered from head to foot in dust, but he was no less regal for the fact. Here was a man who knew who and what he was, and believed in his identity. He looked at Olivia in a way that raised her temperature.

It was humiliating. She'd made herself available, and her wanting was about as subtle as a neon sign in front of a Las Vegas casino. For all of that, Esteban seemed to find her eminently resistible.

"Maria found these things for you and laundered them," he said, tossing a bundle of denim and cotton clothing into her arms. She hadn't noticed that he was holding anything. "Change and meet me in the dining room. We'll have the midday meal and then, after *siesta,* we'll ride out."

Olivia's heart leapt joyously, but at the same time her throat constricted with grief. "Are you saying that you're going to take me back to the United Sates?"

Esteban regarded her for a long moment, his patrician face unreadable, and then shook his head. "No. A band of my finest horses has strayed, to the south we think. I must go after them."

She took a step toward him, then stopped, unsure of her feelings. They were in such a contradictory tangle that she couldn't make sense of them. "And you're taking me along? Why?"

"Because I cannot leave you here."

Olivia swallowed. If only Esteban would do that, she'd have a chance to find the gas pump, fill up the Blazer and make a run for it. "You said yourself I would only be safe within these walls, with guards outside."

He shoved a hand through panther-black hair coated, like the rest of him, with dust. "I would not be able to concentrate on finding the horses if I had to worry about you the whole time I was away. Please. Just do as I have told you."

Ever since Olivia had met this man, it seemed to her, she'd been of two minds. She wanted to escape, mostly to spite the arrogant *leopardo,* she had to admit, and yet the idea of riding with him and his men was like the fruition of a fantasy.

"I'm not a very good rider," she confessed when Esteban was halfway across the room.

He didn't turn around. "I am," he countered and then, as though that settled the entire matter, he strode out.

Olivia went upstairs and untied the string that held the clothes Esteban had provided. There were two worn cotton shirts, long-sleeved, and two pairs of ancient jeans.

She took off her own blouse and slacks and changed into garments that had probably been left behind by some ranch hand who had moved on. He'd been a small man, and though his shirts fit Olivia perfectly, the pants were tight across her hips and the waistband stood out a little in front.

Even so, when Olivia appeared in the dining room ten minutes later as ordered, the expression in Esteban's eyes said he liked what he saw. He rose from his chair, seated her, then sat again.

He'd visited the pool, for the dust was gone from his hair and skin, and his clothes were fresh. Olivia felt envious for several reasons—Esteban had so much freedom, he'd enjoyed the cool privacy of the pond while she'd been sweltering, and she remembered only too well the primitive pleasure of surrendering in the soft white sand.

Maria served a luncheon of sliced fruit, cold cuts and her own newly baked bread, and left the dining room wearing a secretive smile, as though she knew something Esteban and Olivia had yet to even guess at.

"What about Maria?" Olivia asked. "Will she be safe here alone?"

"She won't be alone," Esteban replied, settling back in his heavy, beautifully carved chair to study Olivia with shameless leisure. "I'm leaving two men to keep watch. Besides, Maria is not a target."

After the meal, during which Esteban said remarkably little and yet devoured Olivia with his eyes, Maria came to clear the table. Esteban stood, drew back Olivia's chair and pressed one hand lightly but firmly to the small of her back.

"What . . . ?"

He propelled her through the inner courtyard to the stairs. "It is time for *siesta*," he said. "In Mexico, we rest during the hottest part of the day."

Olivia's heart had stuffed itself into her windpipe. Even the weight of Esteban's hand at the base of her spine had aroused her, as had the sleepy, sensual images the word *siesta* had brought to mind. "I'm not tired," she faltered, testing the waters.

If the brightness of Esteban's grin could have been hooked up to solar reflectors, it would have provided enough power for three states. "You will be," he promised.

He escorted her past her door and through his own, closing and latching the graceful arch of carved wood behind them.

Olivia's cheeks were bright red, and this time she couldn't blame the sunburn. "I'm not your plaything," she whispered, angry because she would be practically anything he wanted and he knew it.

Esteban pulled her plaid cotton shirt from her jeans. "You are like ripe fruit—a sweet, juicy peach, I think. It was all I could do not to lay you out on the dining room table and enjoy you right then and there."

Olivia yearned to defy him, but some elemental part of her nature had taken over and she couldn't. She gave a soft gasp when Esteban gripped both sides of the shirt and pulled, so that the mother-of-pearl snaps gave way. He pushed the fabric back.

Away.

Because of the sunburn and the fierce Mexican heat, Olivia wasn't wearing a bra. Her plump breasts were bare under Esteban's gaze, their pink tips hardening, reaching.

"*Madre de Dios,*" Esteban rasped, sounding stunned, as if a woman's body were a new invention. Then, his hands tight on the curve of her waist, he bent and, using his tongue, teased each morsel until Olivia was leaning back in his embrace, groaning. Just when she was nearly insane with need, he began to suck, gently at first and then with greed.

Presently, he set her on the edge of the bed, removed her sandals and jeans. When she tried to rise, afraid of the force of the passion she knew he could make her feel, he stilled her, placing his hands on her hips. She whimpered and flung both arms back over her head as he nuzzled her, kissed the quivering insides of her thighs, then boldly conquered her greatest secret with his lips and tongue.

Olivia's hands clawed at the bedclothes, and she tossed her head from side to side, wild in her surrender. "Esteban," she choked out. "Oh...*Esteban!*"

He slid his palms beneath her bottom, lifted her slightly, and continued to enjoy her just as he might have enjoyed the ripe, sweet, juicy peach he'd spoken of earlier. Olivia raised her feet to his shoulders, but not in an effort to push him away. She needed to anchor herself to him, to be touching something other than his tongue and his hands.

He slid her closer, then reached up to grip her ankles hard. Olivia shouted with pleasure as her climax first lifted her body high off the bed, then twisted her from side to side. If Esteban was worried that someone would hear, he gave no sign of it. He stayed with Olivia until the last vestige of ecstasy had been extracted, until she lay wilted and half-conscious on the mattress, eyes unfocused, her breathing fast and shallow.

She was vaguely aware of being moved, of Esteban removing his clothes, stretching out on the bed beside her. His hand moved in soothing circles on her stomach, and his nakedness teased her ultra sensitive flesh like the brush of a feather.

"Please," she murmured moments later. That one word was all she had strength for; Esteban had taken everything else.

Still, he knew what she wanted, and he denied her; she felt the shake of his head rather than saw it. "No, *dulce*. Rest now." His voice was gruff, hypnotic. "Rest."

Olivia's lashes fluttered as she fought to keep her eyes open, and even the dangerous realization whispering in the back of her mind could not bring her to consciousness again. She slept, but the cruel knowledge was there, like a burr in the tender folds of her spirit.

To Esteban, this was all a game. He liked to make her respond to him sexually, but he consistently refused to make a surrender of his own. She was a diversion.

She drifted into a fitful sleep, and in her dreams she wept with disappointment and grief.

Olivia awoke at twilight, a sea breeze blowing over her body and her eyelashes wet with tears. Esteban's side of the bed was empty, but the sheets still bore his singular scent and the air was tinged with the scent of his cologne.

Sitting up, her arms wrapped around her legs, Olivia let her forehead rest on her knees and sobbed. It was bad enough that she loved the Leopard and had to leave him, but to realize he'd only been playing with her body and emotions was shattering.

He came in as if summoned by her thoughts, and approached the bed silently. She looked at him with red, puffy, defiant eyes.

"Don't touch me, damn you," she hissed, trying to slide away. "You've had your fun!"

He was quick, like the animal whose name he bore, and before she reached the far side of the bed he'd tangled her in the top sheet and dragged her back.

"What is it?" he demanded. "What are you talking about?"

Olivia tried to fling herself at him—in a passion of fury—but she was still tightly bound in the sheet; it was as restrictive as a straitjacket. "You think it's funny, don't you? Making me want you so much, making me cry out because the pleasure is more than I can bear, then walking away without actually making love to me!"

Esteban might have been an actor instead of a rancher. His face drained of all color and he looked stunned for a moment, then coldly angry. "Did I not please you?"

"Please me?" Olivia was positively livid with rage and hurt, but he still had her trussed up like a chicken in a burlap sack. "You weren't trying to make me happy, you were *road testing* me, like a car you might decide to lease for a while!"

Esteban's jaw clamped tight for a long interval; it was plain he was struggling for self-control. "So," he finally whispered, "it troubles you that I have tried to respect your honor. You do not like being treated like a lady." He gripped the sheet with one hand and began unbuttoning his shirt with the other. "Well, my lovely little captive, have it your own way."

Chapter Eight

Deftly, Esteban flipped the sheet that had enclosed her like a cocoon, in the same way a magician might wrench away a tablecloth without disturbing the china and silverware on top. Unlike the wizard's dishes, Olivia was definitely displaced; she did a complete revolution in the air above Esteban's feather mattress and plopped on her back into its softness, naked as truth.

She swallowed, watching with wide eyes as her captor-host removed his clothes again. Honor demanded that she oppose him, even though, on the deepest level of her awareness, she knew she wanted to lose.

"Don't you even *think* it," she whispered.

His eyes flashed. "By the time I have you," he said, "you'll be begging." He stretched out beside her, cupped the back of her head in one strong hand and kissed her. She tried to keep her mouth shut, but his tongue was too persuasive, too expert at pleasuring her. Finally, with a whimper, she opened to him.

"You are a pompous SOB!" she gasped the moment he freed her.

"*Sí,*" Esteban replied. He seemed to know her protests were hollow, and he smiled at the game. "You are not a virgin, yes?" He inquired practically, when he had kissed and caressed her into a state of near hysteria.

"No," Olivia admitted, moaning the word.

"Then you will be able to take me inside you without pain, and there will be only pleasure," Esteban replied, his voice sleepy and low. He rolled onto his back in a graceful motion and set Olivia on top of him, her legs parted over his hips.

She felt the size and power of him pressed against her belly, and closed her eyes, overwhelmed.

Esteban lifted her slightly, and she felt his manhood move into place like a rocket rolling onto a launch pad.

"Oh, my," she cried in a hoarse whisper, as she felt him glide slowly, powerfully into her.

"Open your eyes and look at me," Esteban ordered, though not unkindly.

Olivia blinked, wonderstruck, and her expression must have been a dazed one. The last thing she wanted to do then was have a meaningful conversation.

Esteban gripped her hips, raising her along his length with merciless leisure, then bringing her down again. When she'd traveled him once, twice, three times, he finally went on. "What am I doing to you, Olivia?" he asked reasonably.

She trembled as a shock of yearning went through her, bit her lip for a moment, and then answered him in two very intimate words.

He let her just sit, filled with his manhood, while he teased her nipples with expert fingers. "Would it be so good between us if I were only using you?"

Olivia didn't trust herself to speak.

Until Esteban held her hips again and gave her three long, mercilessly thorough strokes.

"No!" she sobbed, the word bursting from her in an explosion of desperation and surrender.

"Why not?" He was rubbing her stomach now, making her wait. Mastering her.

Olivia was wild with the kind of primitive need that had probably enabled mankind to survive through so many millennia. "Oh—Esteban—I don't know—I swear I don't know!"

Esteban raised himself to enjoy one of her pulsing nipples for a long, sweetly torturous interval. "I have taken you. From today forward, you will be my woman."

"Yes," Olivia moaned. There was a wealth of meaning in that common word: surrender, joy, defiance, fury.

He twisted, never breaking his bond with Olivia, thrusting her beneath him, and kissed her again, savagely. When he raised his head, he searched her face with unreadable eyes and then gave himself to her, full force, with nothing held back.

Olivia's fingernails dug into the supple flesh of his back—that was something she'd only read about until this glorious, tragic day in the Leopard's bed. The hard, slamming motions of his hips, the rhythmic invasion of his manhood, all of it conspired to drive her wild.

When it finally happened, when satisfaction overtook her, her body buckled repeatedly while, at the same time, her spirit soared. It was as though she'd just jumped from an airplane and found that her parachute wouldn't open, except there was no fear. She tumbled through the sky, end over end, knowing that when she struck the ground there would be another cataclysmic release, then nothing.

It was happening, she was about to collide hard with the earth. Olivia tensed violently in Esteban's arms, gave the keening cry of a wild thing mourning in the dark, and for several seconds she didn't exist because she'd given everything she had and everything she was to the man she loved.

When she returned to herself, Esteban was just crossing the threshold. His head was flung back, his teeth bared, and the muscles in his chest and upper arms stood out as he balanced himself on his hands and lunged deep.

A string of soft Spanish words escaped him as he emptied himself into her, and Olivia couldn't resist caressing him, murmuring tender words as he confronted an elation that was obviously excruciating.

When at last his lean and unabashedly muscular body had relaxed, Esteban collapsed beside Olivia with a despairing moan and dragged her close to him. His embrace was perfect, firm and protective but somehow not restrictive.

Olivia smiled, even though if anything she was in more danger instead of less, and closed her eyes. The velvety breeze sneaked between the woven drapes covering the terrace doors and flowed over her bare skin like lotion.

He was a fool, Esteban thought, lying propped on one elbow, watching Olivia sleep. He'd made up his mind not to have this American temptress—in his opinion, she needed a spanking more than the sweet, fevered exercise he could provide—but in pleasuring her he had created an undeniable need within himself.

Her nipples were peaked, like inviting confections, offering themselves to him. Esteban swallowed, admiring the rest of her small, succulent body. Her hips were wide enough for childbearing and for receiving him, but not broad. Her thighs were like firm cushions, absorbing the impact of his fervor when he mounted her, and her stomach was flat and smooth.

He couldn't help imagining her swelling, ripening, as his child grew within her.

The idea made him hard—hard enough that he wouldn't be able to ride at sunset when they would leave for the southern part of the *rancho,* seeking the lost horses.

He put the animals out of his mind for the moment, valuable as they were, and traced the outline of Olivia's soft, kiss-swollen lips with his index finger. Her lashes fluttered and she looked at him with those marvelous pewter-colored eyes of hers, and she smiled.

Something bitter and rigid melted deep inside Esteban. He tasted her mouth. "I need you," he said in a throaty voice. He hoped the extraordinary truth of the statement didn't show.

"Come to me, then," she replied. "Let me comfort you." With a small, seductive sigh, she wriggled against the sheets, as inviting as the pool on a brutally hot day.

Esteban felt everything inside him tighten and then vibrate at her words, like a guitar string drawn so taut that another twist would either snap that string or break the instrument. With a groan, he gathered her close to him, settled on top of her, devoured her mouth with his own.

She was ready for him, her eyes dreamy, her womanly place moist and warm. With a soft croon of welcome, she arched her back and received him, and Esteban had a sense of returning home after years of wandering.

When her thoughts were finally coherent again, which was a long time later, Olivia was more certain than ever that she had to escape Mexico the first chance she got. Estebar.'s power over her was frightening in its scope, and if she stayed until he'd made her pregnant, his hold would be even greater. Plus, Señor Ramirez led a very dangerous life. To stay would be to share that peril and maybe force a child to share it, too.

She watched as Esteban and his men saddled their horses in the twilight. Olivia supposed she could have dealt with all the other stuff—women were coping with worse things all over the world—but the fact that made her dreams impossible was something else. Esteban would never marry her; she would be the Leopard's woman, but never his wife. Men like Esteban only wed women of their own social status and religion; everyone else would be classified as a mistress.

Olivia had had a fairly broad education; her uncle was an adventurous soul and had taken her on safari in Africa, to see the pyramids in Egypt, mountain-climbing in Tibet. She'd had a number of exciting times on her own, of course, doing research for Uncle Errol's books. For all of that, however, Olivia had never learned to ride.

There must have been a lot of trepidation in her face when Pepito rode over on his overworked horse, leading an energetic little chestnut mare behind him. He spat something in Spanish and tossed the reins to her.

Resigned, Olivia gripped the saddlehorn, as she'd seen the others do, put one foot in the nearest stirrup and hoisted herself up. In the process, she dropped the reins.

The mare danced and sidestepped so much that Olivia was really afraid the creature meant to buck her off, so she took a new, white-knuckled grip on the saddlehorn. Esteban rode over and, with a grin, bent to collect the dangling reins and hand them to Olivia. He ran the tip of his tongue over his upper lip, briefly reminding her, and Olivia felt her cheeks burn.

She saved her pride by turning her thoughts from the wholehearted, lusty way she'd responded in Esteban's bed to the prospect of escape. She had a horse now; maybe she would get an opportunity to ride back to the ranch house, find the gasoline pump, fill up the Blazer and head for home at top speed.

One question gave her pause. What, exactly, was she going to do with the rest of her life?

She was pondering that earth-shattering question when Esteban shouted an order. He gripped the mare's bridle to bring her apace with his own fierce stallion, and Olivia shifted uncomfortably on the hard saddle as she drew certain parallels. Soon they were riding across the sand, Esteban and Olivia in the lead, fourteen armed and mounted men close behind.

Olivia bounced painfully for some time, until she got the hang of slipping into rhythm with the horse. She knew she was going to be sore the next day.

Out of the corner of her eye, she watched Esteban, waiting for him to tire, but the night wore on and he showed no sign of fatigue. Finally, when the moon was high and coyotes could be heard howling their mournful concertos, the band stopped at a rustic cabin that backed onto a bluff. There were a few scrubby trees around, along with some grass, and there was a horse trough that would logically be filled from the rusty-handled pump standing at one end.

Esteban said something to the men, who were eager to water their horses and, Olivia suspected, themselves. Then he swung one leg over and slid to the ground; probably, he had been riding as long as he'd been walking, so comfortable was he in the presence of these snorting, head-tossing, temperamental animals.

Raising his hands to her waist, Esteban lifted Olivia down from the saddle, letting her body slide along the length of his before her feet finally touched the ground. His palms lingered against her sides, and for a moment, he looked as though he meant to kiss her. Olivia wasn't surprised when he didn't; that would have been a violation of the macho creed, showing such tenderness in front of the others.

He gestured toward the cabin, which leaned wearily into the side of the bluff like a traveler who could venture no farther. "Go inside," he said. "There is a lantern and a box of matches on the table to your left."

It all seemed pretty high-handed to Olivia, his assuming she'd obey him like a trained puppy. "What if there are spiders and rats in there?" she whispered, folding her arms.

"I'll protect you," Esteban whispered back, his eyes laughing in the bright moonlight.

"So far," Olivia retorted tartly, arms still folded, "you've been a regular Robin Hood." Then she stomped toward the cabin, hoping the sarcasm in her words would distract Esteban from the fact that she was obeying his command.

Chapter Nine

Inside the cabin, the darkness was thick and the air smelled of dust, mice and long neglect. Olivia yearned to bolt back through the rickety doorway and cling to Esteban like gum on the sole of a shoe, but she could not shame herself that way.

After squaring her shoulders and taking a deep breath, she groped for the matches Esteban had mentioned, found them, struck one against the rough timber of the doorjamb. Weak light flared, along with the scent of sulfur, showing the promised lamp, a table with a candle at its center, two flimsy chairs and a bed with a rope frame but no mattress or box spring.

Muttering, Olivia worked the filthy glass chimney from the lamp base and moved to light the wick, only to have the match burn her fingers and then go out. She swore, hearing skittering sounds behind her in the darkness of the cabin, and the raucous, irreverent laughter of Esteban's men.

How much did she really know about this man? she asked herself, as she felt for another match and finally managed to get the lamp burning. Suppose she had misjudged Esteban Ramirez entirely? Suppose there was a drunken party and he turned her over to his men?

She turned to look at the pitiful room, hugging herself, taking particular note of the impossible bed.

Surely he didn't expect her to sleep there, but if not, where?

Without a squeak of the ancient floorboards or so much as a clink of his fancy spurs, Esteban entered the cabin. Olivia knew when he was there; she felt his presence prickling against her skin like heat from a fire.

He closed the door quietly. "As a boy," he said in a low voice full of remembrance, "this was one of my favorite places. I used to hide here when I was angry or hurt about something, and for a time my grandfather would let me think he didn't know where I was."

Olivia turned, catching a fleeting glimpse of the boy before he took refuge once again in some hidden chamber of his soul. "We're not staying here, are we?" she demanded, to hide a rush of tenderness. It wouldn't do to care too much, not when she would be leaving soon and never coming back.

Esteban sighed, though Olivia wasn't entirely sure he hadn't seen through her ruse. He removed his gloves and the round-brimmed hat that hung down his back from a string when he wasn't wearing it. "Yes," he answered gravely and at length. "For tonight, we are staying here. Be grateful—tomorrow night the mosquitoes will have a much easier time getting to us."

Olivia shuddered, and that elicited another smile from Esteban. He adjusted the smoking kerosene lamp to his liking, then went outside again. He returned minutes later, carrying two rolled blankets, a canteen and a pair of saddlebags.

Even though she was afraid, and certain she'd finally stumbled upon her last great adventure, Olivia was glad to see him.

He went to the rope-bed, gave it a shake to dislodge the worst of the dust, then spread one of the blankets over the top. The other he folded at the foot.

"You're actually going to sleep on that thing?" Olivia inquired, hands on her hips. She wasn't feeling obnoxious, exactly, just tired and testy and scared.

Esteban answered with a nod and, "Yes, *dulce*. And so are you—unless you'd rather curl up with the rats."

Olivia raised an eloquent eyebrow and said nothing, and Esteban laughed. He pulled back one of the filthy chairs at the table and thumped it against the floor instead of dusting the seat.

"Here," he said. "Sit down and I will give you some supper."

Olivia wondered what kind of supper she could possibly get in a place like this. Roast prairie dog? But she sat. She was about to topple over from exhaustion and she was very hungry.

Esteban brought fruit from one of his saddlebags, along with two slightly dented American candy bars, a plastic bag containing several of Maria's fluffy biscuits and some canned sandwich meat.

"What about the men?" Olivia asked, feeling guilty about her greed. After all, there were more than a dozen riders outside, and they might have been questionable types, but they were human, with stomachs that needed filling.

Esteban bent to kiss her forehead lightly. "They have provisions of their own, *dulce*," he said.

Reassured, Olivia ate with gusto. There was no telling what tomorrow would be like, and she needed her strength.

In the meantime, Esteban, evidently feeling no need to eat, went outside. When he returned, he found

Olivia finished with her dinner and pacing the small
expanse of the cabin.

She gave him a pained look when he entered, and he
interpreted it correctly, chuckled and held out his hand
to her. The men had laid their bedrolls out around a
small bonfire, and the horses nickered inside an im-
provised corral.

Well away from the cabin, Esteban indicated a
cluster of bushes. "There," he said.

He waited with his arms folded while Olivia slipped
out of sight and did her business. When they returned
to the cabin, Esteban immediately disappeared again.

Olivia felt deserted, thinking he would probably
play cards with the men all night, but instead he came
back carrying an old basin brimming with hot water.
He dragged one of the chairs over beside the rope-bed,
then set the basin on its seat.

Following that, he crossed the room to blow out the
lamp.

The cabin was in sudden, primordial darkness—
surely a cloud had crossed the moon—and Olivia, who
had been standing near the table, floundered inwardly. It was like being dropped into the utter void at
the bottom of the deepest ocean, a place where the fish
have no need of eyes.

Then she felt Esteban's arm around her waist. He
evidently had the vision of a jungle cat, as well as the
nickname, for he took her easily to the bed and gently
undressed her.

When she was naked, he began to wash her with
warm water and a piece of cloth that was probably a
bandanna. He cleansed her face and hands first, but
then the bath became more intimate.

Olivia shivered.

"Cold?" Esteban asked, his voice seeming independent of his body in that black room.

Olivia shook her head. "No. You're going to make love to me, aren't you?" she asked worriedly.

"Yes, *dulce*," he answered. "Very thoroughly."

"But..." Olivia began in a wailing whisper, "I'll yell—I won't be able to stop myself—and all those men out there will hear me!"

Esteban chuckled, and continued to wash her. "They already know what is happening in here tonight," he said. "As for your yelling, well, you were doing that on the beach, and then again today during *siesta*. It is no secret that you enjoy your pleasures, little one."

Olivia's cheeks were on fire.

He eased her down onto the rope-bed, which felt like a hammock and swayed in a comforting way, and covered her with the second quilt. She heard quiet splashing while he washed, but still couldn't make out even the outline of his body.

"Why did you bring me here?" she asked when she was no longer strangling on her pride.

"I told you," Esteban replied smoothly, joining her. Instead of stretching out beside her, however, he knelt and straddled her, turned her onto her stomach, then lifted her onto her hands and knees. "I wanted to protect you from my enemies."

Olivia felt the tip of his manhood tease her femininity, sucked in an excited breath and squeezed her eyes shut for a moment. "Who will protect me from you, Leopard?" she asked.

He teased her with an inch or so, giving, then withholding, then giving again. "No one," he replied. He eased in farther, and his hands reached beneath to cup her full breasts.

She made a whimpery sound, a sound of frustration and yearning.

"What do you want, *dulce?*" Esteban prompted, knowing very well what the answer was.

"All of it," Olivia burst out hoarsely. "All of you."

Esteban toyed with her nipples while he rewarded her for her surrender, moving deep inside her, deeper than she'd ever dreamed a man could reach.

She gave a small, strangled sob, but it was pure pleasure and Esteban obviously knew that. He withdrew, then gave her even more than he had before. "I'm going to yell," she fretted frantically, seeking him, bucking under him like a mare under her stallion. "Oh, please, Esteban, I'm not going to be able to help it, I'm going to *yell.*"

"Good," he said. "Let the whole world know that my woman is happy in my bed."

Olivia feared she'd go right through the rope-bed and land on the dusty floor, so hard were Esteban's thrusts and so vigorous was her own bounding and leaping beneath him, but somehow the net held.

Finally, Olivia's journey was complete. In those last moments of thunder-and-lightning bliss, her skin was moist with perspiration and musk. She threw herself back against Esteban in a spasm of passion, delighting in his muffled gasp and the subsequent stiffening of his powerful body, and she was still responding moments later while he held her breasts and kissed the damp ridges of her spine.

"I yelled," she said dismally a long time later, when she could speak.

"I'm afraid so," Esteban replied, holding her close against his side. He didn't sound the least bit regretful.

Olivia used what little energy she had left to kick him in the side of the leg. "Macho creep," she said.

He laughed, wrapped his arms around her and dragged her on top of him. "Be careful, or I will make you do it again. Perhaps at a higher octave."

Having no doubt that he could, and would, Olivia forced her ready temper to subside. She made no effort to move off of him, but entangled one finger in the hair on his chest and let her chin rest on his collarbone. "Do you think we'll find the horses tomorrow?" she asked.

Esteban smoothed her perspiration-damp hair back from her face. "Maybe tomorrow, maybe the day after that. We'll find them."

Olivia sighed and scooted up so she could rest her head on his shoulder, wondering what Esteban would say if she told him she thought she'd fallen in love with him.

It would probably be a great joke.

"Sleep," he said, as though sensing her turmoil. Olivia closed her eyes, and when she opened them again, the first light of dawn had invaded the cabin and Esteban was still lying beneath her.

He smiled. "Convenient," he said.

Olivia stared at him and started to wriggle away, but he caught her hips in his hands and held her. He had her again, with finesse, and she buried her face in his neck to muffle the moans the resultant climaxes wrung from her.

After another basin bath, another trip to the bushes, and a largely unhealthy breakfast, Olivia mounted her horse and rode out with Esteban and the others. She was very grateful for the straw hat Maria had given her before they left, because it not only protected her from the sun but hid her face from the gazes of all those curious ranch hands.

When she dared to risk a glance at Pepito, he smiled, and Olivia was mortified all over again. Her reputation was ruined, if she'd ever had one in the first place. She began to think more and more of escaping.

At midday, when the sun was at its zenith, they stopped at a charming old mission house with a bell and white adobe walls. While the horses drank at the trough and the men rested on the brick floor of the shady courtyard, Esteban and Olivia talked with the priest in his chapel. At least, Esteban did. Olivia couldn't make out much of the conversation, so she just sat at the trestle table, drinking deliciously cold water from a plain cup.

"Did the *padre* know anything about the lost horses?" Olivia asked as they left. The old priest had used only one word she recognized—*siesta*—and she suspected she and Esteban would rest until the glare of the sun relented a little.

"I didn't ask him about the horses," Esteban replied, opening a door that led to a plain room decorated only with a crucifix and furnished with two inhospitable cots.

"Then what was all that talk about?" Olivia asked, selecting a cot and sitting down to pull off her shoes.

Esteban gripped the waistband of her jeans and pulled her playfully back to her feet, then not so playfully against him. "He thinks we should be married."

Chapter Ten

The stone floor of the small room, worn smooth by the traffic of many years, seemed to sway a little under the soles of Olivia's feet. At the same time, her traitorous body was fully occupied in reacting to such close contact with Esteban's commanding frame.

"Married?" she croaked, as though she had never heard the word before. She certainly had not expected Esteban to raise the subject, even after their lovemaking.

He touched her nose. "The *padre* says we will surely burn in hell for all eternity, if we don't correct the oversight right away," he told her.

"Now there's an appealing prospect," Olivia answered, trying to keep her voice light.

Esteban smiled and rested his hands on her shoulders. His thumbs made caressing motions in the hollows of her collarbone. "It was probably not as poetic as some proposals," he admitted.

Olivia swallowed hard. "That was a proposal?"

"Yes," Esteban said with a sigh, as though surprised by his own actions. "Marry me, Olivia. Stay with me. Laugh with me, sleep with me, capture the beauty of the land in your art."

She swayed, swallowed again. Sometimes it was such a dangerous thing, hoping. "Esteban, there are so many problems—"

"We will solve them all," he said, his lips warm and insistent and so very close to hers. "Where is it written that all problems, real or potential, must be worked out before the wedding?" He paused, and his sigh moved against her mouth, sending a fever racing through her blood. "What has begun between us will not be stopped, *dulce*. I cannot keep myself from touching you, and yet I was raised to believe that one woman in a man's life must be cherished, honored above all others."

Olivia felt tears of happiness sting her eyes, but she was afraid, too. She reveled in the gentle kiss that followed.

Esteban cradled her face in his hands, wiped a tear from her cheekbone with one callused thumb. "I believe you are that woman," he told her.

She was struck by an attack of practicality. "But we haven't taken blood tests, or gotten a license—"

Esteban's white teeth showed in a cocky grin, and his eyes danced as he scolded her. "How many times must I remind you, my stubborn little desert flower? This is the heart of Mexico—*old* Mexico. Things happen here that could never take place in any other part of the country, let alone north of the border."

Olivia's heart was hammering. She thought of Uncle Errol and the delight he would take in this outlandish situation, and of how he'd always urged her to be bold and take chances, to grasp at life with both hands. She decided to reach out for what she wanted. She loved Esteban desperately, and she yearned to be his wife, as well as his woman.

"All right," she said. "But I'm scared."

Esteban bent his head, nibbled at the fragile flesh beneath her right ear, then confided, "So am I."

They returned to the *padre* and were married in the shady courtyard under a carefully nurtured, leafy tree, and while Olivia didn't understand most of the words, she felt their meaning in her soul. The only thing that kept the ceremony from being perfect was the fact that Esteban had never told her he loved her.

Olivia knew from long experience that nothing in life was perfect, and Esteban *had* said she was "that one woman" in his life, the one to be cherished and honored. She had sensed centuries of tradition behind his words.

"W-would this marriage be recognized in the United States?" she asked, when they were alone once again in the little room with the stone floor.

Esteban folded his arms and cocked his head to one side, looking smug. "It is recognized in heaven. If you returned to your own country and married another man, you would be a bigamist."

Olivia felt herself go pale. She wasn't particularly religious, but she did believe in God and in the sanctity of wedding vows.

He gave another of his Latin sighs and sat down on one of the merciless-looking cots to pull off his boots. That done, he stretched out, apparently to rest. He shifted and sighed while he made himself comfortable, causing Olivia an embarrassing barrage of sensation, then yawned, laid his hat over his face and, without another word, went to sleep.

Olivia could have killed him.

Presently, she lay down on the other cot, her mind spinning, trying to absorb the fact that she was married.

Some honeymoon this was, she thought. Her groom was already asleep, and their marriage bed would be a monk's pallet.

For all of that, she was happy, too happy to sleep. She rose, crept out of the room and went to the low adobe wall of the mission to look out at the desert. She saw a pink flower blooming on a cactus some distance away, and suddenly had to see it up close, touch it, find out if it had a scent. She wanted to bring that particular shade of pink home in her mind and blend a glaze to match it exactly.

She looked around and saw that the mission was deserted—like the Leopard, his men were indulging in their *siestas*. Olivia decided to climb over the wall and check out the cactus flower. She would be back before anyone even knew she was gone, though fear of Esteban's displeasure was not her reason for hurrying—she knew what the relentless Mexican sun could do to her if she stayed out too long.

The desert blossom was so delicately lovely that Olivia's throat constricted at the sight of it, and her eyes brimmed with fresh tears. She was about to go back to the mission, only about a hundred yards away, when she saw a rock formation farther out. It suggested an interesting new shape, one she wanted to copy in clay, and she wandered toward it.

After that, it was the layers of pastel colors against the distant horizon. Olivia was hypnotized, her brain whirling with wonderful ideas, and she kept walking. It was only when she took refuge from the sun under the teetering roof of an old shed with no walls, that Olivia realized the mission was no longer in sight.

She bit her lower lip, studying the rugged and unforgiving, yet beautiful, terrain around her. All she had to do was walk back that way...

Or was it *that* way?

Esteban stretched luxuriously when he awakened from his *siesta*. In the cool of the approaching evening, he and Olivia and the others could push on in pursuit of the stray horses. He glanced at the opposite cot, expecting to see her curled up there, perhaps delectably naked because of the heat, but the bed was empty.

A cold feeling zigzagged through the pit of Esteban's stomach, but he immediately stemmed the panic rising inside him. Olivia had merely awakened before he had and gone off to find the amenities, such as they were in this isolated place. Or she might be sitting quietly in the garden where the *padre* liked to hide away while pondering great mysteries of the spirit.

Someone had set a bucket of cool well water outside the door, complete with a chipped enamel dipper. Esteban brought the *agua* in, drank thirstily, doused the back of his neck. Then he set out to find Olivia.

Esteban was pleasantly waylaid by the *padre,* who wanted to talk about building dormitories and classrooms at the mission so that children could come to live there and be educated. He had spoken with representatives of an organization up north, in Los Estados Unidos, that would be willing to provide books, supplies and a couple of teachers, but money was needed for the buildings. A great deal of money.

Esteban listened, though the whole time one part of his mind wandered the grounds of the mission, seeking Olivia. He nodded at suitable intervals.

"We could house forty to fifty children here," the father concluded in Spanish. "The lost, abandoned ones who would otherwise be alone on the streets of our troubled cities, living by their wits."

Esteban was feeling a strange pulling sensation, as though someone had tied a string around his soul and was now trying to lead him somewhere. "*Sí,*" he answered. "You know I will help. Have you seen Olivia?"

"Your wife?" Padre Tejada teased. "I assumed she was with you, my son."

Esteban could no longer contain his concern—or his rising anger. She had left him, after promising to share his life. It had all been a lie to her, a way to humor the man she regarded as her captor.

Worse, she had deliberately endangered herself. The fierce desert harbored so many evils, so many unexpected pitfalls, and it was so easy to get lost. She could stumble right into the hands of his enemies, or meet up with those characters who had kidnapped her in the first place.

Esteban pushed his hat back off his head so that it dangled between his shoulder blades and stepped into the shadowy quiet of the chapel. He hadn't set foot in a church since his grandfather had died, but the rituals came back to him easily enough.

He dipped his fingers into the holy water in the font at the back of the small sanctuary, crossed himself, genuflected. There were no statues at the altar—those were for more prosperous parishes—but the crude wooden cross on the wall spoke to him as it never had before.

Esteban knelt at the railing beneath the cross and offered the first earnest prayer of his adult life. *Protect her.* His head was bowed, his hands clasped. *I beg You to protect her.*

Nightfall came and Olivia still had no idea which way to go. She remained where she was, thirsty and scared, knowing she would only make her situation worse by wandering. The desert air, so mercilessly hot by day, was cooling off rapidly, and she knew the night would be very cold.

Her mind strayed back to the one before, when she'd tossed and moaned on that rope bed while Esteban taught her one delicious new pleasure after another. She ached to feel his arms around her again.

By now, she reflected, bringing herself back to the gloomy present, her husband had certainly discovered that she was gone. He would assume she had purposely abandoned him, and he might be so angry that he would simply wash his hands of her and not even make the effort to ride out looking for her.

"Esteban," Olivia whispered, but her soul shouted the name.

It grew darker, and she tried to sleep, hugging herself, shivering against the desert chill. The stars overhead seemed enormous, but counting them, a game that had gotten her through some difficult times in the past, was of no comfort.

She dozed, awoke shivering, and dozed again. And then she dreamed she heard a horse nicker and the jingling of a bridle. Something long and steely hard nudged her chest, and that was only too real.

Her eyes flew open. She looked up in horror to find the barrel of a rifle, clearly illuminated in the bright light of the moon and stars, pressing her breastbone. The stock and trigger were in the hand of a man Olivia had never seen before.

He smiled, but made no effort to withdraw the gun. "Ah," he said. "The Leopard's woman." His English was heavily accented but only too clear. He looked around, somewhat theatrically. "Ramirez is not here," he said with emphasis, even though it was obviously a fact he'd long since decided upon. The stranger sighed. "His horses stray, his woman strays. It is too bad. Could it be that the Leopard is not such a man as we have always believed?" With that, the man threw back his head and laughed raucously.

Olivia's first instinct was to panic, but she wouldn't allow herself the indulgence. The rifle still pressed to her chest, she scooted upright, slowly, an inch at a time. If there were other *bandidos,* they were well hidden, for she could see no one but this one man.

"Who are you?" she demanded, as if there were some way she could force him to tell.

"Pancho," he replied, reaching down to clasp her shirt with his free hand. He wrenched her to her feet with an easy, wiry strength. "Are we going to be friends?"

Olivia glared at him to let him know she wouldn't welcome his attentions. "Yes," she replied evenly. "We can be 'friends.' All you have to do is get back on your horse, ride out of here and leave me alone."

Pancho laughed, shook his head. "Too valuable. There is a man who would pay *mucho dinero* for the woman the Leopard loves." His dark eyes glinted, and he stroked the underside of her chin with the edge of his thumb. "It would please him to have you, and to send word to Ramirez that you are enjoyable."

Olivia's stomach roiled, and for a second she thought she would throw up all over Pancho's boots. In that same instant, it seemed that her personal universe had been wrenched into perspective; the mysteries were solved, she knew what was important.

Love. Esteban. The child she secretly hoped she was already carrying.

"The Leopard loves many women," Olivia finally threw out, falling back on bravado. "He will not miss one."

Pancho shook his head and made a deprecatory sound deep in his throat. "No. Esteban Ramirez cares for just one woman, and that is you. We know. We have been watching. Come, we leave now." He tied Olivia's hands behind her back and hoisted her up onto his horse. They set off through the night toward God only knew where.

Olivia was in shock by that time, sick with fear. Something told her that this new man, to whom she was being taken like so much pirate booty, was nothing like Esteban.

At sunrise, they rode over a rocky rise and then down a verdant hillside to where a relatively small but stately brick house stood. From her perspective, Olivia could see a swimming pool and a tennis court and a corral full of sleek horses.

The ones missing from Esteban's herd, some sixth sense told her.

A tall blond man with startlingly blue eyes approached, looked her over as though she weren't human, as though she couldn't understand what his scrutiny meant.

"This is the Leopard's woman," Pancho announced proudly.

The azure eyes lit up. "I see," he said, and although his English was more cultivated than Pancho's, it was still marked by a thick Spanish accent. He ran a hand over Olivia's leg, clenched his fingers around her ankle in a bruising hold when she would have twisted away. "Very good," he said. "We have only to wait. The Leopard will surely appear."

Chapter Eleven

Olivia was doing her level best to keep her composure, but under the circumstances it wasn't an easy task. "What are you?" she asked her new captor, who had dragged her unceremoniously into his house without bothering to unbind her hands. "A drug dealer? A white slaver?"

The Mexican was standing at a beautifully carved sideboard in his airy parlor, pouring brandy into a crystal snifter. He chuckled and raised the glass in a mocking toast. "Nothing so dramatic. I make my living selling weapons and cooperating with certain governments."

Olivia was scarcely relieved by this announcement. After all, she was in the hands of a man who would sell out whole countries if the price was right, not just individuals. "What is your quarrel with Esteban Ramirez?" she asked, partly to stall and partly because of a sincere desire to know.

The mystery man smiled. He was really very handsome, but his looks were spoiled by the essential vileness of his nature, which pervaded the room like a bad smell. "He interfered with a project that would have netted millions of American dollars. I was nearly ruined, and it has taken me several years to regain my financial footing. My design is quite simple, and it is twofold—I will repay Ramirez for the sufferings he caused me, and make certain he cannot repeat his transgressions.''

Olivia felt the color drain from her face. This man meant to *kill* Esteban. The knowledge made her reel inwardly, but on the outside she was deceptively calm. ''He will laugh at you,'' she said, falling into step with her captor's formal, carefully paced English. ''I am nothing to him.''

The monster ran his eyes over her with mingled contempt and interest. ''Even better. You would lie to save the Leopard. My instincts tell me that he will go still further to save you, *señorita*. I believe he might well be willing to lay down his life for you.''

Olivia closed her eyes tightly, fighting for control. She wanted to fall apart, to give way to utter panic, but too much depended on her ability to keep her thought processes clear. Esteban's life, for example, and most likely her own, as well. ''You are wrong.''

''We shall see,'' he responded. ''In the meantime we must make certain that you retain your appeal.'' He set the snifter aside, empty, and clapped his hands loudly, causing Olivia to start. ''Juana!'' he shouted.

A slender Mexican girl appeared almost immediately. ''*Sí*, Señor Leonesio?'' she said.

Olivia could see, even in her state of quiet terror, that Leonesio didn't appreciate the fact that his name had been revealed. Probably, he hadn't planned on introducing himself.

The master of the house blurted an order in rapid, furious Spanish, and Juana winced. Olivia reflected that the girl was probably as much a captive as she was, and felt sorry for her.

When Leonesio had finished his diatribe, Juana turned to Olivia, who was sitting on a small couch, and uttered a single word that was clearly a summons. Her enormous dark eyes implored the prisoner to obey.

Figuring anything was better than staying in Leonesio's presence, Olivia rose, every muscle shrieking with soreness, and followed Juana out of the room and up an elegantly rustic staircase.

"You must not try to run away," Juana whispered in labored English when the two women were alone in an upstairs bathroom. She was cutting the bonds from Olivia's wrists. "The wind brings Leonesio news of everything that happens."

Olivia stared into Juana's eyes, rubbing one aching wrist. "You speak English," she marveled.

Juana shrugged and began filling the big tile-lined tub with tepid water. "Not much. I listen. I say words to my person until I know them like rosary."

Olivia was touched. "Are you . . . Do you love Leonesio?"

Juana made a bitter sound. "He says I will be his woman when I am older. I will be trained to make pleasure."

A shiver went through Olivia. She closed her eyes. "Who is his woman now?"

"He has many." Juana looked at Olivia pityingly. "I think you will share his bed for a time."

Olivia shook her head. "I'll die first."

"He will have you whipped if you say refusing," Juana said in her convoluted English.

The image made Olivia sway. "Dear God."

Juana added jasmine-scented salts to the bath and gestured for Olivia to get in. Although she wanted to rebel in any and every way she could, she was covered with dirt and dried sweat and fear, and being clean might do something to restore her reason.

Olivia took off her shoes, her jeans, her shirt, her underwear, and climbed into the bath. Juana hovered nearby, dark eyes averted, while Olivia shampooed her hair and washed her aching body. After she was finished, a huge, soft, thirsty towel was provided, along with a long, gauzy, white gown, a very expensive lace teddy with the price tag still attached, and a pair of sandals.

Juana led Olivia into a luxuriously furnished bedroom, urged her to be seated at a vanity table and began brushing her hair dry. When she'd done that, she said, "I bring food. Make strong."

The last thing Olivia wanted to do was eat, but she saw the sense in Juana's words. She would need physical strength, and it was crucial that she keep herself from giving in to threatening hysteria. Her own life, and maybe Esteban's, could depend on those things.

She meant to make the most of every advantage and every opportunity, however small. When Juana left the room, turning the key in the lock after she'd stepped into the hallway, Olivia rushed to the French doors that led onto the terrace.

There was nothing below except a big brick patio that extended to the pool. The drop was at least two stories, and if she jumped, Olivia reasoned, biting into her lower lip, she would be veined with cracks from head to foot like an old piece of china.

She went back into the bedroom and paced— thinking, planning, plotting. Coming up with absolutely nothing. Olivia didn't like to admit it, being a take-charge sort of person, but unless Esteban rescued her, she was in for it.

"Leonesio," Esteban said, when at twilight, he and Pepito found the place where Olivia had been taken. In times of crisis, he operated on Murphy's Law: If anything can go wrong, it will. Leonesio de Luca Santana was the most devoted, the most ferociously vengeful of his enemies, and one of Leonesio's men stumbling across the fleeing Olivia would have been the absolute worst thing that could have happened. "The rumors are true, Pepito. He's back."

"*Sí,*" was all Pepito said in response. At Esteban's insistence, they rarely spoke of the old days and the people they had thwarted.

"Go back to the mission for the others," Esteban ordered quietly. "You know where Leonesio lives when he is in Mexico."

Pepito nodded. "*Sí,* the St. Thomas estate." He paused. "There will be a fight," he finished, with a certain relish.

Esteban thought of a battle, imagined Olivia caught in the crossfire and closed his eyes. "Not if we can avoid it," he replied hoarsely. "All I want is my wife, alive and unharmed."

"*Sí,*" Pepito agreed automatically, but he looked skeptical. Men like Leonesio thrived on conflict, and they both knew it.

Esteban gestured for his *amigo* to ride out, then swung back into the saddle and set off toward the luxurious hideaway that had belonged to several owners over the years. When Esteban was a child, the place had been the home of Enrique St. Thomas, his friend. Rico had had a fiery Mexican mother and an equally temperamental French father, and when Esteban and his grandfather had visited, it had seemed that the whole house was charged with the St. Thomases' passion for each other.

Tragically, the explosive couple had perished in an epidemic of influenza about a decade before. As he rode steadily toward Olivia—she was the focal point of his whole existence, the magnet he could not resist—he wondered where Enrique was now. It would be good to see his old friend again.

The darkness was thick by the time Esteban reached his destination. He tethered his horse well back from the inner edge of the lush palm trees and tropical plants that surrounded the familiar house.

There were guards, of course, but if Leonesio's small army was around, there was no evidence of it. Just three sentinels, one leaning against a gatepost, smoking, two pacing the outer grounds.

It was a trap, of course. Leonesio wanted revenge for plans that had been thwarted a long time ago, and he knew Esteban would come for Olivia. He was waiting.

Esteban sighed. He had vowed never to play this game again, but that had been before that redheaded American woman had turned his life upside down. Having no choice, Esteban Ramirez put off his regular identity and became, once again, the Leopard.

Overcoming the guards proved so easy he was almost disappointed.

Dinner was served on the patio at an umbrella-covered table next to the pool, and Olivia was ordered to appear.

She joined Leonesio with cool dignity, her manner even and quiet, but she was aware of every cricket and bird sound in the foliage that edged the low stone wall encircling the grounds. Maybe it was just wishful thinking, but she could have sworn Esteban was somewhere nearby—it was as if she could feel his heartbeat thumping in unison with her own.

"You will share my bed tonight," Leonesio announced, after taking a sip of his claret.

"In your dreams," Olivia replied bluntly. "I'd rather sleep with a lizard."

Leonesio threw back his head and laughed. "So much fire. No wonder the Leopard is obsessed with you."

Olivia forced herself to sip her wine calmly and even to nibble at a few bites of the sumptuous food. "You're building yourself up for a big disappointment. Señor Ramirez has already grown tired of me. By now, he's bought himself another plaything."

"He bought you?" Leonesio set his wineglass down and leaned forward, pleased.

"That idea *would* intrigue you," Olivia remarked. "I'll bet your parents spend a lot of time wondering where they went wrong."

Again Leonesio laughed. "I am exactly what they raised me to be," he responded presently, "but we were discussing your statement that Ramirez bought you."

"Two men kidnapped me off the road when my rental car broke down," she answered, as though such things happened every day. "They sold me to Señor Ramirez, and I escaped him as soon as I could. Only to be captured by you, of course." She paused, sighed philosophically, hoping the enemy would believe her lie about escaping.

Then, suddenly, Esteban was there, vaulting silently over the fence behind Leonesio, and she prayed the knowledge didn't show in her face. "The life of a white slave is not easy, Mr. Leonesio. Or is that your first name? Do you have a nickname?"

The distraction kept Leonesio occupied long enough for Esteban to lock one arm around his enemy's throat and wrench him to his feet.

"*Sí*," Esteban growled, tightening his hold. "This is *el pollo*—the chicken."

Leonesio made a strangling sound and flailed.

Esteban's gaze moved to Olivia, took in her flowing white dress, narrowed. "We will discuss your part in this little adventure later," he said. "For the moment, you will return to the house and remain there until I come for you. Is that clear?"

Olivia wasn't entirely sure that being rescued was going to represent a significant improvement in her circumstances. Esteban was obviously furious, and she could just imagine the blistering lecture he would deliver once Leonesio and his men had been dealt with. She nodded, disappointed that he hadn't embraced her, hadn't even said he was happy she was safe, and went into the house without a word.

She and Juana sat together on the leather sofa in Leonesio's study, waiting. When a gunshot sounded, both women jumped, and Olivia bolted for the door, certain Esteban had been shot, that, for all of it, she'd lost him, after all.

She collided with him in the doorway.

Probably, the shot had only been a signal to his men.

"You do not follow orders very well, *dulce*," he said, his voice gruff.

Olivia hurled herself into his arms, buried her face in his neck. "I'll probably never be very good at it," she said, her voice muffled by his flesh. "But I love you, Esteban Ramirez. And whether you believe me or not, I never want to be away from you again!"

He held her apart from him, searched her tear-glazed eyes somberly. "You will stay? But you ran away—"

"I didn't run away, you idiot. I was looking at cactus flowers and things and I got lost," Olivia blubbered. She drew a deep, shuddering breath. "Before I came to this crazy country and met you, I was living my Uncle Errol's life, not my own. Now, for the first time ever, I'm really *me,* and I don't want to give that up!"

Esteban's smile said he understood. So did his kiss.

One month later...

Uncle Errol was wearing a white Armani suit, perfect for the tropics, and looked as pleased as any mother of the bride.

He'd shipped down Olivia's kiln and potting wheel as soon as she called him from Mexico City and announced that, even though she and Esteban were already married, they intended to have a formal ceremony at the *rancho.*

Olivia smiled, watching him from the terrace outside her room. The whole courtyard was decked out in flowers and ribbons, and long tables groaned under platters of Maria's world-class food. Guests from every corner of the globe mingled, sipping champagne in the late-afternoon sunshine.

Esteban stepped up behind Olivia, slipped his arms around her, kissed the place where her neck and shoulder met. She was wearing a long white dress with an off-the-shoulder neckline, so there was plenty of skin to tempt him.

"Happy?" he asked.

Olivia let the back of her head rest against his shoulder.

"Oh, yes," she answered. "I'm happy."

He turned her in his embrace, gave her a lingering kiss that promised many splendors for the night to come. She was still a little dazed when he linked her arm with his and led her inside so that they could descend the stairs and exchange vows for the second time.

"Just don't expect me to promise to obey," Olivia said.

Esteban chuckled. "I would not believe you for a second, even if you did," he answered. "I love you, Señora Ramirez."

Olivia smiled up at him, with her eyes and her heart, as well as her mouth. "And I love you, my Leopard."

Linda Lael Miller

Mexico has always fascinated me, being a place of vast resources and of ancient mysteries. My experience of the country is regrettably limited, since I've only visited two cities, Nogales and Tijuana. When Silhouette Books asked me to write a story for this year's edition of *Summer Sizzlers,* the land south of the border immediately came to mind.

While I had to depend on research, documentaries and old episodes of *Zorro* and *The High Chapparal* for background, once I began writing about Olivia and Esteban, my fictional Mexico became as real to me as any place I've ever written about. As the Leopard and his woman fell in love with each other, I fell in love with deserts dappled with starlight, with white sand beaches and turquoise seas. I realize now that this story has been brewing in my mind since I read Janet Dailey's wonderful *Touch the Wind* a long time ago. The idea of writing a historical romance within a contemporary delighted me.

So, dear reader, I give you the Leopard and his very independent woman. This is a story of which I am particularly proud, and you have my personal guarantee on this—IT SIZZLES!

Linda Lael Miller

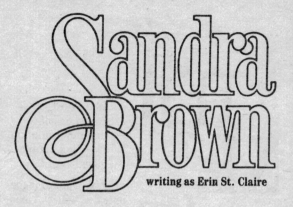